I0694499

Ruin Me, Little Vixen

A Dark Romantasy

J.S. Rodriguez

LITERAL PUBLICATIONS

Contents

Content Warning

Some contents within this book may be triggering or disturbing to some readers. This book is intended for mature audiences only. Reader discretion is advised.

This book contains themes and descriptions of loss/death of family, scenes of trauma, anxiety, mentions of domestic violence, sexual assault, murder, torture, graphic gore, kidnapping, captivity, forced proximity, and descriptions of death that may be distressing to some readers. Please prioritize your mental well-being and do not read if you are sensitive to these topics.

Chapter One

Xavior

"Heal him!" I roar angrily, voice echoing off the stone walls as my hand shoots forward, gripping the healer's throat and lifting him off the ground. His feet dangle wildly, his fingers clawing at my wrist, desperate to pull my hand away. The scent of magic and blood clings to the air like rot, my rage thickening it.

"I can't," he wheezes out. "But I know how we can."

I throw him across the floor, his body skidding across cold marble before he slams to a stop. My eyes snapped back to my brother sprawled on the bed behind me. He has been in a coma for an entire week; the useless healer swore he'd be awake by now, yet here we are. His chest rises shallowly, barely moving, like even breathing is too much effort for him.

My jaw tightens. I don't have time for his pathetic stalling.

"Well?" I growl, impatience burning through me.

"His partners killed the witch," he stammers, flinching as he stands, "but not before she cursed him. The only way to awaken him is with her blood."

My vision darkens. "What good does that do me when they hung the bitch, completely draining her!" I stalk forward, the floor trembling beneath my steps as my shadows stir. "I no longer have any use for you."

My shadows slither up my arms like living snakes, curling over my skin, eager for release. The healer trips over himself, backing away, palms scraping against the floor.

"Wait! Please, I'm not finished!" he cries. I nod once, granting him a final chance. "She had two daughters—the Wixx sisters. You need the oldest. She's the key to removing the curse. You'll have to drain your brother's blood, bringing him to the brink of death, then place an IV into him, and feed her blood into his veins. When her blood replaces what the curse touched... he'll wake."

"That is all? I must drain her completely?" I ask, my voice low.

"Yes," he says quickly, nodding frantically. "You'll need every drop of her blood to cure him. When it replaces the cursed blood, he'll be released from it. Am I... am I free to go?" He crawls toward the doorway like a coward, shaking and desperate to escape. Foolish... he should know better.

"You know too much," I say quietly. "I can't allow you to leave and run your mouth. If anyone learns my brother is like this, his enemies will come to finish him."

My shadows pulse, reacting to my anger like they feel it too. They move around me, waiting for my command.

"I swear I won't speak a—" His voice is cut off with a choking sound as my shadows surge. They wrap around him tightly, squeezing with a lethal force.

His scream rips through the room with the sound of bones cracking. His back folds unnaturally as the shadows crush every organ from the inside out. Blood pools beneath him as he collapses lifeless.

I inhale slowly as if I'd ever trust him to keep this secret.

My most trusted guards stand outside these doors, sworn to protect him while I leave to hunt.

How the hell am I supposed to find the Wixx sisters?

My phone vibrates in my pocket, and I answer without checking who it is.

"Son," my father says, "another coven has been attacked. They called for my assistance. I'll be leaving for a few weeks."

A grin spreads across my face. A coven of witches, what a perfect place to ask around for the Wixx sisters.

"May I join you?" I ask.

I can imagine the shock on his face. I never volunteer to go. I stay here and keep everything in order. I hate his business trips, and I already know who's behind the attacks on the covens, my brother, which is how he got himself into this mess. I never asked what he was doing with the witches. He got what he deserved... but he's still my brother.

My father will be pleased that I want to come. He's part of the council; whenever there are attacks on any of the species, and help is needed, the council gets involved.

"Of course, pack and be ready to leave this evening." He hangs up.

He must never know my brother is in this state. He'd be the first to kill his bastard son. I don't care that he's not my full brother, or that he lacks royal blood. I will not turn my back on him like our father did.

I turn to my brother and whisper my oath, "I promise, brother. She will die at my hands, and I will save you."

I will find the witch who holds the key to my brother's salvation, and I will destroy her. No matter the cost. If she is anything like her mother, she deserves to die, and she will.

I never thought I could hate someone so fucking much without even meeting them, but I do with a passion. These sisters deserve what is coming to them.

Chapter Two

A week earlier...

Amara

"Come on! You're doing a shitty fucking job!" I squeeze my eyes shut, trying hard not to let these stupid tears fall. Why am I always so emotional around her? I swear, I'm never like this. It takes a lot to make me cry, but she makes it so easy. "What the hell did I do so wrong in my life? For the goddess to give me a daughter like you! So weak and useless! You're such a disappointment."

Embarrassment and anger rush through me. I grind my teeth together as I push harder, trying to impress her. The magic flowing through my veins feels good, so addictive. I decide to use my air powers instead of fire. Spinning around, my powers flowing out of the palms of my hand like a whip. It knocks my opponent off his feet, knocking the wind out of his lungs.

My opponent is faster.

He hurls his own wind power at me before his ass even hits the ground, and it wraps around my body tightly, squeezing me till I can no longer breathe. I try wiggling loose, but it's useless.

My mom scoffs, shaking her head before stomping away. Tyler releases me, and I slump forward, dropping to my knees, my hands gripping my thighs as I catch my breath. I watch as my mom disappears, chest tightening. I would do anything to have her approval.

"Don't worry, kid, that was impressive. Not a lot of people knock me down."

"Tell her that," I huff, pointing in the direction my mom disappeared.

"Relax, don't be so hard on her. She's just pushing you because she sees potential. You're strong, but you let your emotions control the magic. You'll get there." He holds out a hand. I hesitate for a second before slipping mine into his, and he yanks me up.

My body falls into his, and I blink up at him. Goodness... he's attractive, and completely off-limits. He works with my dad, who made it very clear that my sister and I are off-limits to all of his employees.

Doesn't mean I can't look.

His brown skin glistens with sweat. My eyes trail down his slim, muscular chest, across his defined abs, and lastly, his basketball shorts. Forbidden or not, I appreciate it. When my gaze moves back up, I catch him looking at me too.

I normally don't train with another person, but when my dad stopped by earlier with Tyler, my mom burrowed him. I've met Tyler a few times before at work functions. My dad isn't the type of man who brings work home with him, but he's been crazy busy lately and always gone. I don't see much of him.

"Anything planned for later?" he asks, stepping back, not caring at all that I just caught him eye fucking me.

"No, not really. You?"

"Let's hang, you're twenty-one, right? What about going to Spades?" I blink in shock, and he grins. Spades is a local bar in town.

"Yeah." I nod; I could use a drink. "Yeah, that sounds like a good idea. What time?"

I step into the bar, scanning the crowd. It's busy. Not surprising for a Saturday night. I find Tyler sitting at the bar. He doesn't notice me until I slide onto the stool next to him.

"I honestly didn't think you'd come," he admits. "You're such a rule follower, and you keep to yourself."

"I'm a rule follower?" I laugh. "No, not at all. I may listen and behave when we're at one of my dad's events, but that's only because I respect him and what he does. At home, I drive my parents insane. Now my sister? She's the rule follower, the angel of the house."

"Good to know." He waves at the bartender, trying to get his attention. I order a rum and Coke, and he gets a beer.

"I have to say I'm surprised you asked me out, you know, since my dad's number one rule is. No talking to his daughters, let alone taking them out."

He shrugs. "It's a stupid rule. You're old enough to decide for yourself. And I want to get to know you better." His eyes move down to my shirt, and he smirks, reading my shirt aloud, "'Big tits, bigger attitude.' Is that so?"

"Sure is, my attitude gets me into a lot of trouble." I smile at the bartender when he hands me my drink. He winks at me before turning away to help the next customer.

Tyler's phone rings, and he grumbles, pulling it out of his pocket.

"Don't answer," I say when his face twists in disappointment.

"I have to, it's my work phone."

"Hello?" He listens, eyes snapping to meet mine as his shoulders tense. "I'll be there in a few minutes." He hangs up. "Someone attacked your house."

My back straightens as I stare at him, processing his words. Then terror slices through me, paralyzing me. "I'll drive you home, since I'm already heading that way. You'll have to leave your car here for the night."

I don't wait for him to finish. I'm already out of the seat, rushing toward the door. He's right behind me. "I'm over here." I turn, following him. He unlocks a blacked-out truck. I jump up with the help of the step bar.

He's in the driver's seat a second later. I ask as he starts driving. "Ana? My dad? Mom?" My hands are trembling as I try to buckle my seat belt.

"I don't know, your dad's fine. He's the one who called. I know this isn't something you want to discuss right now, but this is what we have to tell him: we were in the same bar, you were with friends, and I was alone. I grabbed you when he called."

"Okay, that's fine." I nod, not really listening.

Of course, he doesn't want my dad finding out he took me to the bar. I really don't care. My knee is bouncing, and my fingers are tapping against my leg nervously.

"Hey, it's going to be okay." Tyler places his hand on my thigh and squeezes.

We finally reach my house, and I have the door open before he even fully stops the car. I jump out, rush toward the front door, and fling it open.

My lips part as I take in the scene around me. The living room and dining room are completely trashed. Tables are flipped, lamps are broken on the wooden floors, and glass is shattered all over the floor from a couple of broken windows.

I was just here. *What the hell happened?*

My hand flies to my mouth, keeping my cry stuck in my throat.

"Amara." My dad's arms wrap around me, and I finally release a small cry. He places a soft kiss on my forehead. "You should go back to your dorm; you can't be here right now."

"Ana? Mom?"

"Ana is fine, she wasn't home. The only person here was your mom." He pauses. "We can't find her. We believe they took her."

"Can't I help look for her? I don't want to go back to the dorms and do nothing."

"No," He shakes his head, and I narrow my eyes at him.

"I can help! The more people..."

He cuts me off. "Do not fight me on this! I don't have the time to deal with you. Go back to school, and that is final, young lady!" he snaps before turning, dismissing me. I watch him leave, disappearing around the corner.

Chapter Three

Amara

I exit the girl's dorm building, smiling once I'm outside. I close my eyes, soaking in the morning sun. I head toward the dining hall on the first floor of the Academy's main building, next to the administration offices, while the classrooms sit on the second and third floors. To the right of the main building is the girls' dorm, to the left is the boys', and the courtyard with a large garden that I adore makes a U in between all three buildings.

I don't usually eat here, but I have been for the last few days, for my sister. I know she likes having me close, especially with everything going on. She's scared I'll disappear like mom.

Inside the dining hall, I head straight to the line, grabbing a blueberry muffin and a much-needed cup of coffee.

"Good morning," I mumble as I sit next to Ana. She smiles at me, showcasing our matching dimples, and leans in, resting her head on my shoulder. She is definitely the affectionate one; her love language is touch. "Hey, you okay?"

"I'm fine, I just miss mom."

"Hey, pretty girl." Domanic – Ana's current boyfriend– sits on the other side of her.

She's also the popular one. I've always been more of a loner. Not because I don't like people, but because I prefer books, quiet nights, ice cream, and movies. Although I do enjoy going out sometimes with my best friend, Brandon. He graduated last year, but thankfully still lives close by.

I massage my temples, staring down at my coffee as my thoughts drift to mom. She is still missing. It's been a week since the break-in, and there's no trace. It's like she just... poof vanished into thin air. Dad's been working nonstop, forcing my sister and me to stay out of the way; we're not even allowed to go home.

The double doors on the other side of the room slam open. One of my professors rushes in, panic written all over his face as his eyes sweep the dining hall.

"Go to your dorms and stay there until further notice. This is not a drill. We are under attack!" he shouts.

For a second, no one moves a muscle as we process. Then all hell breaks loose. I jump up, grabbing my sister's hand and pulling her toward the corner of the room.

"What do you want to do? Run and hide or fight? I'll do whichever, but you will stay by my side." I ask as I look around, not releasing her hand. There's no point in running right now. We'd just get trampled. We'll wait for the students to clear before we leave.

I don't know what we're dealing with, but I know I can help, and they could probably use it. Ana can help, too, but she panics in situations like this. The school grades us on crap like this. I always pass. She always fails. She freezes when it matters most.

"I can't," she cries, panting. "But you go and help!"

"No! Are you crazy? I'm not leaving you!"

"Mom will be mad if you hide!"

"I don't care. She's not here; she won't know." I glance around once more, noticing most of the students are gone already. "Come on, we need to get to my dorm."

I pull my sister along, then pause at the doorway. Professors are running down the hall toward the back exit. Is the fight happening there? It would make sense—the woods are the easiest way to sneak in.

"Stay here," I mutter to Ana. "I'm going to see what's happening."

I move toward the back of the dining hall, where a row of windows faces the woods, and sneak a peek outside.

Shit.

My eyes widen when I see a large group locked in combat with five professors. The professors are badly outnumbered. It has to be the same group that attacked our home. These are fully trained warlocks, and the professors are losing. Everyone in the group is dressed in black, their faces hidden behind glossy black skull masks.

"Go. I'll stay right here," Ana reassures me, and that's all I need.

I take off in a run, inhaling deeply as I summon my magic. It warms my veins as it pulses through me. The feeling is exhilarating, my body shivers, and I feel intoxicated.

I step outside, my fire whip forming in my hand, scorching the grass and leaving a glowing trail in its wake. I feel unstoppable.

One of them, I assume it's a man, judging by his massive frame, spots me first and turns toward me.

I lift my whip, giving it a snap, the hiss of it echoes around us, testing its strength, and the man's legs slow as he catches a glimpse of it.

Creating a whip out of fire is nearly unheard of, so I'm not completely surprised that I caught him off guard.

A large grin overtakes my face as I snap my whip toward him. It cracks loudly as it moves through the air. My aim has always been deadly. It wraps around his throat, and my arm pulls back *hard,* slicing through his skin and completely severing his head.

I don't have time to indulge in the addictive feeling as a piercing screech reverberates around me. I turn and spot what looks like a woman––due to her small frame––running toward me, only a few feet away. If she hadn't screeched, I would never have caught a glimpse of her.

She throws her arms up, and a strong gush of wind knocks me over, but not for long. I jump to my feet as the wind she's creating wraps around both of us, circling us like a living thing. She bares her teeth at me, just like the others. A mask covers the upper half of her face.

"You will pay for killing him, you stupid little bitch," she screams, then launches at me with her fist raised, aiming for my face. I spin out of the way at the last second, narrowly avoiding the punch. She wants to fight, but I can't let it escalate to that. I'm no good at hand-to-hand combat without magic.

As soon as she stumbles forward, right where I'd been standing, I act. My whip hisses as it snaps toward her at high speed, wrapping around her midsection. I yank. The flames work fast, burning through her clothes and flesh as she screams in pain. I pull harder, and it slices her in half, cutting off her screams.

I turn to see who's next when a small gasp escapes me as I stare at *him*. His presence commands my attention. I can't look away, even if I want to. I feel his gaze on me, assessing.

He moves across the field with slow, deliberate steps, like he has all the time in the world. Like a predator who's in no hurry because he knows he'll catch you anyway.

Black shadows swirl around his body, making it hard to see him clearly. The grass blackens and withers beneath his boots, killing it instantly with every step he takes and leaving a deadly trail behind. His dark power is overwhelming, drawing me in, tempting me, and making me almost forget where I am and what I'm doing.

"Amara, watch out!" someone screams, snapping me out of my daze.

I spin around, but I'm too late. A massive body slams into me, throwing me through the air. The breath is knocked from my lungs as I crash into the brick wall and hit the ground hard. I try taking a deep breath, but it hurts.

Get up...

I force myself upright, just in time to see the massive body charging at me at full speed. I can't get a good throw while I'm still on my knees, and my legs feel sluggish as I struggle to stand. I don't have time, but I can slow him down.

My whip cracks through the air and wraps around his ankles, sending him crashing to the ground. Professor Maxwell is on him instantly.

I don't watch Professor Maxwell. No, I watch in a mixture of horror and fascination as the man who's covered in shadows raises his hands toward the group.

Darkness snakes down his arms before shooting forward, wrapping around five attackers at once. Their bodies lift effortlessly into the air, legs kicking as the shadows squeeze the air out of their lungs. The fight slowly leaves their bodies, and they slump forward, dead.

"Holy *shit!*" my sister squeals right next to my ear, snapping my attention away from the large shadow man. I didn't even hear her come outside. "That's the Shadow Prince."

My stomach drops. I grab her hand and take off running, dragging her with me. I don't know what I'm running from... the attackers or him.

He is the Shadow Prince, carved from darkness, a darkness that tempted me. It's dangerous and can be intoxicating if you let it in. Beautiful, but fatal if you get too close.

I just know I need to get her away from here. I can come back and help later if it's needed. I'm sure it'll be okay. The Shadow Prince is here, which means the council is probably here, and that also means this is bigger than any of us thought.

Once we make it to my dorm, Ana drops into a chair in the corner of the room as I pace.

Should I go back and help? Is my mom even alive? If I leave, will Ana be okay? What if that group was just a distraction, and there's another group about to attack the dorms? So many questions running through my mind.

I wipe my sweaty palms on my blue jeans and pull my hair into a ponytail. I feel trapped in the small room, the adrenaline still pumping through me, making my heart race.

My cellphone begins ringing in my front pocket. I take it out and see *Dad* written on the screen.

"Amara! Are you safe?" my dad barks through the phone before I can even say anything.

"Yeah, I am, but da—"

"Have you seen your sister?" he cuts me off. "I've tried calling her, but she's not answering."

"Yes, she's here with me." I glance over my shoulder at her, and it looks like she's in the middle of a panic attack, bracing her knees to her chest while she rocks back and forth, her eyes glued on the door. "She's not doing so well. She's scared. I tried helping during the attack, but I had to get Ana out of there. Should I go back?"

"No!" he snaps. "These are very dangerous people, and they've already taken down other covens. I won't have you in harm's way. Stay with your sister and stay safe. I can't lose you, too."

I nod in agreement, then remember he can't see me. "Yes. Of course."

"Promise."

"I promise." I rub the back of my neck before walking to the window and peeking outside. Students crowd the courtyard, phones raised, no doubt recording everything.

Fucking idiots...

"I love you. Stay inside, lock the doors, and I'll come find you when this is over. I'm at the school. I have to go." He hangs up without waiting for a response.

I toss my phone onto the bed and walk back to Ana. Sitting on the arm of the chair, I rub small circles on her back, trying to soothe her. She's always had panic attacks, so we're used to them.

"It'll be okay," I murmur. "Dad is here. Everything will be okay." I promise, my skin still warm and tingling from the use of my magic.

Chapter Four

"**W**ake up!" Lisa's voice cuts through the room as she tries to wake Ana. She's my sister's best friend.

Ana stayed in my room after the attack. Dad came by last night to make sure we were okay. He told us none of the professors were badly injured and that we were on lockdown for the rest of the night.

"What is it?" Ana grumbles. "Don't wake Amara. You know she gets cranky when she's woken up this early!" she whispers a little too loudly.

I sit up, rubbing my face, trying to wake myself up. Fuck, my back is sore. It hurts to move. "What the hell are you doing here, Lisa? I didn't invite you in."

"I let myself in." She shrugs. "It's important. The council arrived last night, and the Shadow Prince is here!" She squeals like it's the best news she's heard all year. She and Ana are two years younger, nineteen. It's their first year at the academy.

"And?" I toss my blanket off and check the time. Shit. It's later than I thought. Classes are about to start. It wouldn't be so bad skipping gym... Not fucking worth it.

Ehh. Maybe it is.

"And?" Lisa rolls her eyes. "He's hot."

"I know," Ana says. "We saw him last night during the fight. He killed five guys in a matter of seconds! It was the hottest thing I've ever seen!"

Her eyes are still red from crying all night, and no, it wasn't because she was scared or because of Mom. She was crying because her douchebag boyfriend called last night and broke up with her. I warned her that all he wanted was a quick fuck. She wouldn't listen. He does it every time, with different girls.

I'm going to kick his ass for hurting her.

I grab my phone and see a message from the school letting us know the lockdown has been lifted.

"Okay, can you two please gossip somewhere else?" I point at the door, and Ana pouts. "I need to get dressed, and I'm in desperate need of coffee."

"Fine. Love you." Ana pulls Lisa out of my room.

I open my social media account and immediately see a flood of posts about the Prince of Shadows. Everyone is raving about him, thrilled that he's here. I zoom in on one of the pictures and instantly understand the obsession.

He's hot.

The literal definition of eye candy. I stare at the dark prince a little longer, wishing I could see what color his eyes are.

No matter how hot he is, I'll stay away. He's dangerous, and his magic is made of pure darkness. I don't know much about shadow wielders, but their shadows honestly scare me.

I decide to check in with Brandon and type a quick text:

Hey, you, okay?

I toss my phone onto the nightstand and grab clothes from my closet. The phone buzzes, and I jump back onto the bed, reaching for it, only to frown at the message from the academy.

> *Classes are canceled. Council meeting at nine a.m. in Coven's Hall. All must attend.*

I groan, slamming the back of my head against my pillow when I realize I have exactly ten minutes to get there. No time for my caffeine addiction.

I pull on leather pants and a gray T-shirt that reads: *Spank me! I've been a bad girl.* I tuck the front into the waistband, throw on my leather jacket, and finish the look with black high-heel ankle boots.

I step in front of the bathroom mirror, debating whether to straighten my wild, wavy hair, but decide against it. I don't feel like putting in the extra effort. I stare at my full lips, wondering if I should wear gloss or lipstick, the only makeup I normally wear, and settle on red.

I used to try hiding the freckles under my eyes and across the bridge of my small nose, but lately, I haven't. And by lately, I mean since my breakup with Jaxon.

He always told me to cover them; always said they weren't sexy. I was stupid enough to listen. I changed so much of myself for him, even as far as cutting my dark hair short, which I hated. Thankfully, it grew back fast.

I grab my keys, step out of the room, and lock the door behind me. My phone buzzes in my pocket. I pull it out and see a message from Brandon.

Brandon:

> Yeah, I'm fine. I just found out what happened when I got to work. Fuck me sideways, that sounds insane. Anyone get hurt? Did you kick ass?

I chuckle, sliding my earbuds in and turning on some music before replying.

> I helped, but not much. I had to get Ana out of there... Did you hear who's in town?

A few people try to stop me to talk, but I ignore them. I'm not feeling social—and honestly, I can't socialize without caffeine.

Brandon:

Duh, bitch! And you better give him my number if you see him! I need a shadow daddy in my life.

I snort, rolling my eyes as I type back.

One, I'm pretty sure he's straight. And two, you have a boyfriend. I'm the one who needs a shadow daddy devouring my body.

I enter the coven's hall and scan the room for a familiar face, but see none. I head toward a deserted corner by the small stage in the front and lean against the wall, waiting for the meeting to start. Resting the back of my head against the wall, I stare up at the glass ceiling. The academy is old, and the room has large trim, huge arched doorways, and dark wooden floors.

Kids think the room is creepy at night and usually avoid it, but I like it. Sometimes at night, I lie on the floor and stare up at the stars. The space is large enough to hold every student in our small academy, which is just a couple of hundred.

A few minutes later, Ana and Lisa walk in. Ana scans the room, and a large smile lights her face when she spots me. She heads my way, holding two cups of coffee. A grin stretches across my face. She loves me, grumpy and all.

"Here." She hands me a cup. "I figured you didn't have time to get one, so I grabbed one for you. Especially since it's my fault you stayed up late last night."

"Thank you! I could freaking kiss you right now." I sip it, groaning as the hot, tasty liquid runs down my throat. Perfection.

"I love you, but please don't," she says, leaning against the wall beside me. I open my mouth to ask if she's heard from Dad, but my attention snaps to the front of the room.

The door at the back of the stage opens, and the council members slowly walk in, taking their seats at the long table facing the crowd. There's a witch, a warlock, a fae, a vampire, a werewolf, a demon, and the shadow king. I've never met them before; our coven wasn't powerful enough to earn their presence. I guess a group of mass murderers killing witches in town is enough to get noticed.

The murmurs around us die instantly. Their power radiates through the room, impossible to ignore. I take my time, studying each one.

Beautiful. That's the only word that comes to mind.

The door opens again, and my heart skips a beat. The energy in the room shifts, suffocating me. I feel his power calling to me. Slowly, I take him in as he walks toward the table, and the pictures on social media don't even come close.

Girls around the room gasp and whisper, and a cocky smirk spreads across his face. He walks with a slight swagger, he knows he's hot, and he commands the room. His tattooed hand rakes through his dark, shaggy hair. It looks like he just rolled out of bed... strong, angular jaw, and fuck... those lips are made for sinful shit.

Is he hot? Hell yes. Arrogant asshole? From what people say, definitely. I don't give a damn whether or not the rumors are true. I don't need another playboy in my life. I've seen pictures of the sexy prince with a different girl on my feed too many times.

He's the definition of a man-whore.

"Holy crap, he's hotter in person!" Lisa squeals, loud enough to make every council member turn. I step back, distancing myself from her.

Xavior—the Shadow Prince—glances over her, then my sister. And then... his eyes don't just land on me, they pinned me in place. Hunger and violence lived in that stare like he was imagining what my blood tastes like or how loud I'll scream.

I can't tell the color of his eyes, but I feel them scanning my body slowly, and deliberately, more than a few times, like once or even twice isn't enough. My heart hammers, and a shiver runs through me. I force myself to stay still, not wanting to squirm under the intensity of his attention. Finally, he meets my gaze. I square my shoulders, lift my chin, and meet him head-on.

I won't be intimidated by him... or his dark power.

"Silence!" My attention snaps to Mr. White, our dean. I don't want my eyes to wander back to Xavior's, so instead, I look down at my cup, nibbling on my lower lip.

"I know this is a lot to take in, and many of you have questions. I assure you, we're handling it," declares the man in the center of the table, a vampire. "We believe it's best for students to go home until the threat is eliminated. We've spoken to your parents, and they've requested that you remain on campus for the rest of the week to allow time for arrangements. By the weekend, you will return home. The council agrees to these terms and will stay on campus for protection. No classes will be held during this time, but you are welcome to use the library, gym, pool, and dining hall. Food will still be served. No visitors, and no leaving campus."

My gaze snaps to my dad, seated between the vampire and the witch. He's trying to look strong, but I can see the strain behind his eyes.

Who will protect my sister and me out here in the middle of nowhere? They've already attacked our home... and who's to say they won't again?

"What about us?" my sister steps forward. "Mom is missing, and Dad is with you. Who will look after us in a house in the middle of nowhere? I don't feel safe there." She walks over and threads our fingers together.

Xavior leans toward his father, whispering something I can't hear. His father nods in response, then Xavior leans over to speak to our dad, who also nods.

"Prince Xavior has offered his assistance and will stay with you when you return home."

I narrow my eyes at my dad. How dare he invite a stranger into our house? "We can stay at Lisa's. We are not living in a house with a complete stranger."

"Amara, this is not up for debate," my dad snaps.

I press my lips together, lean against the wall, and cross my arms over my chest.

"Thank you for your time. Please begin packing."

I storm out of the room, fully aware of Xavior's dark gaze burning into my back. I don't know *how* I feel his eyes on me, but I do. Maybe it's the way he dominates the room. Maybe it's how his power slithers over my skin, sending chills down my spine. Whatever it is, it scares me how deeply he affects me.

I make it back to my room and flop onto my bed, staring at the ceiling as the reality sinks in.

I'm about to be trapped in a house with a dangerously hot stranger. What could possibly go wrong?

Other than the fact that I want to spread my legs for him, beg him to touch me, taste me, and consume me completely.

My phone buzzes, and I grab it instantly, desperate for the distraction.

Brandon:

> **Are you going to the bonfire tonight?**

I tilt my head to the side. *A bonfire sounds like exactly what I need.*

> I wish. But I can't, we're on lockdown.

Brandon:

> **Nope, kids at the school are throwing the party with the help of the sexy ass shadow daddy.**

I sit up, too quickly. My head spins for a second. When the hell did this happen?

> Yes, I could definitely use the distraction. Where will we meet? How will you sneak in?

My stomach growls. It's dinner time, I guess. I leave my dorm and head toward the dining hall.

Brandon will be sneaking in around ten with a friend: a hot, single, straight man, whom he keeps trying to set me up with.

I step into the dining hall, scanning for the one who deserves a swift kick in the balls for hurting my sister.

Finally, there he is. Great, of course, he's with Xavior. That won't stop me.

My eyes flick to my sister's table. She's watching me with a horrified expression, already knowing what I'm about to do. I smile sweetly, arch my brows. She mouths *no*, shakes her head, and slices a hand across her throat.

I straighten my shoulders, swinging my hips a little more than usual. A group of girls huddles around Xavior, all vying for his attention, like a pack of hungry wolves.

Everyone laughs at something Xavior says, and that's when Domanic notices me, my gaze locked on him. His laughter dies mid-chuckle. He mouths, *Oh, shit.* Xavior notices too, and then the entire group parts, giving me a clear path.

"Amara, you're looking mighty fine today," Domanic smirks, though the twitch of nervousness in his eyes gives him away.

I stop a couple of inches from him, placing a hand on my hip, letting my eyes slowly sweep over him, scrunching my nose, looking severely unimpressed. "Domanic," I say, voice dripping with warning. "My sister told me something very interesting."

"Look, I'm sorry, okay. I just couldn't commit to one girl; you get that, right?"

"Oh, I do. But what I don't understand is why you told her you wanted to be with her and her only. And when she gave you what you wanted, you dropped her."

"I tried, I really did, but sex with her was very vanill—"

Before he can finish, my knee shoots up, hitting him square in the balls. He hunches over, gripping himself, and I swing my knee up again. My hands grip the back of his head, slamming it down into my knee.

A vicious smile spreads across my face as I hear the satisfying crunch of his nose breaking. Did he really think I'd let him finish that sentence?

"Next time you talk shit about my sister, try not to ruin my outfit in the process," I say, pointing at the blood on my knee, shaking my head at him. He stares at me, shocked, pained expression as he clenches his broken nose.

"Fuck your outfit! You broke my fucking nose!" he screams.

"You'll live. Unfortunately," I sigh, turning away. He yells after me, calling me a crazy bitch. I ignore him completely.

The entire dining hall is silent as I walk toward the buffet, grabbing a burger and fries like nothing happened. Instead of sitting with my sister, I slip outside, heading straight to my favorite spot in the woods, away from everyone.

I settle at the base of a large tree, resting my back against the trunk. I take a bite of the burger, eyeing the sun through the canopy of the trees surrounding me, and listen to the birds sing their beautiful song.

When I finish, I close my eyes and sigh, fingers brushing the earth beneath me. The air shifts, my senses snap awake. The birds suddenly grow silent. Every muscle in my body tenses when I feel him. I pretend not to notice, staying unnaturally still, hoping that if I ignore his presence, he'll lose interest and leave.

He clears his throat after a few minutes. So, I guess he's not leaving. I finally blink my eyes open to look up at him. He stands a few feet away, his stance wide, arms crossed over his chest, making his blue shirt stretch to accommodate his large shoulders.

His arms and hands are covered in smoky tattoos. They seem to move slightly, but before I can look closer, he unfolds his arms, his chin lifting slightly as he looks down at me. I can't see his eyes since they're covered with black sunglasses.

"Amara, right?"

"Mhm."

"Mind if I join you?" he finally asks after we stare at each other for far too long.

"I do mind, actually." He frowns slightly, brows furrowing.

He's not used to women saying no to him, I'm assuming, but he completely ignores me and plops down right next to me. I narrow my eyes at him, but he doesn't seem to care as he stares at me.

"You were the girl in the field yesterday, right? That fire whip was deadly."

"Yeah, I guess so."

"Did you hear about the bonfire tonight?"

"Yep." I turn away from him, deeply inhaling, as I look back up at the sky. I still feel his gaze on me, his attention turning my blood hot. Is it desire or nervousness?

"Will you be coming? I'm not sure if you were invited, so I am officially inviting you."

"I was invited," is all I say as I stare up at the clouds, wondering why the birds flew away. Can they feel his intimidating presence as well? Probably, animals are very smart creatures.

"You didn't answer the other question." He pushes after a moment.

I sigh in annoyance, tilting my head slightly to look at him. I release a small gasp when I find him inches away from me, too close but not close enough at the same time. His sunglasses are off, resting on top of his head. My eyes connect with his smoky grey ones.

Wow...

"Yeah," I nod, licking my lips. "I'm going with some friends."

My eyes slowly roam across his face, the small shadow of stubble on his angular jaw, his straight, perfect nose. The only flaw on him is the scar running down from his right temple, passing the corner of his eye and stopping at the top of his right cheek, but it just makes him look even sexier to me.

I realize that we are both staring at each other, closely. I clear my throat, setting my hand down to scoot over, but it lands on top of his. I feel a wave of sparks spreading up my arms when our hands connect, making me gasp.

I rip my hand away like it had burnt mine, and being so close to him is all too much for me. I start gathering my trash before jumping up to leave.

As I walk away, he says, "I'll see you later, little vixen."

I don't respond or even look back at him. The way he says, *little vixen...* with pure hunger and a low voice made of velvet sin. It's a temptation, one I have to avoid. I will stay away from him; there is something off about him. He is here for a purpose, and I'm not quite sure what it is.

His presence rattles me. I'm not sure if I should be scared or excited about it.

Chapter Five

Amara

I'm standing in front of my floor-length mirror, chewing my inner cheek. Normally, I don't give two fucks about how I look. Jaxon never made me feel like this. Yet here I am, feeling... something. And no, it has nothing to do with the prince.

I curl my hair into long waves down to my hips. I put on some eye shadow to make my eyes pop, a hint of blush, and gloss on my lips.

I glance down at my outfit: light blue high-waisted skinny jeans—damn, they make my ass look unreal—black knee-length boots, and a white tube top with my strapless bra to give my chest a lift that makes my hourglass figure undeniable.

Yeah, my body looks good. Killer even. But... is it too much?

The door opens. Brandon walks in alone.

"Shit." He stops, staring me up and down. "You are dressed like a god-damn siren. Looking for someone to hook up with or what?"

"Too much, huh? I'll change," I reply, teasing, but there's a smirk on my face.

"No, the hell you will! I'm questioning my sexual preferences. I might totally be bi instead of gay." He glances at me again, clearly impressed.

"Yeah, no. We're not testing that theory. Don't even think about it." I laugh, shaking my head.

"Shit, I'll have the hottest girl there as my date," he says, winking and opening the door for me.

"What happened to your friend?"

"He got a booty call. Said sorry, but that was a better offer. Oh, and David says, 'Hey.'"

We walk through the dark woods toward the academy's border. The coven and the academy hide inside a massive magical dome. On the other side is the human realm. I cross over occasionally, it's fun, and my favorite club and café are there. Humans are easy to mingle with. Students aren't allowed past the protective dome, but that's never stopped us.

The barrier hums low as we step through it. I feel a vibration. The magic brushes over my skin, electric, like static, then it's gone, leaving me strangely bare on the other side. Humans can't see the dome at all. To them, this is just another stretch of woods.

A quick prickle runs down my spine, then it fades. If this is the big, scary ward everyone's worried about, it's seriously overrated. Up ahead, the tree line opens, and laughter drifts toward us.

Brandon drapes an arm over my shoulders as we step onto the sandy beach. My eyes scan the partygoers around the fire, completely absorbed in themselves. I don't see him at first. Then I see him, dressed in blue jeans, a black V-neck, and a leather jacket.

As if he senses me, he turns my way. I quickly look away, keeping my body casual, careful not to show any interest.

"He's looking over here," Brandon murmurs, amusement in his voice. "Pretty sure he's checking me out." I chuckle and nudge him gently, stepping toward the coolers between the trucks and the fire.

I bend, grabbing two cans of beer. I toss one to Brandon, who catches it without missing a beat. I pop mine open, letting my gaze roam over the dancers, trying to ignore the prince's gaze lingering on me.

"Let's go say hi to little Ana," Brandon suggests, glancing over my shoulder. I press my lips together; that's not happening. She and her friends are surrounding Xavior.

"No, let's dance," I counter, but he ignores me and moves toward the group. Tiffany and her friends are approaching, so I sigh and follow Brandon, sipping my beer as I glance at the ocean waves. I stay near the edge, away from the crowd, taking in the night.

Normally, Brandon stays glued to my side, knowing how I feel about parties, but tonight? He's practically glued to the sexy prince. It's hard to blame him. I move away, and shiver as a breeze rolls off the water; the wind is colder this close to the waves.

"Bored already?" a low voice says behind me. I glance over my shoulder to find Xavior standing there. He really does have a talent for showing up when I finally get a second of peace.

"I don't do well in crowds," I say, turning back toward the ocean as the waves rush close to my feet.

"Yeah, I get that. I prefer smaller circles... or none at all," he replies, dropping down beside me. I blink at him, and he chuckles. "What? Don't look so shocked."

"How could I not? You survive off attention like it's oxygen."

"Nah," he says, unfazed. "People just attach themselves. I tell them to fuck off, but the media team edits that part out. My father prefers the polished version." He stares ahead, and with his focus elsewhere, I take in every line of him.

"Polished? That's what you call it?" I snort, studying my beer can. "All I've seen from you is attitude."

"You keep track of me?" His smirk twists, dangerously amused. "Interesting. But yeah, that's my nicer side."

"I haven't been watching you. You're literally everywhere. Hard to miss." A gust of cold wind rolls off the water, and I rub my arms. "And if this is you being nice, I'd hate to see what you're like when you're not."

"Here."

I look over just as he shrugs out of his jacket. I open my mouth to decline, but he moves faster, settling it over my shoulders. His scent hits me hard: cedar, spice, heat, and a hint of something I shouldn't like as much as I do.

"Thanks," I murmur, sliding my arms through the sleeves and drawing the warmth in tighter. The warmth feels... extremely good.

"Xavior." That high-pitched, sultry voice cuts through the air. Tiffany stands behind us in a dress that's basically see-through. Her entire bra outline is visible. Xavior doesn't even look at her. He's staring at me. "Come dance."

"Go," I tell him with a small smile, turning my eyes back to the night sky as I take another sip. "I'm fine."

"I'd rather stay. But thanks, Tiff."

"Come on, Xavy. I'm not taking no tonight. And if you insist on sitting with the loser, I'll stay too." She steps closer, rubbing his shoulders, and he visibly tenses. The nicknames make my jaw tighten. They've definitely spent time together since he arrived. She latched on immediately, and of course, he let her. She's gorgeous... toxic, but gorgeous.

"Please just go," I hiss, unable to hide my irritation. I'd rather swim in the freezing ocean than endure her presence.

He nods and gets up. "I'll be back."

A few minutes later, I glance over my shoulder and see them dancing by the fire. I swallow as a surge of irritation hits me. I stand, brush sand off my jeans, and walk away.

I want space. Not my dorm or this party, so I tip back the rest of my beer, drop the can, and head toward the woods, away from the academy and far from everyone else. A place people don't wander.

As I stride deeper into the trees toward my usual spot, something prickles at the back of my neck. I stop, someone's watching. I scan the dark woods, but nothing. I keep still, but nothing. I tell myself I'm imagining it, shake it off, and walk farther in.

Who the hell gets jealous over a man they barely know? The irritation feels wrong under my skin. I'm so wrapped up in my thoughts, I don't see them until the last second. Up ahead, two men and a woman stand blocking my path, watching me in silence.

"Well," the larger man on the right grins, eyes dragging over me. "Look what we have here."

"You made it so much easier for us, little girl. We had a whole plan on trying to get your or your sister's attention to get you all alone." The shorter pudgy man says.

"But you just walk over to us on your own free will." The woman steps forward, holding what looks like a leather whip.

I call my magic forward, knowing that I'll need it. The warmth spreading through me is a nice contrast to the cold air. I probably won't win this fight. I am severely outnumbered, but I refuse to go down without a fight.

What the fuck was I even thinking wandering the woods alone, when I knew these psychopaths were out here hunting us like animals? They warned us to stay inside the academy's wards.

"I like your whip," I say, nodding toward hers as I take a slow step forward. "Let me show you mine."

Fire moves in my hand, snapping into shape. I crack it against the ground between us, the heat hissing as it touches the dirt. It misses her feet by inches, and all three of them flinch, stepping back.

"Where is she?" I ask, taking another step forward. They obviously know who I am.

"Oh, don't worry," the pudgy man says with a cruel smile. "She's with our friends, safe and cozy."

My grip tightens. My eyes flick between them as I try to come up with a plan. My whip is long enough for two, but the third one could run at me. My best chance is to distract them so that I can make a run for it.

"Lactus!" I shout, throwing my arms up.

The magic surges through me and escapes my palms, but the woman holds up a hand, her lips moving as she whispers a spell.

My heart shutters as I feel my magic bounce back, slamming into me instead.

I scream as my body is thrown through the air, my voice echoing through the woods. Goddess, please let someone hear me. We're not far from the bonfire.

My back slams into a tree trunk, the impact stealing the breath from my lungs. I cry out as sharp, blinding pain tears through me. Then my head whips back, cracking against the bark hard enough to make my ears ring, and black spots swarm my vision.

I blink rapidly, trying to fight the darkness off as panic floods my chest. My whip disappears, my magic slipping through my fingers.

Shit, *shit*.

Fucking shit!

How am I supposed to fight if I can't use magic without it hurting me? She's a reflector... a witch who can turn your magic back on you. It's a rare gift, but badass.

No wonder they took down so many covens.

I refuse to give up.

The large man and the woman stalk closer, my body is slumped uselessly against the tree. I part my lips, pretending to whisper a spell, but instead, I summon my whip.

Ignoring the dizziness, I flick my wrist and let it fly, not caring who it hits.

Luck is finally on my side.

The whip slams into the woman's head, flames erupting as her hair catches fire. The smell of burning flesh fills the air. She screams, clawing at herself as the pudgy man scrambles to put the flames out.

I grin through the pain, forcing the darkness back. There's a deep, nasty, and bloody gap where the whip struck. She won't survive that without a healer.

"Told you my whip was cooler."

My smile drops when the larger man steps closer, his mouth curling into a cruel smirk, whispers, "Dolore," which means pain.

Pain slams inside me. My back arches, it feels like fire racing through my veins, my insides burning like I'm being ripped apart from the inside out. My body spasms violently, screams tearing from my throat as they echo through the woods.

"I hear someone coming!" a voice shouts. "We need to leave, now!"

My vision blurs as I stare up at the crescent moon, the stars blurring together. The corner of my vision starts darkening.

It hurts too much. My throat burns raw from screaming. Is this how I die? Alone in the woods?

"Stop, pl—" My lips move, but the words won't form.

"Grab her! Whoever's coming is almost here!"

My screams fade as the world starts slipping away, but then I see him. Xavior.

He charges forward, shadows swirling around his body, his gray eyes glowing like something feral. An animalistic growl rips from his chest as his shadows surge out, slamming into the two men.

I watch in dazed fascination as the darkness invades them, twisting inside their bodies. Whatever it's doing... it looks like agony.

The woman turns to run, blood pouring down her face, but the shadows are faster. They wrap around her like chains, squeezing, crushing, stealing the life from her.

Then suddenly Xavior is beside me, dropping to his knees. His lips are moving. I know he's saying my name, but I can't hear him.

He's the last thing I see before everything goes dark.

Strong arms are wrapped tightly around me. I groan softly, rubbing myself deeper into the warmth. It feels so good and safe. I blink my eyes open and find Xavior above me, his gaze locked straight ahead. The muscles in his jaw tick like he's barely holding something in.

He's carrying me.

Something shifts along his throat. I squint, then... shit. His tattoos are moving beneath his skin. They aren't tattoos at all. They are shadows rolling under his skin.

My head throbs, and exhaustion drags me down again. I close my eyes, resting my head against his chest, letting myself relax. For the first time since the woods, I know I'm safe. His heartbeat grounds me.

Thump, thump, thump.

When I wake again, I'm lying in a dark room. I blink a few times, letting my eyes adjust, my head fuzzy.

Where am I?

The bonfire, burning jealously, walking into the woods, and the pain, so much excoriating pain, and then Xavior.

I gasp and push myself upright, immediately regretting it as sharp agony shoots up my spine and into my skull. A moan slips out before I can stop it.

"Careful," a low, dark, and groggy voice says from the corner. "Your body needs more time to heal."

I turn my head and find Xavior sitting in a chair clearly not made for someone his size. He looks so uncomfortable, shoulders tense.

I shiver.

The way he tore through two warlocks and a witch without breaking a sweat still plays in my head. I always knew he was powerful—my father never shuts up about it—but seeing it with my own eyes?

It was terrifying.

How can someone hold so much power? He's dangerous, and my gods, it turns me on.

He rescued me...

"Where am I?" My voice comes out harsh.

He stands slowly and moves to my bedside without breaking eye contact. He grabs a glass of water from the table and holds it out.

"The academy's healing center. Your dad and sister were here earlier, but I told them to leave."

I take the glass and drain it, my throat painfully dry. I force myself not to ask the question burning in my chest. *Why are you still here?*

"How long was I out?" I ask instead.

"It's early Thursday morning. You slept through Tuesday night and all of Wednesday."

My gaze drifts down him. He's still wearing the same clothes from the bonfire, wrinkled and worn. I look back up, my brow furrowing.

"And you stayed?"

He swallows, then nods.

"Why?" I press.

He shrugs, rubbing the back of his neck. "Couldn't leave until I knew you were okay."

My heart does this stupid little swell, but I ignore it.

"How did you find me?"

"When the song ended, I went back to where you were. You were gone." His jaw tightens as he looks away. "I followed your footprints in the sand until they disappeared in the woods. Found your beer can. Then I heard you scream." His voice drops. "You were in so much pain."

I flinch at the memory. "Yeah... I was. Thank you."

He shakes his head. "You don't need to thank me. I shouldn't have left you." His hand lifts, hesitating near my face like he wants to touch me, but the door opens.

He growls lowly, annoyed, and immediately clenches his fist and drops it to his side.

A woman in pink scrubs steps in, smiling. "I thought I heard voices! I'm glad you're awake." She looks at him. "You don't need to stay, Prince Xavior. We've got her now."

He looks at me once more, long and unreadable, then nods and leaves without another word.

I almost ask him to stay.

The nurse gives me pain meds and checks my injuries while my thoughts stay firmly locked on the man who carried me out of the woods.

My sister comes by during breakfast and tells me Xavior never left my side, and that when he brought me in, he completely lost it on the healers, demanding they help me, even threatening them when they hesitated.

But why would he do all of that for me?

I don't have an answer, only the stupid butterflies going wild in my stomach every time I think about it.

They discharged me right after lunch, but he never came back to see me.

Brandon sends flowers with my favorite box of chocolates. He feels awful about ditching me, keeps apologizing, but I tell him I don't blame him. I really don't. It makes him feel better, at least.

After leaving the healing center, I decided to go on a walk with my sister. I need to stretch my legs and get some fresh air. Still, my eyes keep drifting to the tree line, like something or someone might jump out. I thought this would be peaceful, but I'm still too raw from the attack.

"Any updates on Mom?" I ask. "How's Dad holding up?"

"No updates," she says. "Dad's been burying himself in work. You know how he gets when he's stressed." She hesitates. "We were so worried about you. The healers were struggling. You were bleeding internally, and your brain was swelling."

My chest tightens with guilt.

"If it wasn't for Xavior, they would've given up," she continues. "Well... they did. But Xavior threatened their lives." She exhales. "I'm honestly glad he was there. Don't ever run off alone like that again, or at least, not until this murderous group is gone."

"I'm sorry I scared you," I say softly. "Did Xavior kill them?"

I slow my steps, looking at her. I already know the men are dead. I watched it happen. I'm just not sure if the woman survived.

"Yeah," she nods. "But it's not over. The teachers said at least ten people escaped during the last attack. Their numbers are shrinking, though."

"Good," I mutter. "Someone in that group has teleportation magic. It's the only reason they never leave a trail."

"Yeah." She kicks a rock. "This whole thing sucks. Why are they even doing this? What did witches ever do? I know we're hated, but not all of us are evil."

"I know," I say. "But some people are raised on hate, and hate doesn't need logic. And power... it corrupts. There are more bad witches than good ones. A lot of us drown in our magic."

"But why not go after the evil ones?" she asks, her voice cracking. "Why hurt the innocent?"

"I don't know," I admit, shaking my head. "Maybe they want to wipe us out before we even get the chance to turn."

She stops walking and turns to me.

"She's dead, isn't she?" Her eyes shine with tears.

"I don't know." I open my arms. "Come here."

She steps into me, and I wrap my arms around her, rubbing small circles into her back. We're complete opposites. She wears her heart on her sleeve and believes in fairytales and mates. Says she can *feel* hers out there somewhere.

Me? I hide everything. I cry alone in the dark... like I can hide it even from myself. I don't believe in mates, and most days, I don't believe in love either.

I've never craved a man's touch... not even my ex.

But gods, ever since I woke up, I can't stop thinking about Xavior's arms around me. About how safe I felt. And it scares the hell out of me.

Should I go talk to him? No.... absolutely not. The thought of embarrassing myself makes my stomach twist, and that's not me. I'm never scared when it comes to men.

After about an hour, we head back. I pause when my eyes meet Xavior's.

He stands ahead of us, our eyes lock. His face is blank, unreadable. I give him a small, hesitant smile... but his upper lip curls into a nasty snarl.

Then he turns and storms off in the opposite direction.

My stomach drops, a sharp, unfamiliar emotion twisting through me. *What the hell?*

I let out a frustrated breath. Ana glances at me, eyebrow raised. I just shrug and keep walking. For a brief, stupid moment, I thought he cared.

Idiot. Why would he? He doesn't even know you.

Chapter Six

Xavior

Finding the Wixx sisters was easy, and getting close to them was easier.

What isn't easy is my attraction to the older sister, Amara.

The younger one is sweet. Both girls are beautiful... but shit. Amara? She's something else entirely, otherworldly. I can't look away, no matter how hard I try.

After the attack, I started watching her more closely. I told myself it was necessary, that it was about protection. I tried to ignore the strange pull, but I fucking can't, and that pisses me off.

I've managed to keep my distance, but that doesn't mean I don't watch her... every fucking move, and every habit. I need to know where she is at all times, more than I've ever needed anything. When she's not in my line of sight, it drives me insane. Which is why I'm currently installing a hidden camera in her room like a damn psychopath.

My hand twitches on the camera. I shouldn't do this. I know I shouldn't. But fuck. My hand keeps moving anyway. I can't stop myself. I've known for a while that I'm not a normal man, but I never considered myself a crazy motherfucker, not like this.

I'm not a mindless monster. I know exactly what I'm doing. I'm keeping her safe because she's the key to saving my brother, but fuck... she's becoming an obsession.

I'll feed my obsession for now. I'll feed *her*, and when the time comes, she'll die by my hands.

The worst part? I don't give a flying fuck.

If I'm losing my mind... if this is full insanity, then let it happen. Because if *she's* my madness...

I'll drown in it with a smile. That's what scares me.

I angle the camera toward the door and her bed, positioned just to the right of it. I don't install a second one facing the closet or bathroom. I'm not trying to be a pervert and watch her shower, though the thought tempts me.

I want her to feel my presence.

Still, if she walks in front of the camera naked, I doubt I'll be able to look away. I've never claimed to be a good man. I'm no saint.

The sound of keys in the lock makes my body tense. She should be at dinner. I should know... I watched her enter the dining hall earlier with her sister.

I slip into the closet, shutting the door just as it opens. Through the slats, I watch her move around the room. I don't know how it's possible, but somehow, she looks even more breathtaking than the last time I saw her.

I love her like this most when she thinks she's alone and visibly relaxes.

Amara has the kind of beauty that borders on obscene. A body built to ruin men, and a face that makes them stupid. Every guy in this damn academy watches her like she's theirs to claim... and she doesn't spare a single one of them a glance.

But what pisses me off the most?

She doesn't look at me either. Not the way I want. The first woman I've ever truly wanted to claim, and she doesn't flinch, doesn't even blush, doesn't try to impress me. She doesn't perform. She doesn't see me.

And God, it's driving me insane.

I bite down on my knuckle as she starts undressing, my heart hammering unnaturally hard. My gaze drags over her body, slow and hungry, pausing on her perky breasts in a white lace bra, then lower, to the curve of her wide hips in a matching thong. White against her brown skin looks sinfully perfect.

Heat slams straight into my cock, making me shudder, making me ache.

She lies back on the bed, knees bent, thighs parted just enough for me to see her lace-covered pussy. I lick my lips, imagining the taste of her. Shit, I'm on fire, and I'm already losing it.

Her body is everything I've ever wanted. My filthiest thoughts, every fantasy. All of it, right there in front of me.

Then she rolls onto her stomach, phone in hand... and fuck, I swear I could die in this closet from wanting her this badly.

Tell me how bad it would really be to open this door, walk over there, and put my hands on that perfect fucking ass.

I swallow as I undo my belt, unzip my jeans, and pull my hard cock free. I'm throbbing, demanding more. I wrap my hand around my cock and stroke, heat pulsing as my eyes stay locked on her ass. For half a second, her laugh flashes through my mind, soft and unguarded.

My grip tightens instead of loosening. I know this is wrong, but I'm losing control... my grip on reality from my desire for her.

I picture myself pulling her onto her knees, sliding those tiny panties aside. *Shit*. I grind my teeth, swallowing my groans as my balls tighten and strands of come shoot out of my tip, painting the back of her closet doors.

This isn't a strategy anymore. No... this is a need.

Her phone rings, and she groans, ignoring the call. Who was it?

I need to get her phone to mirror it to mine. I need to know who she's talking to.

Chapter Seven

Amara

I slam my suitcase shut, zipping it closed before tossing it onto the bed, letting all my frustration bleed into the stupid thing. It's been two days since Xavior started ignoring me and spending time with my sister.

Yesterday, when he and Ana were talking, I walked over and said hi. He didn't even look at me before walking off. Ana actually had the nerve to ask what I did to piss him off.

I tell myself I don't care, but seeing them together hits something raw and ugly inside me, even though she swears it's purely friendly. He never flirts with her, and she doesn't like him that way.

Still, jealousy doesn't listen to logic. It hijacks it and buries it somewhere I can't reach. I want him to notice me. I want his arms around me again. That single moment wasn't enough. One taste wasn't enough.

Does he see her softness and my edge as a contrast? Something safer? Something easier? Maybe, but I'm not here to compete.

You know what? I don't care. Let him keep his strong arms, his impossible grey eyes, his confidence. None of it matters, not really. I roll my eyes at the thought, even as I admit, grudgingly, he's impossible to ignore.

A strange prickle crawls up my spine, the feeling of being watched even alone in my own room. I glance around. Nothing, but still, the unease lingers.

Brandon is picking me up for the town fair soon. I pull my hair into a low, messy bun, leaving a few strands loose around my face. My door swings open, and Ana strides in, balancing two large suitcases and a carry-on.

"You do know we're just going home, and your clothes are there, right?" I rub pink gloss across my lips.

"Yeah, and your point? I need options. You never know when I might need something..." she smirks, "...sexy. Speaking of sexy, you look good."

"Brandon wants to take me out tonight and thought the fair would be a good distraction," I told him how I feel about Xavior. Brandon doesn't understand why he acts like he cares one second, then ignores me the next. He thinks Xavior likes me, and I think he might need serious therapy.

"I want to go, but I don't want to be the third wheel. Maybe I can convince Xavior to come."

"Please don't."

She sighs dramatically. "Fine. Are you ready? Xavior texted me saying he's out front waiting for us." Great. They're texting buddies now.

I shove the irritation down and check my reflection one last time. I'm wearing a white halter dress. It's low cut, flowy, stopping mid-thigh, and my back is completely exposed.

"Yeah, let's go. Brandon will be here any moment." I grab my suitcase, and we leave. A few guys glance my way as we step outside, and I feel a familiar surge of confidence.

I smooth the front of my dress and square my shoulders when I spot him leaning against a blacked-out BMW, arms folded. His black shirt strains over his muscular frame. Dark sunglasses cover his eyes as he scrolls on his phone.

"Xavior!" My sister calls, pushing past me.

He looks up, glancing over Ana before his gaze lingers on me. He lifts his sunglasses without breaking eye contact. I slow my steps as we stare at each other. It's the first time he's looked at me in two days.

"You're all dressed up for just going home."

He hasn't said a word to me in days, so I return the favor. I open the rear door of his car, toss my suitcase inside, and slam it shut.

Is it childish? Maybe. Do I care? Not at all.

Ana looks between us. "She's not coming. She's going out with Brandon."

As soon as she finishes, Brandon's red Mustang pulls up. He jumps out, grinning at me.

I walk toward him with a smile spreading across my face. I've missed him. I throw my arms around his neck; he lifts me effortlessly, spinning me, and I can't help but laugh, letting the joy of seeing him wash over me.

"Beautiful as always, Chicca." He sets me down before glancing behind me. I turn to face my sister.

"See you later," I say, lifting a hand in a peace sign as Brandon guides me toward his car.

"I have a great idea!" Ana calls as Brandon opens the passenger side door. I pause, oh God, please don't. "Why don't we join you? What do you think, Xavior? They're going to the fair."

I narrow my eyes at her, and her smile only widens. *That little traitor.*

I look at Xavior. He meets my gaze, expression sharp. I shake my head no.

He smirks. "Yes, that's a great idea."

I search for a way out. "I don't know, it's supposed to be just us," I say, glancing at Brandon with subtle pleading, but he isn't paying attention.

"You guys can come along if you want," he says, shrugging. "Follow us."

"Cool." Ana nods.

I cross my arms, watching Xavior lift her heavy suitcases. He leans to grab the handle, murmuring something that makes her laugh. He opens the trunk and places her things inside.

I turn away, heading for the Mustang, letting Brandon close the door behind me.

We pull into the crowded fairground parking lot, heading toward the back. Brandon parks and turns toward me, a small pout tugging at his lips. "Are you upset with me?"

"Yes. You were supposed to distract me from him, not invite him along."

"I thought giving him a taste of his own medication wouldn't hurt. You know, make him a little jealous. If I'm right, then he likes you." He pulls down his visor and ruffles his blond curly hair, messing it up.

"Brandon, honey, he knows you're gay. I doubt he's the jealous type, even if he does like me. Which he doesn't."

"No, he doesn't. Look, he got jealous when I hugged you; he wouldn't have gotten jealous if he knew I was gay. I'll do what I do best and flirt." He winks at me, pulling open his door.

I roll my eyes. He's mistaken, but whatever. He opens my door for me and grabs my hand to help me out.

We walk towards the long line, and I see Ana and Xavior already there, talking away. We step up behind them. I lean against Brandon, not for physical support but mental support.

He leans down and whispers in my ear, "You don't need to be jealous." He places his hands on my hips.

If he weren't my friend, I would've punched him.

I close my eyes, shaking my head as I sigh. "I have no right to be. I don't know why I am. It's driving me crazy."

"Well, it seems that feeling is very mutual," he whispers the words before kissing my cheek and straightening.

I open my eyes, and the first thing I see is Xavior.

His dark gaze pulls me in. His upper lip curls back, baring his teeth, eyes burning with something close to murderous rage as he glares at Brandon.

What the fuck... maybe Brandon was right.

Does he feel this magnetic pull between us? Does he stay up late at night thinking of me, too? Is jealousy eating him alive? Am I driving him to the brink of madness?

Jesus, I hope so.

I want him to want me.

It's almost impossible to believe a man like him could be this crazy over me. Not because I'm not pretty or not good enough. No, because men like him don't *do* relationships. He can have any woman he wants. And I'm not the type of girl to share.

Maybe one night with him would be enough to ease the madness inside me.

Xavior pays for all of us, and I drift toward the flashing lights, spinning in a small circle as I smile. I haven't been to a fair in so long, the lights, the laughter, the distant screams of joy.

I look back at our little group. Everyone is taking it all in... except him.

He's staring at me with so much intensity it lights a flame inside me, heat pooling low in my body. As we hold each other's gaze, the noise fades away, and the crowd seems to disappear.

His tongue darts out, licking his upper teeth. The tattoos along his neck and arms seem to swirl beneath his skin.

I love the way his attention feels, like nothing else exists, like *I* am the only thing that matters. And I realize, in that moment, I would gladly give myself to the madness for him.

"Amara!"

I blink as the sounds crash back in. I turn, heat rushing to my face with embarrassment. Brandon... of course, it's Brandon. He's pointing toward the rows of games.

I shake myself mentally and let out a small giggle, jogging toward the nearest booth. Excitement bubbles in my chest, making me feel like a little girl again. I scan the stuffed animals, and my eyes land on a large pink pig. That's the one I want.

I hand the man behind the booth some money. He gives me five baseballs and explains the rules… knock down five clowns for a large prize, or three for a smaller one.

Doesn't sound too hard. He turns the machine on, and the clowns start moving.

Oh, come on.

"You can do it!" I glance back to see my friends watching. I flash them a grin before focusing on the targets. I throw the first baseball. It misses by a mile.

There goes my pig.

I throw the remaining four, but not a single clown falls. My shoulders slump.

This is bullshit. The clowns shouldn't be moving. What a joke.

My body itches with awareness when I feel warm breath tickling my ear, and a pair of large hands grip my hips, the heat of his body pressed against my back.

Jesus, it feels so good. Every inch of me wants to lean back, to melt into him. I don't have to look to know who it is.

Xavior's lips graze my ear as he whispers. "Pick which one you want."

He releases me but doesn't move away. He hands the man some money, then grips my hips again, pulling me tight against his front. My body shivers as I bite my lower lip, holding back a moan.

The man holds out the baseballs. Xavior squeezes my hips once more before reaching past me and taking them. "Hopefully, your boyfriend doesn't get mad."

I say nothing. I can't, feeling completely consumed by his warmth, by the hard line of his body pressed into mine. He straightens and starts throwing. I force myself to focus on the game instead of the sparks igniting low in my belly.

When he knocks down all five clowns, I squeal, bouncing on my toes. I point excitedly at the pig, and the man hands it over.

I turn to Xavior, look up through my lashes, and smile widely. "Thank you."

"Of course. Anything—"

He's cut off when Brandon reaches around him and pulls me away. I point at the massive Ferris wheel in front of us. "Brandon! Let's get on."

He shakes his head immediately, and Ana laughs at his horrified expression. A warlock who can wield magic but is afraid of heights.

"Oh, come on, please!" I try to drag him forward after handing my pig to Ana.

"I'll take you." Xavior steps forward, holding out his hand for me to take.

I hesitate. "Is that okay with you?" I ask Brandon, not wanting to ditch him.

"He'll be fine with Ana," Xavior answers for him.

Brandon nods, agreeing.

I slip my hand into Xavior's, and he immediately pulls me close, wrapping an arm around my shoulders as he guides me toward the line. I stand stiffly at first, my arms awkward at my sides, then, after a moment, I lean into him.

It feels... right. I never loved being in any other man's arms. I always thought I wasn't the cuddly type. I was wrong.

"Have you ever been on one?" I ask after a few minutes, glancing up at him.

He shakes his head. No surprise, this doesn't feel like his scene. "It's been forever since I have. I think I was twelve the last time I went to a fair. I always loved it."

"Why did you stop coming?"

"Training. We were always training. My mom pushed me even when I was young. Dad used to give us days off, but once he joined the council, he wasn't around much to stop her." I normally never tell anyone that; only a few people know how strict my mom was or is. Brandon, Ana, and my dad.

"She didn't push Ana the same?"

"No. She trained Ana, but not like me. Don't ask me why. I used to but she said I was being overdramatic."

Xavior opens his mouth to respond, but the attendant opens the gate and tells us to get in. He drops his arm as he sits, but the moment I settle beside him, he wraps it back around my waist.

The attendant shuts the gate, and we begin moving. I laugh, gripping his thigh as the wheel lifts us higher. I haven't laughed like this in so long. When we reach the top, the ride stops.

"Wow," I breathe. "The view is amazing."

Xavior pulls me closer. "Yeah," he murmurs. "It is."

My heart stutters when his free hand slides onto my bare thigh. Why does he keep touching me?

I turn my head to find him already watching me, we're inches apart. I can feel his breath against my lips.

Kiss me. Jesus, please.

"Xavior," I whisper. His gaze drops to my mouth.

"I don't think I told you how beautiful you look." His fingers lift, brushing a strand of hair behind my ear.

"Thank you," I say softly. "You don't look so bad yourself." I smile. "So, tell me about you."

"There's not much to say."

"Oh, come on. I doubt that. I know you have zero siblings, but what about your mom? Is she back home?"

His body stiffened when I said, 'zero siblings.' Was I wrong?

He doesn't answer. He removes his arm and shifts away, creating distance between us. And suddenly, everything feels awkward. Thankfully, the ride starts moving again.

Chapter Eight

Xavior

Ignoring her for the past few days has been the hardest thing I've ever done. When she isn't looking, I watch her. I follow her, make sure she's safe.

I never thought I'd become a crazed stalker, but dammit, I am for her, and her alone.

Tonight, though, I can't ignore her. Not when Brandon keeps touching her. Every time he does, something foreign and burning creeps through me. Jealousy, I think.

I want to break his fingers for daring to put his hands on her. I would do it too, but I know she would never forgive me if she found out.

You don't need her forgiveness. She'll be dead.

I growl softly at the voice in my head.

She's skipping ahead of the group, clutching the pink pig I won her. She turns and walks backward, smiling at us. "Let's get some cotton candy!"

"Yes!" Ana shouts, grabbing her hand. They rush toward the long line together.

"She's beautiful, isn't she?" Brandon steps up beside me, smirking. "Too bad you can't have her."

He walks off before I can respond, wraps an arm around her waist, and winks at me.

I bare my teeth, imagining all the ways I could kill him, slowly and methodically: ripping him apart limb by limb or crushing his heart until it stops beating for her, until there's nothing left for her to love.

I shove my hands into my pockets and drag in a breath, trying to think of a way to get her alone again. I rake a hand through my hair, frustration clawing at my chest.

"Xavior!"

Fuck. I love the way she says my name.

I wonder what it'll sound like when I bury myself deep inside her, when I make her forget Brandon ever existed.

I watch as she runs toward me, grabs my wrist, yanks my hand from my pocket, and drags me to the front of the line where a bored employee waits.

"Which flavor do you want?" She tries to pull her hand away, but I don't let her.

I lace my fingers through hers, keeping her pressed close. I refuse to let her go back to him. I'm aware of his sexual preferences but it doesn't matter. He still needs to keep his hands off what's mine.

"Nothing for me," I tell the employee, and Amara pouts.

She's creating a monster and has no clue, no idea how close I am to snapping, to losing control completely if he touches her again.

Would she hate me if I locked her away somewhere far? Somewhere where no one else could touch her. Somewhere she'd belong only to me.

"Come on," she pushes. "Have you ever tried cotton candy? If you haven't, you have to."

"Surprise me." Her smile returns, bright and devastating, as she turns to order.

I don't even like sweets, but to keep that smile, I'll eat anything.

I glance at Brandon and smirk.

Mine.

"Hey, Brandon," Ana says, grabbing his arm. "Why don't we go try to win one of those adorable fish?"

She drags him away after they get their cotton candy.

Thank fuck.

Amara thanks the employee and hands me a cone. "It's bubblegum flavor." She wiggles her brows.

I laugh. *Shit...* I haven't laughed in so fucking long.

She tears off a piece and lifts it toward me. "Open up."

And I do. Because I'd do whatever she tells me. I must make a face, because she bursts out laughing. "It's not that bad!"

"It's too sweet."

"Nope, it's perfect." She pops another piece into her mouth and moans softly.

Goddamn... I want to hear that sound again.

"Come on!" She wraps her free hand around my elbow and drags me forward. For someone so small, she's surprisingly good at manhandling me.

She shoves me into a photo booth and climbs in after me. "Scoot over! There's no room for me!"

"Plenty of room, little vixen." I tug her down onto my lap. She lands with a soft gasp, cheeks flushing. "See? Perfect."

She shifts to adjust herself, her curvy ass rubbing against my upper thighs.

"Ready?"

She doesn't wait for an answer. She hits the start button and leans back against me, smiling into the camera. The flash goes off.

Then she turns, grabs my jaw, forcing my face toward the lens. My body shudders when her lips brush my cheek.

The camera flashes again.

She starts to pull away.

My hand tightens on her thigh. My other hand wraps around her jaw, and I crash my mouth against hers.

She gasps in shock... then kisses me back.

Flash.

We don't pull apart. My world tilts with the intensity of the kiss, hunger roaring through me. My body burns with need. My hand slides higher up her thigh, creeping beneath her dress, gripping her hip.

She moans.

There are no words that can describe this feeling. Her lips are impossibly soft and sweet. I taste cotton candy, and fuck, I love the taste of it now. I tilt my head, deepening the kiss. My hand leaves her jaw and tangles in her soft, silky hair, holding her exactly where I want her as my tongue slips between her luscious lips.

This kiss nearly undoes me.

I've never felt hunger like this. Desire slams into me so hard it makes my head spin.

The camera flashes again and again.

The words pound in my skull, screaming for me to acknowledge them. I know what this means, but I can't.

This is impossible. There is no way.

Axel...

I rip myself away, the image of my brother—weak, broken, lying in a coma—slamming into me.

What the fuck am I thinking?

I can't do this, not with her. I'm not allowed to want this. Not with the girl I'm supposed to kill to save my brother.

I should hate her, but I don't.

Fuck.

I snatch the photos as the machine spits them out and shove them into my pocket. I want them... need something to remember this moment, proof it happened.

I stand too fast, sending her tumbling onto her ass, her eyes go wide with shock.

I look away, jaw clenched tight.

"That was a fucking mistake," I spit, venom coating every word. I want to hurt her for making me feel this for breaking something inside me. Like if I hurt her enough, it'll stop hurting me.

Her eyes fill with pain, and my chest tightens.

I freeze for half a second too long, long enough to almost reach out for her. I have to leave now, before I fall to my knees and beg her forgiveness.

I turn my back on her and storm away.

The farther I get, the worse it hurts. By the time I reach my car, my chest feels like it's splitting apart. I slam the door shut.

"Fuck! Fuck! Fuck!" I roar, slamming my fist into the steering wheel with each word, hard enough to bend it. The horn screams beneath my blows.

I collapse back into the seat, chest heaving, and tear the pictures from my pocket... then freeze.

Blood has smeared across the glossy surface.

Across her perfect smile.

I swipe at it frantically with my thumb, only making it worse.

"Shit..."

I drag my thumb to my mouth, licking it in blind panic. As if that could fix it. As if I can clean her without ruining her. As if I can undo what I just did.

Chapter Nine

With the tip of my finger, I trace my lips. They still tingle from the kiss.

I told Brandon and Ana that Xavior got an important call and had to leave. I couldn't tell them what actually happened.

I plaster a fake smile on my face as we play more games, but God... it still hurts.

We stay for another hour before finally leaving. As Brandon drives slowly up our long driveway, my stomach tightens when I see Xavior's car.

It was just a stupid kiss. Not a big deal.

"Good night, Chiccas!" Brandon calls as we climb out of the car. I force a smile and say good night before shutting the door.

"God! That was a freaking blast!" Ana exclaims, climbing the porch stairs. I mumble a quiet agreement as I open the front door.

Everything is spotless. No trace of the chaos from the attack. My heart stutters. When did Dad have time to clean?

"Dad hired someone," Ana explains, reading my expression. "Do you think she's okay?"

I take a deep breath. "I don't know. They're bad people, obviously. If she is still alive, it's for a reason. Come on it's late, let's go to bed."

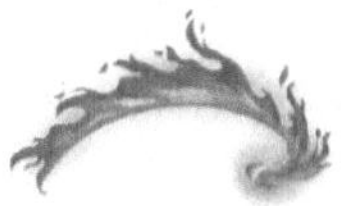

I cover my face with the blanket and let out a long sigh, savoring the comfort. I'm not ready to start the day.

Eventually, I get up, rubbing my tired eyes, and head to the attached bathroom. I splash cold water on my face. I brush my teeth, the routine grounding me.

I need to go for a run. It's been too long, and I can't let fear rule me again. I doubt they'll attack the same place twice.

I pull on tight red running shorts that hug my ass perfectly and a matching sports bra, comb my hair into a high ponytail, grab my phone, and slip on my wireless headphones. Old school rap blares, "Saltshaker." Hell yeah. I'm totally not trying to look sexy for him.

I run downstairs, passing Xavior at the dining table, sipping coffee. I look away, ignoring him, and grab a granola bar and water. I perch on the countertop and scroll through social media.

I'm doing a damn good job ignoring his gaze. It feels like it's burning a hole into my skin. I remember his words from last night. *This was a fucking mistake.*

The kiss was incredible, the best I've ever had, but then he pushed me onto my ass and hurt me. It took everything I had to hold my tears at bay. He doesn't deserve them.

I turn off notifications, shutting the world out. I leap off the countertop and rush through the back door. His presence is suffocating; it's everywhere.

I take off, running hard through the woods. My lungs burn, my thighs scream, but I keep going. An hour later, I finally slow to a stop.

I sink onto the forest floor, staring up at the trees and the sunlight beaming in through the tree branches, enjoying the warmth of it against my skin.

I hear a branch snap and immediately turn my head. I let out a breath of relief when I see a deer walking past. I close my eyes, enjoying this peaceful moment.

I groan, muscles aching, especially my neck, realizing I must have dozed off. When I turn on the notifications on my phone, I freeze. Missed calls a dozen from Ana and an unknown number. It's already late afternoon.

Shit. I've been gone for hours.

I push off the ground and sprint back, hoping Ana hasn't called Dad. He already has enough to deal with.

I make it home and open the back door, and I barely get it shut before I'm slammed against the wall. Hard.

"Where the fuck have you been?" Xavior growls, his face inches from mine. His eyes are completely dark, shadows churning violently beneath his skin. His hands clamp around my upper arms, so tight I'm sure he'll leave bruises.

Fear rushes through me. He's scaring the crap out of me, but he wouldn't really hurt me. Right?

I shove at his chest, but he doesn't budge. "Let me go!" I snap, pushing harder.

"Xavior!" Ana shouts from behind him.

He freezes, then, with a sharp breath, he releases me and steps back.

"We were so worried," Ana says, her voice shaking. "We thought you were taken."

"I'm sorry," I say, rubbing my arms. "I lost track of time."

"Who were you with?" Xavior snarls. "Brandon? Or was it another man?"

The accusation makes my blood boil. "Seriously?" I snap. "If I were, it's none of your business. If I were out there sucking his dick, it's *still* none of your business."

I turn to walk away.

"The fuck did you say?" His voice drops, low, dangerous. A shiver crawls up my spine. I stop, turning around.

"Yeah," I say coldly. "And it felt good too. He bent me over and fucked me so good my legs are still shaking. He couldn't get enough of me." I smile cruelly. "It was hot when he praised me—shouting my name like a goddamn prayer."

Ana stares at me like I've lost my mind. I push past them and head straight for my room.

Behind me, the front door slams. Seconds later, I hear his car roar to life, tires screeching as he tears away.

My hands shake as I strip and step into the shower.

"Okay, what the fuck was that?" Ana demands, slamming the bathroom door open.

"I'm in the damn shower," I snap. "Get out."

"Nothing I haven't seen," she says, crossing her arms. "I'm not leaving."

"It was nothing."

She snorts. "Really? Weren't *you* the one who told me not to be childish when I tried to make my ex jealous by sending him a picture of me kissing someone else?"

I yank the curtain open. She's sitting on the vanity, arms folded. "That's different."

"How?" she presses. "Did you say all that to make him jealous? Because we both know it was complete bullshit."

I sigh. "Fine, I lied. But not to make him jealous. I just wanted to piss him off. He knows exactly how to push my buttons, and I snapped."

Ana exhales slowly. "You two need to talk. I'm not built for this kind of chaos." She hops off the counter. "It's usually me with the bad habits and boy issues. You're the one who talks me through it maybe try taking your own advice."

I'm sitting on the couch talking to Brandon on the phone, telling him what I told Xavior. He's laughing his ass off on the other end. I'm wearing shorts and an oversized T-shirt that I may have stolen from my dad a while back.

"Sorry, girl," Brandon says between laughs. "Your fantasy will never come true."

"Oh, please," I scoff. "If I really tried, I could totally seduce you."

The front door opens. Please be Ana, I'm starving.

Instead, Xavior steps inside.

He crosses his arms and leans against the opening between the foyer and the living room, eyes locked on me.

"Get off the phone." I narrow my eyes, about to tell him to fuck off, when the door opens again.

"Food delivery!" Ana sings. "Oh, hey, Xavior. I got food for you, too."

"Hey, I'll call you later," I say quickly, ending the call. I sit up and hold my hands out for the bag.

"No time to eat," Xavior says flatly. "Your father wants me to start training both of you."

"Right now?" Ana asks. "Can't it wait? I'm starving."

She hands me the bag anyway. I pull out the Chinese containers and set them on the coffee table. There is no way I'm not eating. My dad would never approve of training on an empty stomach and honestly, not a full one either, but that's a tomorrow problem.

"Come on, Ana," I say, patting the seat beside me. "I found a movie."

She hesitates, eyes darting between us. I grab the remote and turn on the TV, but Xavior snatches it out of my hand.

"What the fuck?" I shout, jumping up. "Give that back!"

"Get your ass downstairs," he says, holding it above his head just out of reach. "We have training to do."

"No," I snap. "I'm eating and watching a movie."

"No, you're not." His gaze flicks to Ana. "Go get ready."

I glare at her. *If you leave, I will murder you.*

Her eyes widen, but she turns and heads downstairs. Traitor...

"Fuck this," I mutter. "I'm leaving. Tell Ana I'm staying at Brandon's." I shove past him.

He grabs my arm and shoves me face down on the couch. "The fuck you are," he growls.

I struggle, but he holds me down with one hand on my back and the other holding the side of my face against the cushion. Not hurting me, but not letting me move. "

"Get off me," I snap. "You have no right to hold me down."

He chuckles darkly, "And who's going to stop me?"

He flips me around and nudges my legs apart, settling his hips in between them. His hand wraps around my throat, but not squeezing, just holding, thumb pressing lightly under my jaw.

"If you know what's good for you," he murmurs, voice low and shaking, "you'll break it off with him."

Then he kisses me. It's brutal and overly possessive. Everything I shouldn't want but somehow do.

I kiss him back before I can stop myself, fisting his shirt as heat crashes through me. His hips thrust forward, and with his free hand, he grips the back of my knee, lifting my leg over his waist.

A moan tears out of me. My body betrays me completely, my nipples hard, pulse racing, desire roaring so loud it drowns out reason. I want to drown in it. Let it consume me.

This was a fucking mistake.

The words slam into me like a slap. I turn my head, breaking the kiss. His mouth trails down my neck.

"Xavior," I say, breathless but firm. "Stop."

He freezes, just for a second.

"Stop," I repeat, sharper now.

He doesn't stop, "You feel so good. Don't overthink this."

"No." I shove him back and slap him. "Lacere!" Power explodes from me. His body is thrown across the room.

I don't check if he's okay. I know he is. He should've stopped the first time.

I rush out of the house, and I'm almost to the car when I hear him shout my name raw, desperate, commanding. It nearly stops me...

Chapter Ten

I lay on Brandon's sofa, my thoughts spinning. Am I being childish? My emotions yank me in every direction, giving me whiplash. How can I stay there with him—a man who can unravel me with just a single kiss, breaking down the brick wall around my heart? It's insanity. I have to protect it, especially after he pushed me away.

I told Brandon about the kiss last night and what happened at the house. He thinks I need to talk to Xavior. I told him to fuck off. The unknown number keeps calling me, and now I know it's Xavior.

We're sitting at the small round table, eating breakfast, when my phone rings.

"Morning!" I answer cheerfully.

"Amara! Why aren't you home? Why are you ignoring my orders to have Xavior train you?"

"He's an asshole. Pick someone else, anyone! I can stay at Brandon's house." I pace to the window, staring outside, silently praying he'll agree. Normally, he does.

"Xavior will train you. He's the best fighter I know. And it's safer if you go home. I've got too much on my plate. Please, just listen, this once." His voice carries stress I can't argue with.

"Yes... of course."

I hear him exhale. "Thank you. I know this is hard, but we'll get through it. He's on the way."

I'm about to ask who he means when Xavior's car pulls in. I jump back against the wall, noticing what I'm wearing. Brandon's oversized T-shirt and tiny shorts that hardly cover my ass.

"Dad, my car is here. I can drive myself back."

There's a knock at the door. I shake my head at Brandon, but he doesn't look at me.

Xavior shoves his way inside before the door fully opens, like he owns the place.

"Alright. Call me if anything comes up. Stay safe and listen to Xavior," my dad says, hanging up.

Xavior's nostrils flare as he looks me over. "Get dressed. We're leaving." Xavior says to me without looking away from Brandon, who is wearing a pair of sweatpants and nothing else.

I sigh and start down the hall.

"I'll go with her," Brandon mutters under his breath.

Xavior chuckles darkly. "The fuck you are."

I don't wait for Brandon's reply. Knowing him, he'll just nod; he's not one to push back, especially against someone like Xavior. The intensity of his power makes people submit easily. He's a fool to think I'll ever submit to him.

Even though I nearly did last night. The memory of that sweet, pure ecstasy makes me shiver. I touch my lips. They still tingle. Is this what being addicted feels like? Needing another hit more than air.

I head back to the living room, raising my brows at Brandon. He sits on a dining chair, knee bouncing nervously, as Xavior stands beside him, watching him with pure hatred in his eyes, daring him to move a muscle, more like praying he'll move. It looks like he wants him to move just so he can hit him.

"I'll text you later," I call over my shoulder as I go to the door. Brandon stands, takes a step, but Xavior blocks him. Brandon laughs nervously and sinks back into his seat.

Don't say anything, I tell myself.

Shit, if looks could actually kill...

"Alright, bye." I open the door. Xavior stalks over, jaw ticking, hair messy with a few strands over his eyes. He's terrifying, and maybe I'm a little scared.

Neither of us says a word until I look around the parking lot. My temper is slowly snapping. I grind the back of my teeth as I try to calm down. This man I hardly know is trying to control my every move, and it's getting old, fast.

"Where's my car?" I snap.

"Ana."

Really? Like that's a fucking explanation. *Breathe*, Dad is already under a lot of stress. He has no time to hear about me acting up, and Xavior obviously will tell him.

I scrunch my nose when he opens the passenger door. I slide in, and he immediately leans over me, grabbing for the seat belt.

"I can do that myself, thank you very much!" I snap, yanking it away and buckling in. He snarls and slams the door so hard the car vibrates. I'm honestly surprised the glass doesn't shatter. He drags a hand through his hair as he stalks around the front of the car, looking just as aggravated as I feel.

Yeah, me too, buddy. At least I'm being well behaved, I even said thank you.

I smile to myself as he starts the engine and grabs my phone, connecting it to Bluetooth. *Bullshit* comes on, and I smirk as I crank up the volume. I love this song—perfect for sassy-ass moods. I can't speak for all Latinas, but this one definitely has an attitude problem.

Xavior says something I can't hear. He turns the volume down.

I narrow my eyes and turn it right back up, fully committing to being a brat. He rubs his face in frustration and shakes his head. Don't mess with my music when I'm in the mood.

He pulls over. I glance up and realize we're in front of my favorite coffee shop. I want to go in—knowing full well he won't buy me anything—but my stubborn side wins. I cross my arms and glare out the windshield. I didn't even finish my coffee earlier or take a single bite of my breakfast.

Then I see him walking back toward the car with two coffees and a brown bag. Shock spreads through me as he stops at my door. I roll the window down, and he hands me both before circling the car and getting in.

"I saw you didn't finish your breakfast," he says flatly, already starting the engine.

I open the bag. Sausage, egg, and cheese croissant. A chocolate chip muffin. My favorites. My exact order. My heart swells despite myself. How does he know my exact order?

"Thank you." I unwrap the sandwich and take a bite. God, so good.

I love breakfast food and coffee, possibly too much. But it's not an addiction if you admit it, right?

He doesn't say another word the rest of the drive. Honestly, I don't think he's used to someone who doesn't bow to him. By the time we pull into the house, my sandwich is gone, latte in hand. He even got my customized drink right, which somehow makes it worse.

Xavior gathers the trash before getting out, and annoyingly, my anger dulls just a notch.

"Straight downstairs, little vixen," he orders as we walk inside.

I wrinkle my nose at the nickname. "Don't call me that."

I do as he says, heading straight downstairs. Ana's already there, slouched in a chair, scrolling through her phone. I lean against the wall, crossing my arms.

"Alright," Xavior says, his voice edged with something dangerous. "Since we're all finally here." His gaze flicks to me. "Your father wants me to start training both of you today."

I arch a brow. "Yes, that's what you said yesterday. What kind of training exactly?"

"Combat." He steps closer. Close enough that I catch his spicy, woodsy scent. Fantastic.

I suck at combat training. I'm a horrible fighter. Mom gave up on me a while ago. Ana's even worse. None of this makes sense unless Dad is really desperate or really confident in Xavior.

"Start stretching." He turns and walks toward the mats.

Ana pouts as she stands. "This sucks," she whispers.

"Tell me about it." I pull my oversized T-shirt over my head, grateful I wore leggings and a sports bra. When I turn back, Xavior's gaze drags slowly down my body, heated and unapologetic.

I ignore the way it makes my skin prickle and start stretching.

I don't understand him. He pushes me away, yet looks at me like that. I refuse to be the one to ask... it would be humiliating if I'm wrong.

My phone vibrates. I pull it from my pocket, and Ana leans over my shoulder.

Jaxon.

My chest tightens. I decline the call and shove my phone back in my pocket.

"Why is he calling?" Ana asks.

"I don't know."

"Alright," Xavior says. "We'll start with basic stances."

He sits to remove his boots. I lean forward into a stretch, legs wide, arms extended, lowering my chest toward the mat. I turn my head just enough to watch him. The way his biceps flex as he works the laces loose, the fabric of his shirt pulling tight over muscle, does something to me... something dangerous.

Damn it.

"Alright," he says as he stands, lifting his chin. He widens his stance, crossing his arms as he looks down at us. "Show me your fighting stance."

Why is he so damn hot? It's unfair...

I bend my knees slightly, raising my hands just like Mom taught me. My palms are open, elbows bent, feet grounded. Ana glances over, then mirrors me.

"Wrong." He shakes his head, disappointment clear in his expression. "Everything about your stance is wrong."

He circles us slowly. My pulse kicks up when he stops behind me. I shiver as his hands settle on my waist, firm and deliberate, turning me just a fraction.

"You need to open those legs wider for me," he murmurs near my ear.

My breath hitches.

His leg slides between mine, his foot nudging my feet apart. He kicks my left foot forward just slightly, adjusting my balance.

"Yeah," he says quietly. "Just like that."

Oh, my God...

His breath is hot against my ear. My heart pounds so hard I swear he can feel it through my back. Heat rushes to my cheeks. His hands leave my waist only to grip my shoulders, tilting my body to the side. Slowly, far too slowly, they slide down my arms, his fingers trailing, precise, and controlled.

Goosebumps erupt everywhere he touches.

"Bend your elbows," he says softly. "Keep one here and the other here." His voice lowers. "Look at you, listening. Being so good for me."

My knees nearly buckle.

His hands return to my hips. "Now bend your knees slightly."

I do, and my ass rubs against him.

He lets out a low groan before he can stop himself. "Good girl."

Holy hell...

I glance at Ana. She's focused on her own stance, completely oblivious. She can't hear him. Xavior steps away from me, and I hate how instantly cold it feels without him there.

He moves to Ana, and my jaw drops.

He doesn't touch her. Not like he touched me. He stands beside her, instructing with words only. When he does adjust her, it's quick, hands on her upper arms, impersonal, tilting her slightly before stepping back.

Why didn't he do that with me?

"I'm going to teach you how to block hits," he says. "Keep your arms up and watch your attacker's hands."

He steps in front of Ana and throws his fist toward her face.

I gasp, but he stops inches from her nose.

"I'll do that again. Watch my fist. When I strike, swipe your forearm up to throw my arm off target and twist your head away from the hit."

He strikes again. Ana blocks it, squealing when she succeeds.

"Good," he says with a nod. Then he turns to me and repeats the drill.

I smile when I block him, too. We continue like that for another hour, until his phone rings.

At the top of the stairs, I freeze when I hear him answer.

"Hey, Lacey."

Disappointment crawls violently up my chest, squeezing my heart until it hurts to breathe. He's not mine, I remind myself. I have no right to feel this way.

I sit on the corner of my bed and pull out my phone. My heart jumps when I see Jaxon has left a voicemail.

Don't listen. Just delete it. My fingers betray me anyway.

"Amara," he says after a breath, *"are you okay? I heard about the attack. Please call me back. I just need to hear your voice, to know you're safe. I miss you."*

I groan and delete it. I spent months calling and texting him after he left. He never answered once.

I won't call him back, but I will send a short text:

I'm fine. Don't worry.

Nothing more.

Ana rushes into my room, smiling, and plops down beside me. "Jaxon called me."

"Don't care," I mutter, tugging my ponytail loose.

"He says he misses you. He wants you to call him. He sounded upset."

"Did you tell him to fuck off?" I stand, heading for the bathroom. "I'm done, Ana. I know you liked us together, but he hurt me. I texted him. That's it. I'm taking a shower."

I don't want to have this conversation again. I almost broke up with him once because something always felt off—but Ana talked me into staying. She thought we looked cute together. Thought he was good for me. Maybe he was.

But we weren't right, and whatever I felt for him is over.

Chapter Eleven

I hold my phone in one hand and chew my thumbnail with the other, staring blankly at the empty text bar. I've been avoiding Tyler like the plague, and it isn't fair. I need to talk to him and tell him I'm not interested in anything beyond friendship. Letting him think there's a chance would be cruel. I know what we did was just a get-together rather than a date, but he keeps texting me and asking to hang out more. His flirting is obvious.

I finally start typing.

> Hey, I'm sorry. It's been insane. I'm sure you heard. Can we talk?

I hit send and drop the phone onto my chest. Why couldn't I like someone like Tyler? He actually likes me back.

I fall onto the bed and stare up at the ceiling fan as it spins in lazy circles. I need to get out of this house. Go to the bookstore, find something that'll snap me out of this reading block before I lose my mind.

It's been a week since everything happened. A week of avoiding the grumpy prince every chance I get, and to be fair, he's avoiding me, too. We only speak during training. An hour or two every day. I still run every morning. And Xavior insists I tell him whenever I leave the house and exactly where I'm going.

I hate it, but I do it anyway. Dad has too much on his plate for me to add fuel to the fire.

My phone dings.

Tyler:

> Hey, let's grab lunch in town. How does 12:30 sound?

I agree before I can overthink it. Lunch gives me an excuse to stop by the bookstore, too. It'll be perfect. I stand and walk to the window.

Shit. He's here.

A little white lie never hurt anyone, at least, that's what I tell myself as I get dressed in high-waisted jeans and a white T-shirt that reads *'Spank me; I've been a naughty girl'*. I tie a knot in the front and pull my hair into a high ponytail.

I head down the stairs, hoping I can slip out unnoticed.

"Where are you going?" I freeze with my hand inches from the door handle.

I step back just enough to see into the living room. Xavior is stretched out on the couch, legs spread, looking far too comfortable as he watches TV. He looks... unfairly good.

"I'm going to the bookstore in town," I say. "Is that alright, Your *Highness*?"

His gaze drops to my shirt, one brow arching in quiet amusement. Just because I've been behaving doesn't mean I'm dropping my attitude.

He chuckles softly. "Yeah. You meeting anyone?"

"Nope." I shrug, forcing casual into my voice. "Just need some time alone. I'll be back soon."

He studies me for a moment too long. It's long enough that my stomach tightens. His expression gives nothing away. Finally, he nods.

I smile tightly and turn for the door before he can change his mind. I don't need a warden. I don't need permission. But for my dad—for everything that's already falling apart—I deal with it.

I park in front of the diner where we agreed to meet. I wave when I spot Tyler inside, already seated in a booth near the door. He grins and stands as I reach the table.

"Hey, you look good," he greets, leaning in for a hug.

I hug him back, a little awkwardly, and pull away quickly. "Thanks. You do too." I slide into the booth across from him. "So... how's it going? How's my dad? I'm worried about him. He's pushing himself too hard and barely even comes home."

"Yeah," Tyler sighs. "He's been stressed. Won't give up on the search. He's been staying at Dan's place."

That doesn't surprise me. Dan's his right-hand man and one of his closest friends.

The waiter sets two glasses of water down. "Good afternoon! I'm Josh. What can I get you two to drink?"

"Coffee for me," I say.

"Hot cocoa," Tyler adds at the same time.

Josh nods and walks away. I take a small sip of water, suddenly unsure what to say next.

"How's training?" Tyler asks. "Is Xavior being... respectful?"

"It's been okay," I shrug. "You know me and training. I'm good with the magic side, but the physical stuff still sucks. Xavior's better at teaching than Mom was, though. More patient. I'm actually improving." I hesitate. "He's respectful. Just... really bossy."

"Bossy is generous," Tyler mutters. "I think he's a stuck-up asshole."

"Yeah," I admit. "Depends on who he's around. He's nice to Ana and me. Everyone else?" I shake my head.

"Shit," Tyler mutters suddenly, eyes narrowing as he looks past me.

"What?" I turn, and my stomach drops.

Xavior has just walked in. His gaze locks on me instantly.

Heat crawls up my neck as I straighten, forcing myself to look back at Tyler. Maybe he's just here for lunch. Maybe he won't come over. It's none of his business anyway. Wait... Did he follow me here? No, there's no way he would've done that. He is not a stalker... Right?

Tyler's eyes widen. A large presence stops beside me, close enough that I can feel it. I don't look, but I can feel Xavior's stare burning into the side of my face.

"What's up, man?" Tyler finally says.

Silence is the only response. After a beat too long, Tyler glances at me. I rub my lips together and clear my throat.

"Hey, Xavior. Fancy seeing you here."

"Get up, we're leaving," he demands lowly, dangerously.

"What? No. I'm having lunch." I finally look up at him.

He has a black leather wallet in his large hands, and he pulls out a hundred-dollar bill and tosses it onto the table. He shoves the wallet into his back pocket. Then his hand closes around my elbow and hauls me up.

Tyler stands. "Hey, we're not—"

Xavior shoots him a look sharp enough to shut him up mid-sentence.

I don't fight as Xavior pulls me toward the door. I don't want a scene, but the moment we're outside, I rip my arm free.

"What the hell?" I shout.

"Get in your car and go straight home," he says. "I'll follow you."

He opens my driver's-side door like it's already decided.

I laugh, short and incredulous. "No. You don't get to manhandle me and drag me away from my lunch date. That's unacceptable."

"You lied," he snaps. "That's what's unacceptable."

"To *you*," I fire back. "My dad was fine with it. Why are you acting like this? And did you follow me?"

"Get in the damn car," he growls through clenched teeth, turning to look at me. His eyes are dark, shadows swirling violently beneath his skin, along his forearms, his neck, his throat.

Angry doesn't even begin to cover it.

I don't understand why he's acting like this, or what he expects me to do. I just know I'm sick of it.

"No." I cross my arms over my chest. "I'm not doing this." I refuse to be bossed around because of his possessiveness... we're not even dating. If he gave me a real reason, maybe I'd listen. But he hasn't. I'm not doing anything dangerous. Tyler can protect me, and I know my dad would agree.

"I am this close to losing control." He holds his thumb and index finger a breath apart. "Please. Just get in the car."

The plea catches me off guard. I blink, swallowing hard. I hate that it works, but it does. I get in, and the second I do, he slams the door shut behind me.

What the hell just happened?

I didn't even get the chance to say what I came here to say.

My attitude and Xavior's bossiness don't mix well, but I can't lie to myself. A part of me likes it when he gets like this: angry, dominant, and barely holding himself together. It's infuriating. And it's sexy.

I can't help but wonder what he's like in bed. Would he take control of me, of my body? Give me exactly what I want without me having to ask?

I've never been dominated like that. My ex preferred one position, missionary. I tried changing things a few times, me on top, which I liked, but he always took control back. He was... vanilla. I know that because I've watched porn. He barely touched me, barely explored. He always came too fast, and most of the time I was left needy, finishing myself off after. I've never had an orgasm... not like my fantasy books.

He was my only sexual partner. For a long time, I thought something was wrong with me. Now I know better. He just wasn't it. I need more. And even though I'm not into gambling, I'd bet Xavior would know exactly what I need... how to touch me, how to wreck me, how to make me come apart.

True to his word, he follows me all the way home.

We can't keep ignoring this. It's clearly not working.

I park and climb out, leaning against the hood of my car while I wait. He pulls in beside me, on the phone. Through the windshield, I watch him lean back in his seat, his thumb dragging slowly over his bottom lip as he listens and stares at me.

I look down, kicking at the gravel. His stare is too intense.

I straighten when his door shuts. "We need to talk," I say when he approaches. When he doesn't respond, I push on. "I don't know what's going on, but it needs to stop. You act weird around me—maybe it's because we kissed and—"

He lets out a harsh chuckle. "I don't care about that stupid kiss. You think a kiss is a big deal to someone like me?" His eyes harden. "Maybe I just don't like being around you. Maybe I hate babysitting you. Maybe I'm sick of listening to you whine or maybe--"

"Fuck you," I snap, cutting him off as I turn away.

I was trying to do the right thing. Trying to talk this through because part of me knows he feels something, even if he won't admit it.

Whatever the reason, he doesn't get to hurt me like that.

I won't pretend it doesn't sting.

It does.

The next morning, I shuffle out of my room and head straight for the coffee maker. I barely slept, and I feel like absolute crap. After turning the machine on, I lean against the counter while it brews, staring out the window.

Rain pours down hard, drumming against the glass and roof.

It's perfect for a lazy day.

"You look like crap," Ana says cheerfully as she opens the upper cabinet and pulls out two mugs.

"Jeez. Thanks." I glance down at myself, and my oversized black sweatpants slung low on my hips with a cropped tank. My hair is in a loose high ponytail that's hanging more to the right side of my head since I haven't brushed it.

"No problem. What are sisters for?" She hands me a mug already made exactly how I like it, creamer and sugar. I mumble a thanks. "Want eggs and bacon?"

"Yeah. Sure." I nod. Even though my stomach isn't asking for food, I know I should eat. I skipped dinner last night.

"Morning, Xavior," Ana adds. "We're making eggs and bacon. Want some?"

I purse my lips. I didn't even hear him come in.

Part of me wants to demand we talk. The other part wants to pretend nothing exists between us and hope it fades on its own.

"Yeah," he says. "Eggs and bacon sound good. Thanks."

His voice is low, rough with sleep, and it sends a shiver straight through me. He steps closer to grab a mug, his arm brushing mine as he pours himself coffee. My eyes betray me, hungrily sliding over his biceps. He looks good in his black wife-beater and gray sweatpants.

Why does he have to look like that?

He leans against the counter beside me, close enough that I can feel his warmth. I wrinkle my nose when I see his mug.

"What?"

"Black? No milk or sugar?" I scoff. "That's a crime."

He chuckles, then leans in. His nose brushes my cheek as he murmurs, low enough that Ana can't hear. "Not everything can be as sweet as you."

My breath catches. The whiplash is unreal. Heat floods my body, raising goosebumps along my arms. He pulls back just enough to look at me, but not far enough to give me space. I can feel his breath on my lips.

I meet his gray eyes. The tension between us is razor sharp, tight enough to cut. I know he feels it too.

The front door shuts, and I tear my gaze away from Xavior just in time to see my dad and Tyler walk into the house.

"Cover up," Xavior growls.

His eyes flick to my chest, and he tosses a white shirt at me. He turns immediately and steps in front of me, his broad shoulders blocking my view of them.

Or is he blocking their view of me?

I frown and glance down, heat rushing to my face. My nipples are hard, obvious beneath the thin white fabric of my tank. I hadn't even noticed. When did that happen? And where the hell did the shirt come from? I didn't see him holding it.

Clearing my throat, I pull Xavior's shirt over my head. The fabric is warm, already carrying his scent, woodsy, sharp, and overwhelming. It wraps around me, sinks into my lungs, makes my head spin.

"Hi, Daddy!" Ana beams, rushing forward. "Do you have time for breakfast?"

Her excitement hurts to watch. She misses him, and she's worried.

"Not today, sweetheart." He presses a quick kiss to her head. "I just need to grab a few things from my office."

I bite my lower lip, swallowing the words clawing their way up my throat. *You don't have time to eat with your daughters? Bullshit.*

He disappears down the hall, and I watch Ana's shoulders slump just a little. Enough that it twists something sharp and ugly in my chest.

Chapter Twelve

Amara

A couple of hours later, we're in the basement. I tried to have a lazy day, but apparently, Xavior doesn't do lazy.

"Okay, let's see if you can avoid my tackles. I won't go easy. I'll run at you, and you need to get out of the way." He smirks. Oh, look, we graduated from stance drills. Now we need to dodge a bull. "Who wants to go first?"

"Ana!" I step back, letting her take the center. She glares at me like I betrayed her, then bends her knees, feet shoulder-width apart. I give her two thumbs up. She and Xavior have gotten close over the past week, and yeah... I'm jealous. He's different around her, joking, respectful, patient. With me? He's demanding, bossy, and relentless. Around others, he's grumpy and barely talks. Compared to them, I get the VIP treatment... of misery.

"Ready?" Xavior asks. She shakes her head. "Good."

My eyes widen as he charges, and bam. He slams into her, and the loud thump when she hits the ground makes me flinch. She groans, eyes squeezed shut.

"Get up," he demands, striding back to the other side, unfazed. "This time at least, try to dodge me."

"I did try!" she cries, slowly standing.

He charges again. This time, he flips her over his shoulder. She screams as she's thrown into the air.

Oh, hell no...

Yeah... he's still pissed about my lunch date. I back toward the stairs, panic rising.

His gaze snaps to me. "Don't even think about it."

"I... I don't think we're ready for this," I stammer.

"Too bad. Now sit before I make you."

I glance at the stairs, no way. I know I'll never make it. I drag myself back to the chair, cursing my luck. I don't want to fight him. I know he'll win. I'm not allowed to use my magic on him... he snitched. And I sure as hell don't want to tell Dad about the kiss.

I look over at Ana, sprawled on her back, groaning. Every time he slams her down, I flinch. She whines with each hit. Honestly, I think he's enjoying this.

They pause. Xavior strides over for a sip of water, not breaking a sweat. Ana gasps on the floor, drenched in sweat, barely catching her breath.

I should've listened to Mom when she nagged about training more...

"Ana, you're finished. Go relax." He turns to me, smirk widening. "You're next."

My eyes widen. I shake my head, but his grin grows, eyes promising pain.

"Don't leave me, Ana!" I hiss as she limps past me.

"You're on your own! I'm out of here." She groans, pain lacing her voice. "I'll be in the bath if you need me."

"I... uh, I forgot something. I'll be back." I start to follow Ana out.

"Not a chance. Get over here."

He strides to the middle of the mat. I close my eyes, cursing every decision that led me here. The only small comfort? I'm faster than Ana. Maybe it won't be as bad.

I step onto the mat and glance over my shoulder. He yanks his shirt off. My breath catches. Lord have mercy… the goddess clearly took her time sculpting him. Abs, more abs… tattoos wrapping down massive arms, across broad shoulders. His chest glistens with sweat. The V of his hips disappears beneath gray sweatpants. I want to trace every smoky pattern on his skin.

"You done eye-fucking me yet?"

"You wish. I'm just admiring your tattoos. I've always wanted one," I lie smoothly, forcing my gaze to his face.

"Why haven't you?"

"I'm… not sure," I shrug, keeping my eyes locked on him as I move onto the mat.

"What would you get?"

I step closer, he watches my every move. "A crescent moon with stars… or maybe a flower."

He charges. I turn to run, but he's too fast. I land face-first on the mat, hard… his weight pressing against my back.

"Where?" he murmurs in my ear. His hot breath across my skin sets my nerves on fire.

"The moon on my shoulder blade… or if it's a flower, running down my back with a quote from my favorite book." I glance at him over my shoulder.

He props himself on his left elbow, his gaze sweeping over me. Fingers trace down my spine. Shivers ripple through me. "Here?" His eyes flicker to mine, hunger blazing. His hair is nearly falling into his eyes, and my hand itches to reach out and move the strands.

"Yes." I bite my lower lip; his gaze flickers to the movement. My body flushes, lips tingling, remembering our kisses. I need to get out from under him before I do something stupid.

I spin, my right arm lifting, elbowing him in the ribs. He's caught off guard, and his body rolls off me. I quickly jump up. He chuckles, shaking his head, lying back with his hands on his stomach.

"Come on, get your lazy ass up." I hunch over, hands on knees, laughing. This... this is kind of fun.

"Lazy?" He snorts, springing up and charging like a bull. At the last second, I spin aside, laughing, making him growl low and frustrated.

He tsks, wiggling his finger at me. "Come on, little vixen, hold still for me."

I know he's going easier on me than Ana, but I don't question it. He charges again. This time, I crunch down and kick my leg out just like he taught us. His huge body trips, slamming onto the mat with a thud. I laugh so hard my ribs ache.

He sits up, elbows on knees, running a hand through messy hair. "You play dirty."

His phone rings. He jumps up, digging through his gym bag. "I need to take this," he says, glancing at me.

"Okay." I nod, jogging up the stairs, leaving him behind, heart still racing.

I push open Ana's bedroom door, then her bathroom door, peeking inside. She's still in the tub, eyes closed. I can't tell if she's asleep or not.

"You're already done with your torture?" she says, cracking one eye open. "That was fast."

"Yeah. It wasn't that bad," I shrug. "I was quick enough to dodge him when he charged." I don't mention that he went easier on me. "He got a call and had to take it, so we wrapped up."

"Lucky," she huffs. "I feel like I'm dying."

"I'm going to shower," I call over my shoulder as I leave.

I pull my hair free from its bun and start peeling off my clothes, leaving a trail to my bathroom. I twist the shower handle all the way to hot and step in once steam fills the room, sliding the glass door shut behind me.

A moan slips out when the water hits my skin. I close my eyes, letting the heat soak in. My thoughts drift right back to Xavior. My middle finger traces my lower lip, a habit I've picked up this past week.

The slutty side of me wonders why we're resisting it. Whispering to me, it doesn't matter; it's just sex.

I tell myself the kiss was just a kiss, but that's a lie. It woke something in me, a hunger I didn't know existed. And I know, deep down, that if I give in once, it will never be enough. I can't go down that road.

"I didn't say I was done with you, little vixen."

I gasp, spinning toward the steamy glass. His silhouette is unmistakable on the other side.

"Get out! Why didn't you knock?"

"I can't see anything," he says calmly, leaning a shoulder against the door. His hand presses flat to the glass, as if he's trying to touch me through it. "You left your doors wide open."

My pulse hammers.

"I'll let you off the hook for today," he continues, voice low. "But tomorrow? I won't be taking it as easy."

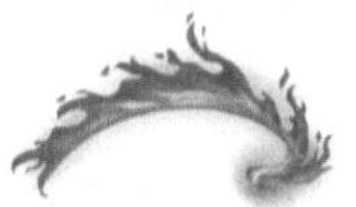

I wipe the sweat off my forehead with the back of my hand. Ana left half an hour ago, and Xavior has been in a pissy mood all day. He definitely wasn't taking it easy on me. I hiss as he throws me against the mat... again.

"Get up," he demands from across the room. I close my eyes, shaking my head. No.

"Now."

"I can't," I groan.

"Don't make me force you again." Last time, it didn't end well. I still remember being lifted off the floor by my ponytail.

"You're such an ass!" I shout, hitting the mat with my palms before pushing myself up to my knees and then to my feet. My sore body protests, but I glare at him. He stands bare-chested, arms folded across his chest. Just like yesterday, he removed his shirt after Ana left.

"Run at me." He spreads his legs, leans forward with hands on his knees.

I sprint toward him, wanting revenge, but then the crazy bastard starts running at me! I spin, trying to get out of his way, but he's too fast. I scream as I wrap my legs around his hips just as my back hits something hard, knocking the breath out of me.

Shit. That hurt.

"Are you crazy?" I yell.

He leans down, brushing a strand of hair from my face. His gaze flickers to my lips for a heartbeat before he grips my waist, trying to lift me but I tighten my legs, refusing to be thrown over his shoulder again. My nails dig into his shoulders.

"Fuck." He groans, he presses into me and I feel him stiffen against me.

I moan; *damn* it feels good.

It only lasts a moment. He grabs me from behind my knees, forcing my legs to unwrap, and throws me across the room. My body slams into the mat again.

"We're done for today." He walks away without a backward glance.

What the heck? Did I piss him off?

I stand on shaky legs. Ana was right this is torture. Every muscle aches. Slowly, I climb the stairs, wishing someone would carry me up.

Fuck it. I sit halfway up, leaning back against the steps. I don't care that the stairs dig into my back. I just need a moment.

"What the hell are you doing?" Xavior shouts from behind me after a few minutes. He must've come back to check on me.

"Go away! I'll be fine, I just need a few minutes."

He mutters something I can't hear and walks down toward me. "Like I'd leave you here to suffer."

"And everyone says you're an asshole," I mutter with a smile as he lifts me. He doesn't meet my eyes.

"I am."

"Okay, fine. You're an asshole."

He clenches his jaw tightly. "I don't want to be an asshole toward you."

"And why is that?" My eyes flick over his throat, wondering what it would feel like to taste him.

He swallows, Adam's apple moving up and down, then gently places me on my bed. He stares at me for a long moment before simply saying, "Get some rest," and walking out, ignoring my question.

Chapter Thirteen

Amara

I wake from a much-needed nap and realize I slept through dinner. It's eight in the evening, and my stomach growls in protest. I drag myself out of bed and into the hallway, stopping short when I notice a closed door across from mine.

Xavior's.

His door is always closed when he's inside and open when he's not. I've thought about snooping more than once, but I chicken out every time. I can only imagine what would happen if he caught me in there without permission. God, I just want to know more about him, but Ana says he hates talking about himself and never gives anything away.

I shut my door and head downstairs.

I preheat the oven and grab a frozen pizza from the freezer. I suck at cooking, and everyone knows it, so they stock frozen dinners just for me. It's embarrassing. I already feel bad for my future husband. Hopefully, he'll be like my dad and actually know his way around a kitchen.

While the pizza bakes, I grab a bag of chips and flop onto the couch. I turn on the TV and scroll through horror movies. Who doesn't enjoy watching something scary alone in the dark?

When nothing catches my eye, I switch to Prime and queue up *Nosferatu*. I've been dying to watch it, but school has kept me too busy. Once the pizza's done, I start the movie and curl up under a throw blanket.

Near the end, I hear a noise.

I look up and scream.

A large shadow stands near the stairs. The lights flip on, and Xavior is standing there, grinning.

"You fucker!" I shout, hurling a pillow at him. "Why are you sneaking around in the dark?"

He shrugs easily. "You weren't in your room. I thought you might've fallen asleep down here."

"And how did you know I wasn't in my room?"

He licks his teeth before looking away. "Your door was open. Your bed was made and empty."

My brows knit together. That doesn't make sense. I swear I shut my door, and my bed definitely wasn't made.

"My bed was definitely not made..."

He shrugs, hiding a smirk. "Just making sure you're okay. Can't have you sneaking off again." He lifts one brow as if daring me to argue. The brief, uncomfortable silence stretches between us, charge and unmistakably intentional.

"Your father is on his way," he adds. "I already told Ana. He has some news he wants to share."

My stomach tightens. "Is it bad?"

"Don't know."

He walks over, and I scoot aside to make room. He drops onto the couch, right in the middle, leaning back until his knee brushes my thigh, even though there's plenty of space.

Not that I mind. I like him close.

Ana comes running down the stairs and takes the spot on his other side just as the front door opens.

"What's going on, Daddy?" Ana stands, then quickly thinks better of it and sinks back down. One look at his face tells me he's in full work mode serious, and distant.

Tyler's gaze flicks to me, then to my shirt. Well... Xavior's shirt. Then his eyes slide to Xavior.

Xavior leans back, his arm stretching behind me along the back of the couch. I arch a brow, but he doesn't look at me. His attention is locked on Tyler, sharp and unblinking.

"We found their hideout," my dad announces.

I straighten, already opening my mouth, but he lifts a hand, silencing all questions. "We're leaving in an hour to search it. Xavior is coming. You both will stay here and stay alert. They know where I live, and if we raid their hideout, they may retaliate. Tyler will stay here for extra protection."

"With all due respect," Xavior says calmly, though there's nothing calm about the edge in his voice, "I'd rather stay. They'd be safer with me here. I don't think Tyler can keep them safe."

"I can keep them safe. What the hell is—" Tyler steps forward, anger flashing across his face. I've never seen him like this. He's always controlled.

My dad raises his hand, cutting him off.

"I agree," he says evenly, "but you and your father are the only two who can blend into the shadows and assess how many are inside."

Xavior's eyes shift to me, dark and unreadable. He hates this, and the idea of leaving me, especially with Tyler. I can see it in the tight set of his jaw, the way his shoulders tense. He's calculating, weighing whether it's worth fighting my dad over.

"Not fair, Dad. We want to come too," Ana snaps.

I nod immediately, my heart already pounding at the thought of being left behind.

My dad exhales slowly, pinching the bridge of his nose, a clear sign he's reaching his limit.

"That might actually be a better idea," Xavior says, turning back to him. "They'd be safer with us than sitting ducks here with someone incompetent."

Tyler's jaw ticks, his hands curling into fists.

"I can remove them from the situation quickly if things go to hell," Xavior adds.

Silence stretches.

Finally, my dad nods once. "Fine. You girls get ready. Xavior—" he gestures down the hall, "—follow me. I have the layout of the house."

An hour later, we park in a large field surrounded by trees. Ana gets out of the car first, and I move to follow, but Xavior's hand shoots out, stopping me. I glance over to see him glaring out the windshield. He's pissed I'm here.

"Do not leave my side. Understand?"

"But—"

"Goddammit. It's not the time for arguments."

I wasn't going to argue; I just wanted to ask what would happen if my dad tried to pull me away. "I won't leave your side, Xavior. I promise." No way in hell would I fight him on this. I wonder why he didn't demand the same from Ana. She's worse than I am in high-pressure situations.

"Good." He steps out of the car, and I stay close to him as we approach the group. Every member of the council is here, dressed in black, swords strapped to their backs, daggers on their thighs, ready for whatever comes.

"Okay, Xavior and Nicholas will go first to check out the hideout. If the coast is clear, Nicholas will send a signal. Ana and Amara stay close to me at all times, got it?"

Xavior steps forward, cutting in before my dad can continue.

"Amara stays with me. I can cloak her with my shadows."

Nicholas, his father, glances at me, his eyes scanning up and down my body. I shiver. He's probably wondering why his son is hellbent on keeping me close. Me too, buddy, me too.

My dad opens his mouth, but Xavior cuts him off again. "It's not up for discussion." He grabs my upper arm, and we move toward the trees. I glance over my shoulder; everyone is watching us. Once we're alone, he stops.

"What was that about? Why are you being like this?" I ask.

"I'm going to wield my shadows now. They'll wrap around us to keep us hidden."

"Will it hurt?" I ask, remembering the pain they can cause.

"No." He steps closer, cupping my face between his hands. I melt into his touch. "Nothing is going to happen to you. I swear."

I close my eyes as his thumbs caress the sides of my face. "Open your eyes."

When I do, I see the shadows wrapped around me like a soft, protective blanket. I laugh as they dance across my skin. Looking up at Xavior, the shadows beneath his skin are moving.

"These aren't tattoos, are they?" I ask.

"No, they're my shadows."

"Your father doesn't have any."

"He does, just not enough to show. They start on the chest, and the stronger you are, the bigger they grow."

"Wow. That's amazing." I hold out my hand, letting the shadows play across my fingers and up my arms. "Are you doing this?"

"No, my shadows have a mind of their own sometimes," he says. "Now come on, we have to move."

"Oh, don't we have to wait for your father?"

"No. He's coming from the east side. We have to stay quiet, okay?"

I nod. He grabs my hand, lacing our fingers together, and we start walking. This... this is the side of him I love being around.

We move silently through the woods, and every shadow and snapped twig makes me jump. My fingers stay laced with his, my other hand wrapped tightly around his forearm like it's the only solid thing left in the world.

We reach the clearing, and I look up at a large, three-story brick house. Vines crawl up the walls, and the grass is overgrown, indicating that it has been abandoned for a long time, but the structure itself remains intact. The windows are unbroken, and the door is still hanging in place, a perfect place to hide out.

One window on the third floor glows with a flickering light, like a fire is going.

Xavior turns, leaning in close enough that his breath brushes my ear. "We're going inside. Stay behind me. If something happens, let me handle it. Don't do anything stupid."

"Okay."

Why did he want me to come along? This shit is scary as hell. I like horror movies, but watching them and *living inside one* are two very different things. This feels exactly like how I always imagined being in one would feel.

We inch forward. I glance around for his father, but of course, I don't see him anywhere. The front door opens with a loud, as fuck creak. There's no one inside. I assumed there'd be a group inside ready for an attack.

We step inside cautiously, moving down a long hallway and peering into each room. The house is still furnished. Dust coats everything, but the furniture has been wiped clean. White sheets that once covered it are discarded on the floor. They were here recently. They just left.

My pulse hammers harder as we reach the basement stairs. The steps disappear into thick darkness, swallowing the light. My fear is eating me alive. "I'm not going down there," I whisper.

"I'll check the basement. You two go upstairs."

I squeal, ripping my hand from Xavior's and spinning around, clutching my chest. "Holy shit—"

Nicholas stands behind me.

"Shit, sorry," I breathe. "You scared me."

"No, I apologize," he says calmly. "I should have made my presence known."

We climb the stairs, every step creaking beneath our weight. I'm back to gripping Xavior, pressed firmly against his back, my fingers locked around his hand. His warmth seeps into me, calming the worst of my fear.

I'm grateful he doesn't complain about my iron grip, because I'm pretty sure I couldn't let go even if I wanted to.

Each room is thankfully empty. I shouldn't be happy about that—it either means they're one step ahead of us, or they left town to terrorize another coven. Which means Xavior would leave. I don't want him to leave. I like seeing his grumpy ass.

We creep down the hall on the third floor, heading toward the room with the flickering fire. Why would they leave it burning? To cover their tracks? Or did they just leave in a hurry, not giving a shit?

Xavior stops in the doorway. I hear a small creaking sound coming from inside. His hand tightens around mine, and his back stiffens. "Go downstairs," he orders, letting go of my hand. I can't see in the room, and he doesn't want me to.

"What? Why?"

"Don't fucking argue with me," he growls, making me jump.

I squeeze under the gap between his body and the doorframe, stepping into the room. My eyes widen at the scene. My hand flies to my mouth as nausea claws at my stomach. I don't even try to hold it in—I vomit onto the floor.

The floor grows blurry as the tears threaten to flow. My body shakes, my heart races. I let out a choked sob. Xavior comes up behind me, rubbing my lower back, whispering softly, "Shh... It's okay, baby. I've got you."

My whole body trembles as the sobs wrack me.

Once I can breathe without vomiting, I spin around, burying my face in his chest, clinging to his shirt.

"Xavior, please..." I whisper, my voice breaking. He knows exactly what I'm begging for. Without hesitation, he lifts me into his arms and carries me out of the room. I try to burn the image from my mind, but it clings, vivid and cruel.

My mom is gone. They have hung her body over the fire. It's still burning, crawling up her legs, consuming her slowly. The creaking I heard was from the rope around her neck, swaying her body back and forth.

Nicholas stops us and begins talking, but I can't focus on the words. My body is still trembling, heart pounding, I'm having a hard time breathing.

Xavior sits me down and kneels before me, cupping my face in his hands. I curl my fingers around his wrists, holding on for dear life.

"Look at me, baby," he murmurs. "Breathe with me. In... and out. Slowly."

He takes a deep breath through his nose and exhales through his mouth. I start to mimic him.

"That's it... You're okay," he whispers, pressing his forehead to mine. "I'm right here. I promise you're safe." My breaths start to even out, just slightly.

"That's my girl," he praises softly, brushing a stray tear from my cheek.

"What's going on?" my dad calls from behind Xavior. I peek over his shoulder and realize we're outside; my back is leaning against the house by the front door.

"We found your wife. She's gone. Up on the third floor." I squeeze my eyes shut, remembering what was in that room.

"Are you okay, sweetheart?" my dad asks. I shake my head, burying my face further into Xavior's chest. I don't care how it looks. I need him close.

"She'll be okay. I'm taking her home," Xavior says, gathering me in his arms and walking away without waiting for another word.

Everything after that is a blur. Ana tries to talk to me, but I stay silent. I don't answer Xavior when he asks if I'm okay or if I need anything.

At home, he lays me in bed and holds me until I fall asleep. Each time I wake, the nightmare of my mom hanging sways in my mind, the low creaking echoing. But Xavior is always there, steady, keeping me anchored in reality.

Chapter Fourteen

Over the past couple of weeks, I have hardly talked to anyone. My dad and Xavior still force us to train, but that's the only thing I do besides lie in bed, staring out the window. I can't get past what I saw. For the first time in my life, I miss her. I even miss her bitchiness.

The nightmares wake me almost every night, but at least I don't scream anymore. Last night, when I jolt awake, I find Xavior sitting in the chair in my room, watching me sleep. He says he's just checking on me. I don't argue. I don't know what hurts more, him being there or the way he leaves without touching me.

This morning, I woke up exhausted from staying trapped in my own head. I need to go out, and I need noise. A club with friends and alcohol. Anything to make my thoughts quiet.

I pull on red shorts and a black sports bra for training, wondering if I should invite Xavior out tonight. He's been sweet. Distant but sweet. And I hate how much I still want him near me.

In the kitchen, he's already there, brewing coffee.

He turns and hands me a mug. "Lots of sugar and milk."

"Thank you." I take a sip, and my chest tightens. This is exactly how Mom liked hers, sweet. Dad and Ana take theirs black.

"Can I join you for your morning run?"

I blink up at him. I thought no one noticed I've been sneaking out early. I want to train harder. Be the person she believed I could be.

"Yeah," I say softly. "That'd be great."

The sun is just rising as we stretch on the deck. Dad had the property warded, no one with dark magic or harmful intent can cross it. He's terrified of losing one of us. Neither of us is allowed to leave without Xavior or Tyler.

"How are you feeling?" he asks.

"I'm okay. I guess." I hesitate for a moment glancing at him. "My mom and I never had a good relationship. She thought affection made people weak. She pushed me harder than Ana. I know she thought it was for my own good, but now that she's gone... I hate that I didn't try harder. I know people have it worse, and I shouldn't be whiny about it."

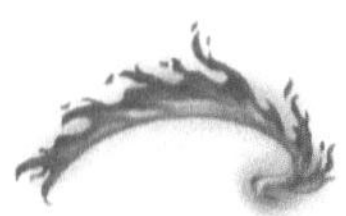

The next day, Ana bursts into my room while I'm getting dressed.

"Xavior has a hot friend over."

I turn toward her, my heart kicking harder than it should. "Oh, yeah?" He never has anyone over. "Is it a woman?" I ask.

"Nope, his name is Zane. Now hurry up, I like him. He makes me feel hot and he's a big flirt."

I sigh in relief, smiling when she does. I'm glad she's doing better. The first week after we found out about Mom, she cried nonstop. It's been rough on both of us, but little by little, we're finding our way back to ourselves.

She looks me over. "You need to tell me where you got that jumpsuit."

I turn toward the mirror. The black jumpsuit clings to me like a second skin. My entire back is exposed, the fabric dipping into a deep V, the seam scrunching just enough to show off my ass. If Xavior insists on pretending nothing happened, then fine. I'll pretend too. He makes me stare at his body. Why shouldn't I make him look at mine?

"I'm ready," I say, turning away.

"Holy cow," Ana laughs. "I never realized your ass jiggled like that. Does mine?"

"Why are you staring at my ass?" I glance over my shoulder, and her head tilts as she watches me walk.

"It's kinda hard not to."

Downstairs, Xavior sits on the couch with his friend, laughing while scrolling through his phone. Zane looks up and whistles low as he stands.

"Well, damn," he says. "Who are you, and where have you been my entire life, doll face?"

Heat creeps up my neck as he approaches, his gaze slow and unapologetic. He's beautiful, light brown skin, shaved head, bright green eyes. He lifts my hand and presses a kiss to my knuckles.

Xavior steps closer, his eyes trailing over me. "Zane," he says, warning sharp in his voice.

"You didn't tell me I'd be training with two Latina goddesses." Zane winks at Ana, then lifts my hand over my head. "Give me a spin."

I arch a brow, glancing at Xavior. I'm surprised he doesn't say anything. I do a spin. "Goddamn," Zane mutters. When I face him again, he's biting his knuckles.

"I'm Amara."

"Fuck," he grins. "Be mi amor?"

I laugh, shaking my head. "I like you."

"You hear that, man?" He taps Xavior's chest. "She likes me. We're going to the club later, you two should come." He slips an arm around my shoulders. "You'll be my dance partner, right, amor?"

I feel Xavior's heated glare burn into my back.

"As long as you're not as mean as Xavior," I tease.

"Damn, man. You're mean to her?" Zane laughs. "You messed up. Don't worry, I'll take care of her. Stretch her out nice and slow before training."

I blush. That sounded way too sexual.

"She's my partner," Xavior snaps. "I already told you."

"Nope. I want Zane. I like that he'll help me stretch."

Xavior growls but doesn't argue. Zane steps onto the mat. "Let's start easy. We'll see how flexible you are, turn around."

I do. He tells me to touch my toes. I bend, palms flat on the mat. He grips my hips, and he leans over me, grabbing ahold of the back of my neck, pushing me down further. At the same time, he pushes my legs apart with his foot. "Just like that," he says and straightens, but stays behind me. "Fuck me, that's perfect. Now hold that for ten seconds."

"All right, time's up." He smacks my ass, and I yelp.

"What the fuck, Zane?" someone growls.

I straighten to find Ana and Xavior watching us. Xavior's anger is a physical thing I can feel it from here. Even I know that went too far. Ana quietly moves to stretch across from us.

"Lie on your back, *mi amor*." Zane ignores him.

I do it cautiously, keeping my eyes on Zane. If he spanks me again, I'm punching him. He drops to his knees, wrapping a hand around my ankle.

"Tell me if I stretch you too much." He winks.

I nod, licking my lips. He lifts my leg, resting it over his shoulder, his body settling over me, face inches away as he stretches me slowly.

"Oh, gosh, Zane," I groan, tapping his arm when my hamstring screams. "You're stretching me too much!"

"You did great," he says casually. "She's flexible, Xavior."

We both glance over. Xavior's jaw is clenched tight, nostrils flaring, fists balled. Zane smirks. "Don't just stand there. Help your partner."

Xavior bares his teeth like a wild animal.

"All right, other leg." Zane turns back to me, repeating the stretch until it burns. "Okay, roll over."

I swing my leg free and end up on my stomach.

Xavior is now pacing like a caged animal, like he's seconds from snapping.

"Okay, ass up." Zane slaps my ass, and Xavior flinches

If this were anyone else, they'd already be dead. Zane has to be important. I know he's poking the bear, but it's not funny anymore.

"I think I'm good to start training," I say tightly.

"No." His voice turns sharp. "You're not getting up until we're finished. Ass up and arch your back. Now." I flinch at his commanding voice. He went from zero to a hundred within seconds.

"Okay! Jeez." I lift my ass. He places a palm on each cheek.

"Um," I frown, "can you not touch my ass?"

"Arch your back," he repeats.

I do, and he hums approvingly. "Yes, perfect."

Then I feel his hips press into me. Okay, enough is enough. He needs to understand boundaries.

I'm about to shove him off when Zane suddenly goes flying across the room. He lands hard... then laughs like a maniac. He wanted this reaction.

"Not funny," Xavior snarls, shadows swirling around him as he stalks toward Zane. "She told you to stop."

I scramble up and rush between them, planting my hands on Xavior's chest, trying to stop him, but he doesn't slow down. His angry gaze is locked on Zane.

Then his shadows creep up my arms, tingling, wrapping around me, pulling me forward until I'm pressed against him.

I laugh breathlessly, looking up. "I think they like me."

His face is still thunderous.

"Don't touch me," he snaps. I yank my hands back like I've been burned and push past him.

"Amara, wait—" His voice softens.

I don't stop. I need to get out of here, need fresh air.

I need to stop this madness. If he doesn't want me, then I need to accept it. Just because he's attracted to me doesn't mean he actually likes me.

I crave affection. I always have. My mom deprived me of it my whole life, and while my dad tried, he was always busy. My love language is touch. I *need* it. And this push and pull with Xavior is destroying me.

I need to ignore it.

I'll ask my dad to let Tyler train me instead. He helped my mom train me before, so why not now? I'll tell him about the kiss. Tell him how uncomfortable I feel.

Decision made, I take off running.

I don't bother grabbing shoes. We own twenty acres, no hikers, no neighbors. Just trees, dirt, and silence. I keep going until my lungs burn, until the house disappears behind me. Ten minutes later, I reach the small stream tucked between the trees.

I hiss when I peel off my socks.

Small cuts cover my feet with dirt and blood. I didn't even feel them. I sink my feet into the cold water, washing everything away, then collapse onto my back and stare up at the sky.

It's a cloudy day. My mind drifts. I'm eight years old. Ana is playing dress-up, twirling in the living room while I scrub paint off the walls. It isn't fair... *she* painted them. Mom walks in and tells Ana how pretty she looks.

She never calls me pretty. Thinking she's in a good mood, I drop the cloth and run into the living room, grabbing a pink dress. *Mom, what about me? Do I look pretty?*

She takes the dress from my hands. *No. The dresses are for Ana. Finish cleaning.*

The memory still burns.

A branch snaps.

I sit up fast, heart stuttering. "Hello?" I scan the trees, standing slowly.

Nothing. It was probably a deer. I turn back toward the stream, but freeze. There's a man standing on the opposite bank.

I gasp. "Oh, goodness! You scared me." I laugh weakly, pressing a hand to my chest.

"Good," he says, lips curling into something cruel. "That was the intention." Then he lunges.

My heart stops.

How...? My dad warded our land. No one is supposed to be able to get in.

He grabs my throat and lifts me off the ground. I claw at his hands, terror flooding me as his fangs extend.

Oh god... Vampire.

"Lacere!" I scream.

My magic explodes outward. His body flies back, disappearing into the trees as I crash onto the ground, gasping. But vampires are fast... too fast.

I need to run. I scramble up and sprint toward the house, fumbling for my phone and calling my dad. It goes straight to voicemail.

Shit.

"Xavior," I breathe, hitting his contact and putting it on speaker as I run. I manifest my whip, magic snapping to life around my hand.

"Amara, where the hell did you go?" he answers, relief nearly drops me to my knees.

"Xavior!" My voice is full of panic.

"What's wrong?"

I dare to look behind me and see the vampire chasing me. I trip, crying out as I hit the ground. Pain runs through me, but I scramble up and snap my whip at him. He dodges it with blurring speed.

Shit... my whip won't work. He's too fast. I back away, heart slamming against my ribs, my foot catches on a tree root. I go down hard, landing on my ass as my phone flies from my hand.

"Such a pretty witch," the vampire hisses, looming over me. "I wonder, will you taste as sweet as you look?"

"Amara? Who said that?" Xavior's voice crackles through the phone.

I don't look away. I can't. Looking away would be deadly.

"Please," I whisper, shaking my head at the vampire, searching his face for even a shred of mercy. My fingers finally close around my phone. "Xavior, help me!" I scream.

"Fuck!" he shouts. "I'm coming, baby. Zane, I need you to follow her scent."

Relief barely has time to register before I spin, trying to get up, but I'm tackled from behind.

"Don't worry," the vampire groans against my neck, breath hot and foul. "We're going to have a lot of fun."

He grabs my chin, forcing my face to the side. His eyes glow red, bright, and hungry. Hungry means weak.

"Don't touch her!" Xavior roars.

The vampire chuckles. His grip shifts, fingers crushing my throat as he lifts me, pressing my back against his chest. One arm locks around my abdomen. His nails dig into my neck, sharp and unforgiving. I whimper, the pain stealing my breath.

"Bye-bye, lover boy."

He flings my phone away and takes off running. The world turns into a violent blur.

Think. *Think*! I reach back, clawing at his face, finding his eyes. My thumbs drive into them as I call to my fire magic.

He screams. My heat surges, burning his flesh. He drops me.

I spin around just in time to see blood streaming down his face, leaking from where his eyes were.

"You bitch!" he snarls. He's on me before I can move. His fist slams into my face. My head snaps sideways, ears ringing. He grabs my hair, yanking my head back.

I stare in horror as his fangs extend even longer. I shake my head. "No—"

He bites into my neck. Agony burns into my neck and spreads through me. I scream.

"Conteram collum tuum!" I try to shout, but it comes out weak. His bones crack, and he collapses, dragging me down with him.

His neck is broken. It won't kill him, but it buys time. Mere minutes if he's old. Hours if he's new. My heart pounds in my ears.

His fangs are still embedded in my neck. Just do it.

I grab his face with both hands and rip him away.

I scream as pain tears through me, raw and blinding. Birds explode from the trees as an answering roar echoes through the woods.

Xavior.

I stagger to my feet, the world spinning violently. My legs barely hold me.

One step. Then another. But the ground tilts, and my vision darkens.

I fall, and everything goes black.

Chapter Fifteen

Xavior

I turn my shadows into wings and fly, following Zane's massive black wolf form as he tears through the woods, locked on Amara's scent. I'd never be fast enough to keep up with him on foot.

He stops suddenly and howls.

I land hard, scanning the ground. Her phone lies discarded among the leaves, along with blood.

A low growl rips from my chest as Zane sniffs frantically, circling, trying to catch their direction when my phone rings.

"Alexander," I answer.

"Tell me you found her."

"Not yet," I say tightly. "I found her phone and blood. A lot of it."

Zane snarls and bolts.

"Find her," her father orders. "I'm on my way."

I hang up and force my shadow wings open again, letting them haul me into the air. I've tried flying before and failed every time. It takes an obscene amount of control and power. Most shadow wielders never manage it.

Neither did I. Until now.

Rage surges through me, sharp and uncontrollable, and my shadows respond instantly. They know who she is to us, even if I refuse to acknowledge it.

I won't acknowledge it. I can't.

I refuse to choose her over my brother.

A scream tears through the woods, raw and full of agony. My chest tightens at the idea of her being in pain.

I roar back.

We're close.

Zane howls again, and I drop from the sky. The vampire lies twisted on the forest floor, neck snapped at an unnatural angle. Not dead, not really, but his mouth is smeared with blood.

My vision goes red.

Zane shifts, naked and human once more.

"Where is she?" I demand.

I don't wait for an answer. "Amara!" I shout, spinning, and then I see it... a blood trail. I follow it at a dead run.

"I'll stay here," Zane calls. "In case he wakes up."

I don't respond.

A minute later, I find her. She lies crumpled on the ground, a pool of blood spreading beneath her. Tears cling to her lashes. Her skin is pale, too pale.

She looks heartbreakingly beautiful.

What if I'm too late?

No. No...

I drop to my knees and pull her gently into my lap, cradling her head against my thigh.

"Come on, baby," I beg, gripping her wrist. "Please."

Her pulse is there, but weak. Terrifyingly weak.

This is my fault.

I search for the wound and find the gaping bite at her neck. She's losing too much blood.

My shadows surge forward on their own.

"No," I snarl, trying to rein them back. I've always been able to control them. "Stop!" I scream.

They ignore me. I freeze as they press against her wound, sealing it, slowing the bleeding. They're healing her. My shadows don't heal. They destroy.

"What...?" My breath shudders.

I gather her into my arms and press a kiss to her cheek. "I'm here, baby." I carry her back toward Zane.

"Shit," he mutters when he sees her. "That's a lot of blood."

"No shit," I snap, fury flaring again at him, at myself, at everything.

I form the wings once more and launch into the air without another word. He'll deal with the vampire. He knows I'll want revenge.

I thought I knew everything about my shadows. Apparently, I don't.

I land hard on the ground, my legs wobbling as I try to keep myself upright. Alexander and Ana burst out of the house. Ana's eyes are wide with tears, her bottom lip trembling as she takes in Amara, limp in my arms, her pale skin smothered in blood.

"Please... tell me she's alive," she whispers. I don't blame her. Amara looks dead.

"Barely," I growl. Alexander steps closer, reaching for her, and I tighten my grip, snarling. "Did you bring a healer?"

"Yes, inside," he says, rushing back into the house.

Two healers wait in the living room, their eyes widening at the sight of her.

"Get the fuck up," I bark, and they jump, startled. I gently place her on the sofa and step aside. They block my view, but I circle behind the sofa, gripping her hand with both of mine. Ana sits at her feet, rubbing her shins, while Alexander paces.

"Who was it? The rebel group?" he asks.

I watch the blue light from the healer's hands hover over her wound. The wound is halfway closed when they stop.

"The fuck? Did we tell you to stop?" I growl.

"We need a break, Prince Xavior," the younger blonde healer says, bowing slightly.

I stalk around the sofa, gripping their necks not enough to hurt, just enough to show I'm fucking serious. I push them back.

"Do your fucking job, or I'll let my shadows come out and play." My whisper is low and deadly. Their eyes widen, and they nod, lifting their hands to continue.

"That's what I thought. You don't stop until she's fully healed. Something happens to her, you die." I cross my arms over my chest, eyes locked on them.

Zane enters silently, dragging the vampire by his fangs, snout covered in blood. He drops the vampire and shifts, moving upstairs without a word, probably for clothes.

"I'll tie him up in the basement," Alexander murmurs, lifting the vampire by the collar.

"I'll be down once Amara's healed. Don't kill him, I want to take my time."

Ana gasps, wide-eyed. "Are you going to torture him?" She rubs Amara's feet gently.

"He nearly killed her. What do you think?" I snap.

No one touches her and gets away with it.

Chapter Sixteen

Amara

I blink a few times, but the bright sunlight streaming through the window is too harsh. I roll onto my stomach, burying my face in the soft pillow. Drool slips from the corner of my mouth, and I feel utterly comfortable. Maybe just a few more minutes of sleep...

A blood-curdling scream shatters the quiet, and my eyes snap open. What the hell was that?

"Amara!" Ana's voice screams across the room. She jumps up from the chair in the corner and rushes to me, wrapping me in her arms. I frown but hug her back anyway, rubbing small circles on her lower back.

"Are you okay?" I murmur, confusion tugging at my lips. Why is she crying? My brain feels foggy, like I'm swimming through cotton.

"You don't remember? You nearly died! You scared the hell out of me!" She pulls back, wiping tears from her cheeks. My mind scrambles, running barefoot through the woods, upset over Xavior, and then...

Oh. The vampire.

I gasp, my hand shooting up to the spot where he bit me. The burning memory hits, but my skin is smooth. No mark, no pain, nothing.

"Xavior and Zane found you. Dad's here, too. The healers fixed you. There isn't a single mark."

Another scream rips through the house. This one isn't my imagination. "What was that?"

"Oh..." Ana rubs her shoulder, looking away, uncomfortable. "Well... Xavior's kind of... torturing the vampire for what he did to you. They've been at it all night."

"What?" I stand too quickly, and the room tilts. I wobble, giving myself a moment to regain balance, then push myself forward. Ana trails behind, telling me to rest, but I ignore her. "Where are they?" I call over my shoulder.

"In the basement, but you need to be in bed. You lost a lot of blood yesterday," she warns.

I open the basement door and freeze at the next scream. My heart jumps into my throat. I scan the training area, empty. My eyes catch the far side of the room, and I run there, pushing a door open.

I gasp.

The vampire hangs, arms above his head, and chains wrap around his wrists, holding his body, feet not touching the floor. His body glistens with sweat and blood. Xavior stands before him, a curved knife in hand, shadows swirling around him like a living tornado. He slams the blade into the vampire's throat—the same spot he bit me—and the creature screams, begging him to stop. My dad and Zane watch silently from the back corner.

"Xavior. Stop!" I step further into the room, voice shaking.

Xavior turns his head, dark eyes flashing with anger. Shadows ripple across his body, making him look deadly, untouchable. My heart skips a beat. I take a step back, unease gripping me.

"Amara," he breathes, his face softening as he walks toward me. His hands—still smeared with blood—cup my face as he looks me over. "You should be resting. When did you wake up?" His thumbs brush along my cheeks, slow and careful, and his shadows follow, curling around me, caressing my body like they're trying to soothe me.

"Not that long ago. I heard his screams," I say quietly. "Ana says you've been doing this all night. Don't you think it's time to stop?"

His gray eyes darken, shadows swirling inside them as his face twists feral. The shadows around his body tighten, restless.

"This is what happens when someone dares to touch what belongs to me," he says coldly. "I kill. And it's not pretty. It's bloody. Painful. I like to take my time." His voice drops. "I'm going to make him suffer for touching you. Go back to bed."

I glance at the vampire. His body is already healing, but the pain echoes around him. His breaths are ragged, each one a struggle. I wouldn't wish this kind of suffering on anyone.

"Please," I whisper. "Stop. He's had enough. No more."

Xavior stares at me for a long moment, long enough that anxiety tightens in my chest. When he doesn't answer, I try another way. "End this," I say softly, "and take me to bed. I'm tired."

"Finish him," he orders over his shoulder.

Then he bends and lifts me effortlessly into his arms, cradling me against his chest. I sigh despite myself, my body relaxing in his warmth as I rest my head against his shoulder. He carries me up the stairs like the world beyond us doesn't exist.

"I tried stopping her, but she wouldn't listen," Ana says when we pass her.

"Make her some breakfast," Xavior says without slowing.

I roll my eyes. He's so damn bossy. "Jeez, you could've said please."

He frowns down at me like the word is foreign. After a moment, he clears his throat and turns to Ana. "Can you please make her some breakfast?"

Ana laughs.

"See? That wasn't so hard."

He grunts, jaw locked tight. His anger still rolls off him in waves. "Are you okay?" I ask gently.

"I'd rather not talk about it."

"Yeah," I nod. "Of course."

He sets me down on my bed and sits beside me. "Are you hurting anywhere?"

"No. Just a little sore." My hand drifts to my neck, to the spot where the vampire bit me. The memory makes me flinch. "It was... really painful."

His nostrils flare. Without a word, he stands and leaves.

This is what happens when someone dares to touch what belongs to me...

I swallow hard.

Is he talking about me?

Does he think I belong to him?

It's been a week since the vampire attack. They still can't figure out how he got past the wards. I've stopped running in the mornings, too scared of what could happen.

Zane invited Ana, Brandon, and me to the club tonight for Xavior's birthday. I'm excited. I got Xavior a small gift—a black necklace with a sword charm. I know he has a thing for swords; it's the only weapon he uses besides his shadows. I even made a tiny replica of his favorite one, capturing every detail.

"Put your left foot forward and tilt your body to the side," Xavior barks, standing a foot away. He directs my stance without touching me. It hurts, the barrier he's put between us, but I know it's necessary. We can't keep doing that push and pull. Even though I want more, I'm happy to have him as a friend, and I won't push him. One day, someone will want me for me.

We're outside practicing knife throwing. The target stands ten feet away. I throw, and the hilt hits the target with a loud thump and falls to the ground. Ana actually gets the blade in the target. I growl in frustration, picking up my knife.

"Xavy!" A high-pitched voice rings out, piercing my ears. A blur runs toward Xavior, and she jumps on him, wrapping her long legs around his waist. "Happy birthday, big man!" she giggles and kisses him on the lips. He turns his face without returning it, unwraps her legs, and steps away.

"Lexie, what are you doing here? Training's over," he says, dismissing us without looking away from her.

My heart shatters all over again. I rub my lips together. He's not yours. There's no reason to get jealous. I haven't seen her face, but her body is perfection: tall, skinny, model-like. My hand clenches the knife's hilt, and I storm away without a backward glance. Of course, he has a girlfriend. That explains why he keeps pushing me away. I'm so stupid for not thinking of that being a possibility.

I stand in front of the mirror in nothing but a bra and panties. Maybe he prefers skinny girls, not that I'm fat, but I'm a size six, with very curvy hips. Nowhere near model-like. Nowhere near her. She's probably a size one.

I stare at the outfit I got online for tonight. At least I'll look badass. I pull on the black skirt, but it's too tight. I grumble silently, loosening the ties, and thank God, it works. Now I can wiggle it on.

I tilt my head, chewing my lower lip. Shit, I have to take off my panties. The skirt has ties lacing up each thigh, curving upward, showing my hip bones, the waistband of my panties peeking out. I slip them off.

I remove my bra and layer on my shirt, a plain black crop tank top under a leather corset. I tighten the laces, making it lift my girls perfectly. I put on my four-inch heels and straighten my hair.

There's a knock. "Come on! Everyone's ready!" Zane calls.

"I'm almost done. You can come in," I reply, adding pink lip gloss.

The door opens. "Fuck me sideways! Are you trying to give every man in the club a heart attack?"

"Oh, shut up! Is it too much?"

"Yes, it's too much... but perfect." He smirks. "God, if Xavior wouldn't kill me, you'd be mine."

"You're overdramatic! He wouldn't kill you," I tease, fastening the little black choker around my neck.

"Whatever you say, little killer. Come on, everyone's downstairs waiting... if we even leave."

"What do you mean?" I grab my clutch as we head out.

"Nothing," he says.

At the bottom of the stairs, my eyes lock on Lexie next to Xavior. He's whispering something in her ear, and she laughs. She's wearing a short red tube dress and matching lipstick, beautiful, innocent, girl-next-door vibes. My face and body scream sex appeal; there's nothing innocent about me. I look like a porn star.

I look away from the perfect couple and glance at Ana in her pink spaghetti-strap dress. I don't know how her tiny straps haven't snapped, or her tits haven't escaped. It's impressive.

"Everyone ready?" Zane asks from behind me, hands on my shoulders. I feel Xavior's attention like a soft heat, roaming down my body. I glance at Zane and nod. This is fucking awkward.

I grab one of Zane's hands, pulling him down the stairs. I push past the perfect couple, avoiding Xavior's eyes. He'll see jealousy burning in mine, and I won't let that happen.

"Zane," Xavior says, low and intimidating, with warning as we pass.

"I had nothing to do with this," he mutters.

"I'm driving," I tell Ana. We need separate cars. I refuse to be stuck in a small car with them.

"Are you coming with us?" I ask Zane.

"Fuck yeah! I want the two hottest girls in the club in my arms," he says.

"No, Zane's coming with us," Lexie dismisses him, pissing me off.

"He's a big boy; he can decide for himself," I snap. Ana's eyes widen, but she says nothing. She climbs into the backseat, and I open the driver's door, carefully climbing in and pulling down my skirt. "Need to be careful since I'm not wearing panties."

Fuck, did I just say that out loud?

"What?" Xavior shouts, storming toward the car. I slam the door shut. Zane is laughing, climbing in beside me. I start the engine, doors locking just as Xavior tries to open mine. I smile sweetly and wave.

Worry about your girlfriend, not my panty-less situation.

"Open the fucking door, Amara."

I turn up the music. "Can't hear you!" I point at my ears and push the gas.

"Have I ever told you how much I fucking love you?" Zane laughs.

"Aw, Zaney! I love you too."

I wasn't trying to provoke him, but I'm not letting his weird possessiveness ruin my night, especially with a girlfriend in the picture.

We make it to the club in the human realm before Xavior because I drive like a maniac, and yes, I may have used a little magic to flip the red lights green. We sit at the bar, and I've already downed four shots. My body is starting to feel the alcohol buzz. Brandon called on our way to pick him up and said he wasn't feeling well, so he isn't coming.

I lean against the bar, scanning the dancers, when I feel the air shift. He's here. I'm always aware of his presence. My body responds before my brain can. I glance over to see his angry gaze locked on me as he stalks forward. Lexie struggles to keep up with him in her killer heels.

I roll my eyes. "Great... buzzkill's here," I mumble to Zane. He looks up and smiles when he sees Xavior.

"Took you two long enough," Zane says as they get close.

I watch Lexie leaning against Xavior, claiming him with her body language.

Fuck you, bitch.

"I wanna dance," I murmur, pressing against Zane. He wraps an arm around my waist.

"I'll take good care of her," Zane smirks at Xavior, then glances down at me. "Mr. Buzzkill doesn't dance."

"Who's buzzkill?" Xavior finally asks, tearing his gaze from me for a moment.

"That's your new nickname," Zane says with amusement.

"I dance," Xavior counters defensively, eyes flicking back to me.

"Sure, you do," Zane snorts.

I pull away, walking backward through the crowd of dancers, shaking my hips, curving a finger at Zane. "Come get me, hotshot," I tease before slipping into the crowd.

By the time they reach me, I'm grinding against a cute guy, his hands on my hips, whispering nonsense in my ear and telling me how hot I am.

Not hot enough for the man I truly want.

Xavior narrows his eyes at the guy and steps forward, but Lexie grabs his arm, whispering something. He listens, still glaring at me. Yes... I want him to rip this guy off me and take me home. But instead, he presses Lexie against him, dancing with her while never taking his eyes off me.

I turn in the man's arms, avoiding Xavior's gaze, but he keeps staring. The stranger grips my ass, making my blood boil. "We're done," I growl, slapping the side of his face. He smirks.

"Get lost, fuckface," Zane growls, pulling me from the man's grip.

"Fuck off, man. She's mine for tonight." His grip tightens, pulling me forward.

"She's not yours," Xavior snarls, his hand shooting forward to grab the man by the throat. "Let her go."

The man finally releases me, his face red. Humans surround us; we can't use magic. Xavior releases him, and he collapses to the floor.

Turning to me, Xavior's voice is sharp. "Do you always let strange men touch you like you're some kind of whore?"

I flinch, stepping back.

"Not cool, man. Not cool," Zane snaps, pulling me away.

Xavior rubs his face, frustrated.

I pull out his gift from my clutch and throw it at him. He catches it, looking down, then back up at me.

"Amara... shit. I didn't mean that, I just..."

I cut him off. "Happy birthday." I turn, and walk with Zane to another part of the dance floor. Ana follows, leaving them behind.

We all dance together for a long time, laughing and having fun. Xavior and Lexie had walked off the dance floor a while ago. I'm starting to lose interest, but I plaster on a smile, not wanting to ruin everyone's night. I remind myself why I don't dance with strange, drunk men in clubs, they get handsy and disrespectful.

"Alright, time for the cake!" Zane shouts, grabbing mine and Ana's hands. We giggle at his excitement as we follow him.

"Did you really get a birthday cake?" Ana asks, wiggling her brows. She loves cake.

"Yep!" We climb the stairs to the VIP lounge, where I see Xavior and Lexie sitting on a leather couch. Lexie is talking a mile a minute, not caring that he's ignoring her completely. Xavior, meanwhile, is holding the necklace, staring at it.

Ana and I sit in the leather chairs opposite them. I grab the pitcher of iced water, and fill a glass, trying to act casual.

"Thanks for the gift, Amara. I love it," Xavior says, putting the necklace around his neck.

I look away, sipping my water silently. He called me a whore earlier; I've been called that before, but never by someone I trusted so much. It still stings.

Out of nowhere, a group of women walks into the lounge, carrying a two-tiered cake covered in candles, singing happy birthday. I glance at Xavior and catch him smiling as he watches them set the cake down.

Gosh, I love that smile.

Zane plops beside him, grabs the side of his face, and messes up his hair while rubbing the top of his head with his knuckles. Xavior laughs and shoves him off. Lexie grins at me, throwing both legs over Xavior's lap and pulling him in for a cheek kiss. Zane frowns at me.

I look away, clearing my throat. "I need to use the ladies' room. I'll be back!" I flash a wide smile and rush down the stairs. I can't watch them anymore; I need to get my mind off him.

I need to show him what acting like a whore really means.

I'm not doing this for him. I'm doing it for me. He doesn't need to know. I won't ruin his birthday. I just want to get over him, and I hope this works. Brandon says it helps—he always gets over an ex by hooking up with someone else—so maybe it'll work for me, too.

Chapter Seventeen

Xavior

I watch Amara walk away, my hand lifting to clutch the necklace she custom-made for me. I've been keeping my distance from her, and it's killing me. I don't know what to do anymore. Part of me would rather leave my own brother in a coma than hurt her, but I can't betray him. I won't.

I hate that I have to hurt her. She isn't some evil monster, yet I still have to avoid her because she has the power to ruin me. She is temptation wrapped in fire, and I am far too willing to sin for a single touch. Her kisses are poison. Her touch could destroy both my brother and me.

In the end, someone has to die. I wish it could be me instead of her.

I start to stand, needing to follow her, just to make sure she makes it to the bathroom safely, but Lexie grabs my arm and pulls me back down. I frown at her. She only smiles. She's been far too touchy today. I told her to knock it off, but that went out the window the moment I danced with her, trying to make Amara jealous.

Lexie knows we're just friends. I made that clear a long time ago. I fucked her once, a mistake, and she knew exactly where I stood before it ever happened. Still, she got attached. That's why I put distance between us this past year. I've barely spoken to her.

Her showing up this morning caught me off guard. We've known each other since we were kids, and I missed her friendship. I hate that I ruined it over one drunken night.

Sleep has been hell lately. Every time I close my eyes, I think about Amara. About that kiss. The one that shattered my control and sent my world spiraling. I don't understand why my shadows react to her the way they do. They crave her touch as much as I do.

When I told Zane, he said the word I despise most. Mate.

Impossible. I don't want one, never have. Mates are weakness, chains. I never even believed they existed, just a fantasy invented by weak hearts.

"She's been gone a while," Zane says, glancing toward the stairs. I scan the room. He's right. "I'll go look for her."

I nod, planting my elbows on my knees and rubbing my face, irritation simmering beneath my skin.

"Calm down," Lexie murmurs, lowering her voice, trying to sound sensual. It makes my skin crawl. She's not wrong, I'm wound tight, and I'm not having a good time.

I wanted to stay home the second I saw Amara dressed like that. Like some kind of sex goddess. My cock twitches at the thought of her, no surprise there. It always does. Showing off those dangerous curves, like she doesn't even realize what she's doing to me.

Does she do it on purpose? Does she know the effect she has on me?

If Zane hadn't planned this stupid party, if he hadn't been so damn excited, I would've kept her home with me.

Every man and woman in this place breaks their neck to watch her walk by, like a siren singing a sweet melody, drawing everyone in. I want to take her home. Chain her to my bed. Hide her from the world. Claim her in every way possible so there's no doubt she's mine.

I left the dance floor because if I saw one more man touch her, I would kill him on the spot, especially knowing she's bare beneath that tight skirt.

I can't ruin this night for Zane. But God help anyone who touches her again.

"I can't find her; I even searched the bathrooms, but the women weren't too happy." Zane rushes over.

I stand so fast the chair scrapes the floor, shoving Lexie off my lap. She has no right to be there anyway. I was lost in my thoughts, completely unaware she'd gotten that close. She hits the floor with a yelp. I don't give a shit.

Ana snickers around a mouthful of cake, eyes locked on Lexie sprawled at her feet.

I pull out my phone and dial Amara.

"What the fuck?" Lexie screeches from the floor, holding out her hand for help. I ignore it, turning my back on her and stepping away from the group. She growls behind me.

"Hello?" Amara answers, then giggles. "Hold on—stop for a minute, I'm on the phone."

"Where are you," I demand, "and who are you talking to?"

"Oh, it's Mr. Buzzkill!"

My eyes narrow. My jaw tightens. I hate the nickname. Can't she see I'm only trying to keep her safe? Keep her *mine*. I can be fun when she knows who she belongs to.

"Where are you?"

"Oh, sorry. I left the club. You were too busy with your girlfriend to notice."

"She's not my girlfriend," I snap. "Tell me where you went."

"I left with someone. We're going to his hotel room."

Something inside me snaps.

My blood boils, rage flooding my veins as my shadows whip violently around me, my vision darkening.

Kill. Kill. Kill.

"Tell me you're lying," I say, my voice no longer sounding like my own. It's low, with a deadly edge. "Fuck, Amara. *Please* tell me you're lying."

"Nope. I need to fuck someone to get over you."

To get over me?

"Come on, get off the phone," a man's voice says in the background.

The call cuts off.

I stare at my phone as my grip tightens until the screen cracks beneath the pressure.

"Xavior... what's wrong, man?" Zane steps closer, then freezes. "Oh shit. It's bad."

"She left with someone," I bite out. "Ana, come on. We're leaving."

"Fuck," Zane grumbles. "I can't even shift to track her; too many humans. But I gotta be honest, man... You had it coming. You shouldn't have paraded Lexie around like that. You're clueless."

"What do you mean?" I stop mid-step, turning to him.

"She was jealous," he says flatly. "Ana told me Lexie kissed you right in front of her."

"She was jealous?"

The word hits harder than I expected. Yes, she saw that, but she also saw me reject Lexie. I would've stopped it if I'd known what Lexie was about to do.

"Yeah," Zane continues. "And you let Lexie touch you all night. Salt in the wound. Amara *likes* you, man. You can be really fucking dumb sometimes."

My chest tightens.

Now I understand why she wants to get over me.

I knew she was attracted to me, but jealous? The girl hides her emotions like a pro.

Fuck.

We pile into the car, and Amara's still parked at the club. Everyone's too drunk to drive except Zane. I sit in the passenger seat, hands clenched into fists, while Ana and Lexie sit in the back.

"Hey... It's okay," Lexie murmurs, leaning forward and rubbing my shoulders.

I growl and shrug her off. If she hadn't shown up, this never would've happened.

I forgot why we drifted apart, why I pushed her away. She never took no for an answer. She kept pushing. Sleeping with her only made it worse. I always felt guilty for not feeling the same, but enough is enough.

"Get your fucking hands off me," I snap. "You need to leave and never come back."

She whimpers, shrinking into her seat. Zane shoots me a sideways glance that says *about time*.

Lexie wipes at her eyes as the road stretches long and dark ahead of us.

Silence fills the car, thick, heavy.

I reach into my pocket, my fingers curling around paper—the photo booth strip from the fair presses against my palm.

I don't pull it out. I don't need to. I can already see it, her smile, bright and unguarded.

The damn blood stain is still there.

I close my hand around it slowly, jaw tightening as the realization sinks in.

I didn't lose control tonight.

I lost it the moment she started to matter.

Chapter Eighteen

Amara

I giggle as he kisses the side of my neck, the sound catching in my throat when his fingers pinch my nipple. I'm straddling his lap, still in his car, parked in front of the hotel. He keeps telling me we should go inside, but I keep distracting him. I'm not ready. He bites the sensitive skin beneath my ear.

"Xavior," I moan.

My hands slide up, reaching for his soft, silky hair, but instead, my fingers meet a smooth, shaved head.

I frown, blinking through the haze.

"I'll be whoever you want me to be, sexy," he murmurs. "Let's go inside."

The fog clears all at once.

Panic floods my chest. I shove the door open and scramble out of the car, my heels barely touching the pavement before I'm running. Tears blur my vision as I sprint down the sidewalk. It will never be him.

"Hey! Where are you going?" the stranger shouts. I don't stop.

My hands shake as I pull out my phone, scrolling frantically until I find Brandon's number. I beg him to come get me. Thank God he's in town.

What was I thinking?

What in the fuck was I thinking?

I sit on a park bench, elbows on my knees, burying my face in my hands as my chest heaves. Never, *ever*. Make big decisions while drunk and jealous.

Brandon picks me up ten minutes later. We go back to his apartment. We eat ice cream straight from the carton while I ramble about Xavior and his perfect girlfriend, the way he looked at me, the words he threw at me like knives.

An hour later, I'm finally ready to go home. He drives me, and I don't say a single word the entire way. I pray everyone is already asleep. I pause on the porch, slipping off my shoes so they won't click against the wooden floors, then ease the front door open.

"Amara."

I freeze. Xavior is sitting on the couch, already watching me. He rises to his feet, moving toward me with purpose, but like the coward I am, I bolt for the stairs.

I barely make it to my room before slamming the door, but his hand stops it. He steps inside, closing it behind him, the soft click echoing too loudly in the quiet room.

"Get out," I groan weakly. I don't have it in me to fight. I toss my heels into the corner and sink onto the edge of my bed, rubbing at my temples.

"Did you fuck him?" His voice is rough and strained, like the words physically hurt to say.

"Who I fuck is none of your concern," I snap. "You should be with your girlfriend."

"You're jealous." It isn't a question. I don't answer.

I hear him move closer, and his black boots stop toe to toe with my bare feet. He grips my chin and tilts my head back, forcing my gaze to his.

"I am jealous," he says, his voice low and dangerous. "Outraged, all I see is red. And dangerously aware that someone else thought he was allowed to put his hands on you." His eyes burn into mine. "That will never happen again. And let me tell you one thing, Amara. I will find him, and I will kill him. I'll give him a slow, painful death for touching you. It doesn't matter if you wanted it or not."

My eyes widen at the violence in his confession, my breath catching. "But why?"

"She's not my girlfriend." He ignores the question, and I don't push. My mind goes blank as his thumb brushes my lower lip. My eyes flutter closed, my body betraying me as I lean into his touch. "I don't want her the way she wants me. I told her that a long time ago. And when I found out she was upsetting you, I sent her away. She's never coming back."

"We never made it to his hotel room," I whisper. "We kissed... and I ran."

His nostrils flare, his eyes darkening, not relieved, but furious.

I flinch as his thumb wipes harshly across my lips before his hand slides to my throat. A low growl leaves him, and then his mouth crashes down on mine, rough, demanding, unforgiving. I know he's trying to erase the memory of another man's kiss.

When we finally pull apart, we're both breathing hard, staring at each other, the air between us heavy and charged.

"Go out with me," he begs before kissing me again. "We'll do whatever you want," he murmurs against my lips, kissing me like he can't get enough.

I don't answer. My head is spinning, desire fogging every rational thought.

"Say yes." He pulls back just enough to search my eyes.

"Yes."

"Thank fuck." He kisses me again, harder this time.

His hand releases my throat and slides down, fingers digging into my thighs as he pulls them apart. "I'm going fucking mad with need," he growls. "You drive me to the brink of insanity. You're all I think about. I'm doing crazy things I never would've done, my rational thoughts are gone."

His voice drops, thick with desire. "I never wanted to lose control. Never wanted to go mad." His mouth trails along my jaw, down to my collarbone, biting and licking until I hiss. "But I'll gladly lose myself to this madness. Give up my sanity as long as you're by my side."

I close my eyes, tilting my head back, moaning as my legs wrap around him, desperate to feel him closer.

"I tried to stay away," he murmurs. One hand slides down the back of my thigh while the other creeps higher, dangerously close. I lift my hips, seeking friction, aching where I need him most.

"I know I don't deserve you," he continues, his voice rough, possessive. "But I'm done fighting this. You're mine, Amara."

His hand pauses. His thumb begins to trace slow circles high on my inner thigh, so close that it makes me tremble. "And the next man who touches what belongs to me," he adds softly, "is dead."

He pulls back, locking eyes with me. "Do you want me to stop?"

His swollen lips are torture.

"No," I whisper.

His pupils blow wide. He inhales sharply before crashing his mouth onto mine again, kissing me like a claim. Then, finally, he spreads my wet pussy lips apart, and his fingers slip between them, finding my swollen clit.

We hiss at the same time.

My head falls back against the bed as he circles me slowly, deliberately.

"So, fucking wet for me," he groans, and leans over me, kissing and sucking along my throat, working his way down. His free hand tugs my shirt aside, freeing my breast.

"Oh, God," I moan as his mouth closes around my nipple, licking and sucking while his fingers move faster, dragging stars across my vision. He teases my entrance, just enough to make me ache.

"Please," I whimper.

He slides two fingers inside me.

"Shit," he curses as my walls clamp down, pulling him deeper. "So, fucking tight," he groans, pumping his fingers slowly, relentlessly, driving me higher with every stroke.

"Xavior," I cry out. I'm right on the edge, teetering on pleasure so intense it threatens to tear me apart, but then he pulls his fingers out.

I open my mouth to curse him, but the words die when he lifts his hand and slides two fingers into his mouth, sucking them slowly.

His eyes fall shut as he groans. "So, fucking delicious."

He thrusts his hips forward, pressing his hard cock against me, and I moan. God, it feels so good.

"Do you feel what you do to me?" he growls against my ear. "I've dreamt about how you'd taste since the moment I laid eyes on you. And fuck..." He exhales sharply. "You taste even better than I imagined."

"Kiss me," I plead.

He does. His mouth tastes like sin. I lift my hips, rubbing myself against his hardness, desperate for more. I swore off men, but I can't resist this pull, this hunger that refuses to be ignored. I'm done fighting it. I want this spark to burn until it consumes me completely.

He pulls back, settling onto his knees between my thighs. "Too much fucking clothes," he gripes, already reaching for my corset.

I watch him unlace it, his focus intent, almost reverent. I can't believe this is happening. He's really going to be mine.

"Finally," he growls, his eyes flicking up to mine before he hauls me upright and strips both shirts from my body in one motion. I fall back onto the bed, breathless.

His gaze darkens as he takes me in, completely exposed, my skirt bunched at my hips.

"I've thought about you like this," he rasps, "lying underneath me, naked and at my mercy." His hands cup my breasts, squeezing them before his thumbs brush my nipples. "God, my thoughts didn't do you justice. You're perfect. Every fucking curve." His voice drops lower. "The gods made you just for me."

The awe in his eyes, like I'm the most beautiful thing he's ever seen, undoes me. My head falls back as I moan his name.

"Perfect," he murmurs, almost to himself, before taking my nipple into his mouth, lapping and sucking until my pussy throbs with a pulse of its own.

I look down at him and... *shit*. He looks devastating like this, his dark gaze locked on me while he devours my nipple.

I fist his shirt. "I want this off. Everything off."

He rises slowly, looming over me like something feral, like a wild beast, breathing hard as his eyes drag over my body again and again, unable to look away. His gaze dips between my thighs, and a deep groan rips from his chest.

I kick off my skirt as he yanks his shirt over his head and makes quick work of his jeans. "I want to take my time," he admits, rough and honest. "Explore every inch of you. But fuck I'm too desperate to be inside you."

His phone starts ringing. He pulls it from his pocket, shuts it off without a glance, and tosses it behind him. It hits the floor with a dull thump.

"What if that was important?" I ask softly.

"I don't give a fuck," he growls.

I swallow as his pants hit the floor. I can't look away as his eyes slowly devour me again, taking in every inch, claiming me with nothing but his gaze.

There's an intense, possessive look in his gray eyes, and it's enough to unravel me completely.

"Beautiful," he murmurs, so low I almost miss it.

He spreads my legs wider, his teeth catching his lower lip as his gaze drops between my thighs, and damn, it makes him look hotter than sin. I don't question it for a second. I know he likes what he sees. It's written all over his face.

"Xavior," I whimper.

His eyes snap back to mine, dark with hunger. "Kiss me."

He lowers himself between my thighs, bracing his elbows on either side of my head before capturing my mouth in a kiss that steals my breath.

My hands grip his shoulder blades, trailing down his back as I wrap my legs around him. His hard cock brushes my inner thigh, making me gasp. He shifts his weight, reaching between us, watching himself as he rubs the head of his cock through my pussy lips before lining up with my entrance.

"Wait, what about a condom?"

"I'm not using one." His voice is firm, unapologetic. "I need to feel you. No barriers. I'm clean. I know you're clean. And you're on birth control."

My breath stutters. How does he know that?

"Tell me you want this." He looks straight into my eyes.

I nod, dizzy with need.

"Use your words, Amara."

The way he says my name sends a shiver through me.

"Yes," I gasp. "I want this. I want—"

He doesn't let me finish.

He thrusts into me brutally, and I scream as the burning stretch steals the air from my lungs. He's so big—it hurts, almost too much—until he hits something deep inside me, a place no one has ever reached before. My eyes roll back as my body clenches around him, instinctively sucking him deeper.

Xavior throws his head back, releasing a raw, animalistic growl. The muscles in his neck strain as he grips me tighter. He doesn't wait for me to adjust. He pulls almost all the way out and slams back into me, sending a shockwave of pleasure straight down my spine.

Sounds I've never made before spill from my mouth, uncontrollable.

"So tight," he groans. "You feel so fucking perfect, baby."

I wrap my legs tighter around him as the pleasure overtakes me, overwhelming and all-consuming. The way he's pounding into me, merciless and rough, hurts so good. He fucks me hard, violently, and I already feel my orgasm climbing fast.

"Xavior, please..."

I don't even know what I'm asking for. He doesn't slow down. If anything, he drives into me harder, deeper, pushing me straight to the edge. I close my eyes as my head spins, my body trembling beneath him.

"Open. Your. Eyes." Each word is punctuated by a hard thrust.

I moan at the sensation. "Now, Amara," he demands.

I force my eyes open, locking onto his. His jaw is clenched tight, gray eyes burning into mine. He palms my breast, rolling my nipple between his fingers, and my back arches as a silent scream tears from my throat.

My body starts to pulse around him, clenching uncontrollably.

"Goddamn," he groans.

Then the orgasm hits me, hard. I scream his name over and over, like a prayer. I can't stop chanting as pleasure rips through me.

Xavior follows me over the edge, slamming into me once more as his head snaps back and comes with a roar. I feel him throb inside me, filling me.

He loses control, and his shadows explode around us, wild and violent. The lamp crashes off the nightstand and shatters against the floor, glass scattering.

Slowly, he pulls out of me.

He stares down at me with something close to awe, chest heaving, lips parted as he catches his breath. Strands of hair fall into his eyes as he looks at me like I'm something sacred and dangerous.

"I'll be right back," he murmurs, kissing my cheek before leaving the room.

I stand on shaky legs, smiling to myself. That was the most intense pleasure I've ever experienced. He knows exactly what he's doing, how to make a girl come undone without needing direction. No wonder he's such a cocky fucker.

I just hope he doesn't decide this was a mistake.

I clean myself up, then pull on his T-shirt, the one I've been wearing every night since he gave it to me, and hurry back to bed, burrowing beneath the blankets.

He returns a few minutes later wearing nothing but gray sweatpants, carrying a broom and dustpan. I watch silently as he sweeps up the shattered remains of my lamp. When he's done, he sets everything aside, pulls back the covers, and slides in beside me.

"Sleep," he whispers against my ear. I snuggle closer, resting my head on his chest, drifting off as his fingers comb gently through my hair.

When I wake, sunlight floods my room, but I'm alone.

I sit up as raised voices reach me, Xavior shouting at someone. I rush down the hall to the guest room where he sleeps. The door is wide open, and he's pacing, phone pressed to his ear.

"No, there has to be another way. I can't go through with the plan anymore," he snaps, running a hand through his hair. "How much time does he have?"

He goes quiet, listening. "I need more time," he growls. "Fine. I'll do what I can." He ends the call sharply, rubbing his face with his palm.

"Is everything okay?" I ask softly as I step closer.

He turns, his eyes flicking over me before settling on my face. "It will be." He pulls me into his side, kissing my temple.

"What time is it?"

"Almost eight. Do you want breakfast?"

"I need a shower first."

"Let's clean you up," he says.

Before I can react, he hoists me over his shoulder, making me squeal. Moments later, I hear the shower start. He sets me down, pulls my shirt over my head, and turns me toward the spray. I glance back, then quickly look away, heat flooding my cheeks as he steps out of his sweatpants.

Oh God... he's coming in.

He grips my hips gently, guiding me beneath the warm water and closing the door behind us. I wrap my arms around myself, suddenly unsure, and turn to face him. I've never showered with someone before. I don't know what to do.

His eyes narrow. "Don't ever hide yourself from me, Amara," he growls gently.

He lowers my arms and reaches for the body wash. My gaze drifts over him, taking in every hard line and taut muscle. Everything about him feels unreal. My eyes widen when my eyes lower. *That fit inside me?*

"Do you understand?" he asks.

"Yes," I answer.

I jolt when he turns me around and begins rubbing the body wash over my shoulders, releasing a low groan as he massages them, working into my upper back. His hands move slowly down my arms, kneading each muscle before carefully massaging my fingers. He repeats the motion on my other arm, unhurried, deliberate.

He pulls me back against his chest, resting his chin on my shoulder as he watches himself clean my stomach and sides. A breathless moan slips from me when his hands move to my breasts, taking his time, giving each one careful attention.

"Spread." His hand smacks lightly against my inner thigh. I obey, opening my legs.

"That's my good girl."

He leans down, gripping the back of my knee and lifting it slightly, spreading me wider. His free hand slips between my thighs, and I rest my head back against his chest, turning just enough to look up at him.

His focus is locked on his hand as it moves over my body. I watch his nostrils flare when his fingers work the body wash between my pussy lips. I'm still sore, tender, but desire curls low in my belly, slow and insistent.

With a growl, he spins me around and drops to his knees, shocking the hell out of me. Men like him don't kneel for anyone, ever.

He lifts my leg, setting my foot against his chest as I lean back against the cool tile, water streaming between us. His hands move from my knee down to my calf, slow and reverent, until he reaches my foot. He lifts it, massaging my sole with careful pressure.

"This is the best full-body massage I've ever had," I murmur, my voice husky with need.

"You deserve it," he says, pressing a kiss to my shin before repeating the same treatment on my other leg.

When he's finished, he releases me, and I step beneath the water, rinsing away the soap. He stays on his knees, watching me like he's caught in a daze.

I move closer. He looks up at me as if I'm everything, like nothing else exists. There's something empowering about seeing a man like him on his knees, taking care of me, and looking at me that way.

His head aligns perfectly with my breasts. A snarl curls his lip before he surges to his feet, taking my nipple into his mouth as he rises, towering over me once more.

I love how wild and animalistic I make him. I love that I do this to him—that he loses control, that I push him to the edge of madness. I've always craved a powerful man willing to burn the world for me, and he exceeds every fantasy. He won't let anyone hurt me. He would kill for me. He *has* killed for me.

He lifts me suddenly, pinning my back against the tile. One arm hooks beneath my knee, lifting it as I wrap my other leg around his hip. He lines himself up and thrusts into me without warning. I hiss at the sudden intrusion.

"Fuck..." he growls, baring his teeth as his head tips back and closes his eyes. He stays still for a moment, breathing hard, like he's trying to enjoy the blissful feeling. When he looks down at me again, his face is full of pleasure.

He pulls back and slides in slowly this time, watching the way we move together. It's different from last night, slower, almost tender.

"You're mine now, Amara," he murmurs. "I'm never letting you go. No matter what."

Pleasure washes through me at his words, even as a flicker of nerves spreads in my chest. I shove the feeling aside.

"What if I don't want to be yours?" I ask not entirely seriously, not entirely teasingly either.

His eyes narrow. He drives into me hard, forcing a whimper from my throat.

"Too fucking bad," he snarls. "You're mine whether you want to be or not. There's no going back."

My heart pounds as heat tightens in my chest. I love this side of him. His mouth crashes against mine, brutal and claiming, like he's sealing the truth of his words with his lips.

Chapter Nineteen

Amara

Xavior chuckles softly when my knees buckle as he sits me down. He helps me out of the shower, steady and careful, and sits me on the edge of the vanity, then grabs two towels. He wraps one around me first before quickly drying himself, his eyes never leaving me, like he can't get enough of me or he's afraid I might disappear if he looks away for too long.

Once he secures the towel around his hips, he steps closer, bracing his hands on the countertop beside my thighs. He leans in, pressing gentle kisses along my jaw, down the curve of my neck.

"Mmm… delicious," he groans against my skin.

I've never felt so wanted in my life or desired. Yearned for and it's intoxicating.

"Do you normally lose control of your shadows like that?" I ask quietly. When he came inside the shower, they wrapped around us with such force it knocked the air from my lungs. For a full minute, I couldn't breathe, and panic clawed through me before it faded.

He drops his forehead against my collarbone, shaking his head. "Baby, I've never lost control of my shadows. Not once, until you." His voice is rough, honest. "You make me lose control in every way imaginable. I'm completely under your wicked spell, little witch."

My heart stutters at his confession, my body shivering in response. I never knew I had this effect on him. Had it always been there?

He pulls back, bends down, and opens the cabinet beneath the sink, grabbing another towel. He dries me slowly, deliberately, taking his time, pausing every now and then to press soft kisses against my skin. I want to stay in this moment forever.

"Are you sore?" he asks, glancing up at me from where he presses a gentle kiss to my inner thigh.

I lick my lips and nod. "It's okay, though. I can go again." I was sore before the shower, more so now, but it barely matters with the way he's looking at me. The way he's worshipping my body.

"No," he says firmly, but gently. "You need time to recover. It can hurt if you don't." He straightens, lifting me easily from the counter. "Let's get you dressed. I'll get you some pain relievers."

He carries me into my room and sets me on the bed with care.

God... I love the way he cares.

I watch as he walks to my underwear drawer and pulls out a matching set. I arch a brow. "How do you know where my underwear drawer is?" I half-tease. "Have you been snooping?"

"Yes," he says easily, like it's nothing, heading toward my closet.

That stops me cold. "When?"

"When what?"

I release a frustrated breath. "When did you snoop?"

"The night of the fair. After I left," he replies calmly. "I came straight here and looked around."

He kneels in front of me and helps me into my panties and shorts. I stand so I can pull them up fully, and he presses a soft kiss between my breasts.

"Why?" I demand. "Did you search Ana's room? My parents' room?"

He straightens, inhaling sharply, irritation flashing across his face. "Does it matter?"

"Yes!"

"No. I only searched your room. Arms up."

I lift my arms, and he slides my bra on, his fingers brushing my skin. I turn so he can fasten it, and he moves my damp hair over my shoulder, kissing the back of my neck. When he's finished, I spin around, cocking my hip and crossing my arms.

He runs a hand through his hair and exhales. "You want to know why?"

He steps closer, bending so we're eye level. "Because I've been completely obsessed with you since the moment I saw you with that fucking fire whip, killing without breaking a sweat." His voice drops, intense. "It was sexy as fuck. I needed to know everything about you." His jaw tightens. "You've been driving me insane. You're all I think about. I can't get enough."

He leans in closer. "Like I said before, I'm under your spell. And I never want to be released from it."

"Why have—" He cuts me off with an earthshattering kiss. I grab his shoulders, opening for him as our tongues clash. He grips my jaw, tilting my head back, devouring me like he's trying to silence the question entirely.

He pulls away first. "Time for breakfast."

Then he walks out of the room like nothing just happened. I stand there for a long moment, stunned. He's felt this way the entire time... so why has he been pushing me away? And he *knew* I was going to ask. He avoided it with a kiss.

I shove on the oversized sweater he picked for me and head downstairs, determination hardening my steps. I'm getting answers. He's in the kitchen now, wearing blue jeans and a white T-shirt, buttering a pan while the mixer hums.

I storm over and slap my hands on the island. "Why?"

His shoulders go rigid. The spatula stills in his hand. "Not now, Amara."

"No. I want to know why you pushed me away if you felt this way about me."

"I said not now," he repeats, voice tight. "And you need to listen to me."

"I'm not letting it go. I have a right to know."

He snaps, finally turning. "I don't have to tell you shit."

My chest tightens. I press my lips together, then turn and walk out of the kitchen.

"Amara."

I ignore him and stomp upstairs, my footsteps loud against the floor as I put distance between us. I slam my bedroom door shut and lock it.

My heart is pounding, too fast like my body knows something my mind is still trying to catch up to. He wants me. I know that now. Not in a casual or fleeting way. No, it's an obsession and dangerous.

The way he said it, the way he looked at me, it wasn't a confession meant to comfort. It was a truth that slipped out before he could stop it. And yet he still won't tell me the one thing that matters.

That refusal irks me more than his temper, more than his secrecy. If this were simple, if it were harmless, he wouldn't be shutting me out like this. He wouldn't be dodging my questions or shutting conversations down the moment they get too close.

My instincts are sharp and insistent, tight in my chest. I've learned to trust that feeling. It's never screamed this loudly without reason.

Whatever Xavior is hiding, it isn't small. It isn't something that can be brushed aside or explained away with time and patience.

And somehow, deep in my gut, I know... it has everything to do with me.

Half an hour later, the door handle turns, followed by an annoyed growl. "Amara, open the door," Xavior says, his voice calmer than it was in the kitchen.

"I'm not ready to see you. I need some time alone to cool off," I call back, my eyes glued to the movie playing on my laptop. I lost my appetite. Do I feel bad that he made me breakfast and I didn't eat? Yes, but I'm too angry to care. I can reheat it later.

Something snaps.

The door slams open, smacking hard against the wall. "Do you really think a locked door will keep me away from you?"

"Xavior, get out! You need to respect my need to be alone."

"Fuck being alone. You can cool off with me in here." The way he says it makes it clear this isn't a suggestion.

He walks over with a plate of pancakes and a mug of what I assume is coffee, setting the mug on my nightstand. "Eat." He places the plate on my lap and sits beside me. I bite my lower lip, hating the way heat settles low in my stomach. I can't believe this is turning me on.

"So freaking bossy." He slams my laptop shut and tosses it onto the other side of the bed.

"That was mean," I pout.

He opens his palm. Two small pills rest there. I take them, grab the water bottle from my nightstand, and swallow.

"Eat the damn food."

"But—"

"I don't care. You haven't eaten anything since yesterday morning, and that hardly qualifies as breakfast."

I nod because he's right. I pick up the fork and start eating. How did he know?

The thought should comfort me. Instead, a chill slides down my spine. He had to have been watching me closely to know that. Tracking me. Noticing things I didn't realize anyone else could see.

The unease tugs at the back of my mind, sharp and insistent again, but I shove it away. I don't want another fight. Not now.

"Thank you," I murmur. "It's amazing. But I'm not over what you said earlier. You do have to tell me. It involves me. I can't start a relationship with you when there are secrets."

His phone rings. He pulls it from his pocket and glances down at the screen. "I need to take this. I'll be out back if you need me." He presses a kiss to my temple and leaves.

Saved by the phone.

I hardly pay attention to the movie as last night slams into me. I had sex with the one and only Shadow Prince. And he said I'm his now.

How do I feel about that?

Normally, I hate being told what to do or how to feel. I'm sick of it. But at the same time... I love it when he dominates me. When he bosses me around like he knows exactly what I need before I do.

What scares me is how much I trust him with my life, with my body, with everything. Butterflies erupt in my stomach, wild and uncontrollable, and I smile, letting out a quiet squeal like a teenager whose crush just said hi. I don't regret a single moment.

The doorbell rings, ripping me out of my thoughts. I groan softly and head downstairs, pulling the door open without checking first.

"What the hell are you doing here?" I cross my arms over my chest when I see who's standing on my porch.

"I've been trying to get a hold of you," Jaxon says. "I needed to make sure you were okay."

Those baby-blue eyes hit me full force. He shoves his hands into the pockets of his jeans, shoulders hunching slightly, like he's disappointed by my reaction. What did he expect? That I'd throw myself into his arms?

"I didn't reply for a reason, Jax," I say flatly. "Now, please leave." I hesitate, "before my possessive... friend, or whatever he is, sees you."

"Don't be like that." He steps closer, too close.

I step back, but he mirrors me. My back hits the wall, and before I can react, his hands come down on either side of my head, boxing me in. He stares at me, searching my face, and my pulse spikes. I can't read his expression, and that makes my skin crawl.

I glance past him into the house. Where is Xavior?

"God, Amara," Jaxon breathes, cupping my jaw and tilting my head back until I'm forced to look at him. "You're still so beautiful. Damn, I've missed you." His thumb brushes my cheek. "I'm sorry for what I did. I was stupid for thinking there'd be better out there in the city. No one even comes close to you."

My stomach twists.

"I planned on coming back after school ended," he continues, smiling like he's already won. "But when I heard you got hurt, I came as soon as I could." His eyes soften. "Go out with me. Let me show you how sorry I am."

I open my mouth—

"She's moved on." The voice behind us is pure venom.

My head snaps to the side. Xavior stands a few feet away, shadows curling violently at his feet, his murderous gaze locked on Jaxon. His upper lip curls as he bares his teeth.

"Now take your hands off her," he snarls, "before I break them."

Jaxon scoffs, finally turning. "Who the hell are you?"

"You need to leave," I snap, my patience gone. His pretty speech is far too late.

"I'm not going anywhere," Jaxon growls. "You're mine, Amara. I had you first." He leans into me, pressing his hips forward. "Tell this prick to leave, and I'll remind you who fucks you the way you deserve."

I snort despite myself. Compared to Xavior, he was pathetic.

But before I can tell him exactly where he can shove that memory... Everything goes dark.

I blink a few times. Did the power go out?

Then the air shifts violently. My hair whips around my face as shadows explode forward, slamming Jaxon into the wall with brutal force. Drywall cracks and crumbles, raining down to the floor as his body hits with a sickening thud.

"Come here, Amara."

Xavior's growl is deadly. Power and fury radiate off him in suffocating waves, raising goosebumps along my skin and nearly locking my knees in place. I've always known he was strong. He is the Shadow Prince, after all, but this... this is so much more than I ever imagined.

"Amara!" he snaps.

His eyes, dark and roiling with shadows, finally find mine. The moment they do, something shifts. The violence eases, and his gaze softens. "I won't hurt you," he says, quieter now. "Please, come here."

"I know you won't." Not wanting him to mistake my awe for fear, I step toward him. He spins me around and pulls my back against his chest, wrapping his arms around me like a shield.

A muffled scream tears through the room. I look up in horror. Jaxon is pinned to the wall, his body spasming violently, feet dangling off the floor as shadows pour into his open mouth. Panic floods my chest.

"Xavior, stop!" I cry. "You're killing him!"

"Relax, baby." His lips brush my ear. "I'm not killing the son of a bitch. This is a warning."

The shadows finally release Jaxon. He collapses to the floor, gasping for air, his skin a sickly gray.

My stomach churns. The shadows still lash around him, restless, waiting.

"She's not yours," Xavior says coldly. "She's mine." He kisses the side of my neck, and I bite my lip to keep a traitorous moan from slipping free.

Jaxon stares up at him with rage-filled eyes, the same look he used to wear right before a fight. But even at his strongest, he was nothing compared to Xavior.

As Jaxon's color slowly returns, I exhale shakily. Death has been following me around lately. I don't want any more blood.

"Tell me you want me, Amara," Jaxon says hoarsely, standing on unsteady legs and reaching for me. "I'll fight for you. We can be happy again."

Xavior stiffens behind me, his grip tightening, a silent promise that he won't let go without a fight.

I hesitate.

Not because I want Jaxon, but because I don't know how to say goodbye without hurting him. I see the vulnerability in his eyes. He really does miss me.

I take too long.

Xavior's hold becomes almost painful as his mouth brushes my ear. "Tell him to leave," he murmurs. "Before I kill him. I won't let him have you. Even if that's what you want."

The threat is so quiet it chills me.

"I'm sorry, Jaxon," I say quickly. "I've moved on. I'm with Xavior."

Xavior exhales, tension draining from his body. A smile curves against my neck cruel, satisfied. Definitely meant for Jaxon.

Jaxon's face hardens. "You'll come running back when he breaks your heart," he spits. "I'm the only one who knows what your body needs."

Then he storms out, slamming his car door and peeling out of the driveway.

I try to step away, irritation bubbling up, but Xavior tightens his grip like he's afraid I'll disappear. Softening, I lean back against him and rub his arm. "He's gone. It's okay."

I kiss his cheek. He loosens his hold but doesn't release me. "You hesitated."

"I know, but—"

"How many times do I have to tell you?" he cuts in. "I'm not letting you go." The next thing I know, I'm thrown over his shoulder.

"Xavior, what the hell are you doing?" I shout.

He doesn't answer. The bed bounces as he drops me onto it. Before I can react, he flips me onto my stomach and lifts my hips, so my ass is in the air. What in the...

Smack.

I cry out as sharp heat blooms across my skin.

Smack.

Smack.

Each strike burns hotter than the last, his anger unmistakable. "That's for hesitating." His voice drips with desire as he rubs my right ass cheek, the one he just spanked. "You are mine. This ass is mine, this pussy," he cups me possessively, "is mine."

He starts rubbing my clit through my shorts. My back arches instantly, a moan tearing from my throat. Then he smacks my pussy.

I hiss, the sharp sting shocking me. My thoughts scatter, confusion tangling with heat. Is he punishing me?

Smack.

Smack.

Smack.

Three more times, each one harder than the last. Tears sting my eyes, my body trembling beneath him. "And that's for letting him touch you."

It hurts, but God, it turns me on just as much.

"You like that, don't you, my little slut?" He settles behind me on the bed, pressing his hard cock against my ass. He doesn't give a single fuck that I'm still sore. He's going to take me anyway just to prove a point.

His arm wraps around me as his hand slips into the front of my shorts, shoving my panties aside. His fingers dip inside me, and he makes a sound somewhere between a growl and a groan.

"So, fucking soaked," he murmurs. "Just for me, right, baby?"

"Yes, just for y—" my moan is cut off as his fingers pump into me a few times before pulling out to circle my clit instead.

I push my ass back into his jean-covered dick, wiggling, desperate to feel the way he stretches me.

"Let me remind you who owns this pretty little pussy."

He slips his hand out of my shorts, then mutters, low and hungry, "Fuck... you're so damn delicious."

He yanks my shorts and panties down, baring me completely. His hands grab both my ass cheeks, jiggling them as he groans, "*Fucking* perfect." Another hard smack lands. "Tell me who you belong to."

"You," I whimper. "Xavior. Please."

Chapter Twenty

Xavior

My teeth sink into my lower lip as I watch her ass jiggle, painted red with my handprints. I squeeze both cheeks hard, then let go. I undo my belt without tearing my eyes away from her flawless body.

I'd never admit this out loud, but I nearly came in my pants just from spanking her. I'll never get over how fucking perfect she is. Every curve, every sound. She's every filthy fantasy I've ever had made real. *Better*.

I free my hard, aching cock and step in close behind her, eagerly anticipating the bliss of her tight pussy squeezing me like a goddamn vice.

I can't lie, ever since I felt her pussy, it's all I fucking want. I want to be inside her constantly. Waiting all day damn near killed me. She needed time to recover, but all I could think about was burying myself back inside her.

Best fucking pussy I've ever had. And that's saying something. I rub the head of my cock over her glistening clit, slow and deliberate, watching her react before lining myself up with her entrance.

Then I thrust. One hard snap of my hips and I'm inside her.

Her pussy clamps down instantly, tight as hell, fighting the intrusion like it doesn't want to let me go. I force my way in, inch by inch, and fuck, she sucks me in like she was made for my cock. *Goddamn*. So perfect, so tight and warm.

This has to be what heaven feels like.

I tilt my head back and groan deep in my chest, staying still not to let her adjust, not even a little, but because if I move, I'll blow my load like a two-pump chump.

I hiss when she arches her back, pushing me even deeper. I grip her hips hard to hold her still. She has no idea what she's doing to me.

She whimpers my name.

I know exactly what she's begging for. So I start fucking her, hard and fast.

I pull back just enough to watch myself slam into her over and over, the headboard crashing against the wall, her ass bouncing violently with every thrust. Skin slapping skin. *Mine*.

It's the hottest fucking thing I've ever seen.

"Jesus, *fucking* fuck," I growl through clenched teeth when she fucking squirts.

The sensation nearly takes me out. Pleasure rips through my spine so violently that my vision blurs. I bite down hard on my tongue, the metallic taste of blood flooding my mouth as I fight to keep from exploding inside her.

Not yet. I'm not done with her.

I pull out and flip her over, settling between her thighs before slamming back into her. My lips crash into hers, my tongue forcing its way into her mouth, tasting her as I fuck her brutally.

She claws down my back, moaning into my mouth, and I thrust harder.

"Who does this pussy belong to?" I demand. I don't care that I already asked. I need to hear it again.

I lean back, eyes locked on where our bodies connect, watching her tits bounce with every snap of my hips. Sweat slicks her skin, glistening under me.

Mine.

My nostrils flare as possession burns hotter in my chest.

I thought I was obsessed before.

Fucking her made it so much worse.

"You," she moans. "All yours." Her eyes flutter closed.

I growl. "Open your eyes." I snap my hips into her harder. "Watch me fuck you. Watch who makes you feel this good. He'll never touch you the way I do, never please you like this. Don't ever fucking hesitate again."

Jealousy burns hot and vicious in my chest. The memory of her hesitation claws at me, enraging me all over again. How could she doubt who she belongs to? Does she still want him?

"He can never make me feel the way you do," she gasps, eyes locked on mine now. "I'm yours, Xavior. I don't want him. I want you."

Satisfaction rips through me.

Her pussy clamps down hard, pulsing around my cock as she comes apart, screaming my name like a fucking prayer.

"That's right, baby," I snarl. "Scream for me."

One more brutal thrust and I lose it. My cock throbs deep inside her as I explode, the release tearing through me so violently my vision whites out.

My shadows surge free, wild and uncontrolled, whipping around us. Her coffee cup is ripped from the nightstand and smashed against the floor, shattering into a million pieces as I roar through my climax.

My head spins. I squeeze my eyes shut and drop my forehead to her collarbone, breath coming hard and uneven.

Fuck. That was... intense. Too fucking good. I've never had an orgasm like that in my life, not until her. She wrecks me. Forces my power out of me with nothing but her body and those sounds she makes.

I pull her closer, her warmth heavy and real against me. Her breathing slowly evens out, soft and trusting. Too trusting. She's already drifting to sleep, giving herself to me in a way she shouldn't, in a way I haven't earned.

The jealousy doesn't fade like I expect. It tightens instead, coiling hot and restless beneath my skin. I've never felt anything like this, this need to protect, to possess, to destroy anything that even thinks about taking her from me.

I hold her there, listening to her breathe, and the thought slips in uninvited.

What would I do if she tried to leave?

My jaw tightens as the answer settles in, quiet, absolute.

I would stop her.

And the most terrifying part isn't the thought itself.

It's how calm I feel once I accept it.

Chapter Twenty-one

Amara

I stand in the middle of the kitchen scowling. What did I do so wrong? All I did was put the damn thing in the panini press.

So why the hell did it burn?

Xavior rushes downstairs, relief washing over his face the second he sees me. The tension in his shoulders melts away as he drags a hand down his face and shakes his head like he'd been bracing for something worse. My scowl deepens.

I plant a hand on my hip and let my eyes trail down his body. He's only in boxers. I mean… what if Ana were here?

"I thought you left," he says finally.

"Why would I leave?" I tilt my head. When I woke up, he was still asleep, and I was hungry. So, I figured I'd come down and make us a late lunch.

He clears his throat and looks away. "Nothing. What's burning?"

"I was hungry, so I turned the panini press on," I say, waving at it as it finally stops smoking. "I turn my back for not even a minute, and it starts burning. I swear that's all I did."

"Mhm." He arches a brow. "Are you sure it was just a minute? Were you... distracted at all?"

"Yes," I hiss, then sigh. Okay, maybe not just a minute. "I mean, maybe a few minutes. Brandon called, but it wasn't me. The damn thing is defective." I pout.

"I don't think so," he says dryly. "It's brand new. I just bought it."

"No, it wasn't me. I was distracted for not even five minutes."

His lips press into a thin line, fighting a smile. I narrow my eyes at him.

"Stupid defective panini press," he complains, lifting it and tossing it straight into the trash. "Why don't you have a seat? I'll make lunch after I put on some clothes."

He steps closer, grabs my hips, and kisses me, sweet, brief, domestic in a way that makes my chest ache.

"Yeah," I say. "That sounds like a good idea."

Especially since everyone in my family has banned me from using anything other than the microwave. Not that he needs to know that. He disappears upstairs, and I grab my phone. Brandon must've hung up. I'd been in the middle of telling him I had sex with Xavior, right before he started begging for extremely inappropriate details.

That's when I forgot about the panini press. By the time I finish cleaning, Xavior strolls back into the kitchen looking unfairly good in a light blue T-shirt and jeans. He usually wears dark colors, so the blue hits different. He winks at me, relaxed and playful.

I've never seen him like this, so at ease. He's usually alert, tense, always watching. I like this version of him. And I hate that a small part of me wonders who else gets to see it.

"I never got to thank you for the pancakes," I say. "They were to die for. I didn't know you could cook."

"No need to thank me." His gaze lingers. "There are a lot of things you don't know yet."

The truth of that hits harder than it should. I gave my body and my trust to someone I barely know. He must see it on my face, because he steps closer, lifts me onto the counter, and rests his hands on my bare thighs.

"You know me better than most," he says quietly. "We'll get to know each other. I'll tell you whatever you want to know. So what are you in the mood for?"

"Hm." I tap my chin, making him smile. "Grilled chicken sandwich?"

"Coming right up."

"Oh, and brownies." I pause. "Wait. Can you bake? Because I may or may not have set an oven on fire once. I'm pretty sure it was faulty wiring," I add quickly. "Or the oven was just... old."

That makes him laugh for real, deep, and unrestrained. My heart skips. I want to hear that sound more often.

"Those damn humans really need to stop making shitty ovens and panini presses."

"That's what I'm saying!"

"You have me now, baby." His voice softens. "I'll make you anything your heart desires."

My heart melts completely. I watch him cook, and honestly? Watching a man cook just for you is one of the hottest things on earth.

"Don't you dare," I gasp when he tries to rinse the brownie batter spoon. He arches a brow and hands it to me. "Licking the spoon is the best part."

I slide it into my mouth. His pupils blow wide. His hands grab my hips, yanking me to the edge of the counter as he presses his hard-on against me.

...Is he hard just from that?

"No," he murmurs, voice low and rough. "I've been hard this entire time. You look so damn sexy in my shirt."

He must've read my mind. He leans in to kiss me, but the back door opens. He groans in pure annoyance, and I can't help smiling.

"Whatcha cookin'? Smells good." Zane strides in, and my face instantly heats. I cover my eyes with my hands.

Xavior told me that Zane wanted to sleep under the moon last night in his wolf form. I've never been around wolves before, but I know enough to understand they like being outside, surrounded by nature, especially during a full moon.

"What the fuck, Zane?" Xavior snaps. "Put some damn clothes on."

"Aw, come on," Zane grins. "It's not like she doesn't enjoy the view, right, Amara?"

"No. I really don't," I say quickly. I drop my hands just in time to see Xavior step fully in front of me, blocking Zane from view completely.

"Jeez. Way to ruin someone's ego." Zane mumbles.

"Don't ask questions if you don't wanna hear the truth."

"Damn," Zane grumbles. "I had to deal with one smart mouth, but now there are two of you. Bullshit, if you ask me."

"Good thing no one asked you," Xavior deadpans, crossing his arms.

"I'm home!" Ana sings, strolling in. She freezes. Her eyes widen as they slowly drag down Zane's naked body.

"Oh," she purrs. "What's going on here?"

I groan. There goes our alone time. I knew it couldn't last, but I wasn't ready for it to end. And I still hadn't asked the most important question.

What exactly are Xavior and I?

"These two are no fun," Zane says. "Nothing but prudes. Nudity is natural."

Xavior snorts, and I bite back a laugh.

"I think it'd be really fun if we all went skinny-dipping," Zane adds. "Might help with those purity attitudes."

"Not happening," Xavior growls, no humor left in his tone at the thought of me naked anywhere near Zane.

"See?" Zane shrugs. "No fun." He walks out of the kitchen, his bare ass on full display. I can see why he has absolutely no problem with walking around nude; he has a nice body.

"So," Ana says, strolling into the kitchen, her gaze bouncing between Xavior and me. I hop off the countertop and squeeze past Xavior to face my sister.

"Jaxon called," she says. "He sounded pretty upset."

"Yeah," I say. "He came over. Asking for forgiveness." I glance at the brownies as Xavior pulls them out of the oven. Yum... of course he's good at everything.

"And I assume that didn't go well?"

Before I can answer, Xavior grips my hips and pulls me flush against him.

Oh. So, we're not hiding this. Annoyance flares. He should've checked if I was okay with announcing whatever *this* is to my family.

"Um?" Ana's eyes widen.

"Well," I start, unsure. "Xavior and I—"

"We're together now," he says calmly, answering for me. "I actually wanted to talk to both of you. Something's happened, and I need to go home."

My chest tightens. He's leaving. His grip on my hips tightens as if he feels it too.

"I was hoping you two would come with me," he adds. "I already spoke to your father. He agreed."

"Heck yeah!" Ana squeals. "I've always wanted to visit the Shadow Territory!"

"As long as Dad's okay with it," I say with a shrug.

Truth is, I'd rather go than stay here while he leaves. Who knows how long it'd be before I see him again? He doesn't live here. Eventually, he'll have to go back permanently. Am I setting myself up for heartbreak?

"Good," he says. "Go get packed. We're leaving tomorrow night." He spins me around easily. "I'll be back soon," he says softly. "There are a few things I need to take care of. Don't wait up."

He kisses me, quick, possessive, then walks out of the kitchen. I watch until the front door closes. I already miss him. Maybe it's too late.

I think I'm already falling for him.

"Okay, tell me *everything*!" Ana squeals the second the front door clicks shut.

I roll my eyes, grabbing a brownie and taking a bite.

"Holy shit... that's hot!" I hiss, sucking in a few sharp breaths as my mouth burns.

"No shit," she says, laughing and shaking her head. "He *just* took them out of the oven. How many times do you have to burn your mouth before you understand they need to cool down?"

"How am I supposed to let them cool down when they're sitting right there?" I argue. "Looking all chocolatey and scrumptious? That's cruel. That's like putting a piece of cheese in front of a mouse and telling it to sit and *stare* at it before it's allowed to eat."

"Jesus, Amara. It's only a few minutes."

"Nah, I'm with Amara." Zane strolls back in, thankfully wearing jeans this time. He grabs a brownie and takes a massive bite.

Instant regret.

"Hot *damn!*" He hisses, spitting it back onto the plate. "That's hotter than hell itself!"

"Seriously?" Ana mutters, completely unimpressed, shaking her head at both of us.

"So," Zane says, smirking. "You and my boy finally broke all that sexual tension? About fucking time. He was going insane." He twirls a finger by his ear.

My scowl snaps into place. "How do you know? Did he *say* something?" I really don't like the idea of Xavior announcing our sex life to anyone.

"Nope," Zane says casually. "I came home last night, and you were pretty loud. Crying out his name like he's some kind of sex god answering all your prayers. I turned around and slept outside."

"Oh." That's... all I've got. Heat floods my face and sinks straight into my chest. Was I really *that* loud? God, that's mortifying.

I clear my throat. "I, uh—I'll be back."

I grab three brownies and bolt upstairs while both of them burst out laughing behind me.

After hiding in my room most of the day, I decide it's time to make an appearance. I lean against Ana's open door and find her sitting on the floor, surrounded by a pile of clothes.

"You don't need that many options," I say, smiling at the stress etched on her face.

"I need options. What if I meet my mate?"

"Oh, come on. You still believe in that load of crap?" I tease. She's completely convinced she'll meet her mate, and it'll be straight out of a fairytale. I'm the opposite, though. I won't lie, for a brief moment, I thought Xavior might be mine. The way my body hums when I'm around him is intense, especially when I first saw him. I wanted nothing more than to touch him, kiss him... but he didn't seem to feel the same.

"How could I not? There are plenty of people who claim their mates. I mean, look at werewolves! Just ask Zane."

"Werewolves are different. The goddess gives every wolf a mate. Vampires sometimes get them. Demons, less often. And us witches? Hardly ever."

"You're wrong. I feel it deep in my soul. I know I have one, somewhere out there, and I'll meet him soon."

"When was the last time you met a witch who found a mate?"

"Whatever, Amara." Her shoulders slump, and the small smile on her lips fades into a frown, tugging at my chest.

"I hope for your sake it's true. I don't care about meeting mine, but I pray you meet yours. Every strong male is granted a mate, they say... so maybe yours is a strong, hot prince, or a king, or a warrior, just waiting for you. I mean, look at Rosa and Dimitri! And Azrael and Bella."

"Really? You think so?" Her eyes light up, gleaming. "See why I want to leave this place? I'll never meet my mate here. No one important comes to a small coven. Well... until now. But everyone who's going to show is already here, and trust me, I introduced myself to each of them, handshakes, smiles, zero sparks, not even a static shock!"

"I'm sure you did." I grin. "The shadow realm is definitely filled with important people... especially warriors."

I don't really know much about meeting your mate. We had an entire boring class on it, but I zoned out the whole time. Why listen to nonsense?

"Don't you need to pack?" she asks.

"I never unpacked in the first place." I watch as she pulls her suitcases out and begins folding her clothes, still grinning, still hopeful.

"Okay, tell me *everything* that happened last night. I left because the tension vibrating off Xavior after you walked out of the club was way too much for me to handle."

"When I came home, he was waiting for me in the living room. We argued a little, and he told me Lexie isn't his girlfriend."

"No crap. I could've told you that. He kept pushing her off him. She was *desperate* for his attention."

I grimace. How did I not notice that? "Anyway, I told him I kissed that guy, and he got jealous. Like... possessive. Very possessive."

Ana cuts me off, eyes lighting up. "God, that's so hot. That's *exactly* what I want: a hottie who's possessive of me."

I smile despite myself. I know I'm lucky. Maybe not every girl's dream, but definitely mine. "Anyway," I continue, "he kissed me, then asked me out, and then—"

"And then *what*?" she gasps. "Was Zane right? Did you have sex?"

"Ana, if you'd stop interrupting, you'd know." I sigh, then cave. "Yes. We did."

She squeals, wiggling like she might combust. "Don't stop packing, keep going!"

"Not yet. I need details." She throws clothes into her suitcase without even looking. "Does he fuck the way he looks like he'd fuck?"

I know exactly what she means: the swagger, the confidence, the way he just *exists* like he knows what he does to people.

"Yes. Gods, yes. If not better."

She shrieks, legs kicking. "Oh my God!"

"It was mind-blowing. Twice last night. Once this morning."

"Better than Jaxon?" she demands. "And how big is he exactly? I bet it's huge."

"Ana!" I throw a pillow at her. "I am *not* answering that last one. But yes, way better than Jaxon. Like, makes me forget my own fucking name better. My toes curled. I saw stars."

She stares at me, stunned. "Holy shit. Please tell me he has a brother. I need sex like that in my life."

We dissolve into laughter, talking for hours until exhaustion finally wins. I fall asleep beside her, curled into her bed, waiting for Xavior.

He never comes home.

Sometime later, someone lifts me up. I groan softly and instinctively snuggle into a warm chest. I don't need to open my eyes to know who it is.

He lays me down gently and pulls me against him. I rest my head on his chest and fall back asleep, safe and heavy with him around me.

"Amara," someone whispers in my ear, sending shivers down my spine. I moan, pressing closer to his touch without opening my eyes. "I'll be right back, little vixen. I have a few things I need to do."

I open my eyes and pout, not wanting him to leave. Waking up in his arms feels intoxicating. "A few more minutes... what time is it?" I beg.

He shakes his head. "I can't stay, but it's five in the morning. Go back to sleep, I'll wake you up in a couple of hours."

I grin wickedly and straddle him, rubbing myself against his already hard cock.

"A few more minutes wouldn't hurt, I suppose," he whispers, eyes smoldering with desire. His hands land on my thighs, thumbs tracing tiny, teasing circles into my skin.

"No, you're right. You're busy. You should go take care of whatever it is you need to do." I try to climb off, but his grip tightens, holding me firmly on his lap.

"Don't tease me, baby. I'm barely hanging on as it is; you have no idea how crazy you make me."

He grips my hips, moving me against his hard cock. My hands trail down his naked chest, over the ridges of his abs, feeling him shudder beneath my touch. I smile, loving how I affect him as much as he affects me.

I pull back and lift my sweater over my head, revealing my bare breasts. His gaze darkens, and he sits up, taking one nipple into his mouth. I cry out as my pussy throbs, desperate for him. His hand grips my hair, tilting my head back until my spine arches and my eyes are looking up at the ceiling.

He releases my nipple and moves to the other, sucking it into his mouth while his free hand cups my breast, spreading the saliva he left behind over the hardened peak. My hips move instinctively, grinding against him. I've always loved being on top, but Jaxon never cared he needed control. I hope Xavior enjoys it.

"Let me ride you," I beg.

He lies back immediately, hands scrambling to lower his sweats, freeing his hard cock, then pushes my shorts and panties aside. His movements are frantic, desperate, like he'll combust if he doesn't feel me around him. He doesn't waste any time; he quickly grabs his cock and holds it up for me.

"Come on, baby. Slide down on it. Use me," he groans, his voice thick with need.

My body shivers at his words. I lift myself, pressing the tip of him against my opening, and slowly slide down.

Holy shit. I moan, eyes rolling to the back of my head as he stretches me wide, making my body tremble uncontrollably. Jesus, it feels so, *so* good.

His hooded eyes lock onto mine as I begin moving my hips, slowly at first, savoring every inch. Once the burn eases, I pick up speed, chasing the rising sweet pleasure, higher and higher. My hands dig into his chest as I adjust my hips before slamming down, hard. I moan as his cock hits deeper than ever before.

"Fuck..." He groans deeply, voice ragged. "Yes, do that again, baby. Again, please."

I repeat the motion, faster this time, and he rumbles, vibrating through me as his pleasure spills over. My heart clenches watching him, his eyes shut, lips parted, head thrown back against the pillow, completely lost in ecstasy.

It's intoxicating, knowing I'm the one driving him wild. I ride him harder, faster, feeling every shudder, every groan, every tremor, wanting to push him even further.

"Amara, shit, Amara. You feel so good, so damn incredible." His hands tighten on my hips before releasing them to cup my breasts. One flick of his fingers on my nipple unravels me completely. My body tenses as an orgasm hits like a thunderstorm, lighting me up from the inside out.

That's when I notice Xavior's shadows crawling out of his chest, wrapping themselves around my arms. They swirl around us, tugging at my hair in the light breeze. I know I should be scared. Shadows are deadly, especially when they enter your body, slowly poisoning your organs, but I'm not. Not when it's him.

"Xavior!" I cry out, over and over, as a second orgasm slams into me with full force, stealing my breath, blurring my vision, and ringing my ears. I'm lost in pure, blissful ecstasy. I feel him follow me over the ledge. He roars my name and it vibrates against my chest as he forces my hips to keep moving while I'm completely paralyzed.

My limbs weaken, and I slump against him. He wraps me in his arms, holding me close as my eyes flutter closed. Even though I'm still riding the aftershocks, I slip into sleep, completely sated and utterly wrecked.

Shit. That was so intense it knocked me out completely.

Chapter Twenty-two

A door clicks shut, and I roll to my side. My eyes open, but I immediately slam them shut due to the sun beaming through the window. I groan, lifting my hand to block the sun and reopening them. I'm inside Xavior's room.

I stand, grumbling when my legs shake slightly. Looking at the clock on the nightstand, it's six am. I fell back to sleep for an hour.

That's when I notice the nightstand drawer isn't fully closed. Just a sliver, barely noticeable. Something pale catches my eye through the gap, and for a second I think it's nothing—paper, maybe, or a reflection from the window—but then I realize it's a face.

My face.

A strange chill slides down my spine as I lean closer and pull the drawer open the rest of the way. Inside are photo booth strips, slightly bent at the corners like they've been handled more times than I want to think about: the fair, the booth, me smiling widely, unguarded, and Xavior beside me, his expression softer than I've ever seen it.

And then my eyes snag on something else.

A dark smear cuts across the glossy surface, right through my smile. I swipe my thumb over it without thinking, my stomach dropping when it doesn't come clean. The color is wrong—too dark, too dull.

Blood.

My pulse stutters, a hollow, uneasy sensation opening beneath my ribs. I tell myself it's nothing, an accident. Someone else's blood. Anything that makes sense, but the wrongness lingers anyway, quiet and heavy.

I slide the photos back into the drawer and push it closed exactly the way I found it. My hand lingers there a moment longer than necessary before I pull away.

I shake myself off, my gaze drifting to the door. Why is Xavior up so early? What does he have to do at this ungodly time? I pull on a white button-up I find draped over a chair, tucking the front into my shorts. It's too big, slipping off one shoulder as I head down the stairs to see what he's up to.

I pause on the last step when I hear a voice I don't recognize, shouting. Does he have company?

Slowly creeping down the long hall where the voice is coming from inside my dad's office. I see Xavior sitting behind Dad's desk, and it appears that he's on a video chat.

I start turning around to head back upstairs. I have no right to be eavesdropping on his meeting, but as I take my first step, I hear my name. At first, I think he's calling out to me, but he's not.

He's talking about me...

I lean against the wall beside the door and listen. If it's about me, I have every right to know why they are arguing.

"We can't use Amara; there has to be another way."

"There is no other way! The witch is dead, and we must save your brother! We need Amara to finish what the witch started." The voice on the computer cracks like a whip, sharp and accusing. "Would you rather your brother die instead of her? Figure out which you'd prefer, because if you choose her, you are abandoning your brother. The way your mother abandoned you."

My breath hitches. My stomach twists into tight knots. My heart stutters violently, and my knees weaken as the words sink in. I grip the wall, nails digging into the paint, trying to steady myself.

"Do not fucking raise your voice at me!" Xavior growls. His anger reverberates through the room like a physical force. "Of course I don't want my brother to die!" I hear the heavy slam of something being hit in his fit of rage.

"I apologize, sir. Your brother is running out of time. Amara must die; she is the key to this curse."

My vision blurs. My heart hammers so loudly in my ears, I'm sure it will burst through my chest.

"I will do what must be done to end the curse, no matter what. He is my brother; I will not abandon him." Xavior's voice is iron, every word an unbreakable promise.

No... no... oh God. I feel bile rise as the truth hits me, and I have to swallow it down. I fell in love... with my own executioner.

I stumble backward, legs moving on autopilot. I need to get Ana—and me—out of this house, immediately.

He manipulated me, and I fell for it. For him.

My body shakes uncontrollably, lightheaded and cold, chest tight as if my ribs are being crushed. I force my way up the stairs, each step deliberate but trembling beneath my weight. My mind races with worst-case scenarios... what if we're caught? What if...?

I reach Ana's room and yank the covers down, shaking her awake.

"What? What is it?" she murmurs, blinking, still half-asleep. "Why are you crying?"

I touch my cheeks. I indeed have tears. I hadn't even realized. My panic flares even hotter.

"We need to leave. Now!" I throw the blanket off her, dragging her legs off the mattress.

"What? Why?" she asks, voice rising. I clamp my hand over her mouth, heart hammering in terror. I glance over my shoulder, half-expecting Xavior—or worse, someone else—to be standing there, waiting.

"Shh! I'll explain later. Get up!" I hiss, letting urgency squeeze through my words.

She scrambles, nodding, trusting me even in confusion. I dash to the shoe rack, yanking out a pair for each of us, throwing them in front of her. My hands tremble violently as I try to tie mine, but the laces twist and knot in my shaking fingers. I give up. Untied. I glance at her, and she's watching me like I've lost my mind.

"Now! This is serious, Ana!" I warn, she slips them on. As soon as she's done, I grab her hand, pulling her out of the room.

We tiptoe down the hall, ears straining, bodies tight with tension. I peek around the corner, scanning the stairs. Nothing, it's clear. I glance over my shoulder, pressing a finger to my lips. She nods.

We move slowly down, muscles coiled, nerves buzzing. The front door looms like a trap, and my heart races faster with every step.

We need to get outside and to our car quietly, and then gun it, because he'll hear the car turn on. I look over the banister down the hall toward my dad's office, squeezing Ana's hand for comfort. My body trembles, cold sweat prickling my skin. I can't believe I slept with him. I can't believe I trusted him.

Now is *not* the time.

We move to the front door and open it. The squeal of the hinge makes me cringe—shit, I never realized it was that loud. I peek over my shoulder, expecting him to appear, but the hall is empty.

I point to our car, and Ana nods, understanding. We tiptoe down the porch stairs, not even bothering to close the door, and once our feet hit the grass, we take off running.

Ana reaches the car first. My skin prickles, and my heart stops. I look over my shoulder.

Xavior stands in the open doorway, shirtless, shadows curling around him. His muscles flex with every calculated step. Calm and composed, his head tilts slightly, and when our eyes meet, a wicked grin stretches across his face. "Where are you running off to?"

I ignore him, shoving the driver's side door open. The keys are in the ignition, as always. I hit the brake, press the start button, and the engine roars to life.

"Hurry!" I shout as Ana climbs in. My stomach twists as I glance back toward the house, and my chest tightens when I see him sprinting toward us, each step deliberate, unflinching. I slam the gas pedal, tires squealing as I turn the wheel and speed off.

Oh, God. My heart feels like it's shattering. I press my hand against my mouth to muffle the cry threatening to escape.

"Tell me what's going on!" Ana shouts, looking behind us.

I grip the wheel until my knuckles ache. "I heard him on the phone."

"Who? Xavior?"

"Yes," I hiss, panic coiling in my chest. Where the hell am I going? Brandon's apartment? Lisa's house? Those are the only two places that will let us in. We can't go to Dad's. Not right now. I need a minute to think without being hounded.

"Amara!" Ana snaps, fear sharpening her voice. "Tell me!"

"He was on a video call in Dad's office," I say, struggling to steady my breathing. "The guy on the other end said something about Xavior needing to hurry... that he needs to kill me to save his brother from a curse."

"What?!" Her eyes widen. "Are you sure?"

"Yes! I heard it. Xavior hesitated at first, said they had to find another way. But the man insisted there was no other option and asked him if he'd abandon his brother to die. He said no. He said he wouldn't abandon his brother for me." I swallow, my throat tight. "That's why I ran and grabbed you. That's why he had us pack. He's taking me to my death—literally."

"Uh, Amara, what's going on?" Ana panics, her head whipping from window to window.

"Shit," I mumble as the road ahead darkens unnaturally. My foot eases off the gas, the car rolling to a slow stop.

I can barely see. The air thickens, turning grey and heavy, smoke curling around us until even the headlights grow smaller. I twist in my seat, peering out the rear window.

My stomach drops.

It's Xavior.

His shadows spill across the road, thick and choking, crawling forward like something alive. He walks through them at an unhurried pace, each step measured—calculated—as if he has all the time in the world. As if we aren't running from him at all.

I glance ahead. I *could* try to gun it, but the road is barely visible now. One wrong move and we'd wreck. Trap ourselves.

My pulse screams in my ears as I make a split-second decision, not caring how reckless it is.

"Ana," I say quickly, already reaching for the door, "I'll distract him. You go get help. I love you."

Before she can respond, I shove the door open and take off running.

"Amara!" she screams behind me, but I don't stop. I can't.

I know he'll follow me. He always does.

I need him away from Ana because if he catches both of us, there is no escape. There is no escaping Xavior or his deadly shadows.

I don't have to look back to know he's chasing me. I can *feel* him—his focus, his intent—burning into my spine like a physical touch.

The woods loom ahead, dark and familiar. They're my only hope.

I know these trees. Every path, every turn. He doesn't.

Branches claw at my arms as I plunge into the forest, my lungs burning. The feeling of his gaze disappears as soon as the woods swallow me whole, and it makes me nervous.

My heart stutters, fear blooming sharp and cold in my chest. I slow just enough to listen, my breath shaking.

Please don't circle back for her.

Please let the chance I gave her be enough.

I spin in a circle, chest heaving, my heart slamming against my ribs. Which way? Toward town or deeper into the forest? Fear trembles through every muscle as I force my legs forward, running away from the faint lights of the road. There's a small cave nearby. I just need to reach it.

After what feels like miles, I slow, pressing my back against a tree. My fingers dig into the rough bark, grounding me with the sting of pain, a reminder that I'm still alive. My lungs burn, my chest heaves, but for a brief second, I think I might have lost him.

Then I hear it, a voice, calm and smooth, yet edged with danger. It rumbles through the silence around me with a razor-sharp intensity.

"Amara..." The word rolls around me, warm and deadly at once. "You're just making this harder on yourself."

I press myself tighter against the tree, my nails digging into the wood until they draw blood. "As much as I've enjoyed this little cat and mouse game..." His voice drips with amusement, but there's menace beneath it, coiling around my spine. "...I'm growing bored."

He's too close.

My stomach drops as I feel the slightest brush against my bare legs. Shadows. His shadows are crawling up, wrapping around me like icy tendrils. My eyes widen in horror.

"My shadows will always bring you back to me."

I can't give up. I take off running, but before I can put any distance between us, something slams into my back. Pain explodes along my skull, my forehead smashing into the earth. Dirt fills my mouth, and I gag.

"There you are," he murmurs lowly in my ear. I ignore the pain, struggle, bucking, kicking, trying to throw him off, but he's strong, terrifyingly strong.

I could use my magic, but the thought of hurting him is unbearable. I scoff, internally shaking my head in disappointment at myself.

"Enough!" Xavior growls, his arm snaking around my waist. He lifts me with brutal ease and spins me around, my back slamming into a tree. Pain spikes through my spine. He grips my jaw, pressing his body against mine, pinning me still.

"You think you can run from me? *Leave* me?" His nose brushes the line of my jaw. His fingers tighten slightly around my throat, reminding me of just how small and fragile I am. My body shivers in fear, my mind screaming. *Is this where I die?*

"You're mine. There is nowhere you can hide where I won't find you."

My body betrays me. Every nerve screams in defiance, yet heat pools low in my stomach. My back arches involuntarily, betraying my terror with a traitorous pulse of desire. I pray he doesn't notice.

"Mmm... does my little vixen enjoy being chased?" His lips brush along the length of my neck, tongue warm and wet. My head falls back, and I can't stop the shiver, the moan that escapes my throat. "Such a naughty girl for me."

I jerk my head to the side, pushing against him with everything I have.

"Fuck you," I spit, pressing my hands flat against his chest and shoving, pushing him back an inch, but only an inch.

He snarls and spins me around, lifting me until my feet leave the ground. His arm locks around my waist as he raises his free hand, drawing it through the air in one slow, deliberate arc.

The shadows respond instantly.

They tear themselves off the forest floor and crawl upward, twisting together until the air in front of us splits open. Darkness spreads in a wide black circle, swallowing the light, like it's pulling me in.

I press my back harder against him, terror freezing me in place.

"Please... no. Stop, Xavior," I choke.

"I'm sorry, my love," he says quietly. "It has to be done. I'm taking you somewhere you cannot run from me."

"Wh–where?" I stammer as I stare at the dark but beautiful city in front of me.

A city rises out of the darkness before us, it's enormous. Dark, stunning, and intimidating all at once. Four massive structures surround a large castle at its center, its towers stretching high with sharp spires that disappear into thick black fog. The windows are tall and arched, carved with gothic detail that makes my chest feel tight.

Outside the black metal gates sit rows of small red-brick homes, tucked beneath the castle's shadow like they know better than to stand out.

"The Shadow Realm."

I scream as Xavior steps forward, closer to the portal. I beg him to stop, but he doesn't; his grip tightens as he leaps.

Cold darkness crashes over me, dragging me down as if it has hands. I fight, but his hold is iron, the world ripping apart around us.

The ground vanishes. Wind slams into me, stealing my breath as we fall. Panic tears through me.

This... this is the worst possible outcome; one so awful I didn't even imagine it. The darkness swallows me whole, and I black out.

I should've risked the car wreck instead of jumping out of the damn car.

Chapter Twenty-three

I stretch and roll to my side, burying my face into the soft pillow, groaning. Goddess, this pillow is so comfortable. I sink deeper into the mattress, feeling the silk sheets slide over my skin. It's hard to leave this warmth, but I know I can't stay here forever. But a few more minutes won't hurt.

Then the memories hit me, sharp and painful, flooding back all at once. It was a dream, right? There is no way I'm in the shadow realm. No possible way Xavior would do that. I mean, right... *right*?

My eyes snap open. I'm in a large room with stone walls, lying in a huge canopy bed. There is a large wooden fireplace directly in front of me with a fire that crackles softly, two small sofas, and next to them, a large wooden door. To my right is an arched window with two smaller ones on each side, and to my left is another wooden door.

I look down to see that I am wearing a cream silk tank top and matching shorts. I push myself out of the bed, my feet hitting the cold stone floor. The chill creeps up my spine, making me shiver.

What the hell is this place?

I dart to the window and press my palms against the cool glass. The fog outside is thick and unrelenting, swallowing up the world. It's hard to make sense of the world outside. Nothing looks real, just a haze of shadows.

I take a few steps toward the door by the fireplace, but the moment I open it, I realize it's just a fancy bathroom with a clawfoot tub. *I can't be here. I can't be in this world, in this place, with him.* My pulse speeds up, and I feel a knot of panic twist in my stomach.

I try the other door. It doesn't open. *Of course it doesn't.* I turn the handle harder, but it's locked. "Hello!" I scream, my voice cracking in frustration. "Let me out of here!"

Nothing.

I step back, the panic rising in my chest. I can't breathe. I can't think straight. *I'm trapped.* I rush to the windows, pressing my face against the cool glass, desperate to see more, but it's all just fog, stretching endlessly. The garden below seems to go on forever. I can't even see the ground past a few feet.

I tear my eyes away from the window and focus on the room around me again. *I'm trapped here. This is real. Xavior betrayed me.*

I back away from the bed, but then the door creaks open, and I freeze.

A woman walks in, holding a tray of food. She's older, wearing a black dress with a white apron, her steps careful and deliberate as she moves toward the table. Her eyes never meet mine. She looks... scared? Or maybe just... nervous?

She bows slightly before she says, "Your breakfast is ready, Miss Amara." She shuts the door behind her and walks toward the fireplace, and sets the food tray down on the wooden coffee table between the sofas. She removes the cover, and I see a stack of pancakes with whipped cream and berries. It looks to die for, a small cup of coffee or maybe tea, and a glass of orange juice. She starts walking towards the door.

What the actual fuck...

"Hey, wait! Where am I? And how did I get here?" She doesn't answer, avoiding my gaze, as if I'm something she doesn't want to deal with. She makes it to the door and taps on it lightly. "Hey, I asked you a question!" I snap, walking over to her, but the door swings open before I get too close. I see a huge, burly man in all black standing there. She walks out, and I try to go after her, but the man quickly slams the door shut.

"What the hell? Let me out!" I shout, banging on the door. I scream in frustration when no one responds.

Calling to my magic with my palms facing the door, I whisper, "Apertis!" which means open. My heart sinks when nothing happens, "Apertis!" I growl angrily, "Apertis!" I scream, but still nothing.

My magic isn't working. They must've spelled the room so no magic can be used. I run to the bathroom to look and see if there's a window I can jump out of, but there isn't.

I'm trapped. Oh my gosh, my panic grows, my chest feels tight, I can't freaking breathe. It's okay, just breathe... I sit down, my knees against my chest. Inhaling through my nose and exhaling through my mouth, like Ana does during a panic attack. After a few minutes, it works. Freaking out isn't the answer.

I stand, pacing around the room. Xavior kidnapped me and forced me through the portal. I'm in the shadow realm. I can't escape. Where would I go? I don't know anything about this realm or about the monsters that live in those woods.

Those thoughts keep circling in my mind as I pace, and finally, I sit down on one of the sofas staring at the cold food as my stomach rumbles. I reach for it, picking up the fork.

What if he poisoned it?

I cover the tray with its lid and slump against the wall, my mind spinning with the same thoughts over and over. Hours pass. Or maybe it's just minutes. Time feels different here. I don't know what to do.

Finally, the door opens again. The woman from before walks in, setting another tray down, this time with lunch. She doesn't look at me, just places it down and turns to leave.

"Please," I beg, my voice trembling, my hands shaking as I look at her. The woman places the tray on the table, and I can barely keep myself together. "Tell me who brought me here. Tell me where I am."

She stays silent, her eyes downcast. She says nothing as she removes the lid from the breakfast tray. She frowns slightly, almost as if she's trying to figure out what to say.

"Miss Amara, you must eat," she says softly, almost apologetically.

"No!" I shout, my voice cracking. My throat feels tight as my heart pounds, a storm of anger and fear building inside me. "Answer my questions!"

I stand, my body moving almost on instinct as I march toward her. Her eyes widen in fear, and she stumbles back, quickly grabbing the tray and spinning toward the door, trying to escape. My pulse races, and I act without thinking. I grab her, my fingers digging into her upper arm as I shake her, desperately pleading, "Tell me!"

"Guards!" She cries out, her voice full of terror.

"Tell me who brought me here!" I scream again, my throat raw. But before she can answer, a pair of rough hands grab me from behind, yanking me away from her with painful force.

I thrash, screaming, "Let me go!" as I try to break free, but it's no use. I'm being dragged back toward the bed, forced down onto the mattress with a brutal shove. My body is limp, but my heart is pounding in my chest. I spring up, my eyes darting toward the door, but another man in black exits, slamming the door shut behind him with a finality that echoes in my ears.

"Fuck you!" I scream, grabbing a pillow and throwing it at the door with all my strength. It hits with a soft thud, the sound barely registering over the fury that fills me. I punch the mattress, again and again, feeling my frustration boiling over with no outlet.

I lean against the wall behind the door, time stretching out painfully around me. Hours? Minutes? It's impossible to tell. Every second feels like an eternity. Finally, the door creaks open again. The woman steps inside, a new tray of food in her hands.

I spring to my feet before she can even get the door halfway closed. In a fit of rage, I shove her. She stumbles, falling to the ground with a crash. The tray goes flying, landing with a loud clatter as food spills everywhere. She cries out, but I don't care. I rush past her, but the two guards are already blocking the door.

I take in my surroundings for the first time: a large hall, the same cold, unfeeling stone walls as the room. The dark wooden floors look like they've seen years of use, but still, they're cold. Everything about this place feels suffocating, and it makes me want to claw my way out of here, even though I have no idea where to go.

"Let me go!" I yell, trying to push past them, but they grab my arms. Their grip is like iron, and I struggle, but it's no use. They drag me back into the room like I'm nothing more than a rag doll.

"We must tell Prince Xavior that she is refusing to eat." The guard's voice is cold, detached.

"Tell him that I said go fuck himself!" I snarl through clenched teeth, but, of course, they ignore me. The woman, silent and afraid, is allowed to leave before they finally release me, slamming the door shut behind her.

I storm toward the table, my hands shaking with rage. I grab the tray of food and hurl it at the wall. The plate smashes, food splattering in all directions. The loud crash of the tray hitting the floor seems to reverberate through the room, and I scream, grabbing at my hair. My fingers twist in the strands, pulling until the sharp pain shoots through my scalp, distracting me from the ache in my chest.

I can't stay here. I can't.

I rush to the bathroom, slamming the door behind me, locking it with trembling hands. The cold stone feels like it's pressing in on me. I sink to the floor, my body wracked with sobs. My breath comes in short gasps, ragged and violent. The tears pour from my eyes, hot and relentless.

I cry for what feels like hours, my sobs echoing off the walls, but the emptiness in my chest remains.

I am a prisoner.

Will I ever be free? Will he ever let me go? Or is this my life now?

The thought of dying here makes my chest tighten with fear. I thought Xavior cared for me, but this... this is something else.

Did Ana make it to safety? Or is she still out there, somewhere, alone?

I curl into a ball, my arms wrapped around my knees as I rock slightly, trying to find comfort in the darkness. My stomach growls loudly, painfully, but I refuse to eat.

I won't let them break me, not like this. No matter how hungry I am, I won't give in. I won't let them win.

I close my eyes, forcing myself to breathe. I'll hold on. I have to.

Chapter Twenty-four

Amara

I'm jolted awake by a growl so deep, it shakes me to my core. The sound reverberates through the room, followed by a sharp crack, like thunder. My heart stutters in my chest. Another bang, and the bathroom door shatters as it's slammed against the wall. My breath catches, my pulse racing as my eyes fly open in panic.

The door is smashed open, and there he is. Standing in the doorway, tall and imposing, his eyes burning with a mix of fury and something darker. I freeze, every muscle in my body locking as a wave of terror crashes over me. My back hits the cold edge of the bathtub as I scramble, trying to put distance between us, but I can't escape him.

I start to tremble, my breath coming in short, desperate gasps. "No," I whisper, more to myself than to him. "No, please..."

His gaze softens for a moment, a flicker of something like guilt crosses his features, but it disappears almost as quickly as it came. He steps forward, and I instinctively recoil, my heart pounding as if it wants to escape my chest.

"Amara," he says, his voice low, almost soothing, but there's a harsh edge to it that makes my skin crawl. It's as if he's trying to comfort me, but it only makes my blood run cold. "We need to talk."

"No!" I shout, pulling my knees tighter to my chest, wrapping my arms around them as though I could protect myself from him. "Don't come any closer. I don't want to hear it!" My voice cracks, the words coming out desperate, as if begging him to stop. I can't bear the thought of being near him, of hearing his excuses. I'm shaking so hard I can hardly hold myself together.

He stops. There's a beat of silence, the kind that presses down on you, suffocating. "Fine," he spits out, his jaw tightening. "But you need to eat."

"Eat?!" I laugh bitterly, the sound empty, harsh. "So, you can poison me? I'm not that stupid, Xavior. You won't get me that easily." My voice trembles with a mix of fear and hatred. The words hang between us, thick with distrust. "You're not going to win. Not this time."

He flinches, just for a moment, but I see it, and I take some dark comfort in it. The small victory is fleeting though, and it doesn't even come close to erasing the ache inside me. The pain of his betrayal, the way he's torn my world apart. My heart feels heavy, like it's breaking all over again. I squeeze my eyes shut, not wanting him to see the tears threatening to spill, but I can't hold them back for long.

Before I can even process what's happening, I feel his hands, warm, and strong, on my arms. My breath catches, and every muscle in my body locks up. I should be fighting, pushing him away, but my body betrays me. His touch sends an unwelcome shock of heat through me, the familiar pull of his strength reminding me of everything I've lost. The tenderness of it... I can't stand it, but I can't ignore it either.

I lash out, my feet kicking wildly as I try to shove him away. "Don't touch me!" I scream, my voice raw, but it's useless. He's too strong, his grip too firm. I kick, I struggle, but it does nothing. He lifts me, like I'm nothing, like I'm weightless, carrying me out of the bathroom and into the room. I kick and scream the entire way, but it doesn't stop him. I'm powerless. I'm trapped. My screams echo in the hollow space, but he doesn't seem to hear me.

When we reach the sofa, he lowers me onto it gently, as if I'm made of glass. His hands leave me, but his presence lingers. He kneels in front of me, his eyes never leaving mine, searching for something in my face, answers? Regret?

I flinch as his hand reaches toward me, and I instinctively pull back. It's a reflex, but it's also the pain of what he's done, the way he's shattered my trust. The disappointment that flashes in his eyes makes my heart twist, and I hate him for it. For making me feel anything, but I refuse to show it.

He turns away, and when he looks back, he's holding a plate of French toast. The golden slices are topped with strawberries, whipped cream, and syrup, something sweet and comforting. I hate that it looks so good.

"Please eat," he says, his voice softer now, but there's an edge to it, a command. "I didn't poison the food."

I snort, bitterness bubbling in my throat. "Like I'll ever believe you. I'd rather starve than ever trust you again." I turn away, eyes fixed on the window, refusing to let him see the way my hands are trembling. The silence between us stretches, thick with tension. I'm waiting for him to break, for him to give me some kind of answer, some kind of explanation. But there's nothing.

"Eat," he says again, this time his voice tinged with anger. The command is sharp, like a knife, but I don't answer him.

A few more minutes pass. Then, without warning, his hand is on me again. He cups my jaw with surprising force, making me look at him. I try to pull away, to escape his grasp, but it's no use. His hold is too tight, and I'm trapped in his gaze. And that familiar, unwanted heat spreads through me again.

He picks up the fork with his free hand and cuts into the French toast then lifts up a slice before turning back to me, pressing it against my lips. "Chew," he growls, his voice dark and commanding. I try to pull away, but his grip tightens, forcing me to open my mouth. Before I can protest, he shoves the food inside, his palm pressing against my mouth, taking my attempts to spit it out.

"Chew," he repeats, his voice low, almost feral. I try to shake my head, but I can't. Tears start to fall, hot and frustrated, and I can't stop them. I feel so small under his touch, so helpless. But I chew, slowly, deliberately, forcing myself to swallow each bite even though it feels like a betrayal. My body shakes with the effort to control myself, to not lose it completely.

When it's finally over, when the plate is empty, I push him away with every ounce of strength I have left. I kick him hard, and he stumbles back. I use the moment to scramble off the couch, rushing to the other side of the room, my heart pounding, my chest heaving with raw emotion.

"I wish it could be different, but it can't. I don't want to hurt you, but I don't have another choice. Don't make this harder than it needs to be." His voice is low, almost pained, but there's no mistaking the finality in his words. It feels like a judgment.

I swallow the lump in my throat, my chest tight with something close to fury. "Oh, I am so sorry that I'm not just going to sit here and let you hurt me," I say, my voice dripping with sarcasm. It's the only defense I have left, the only thing I can cling to. I refuse to let him see how much his words cut.

"Then we'll do this the hard way." His words hit me like a slap, cold and unforgiving. I don't respond.

I don't have anything left to say, nothing that would change his mind. Instead, I press my back into the wall, my arms wrapped tightly around myself in a desperate attempt to shield the broken pieces of my heart. My gaze falls to the floor, and I feel the weight of my own helplessness crashing down on me.

I hear him take a step closer, but I refuse to look up. I won't give him the satisfaction of seeing me break.

For a long moment, he just stands there, the silence thick between us. It's as if he's waiting for me to say something, to beg for mercy, but I'll never do that. Not for him, not after everything.

Finally, I hear his footsteps as he turns and leaves the room, the door clicking shut behind him with a finality that sends a shiver down my spine. The sound echoes in my ears, a stark reminder that I'm alone.

My knees buckle, giving out beneath me, and I collapse onto the cold floor. A wave of emotion crashes through me all at once, relentless and overwhelming. I press a hand to my chest as my breath stutters, my body trembling with the force of it as sobs tear free.

Is he really going to kill me?

The thought lodges itself in my mind, cold and cruel. The question hangs in the air, unanswered, suffocating the air around me as my heart fractures all over again. The weight of his betrayal, of everything that's happened, slams over me, and I'm powerless to stop the grief from spilling over.

I've been locked in this cage, in this nightmare, for what feels like forever. And now, it's like the final piece of my world is crumbling. I thought I knew him. I thought he would protect me.

I try to steady my breath, but the fear, the uncertainty, the helplessness, it's all too much. I curl into myself, my arms hugging my knees to my chest as if I can somehow hold myself together.

I don't know what's going to happen next. But I know one thing for sure: I won't give him the satisfaction of seeing me break completely. Not yet. Not ever.

Xavior comes back hours later with another tray of food. His eyes sweep the room, scanning for me, until he finally spots me curled up in a dark corner. His frown deepens. He sets the tray on the table and strides over.

I shake my head, pressing my lips into a tight line, but he doesn't seem to notice or care. He picks me up effortlessly, and I can't help the startled scream that escapes me. Of course, no one comes.

"Am I going to have to force-feed you again?" His voice is low, calm, but the weight behind it makes my stomach twist. He sits me on the couch and slides in beside me, placing the tray between us.

I inch away, hoping distance will make him relent. My eyes dart to the sandwich, turkey, I think, and a pile of chips. Reluctantly, I lift the plate, moving to the other sofa, eating in silence while staring at the floor. Every bite tastes bitter, but I can't escape the sharp awareness of him watching me.

"Is there anything else you need? The bathroom is fully stocked, and the closet is full of clothes for you." His tone is deceptively casual, but every word carries the quiet force of command.

I say nothing. My throat tightens.

He growls, lifts the empty plate, and walks out. I sink back into the couch, silent, wondering how long I can keep up this stubborn act before he decides I've pushed too far.

Five days. I have been here for five days; every day is the same. Xavior comes into the room with food like clockwork. Always making sure I eat every last bite. I ignore his attempt to talk. His attitude is always different. Sometimes he's sad and hurt when I ignore him, or he grows angry. The depression is slowly creeping its way in.

I'm standing by the arch window, gazing at the beautiful garden below, when the door opens. I don't turn to look, not caring who it is, "We can go down and eat outside by the gardens if you'd like." Xavior's masculine voice says close behind me, making me shiver slightly. My mood shifts, feeling surprised. He'll take me outside...

I release a long, sad sigh, no. I walk around him, sitting on the sofa, looking at the pasta.

"I know it's your favorite." He sits across from me. I watch him lean forward and rest his elbows on his knees in the corner of my eye. I haven't looked directly at him since he force-fed me. I pick up the glass of water, taking a sip before I begin to eat the pasta, and just like before, I taste nothing. It's like my mouth grew numb.

We sit in silence as he watches me eat, never once taking his eyes off me. I need to ask him if my sister is okay and much more. The first question I ask is in a small voice, "When are you letting me go?"

"Amara, look at me."

"Why are you doing this to me?" I scream, picking up the plate and throwing it on the ground. I know I'm acting like a toddler throwing a tantrum, but I can't take it anymore. The broken heart, the not knowing, being kept prisoner by the man who wants to kill me. The man I love. He's dragging it out, and it's driving me crazy. Why hasn't he gotten it over with? Why does he sit with me every day and watch me eat? It doesn't make sense.

"Get it over with or leave!" I scream, pointing at the door. I can't stand to be alone with him; it's too much. I turn my back on him and hold myself tightly as I cry silently.

After a few minutes, I hear the door shut. He leaves, taking my broken heart with him because it belongs to him. No matter how much I try to lie to myself, even after what he did to me.

I crawl into bed, staring out the arch window, feeling completely numb as I watch the sunset. A while later, I drift off to sleep.

I wake up the next morning, and the sun is beaming down on me, making me slam my eyes shut. My head is pounding painfully.

I slowly sit up to see that the pasta mess had been cleaned up, and the broken bathroom door had been fixed. How did I sleep through all of that?

The door opens, and the same old woman walks in with a tray of food. I frown, looking out the door, but there's no sign of him.

"May I please get some medication?" I ask her, and this time she doesn't ignore me. She actually looks at me. "I have a migraine; anything will do."

"Of course, I'll be right back." She leaves, and I hear her say something to the guards, but I can't hear what as the door closes. I lick my lips, stand up, and walk towards the tray of food: eggs, bacon, and toast. I begin eating, even though he isn't here. I know the woman will tell him, and he'll force-feed me again. I never want to experience that again. It was too humiliating.

When the woman comes back, she has a small white plastic cup in her hand. She places it on the table and bows slightly before walking out. I pick up the small cup to find two small pills. Picking up the orange juice to swallow the medication, and that's when I notice a note on the tray. I frown, picking it up.

> *Amara,*
>
> *I apologize, I couldn't make it for breakfast. Something important came up, and it needed my immediate attention. Please eat, little vixen. If you finish your meal, I told your guards that you are allowed to walk the gardens.*
>
> *Xavior.*

My heart pounds excitedly. I rush to eat, and when I'm finished, I walk to the bathroom. For the first time, I go into the closet. He's right, it's filled with all types of new clothes in my size.

I pick something comfortable: grey joggers and a white tank top. I go back to the bathroom and turn on the water to shower. I lay the clothes on the countertop and look at my reflection in the mirror while I wait for the water to heat. I look horrible; my skin is pale with dark circles underneath my eyes. I remove my hair from the bun it's been in for days and rummage through the drawers looking for a brush. I find one, and I start brushing my hair, flinching at the tangles.

The room starts to fill up with steam. I remove my clothes, climb into the shower, and groan when the hot water touches my skin. I'm surprised to find brand-new bottles of the same scent of my shampoo, conditioner, and body wash from back home. Jesus, he was overly prepared for me. He knew he was going to take me, but for how long? He never cared about me, did he? He was faking the entire time. I should have known a man like that would never bend over backward for someone like me.

My mom never even thought I was enough. I was a fool. It was so easy for him to take advantage of me; it's almost laughable. I craved to be loved and accepted, so all he needed to do was show me a little attention and whisper a few sweet words, and I was a goner. I wrap my arms around my midsection, needing comfort. I take my time washing my hair and body, knowing it badly needed a good wash.

I feel so much better after the shower. I put on my clothes. The joggers sit low on my hips, and the tank top is short, showing an inch or so of my lower stomach.

I walk over to the door, and surprise fills me again when it opens; the guards look down at me. They are both young but still older than me, maybe mid-twenties. They are both very handsome; one has dirty-blond, shaggy hair with a strong bone structure, and the other has a short buzz cut with dark eyes and high cheekbones.

"I ate my breakfast," I say in a strong, confident voice that surprises me. "I'd like to walk the gardens."

"Very well, follow us." The blond says with a heavy Australian accent and begins walking. I follow him as the other guard follows close behind. I take in the stone walls and hardwood floors, similar in style to my prison. The hall ends, and a curved staircase follows.

I grip the railing as I begin walking down the steps. The stairs led to a large entryway with a giant gold chandelier. A large floral rug sits in the center of the room with a small round table.

I don't have time to take in more details as the guards rush towards the back of the house. We pass a sitting room, a large library, and finally, I see a set of arched glass doors leading to the backyard.

When the guard opens the door, I inhale deeply, groaning at the earthy scent. I have missed it like crazy the last couple of days. I hurry out and find the garden immediately. Rushing towards it as nature calls out to me, beckoning me forward.

Reaching the garden, my fingers softly grazing the flowers, making me feel alive again. Everyone knows how cruel it is to keep a witch from nature. We need it as much as we need air to breathe; even witches that are thrown in prison have access to a makeshift forest within the prison walls. I fall to my knees, crying out when my fingers dig into the soil, feeling my magic spark through me.

I lift my head, staring at the woods, thinking of escaping. It'll be stupid, there's no point. I don't know where I am. They'd catch me, and I'd be stuck inside those four walls again. The guards catch up to me, finally standing there watching me for a moment before turning around and giving me some privacy.

I sit outside for the rest of the day. The guards don't complain a single time until sunset. The one with the buzz-cut turns to tell me. It's time to go back in. I frown but get up and follow them inside.

Chapter Twenty-five

Amara

I wake up to a loud squeak, like wood scraping against wood. I sit up, blinking as my eyes adjust to the darkness. Xavior is sitting on a small chair beside the bed, sleeping.

He shifts his large body in the tiny chair, and the chair scrapes against the floor, repeating the sound. I swallow hard. He must've fallen asleep watching me.

I should find that creepy, but I don't.

The idea of him watching over me—of not being alone—settles something in my chest.

Stupid.

I lie back down, rolling to my side and slowly drift off as I stare at him.

When I wake up again, the sun is shining brightly, and Xavior and the chair are gone. Has he done that every night since I've been here?

The door opens, and Xavior walks in with a tray of food. That's when I really look at him and notice the dark circles beneath his eyes; he looks exhausted and... defeated.

"Did you enjoy the garden?" he asks.

I sit up, still wearing the joggers and tank top. His gaze drifts over me, slow enough that he trips on the rug near the sofas.

"It was fine, I guess," I say with a shrug.

He sets the tray down and lifts the lid, revealing a sausage, egg, and cheese sandwich with tater tots. I pick one up, my appetite suddenly gone. I clear my throat. I can't put this off anymore.

"Where's Ana?" I keep my eyes on the food, avoiding his stare. "Did you go back for her?"

Please tell me she's okay...

I don't think I can survive losing her, too.

"I didn't go back for her," he says calmly. "Maybe I should. It might keep you in line. This bratty attitude isn't attractive."

My stomach twists, nausea creeping up fast. "Is that a threat?"

"No," he replies flatly. "It's a statement. One I might follow through on if you don't behave." He stands, stepping closer. "You act like you can ignore this. Ignore us. There is no ignoring us."

"I can ignore this if I want to," I snap. "Why does it even bother you? I'm not yours anymore. Just tell me what's next. What is the point of all of this?" I gesture around the room, my breathing picking up despite my effort to stay calm. I press my lips together and stare down at my bare feet.

"You are mine," he snaps, something wild breaking through his composure.

"I am not yours." My voice shakes with anger now. "You lost that privilege the moment you decided I was expendable. The moment you decided I had to die."

I turn away, heading for the bathroom. I need space. It's the only place I can escape to in this fancy cage.

He laughs softly behind me, bitter and hollow.

"That's where you're wrong, Amara." His voice drops, cold and lethal. "You're mine whether you like it or not."

His hand clamps around my arm, spinning me back toward him. His dark eyes are unhinged now, control fraying at the edges.

"You're fucking crazy."

"Don't care," he bites out, jaw clenched. "You're not leaving me. Even if I have to keep you locked up forever."

He releases me and walks out without another word.

The door opens, and I spin around.

The two regular guards step into the room, move to the side, and allow Xavior to enter. My heart flutters violently in my chest, like a wild bird trapped in a cage.

The expression on Xavior's face makes my blood run cold. It's one that could haunt me, one I've never seen, cold, emotionless, and cruel.

He's the shadow prince, not the man I came to know. I step back, dread settling deep in my gut. Something is wrong. I can feel it.

"Xavior?" My tone is full of uncertainty.

He jerks his chin in my direction, and when he does, the guards move forward. I stumble backward, quickly. My feet catch on each other, nearly causing me to fall. The next thing I know, they are there, gripping my elbows.

Dragging me forward, and my fight or flight mode kicks in. I fight, trying to yank my arms out of their iron grip, but it is useless.

"Do not hurt her." Xavior growls, watching me struggle as if he cares.

I throw my weight down, trying to slow them, but they keep dragging me, my feet scraping uselessly behind me. "Stop struggling, it will only hurt you more."

"Fuck you, Xavior," I spit, squeezing my eyes shut to hold back the tears that blur my sight. He will not see me break.

I fight the entire way down the stairs. I reach for my magic—but it refuses to answer. Still, I can feel it there, beneath the surface, pressing and restless, desperate to break free.

We turn in the opposite direction from where they took me to the gardens earlier. My body trembles with fear. What is he going to do to me? I can feel his stare burning into my back as he watches me struggle.

Is he enjoying this?

I gave myself to him.

I fell in love with him.

Am I so deprived of love that I didn't see this betrayal coming? See the monster lurking beneath the beautiful lies? I ignored the signs––the cracks in him I didn't want to see, signs of a psychopath.

A sob threatens to tear from my throat, and I nearly choke on it as I force it back down.

My gaze snaps to a body lying motionless at the center of a canopy bed as we enter a room far larger than mine. The layout is the same. The furniture is identical.

As we move closer, I see it, the resemblance. The same dark hair, same structure. This is him. The brother my mother cursed. Now I'm paying for the sins she left behind. My struggle fades as I stare at him, frozen. He looks peaceful, lost in sleep. His skin is pale, his features softer than Xavior's rounder, almost innocent.

But I've learned how deceiving appearances can be.

Xavior's warmth presses into my back, and my body goes rigid, bracing for what comes next. Will he make it quick? Will it be painless?

"Meet Axel," he growls against my ear. "My brother, whom your mother cursed and reduced to this. I should fucking hate you for what she did," he continues, his voice softening, almost apologetic. "But I don't. I'm sorry for what I have to do. Please forgive me, my sweet vixen."

Before I can respond, his hand clamps around the back of my neck and forces me face down onto the mattress beside his brother. My hips buckle as I try to push him off, but his grip tightens, his weight pressing me into the bed. I turn my face to the side, gasping, trying not to suffocate against the blankets.

"Please don't, Xavior." I cry out. I'm not ready to die.

"Shh. It'll be fast." He leans down and licks the tears from my cheek.

"Are we ready, Prince Xavior?" A woman's voice asks from behind us.

"Yes." Xavior looks away from me and grabs my left hand, forcing it flat against the mattress.

The betrayal hits all at once, sharp and suffocating. It hurts too much. Fear and rage collide in my chest, heating my blood until it feels like it's boiling. But it isn't just anger rising now.

My magic surges.

It bursts through the barrier holding it back, fire building with my fury. The heat rushes down my arms and explodes from my hands, flames tearing through the blanket beneath me.

Xavior's weight disappears as he pushes my body off the bed before the flames engulf his brother.

I hit the floor hard but scramble up instantly, spinning around in time to see Xavior rip the burning blanket away from Axel. I reach for my magic, for anything, but it sputters, nothing more than a useless flicker before dying in my hands.

I turn and run for the exit without looking back.

"Amara." The single word booms through the room, freezing me in place. "I will kill her." Ice floods my veins as I look over my shoulder.

Ana.

She's trapped in Xavior's grip, struggling as he holds her tight.

"Don't worry about me, *go*," she screams.

"Shut up," Xavior growls, his fingers tangling in her hair. He yanks her head back, ripping a whimper from her throat. "Be a good girl, Amara," he continues calmly. "Bring that sweet ass back into the room." His lips curl into a deadly smirk.

I do exactly what he says.

I walk back toward him, never breaking eye contact not even for a second.

"Have a seat." The woman in the black dress gestures toward a leather chair beside Axel's bed.

"Take her away," Xavior orders another guard.

Ana screams my name as she's dragged from the room, her voice ripping through me. I don't react. I force myself into the chair, staring straight ahead at the wall. If I fight, if I say anything, I risk her life. I won't do that. I can't.

"Are you taking her back home?" My voice sounds distant.

"Yes," Xavior says. "As soon as this is over. She will not be harmed. You have my word."

A laugh threatens to escape me, but I swallow it down. His word means nothing. Still, I cling to it because I have nothing else. He has no reason to hurt her now. I repeat that thought in my head like a prayer.

The woman steps closer. I barely feel her fingers press against my skin before a sharp pinch on the top of my left hand. I flinch.

"The needle has been inserted," she says calmly, as if she's talking about the weather. "We'll use magic to make the blood flow faster. It'll be over quickly."

A broken sob tears from my throat before I can stop it. My chest tightens painfully as the reality settles in.

This is it.

This is how I die.

Drained dry by the man I love, alone and forgotten.

Xavior kneels in front of me, his eyes searching my face. "Look at me," he says, his voice strained, almost desperate.

I can't. I refuse. I stare past him at the wall behind his head as tears slide down my cheeks and drip onto my lap. If I look at him, I'll break.

"If my mother cursed your brother," I whisper, my throat burning, "then why are you doing this to me?" I swallow hard. "How am I connected to him?"

"He's part of the rebel group attacking the covens," Xavior explains.

My mouth falls open in horror. I don't bother hiding it. He sees my reaction and shakes his head quickly.

"I had nothing to do with the rebels," he says. "I swear."

"I still don't understand," I murmur weakly. "What does this have to do with me?"

"Your mother was tracking them after an attack," he continues. "That attack weakened my brother's team, making it easier for her to follow them. A fight broke out. She cursed Axel before running—she was badly outnumbered."

He exhales slowly. "His friends came straight to me after that. The other half of the group tracked your mother down and took their revenge. Before she died, she told them your blood was the key to waking Axel."

Silence stretches between us.

"I'm sorry, Amara," he says quietly.

"I hate you," I whisper. The words feel heavy, useless, but they're all I have left.

The room begins to tilt. My vision blurs around the edges. My heart races wildly in my chest before slowing, my breathing following its uneven rhythm. My limbs feel heavy, numb, like they no longer belong to me.

Darkness creeps in, soft and suffocating.

I let it take me.

Chapter Twenty-six

Xavior

"**I** hate you." The weak whisper shatters my heart. I did not think it would be this hard.

"I hate myself for doing this to you." I catch her as she slumps forward. I cradle her weightless body closer to my chest.

I wish she would open her eyes; I need to see them once more. I also wish she would say that she didn't mean those hateful words.

I despise seeing her like this and knowing that I am the reason for it.

My hand circles around her wrist, and I can no longer feel her pulse. It's too faint. My chest constricts painfully, the hole in my heart grows, and it aches. I press my forehead to hers, closing my eyes as I breathe her in.

"I am so fucking sorry." I turn around, sitting in the recliner with Amara on my lap, nodding at the nurse. "I am ready." A small prick stings my hand as she shoves the needle into my vein. I watch as my blood moves through the clear tube and into Amara's needle.

"What if it doesn't work?" asks Zane, who is watching from the doorway.

"It has too."

Because if it doesn't, I don't deserve to live.

Chapter Twenty-seven

Amara

My head pounds painfully; it nearly takes my breath away. I try blinking my eyes open, but they're too heavy. A low whimper escapes me. Why does it hurt so much? I search my mind trying to put the pieces of the puzzle together.

How am I alive?

I gasp, forcing my eyes open and sitting up.

I look around the room, and my eyes land on Xavior, who is sleeping in a chair next to me. Disgust and hate run through me. I need to get away. I don't know how I am still alive, but I can't stay here with this monster.

I stand quickly, but quietly, ignoring the dizziness as I wobble across the floor. I am back in my prison. I test the door handle, and it twists. I exhale. Thankfully, it's not locked. What I find strange is that no guards are standing by the door. I don't question it. I rush down the hall, keeping close to the shadows. I cling to the railing of the stairs as I walk down them. I must go slow; the dizziness is making this nearly impossible.

My bare feet touch the wet grass, and I nearly cry out. I fucking made it! The fog thickens suddenly, curling too close around my ankles, and my magic stirs. It feels wrong.

I glance around, my skin prickling. I need to keep running. I don't know where I'm going, but I head for the woods in front of me.

They stretch on forever from my prison window, dark and endless, but I'd rather be lost than trapped.

I will escape, or I will die trying.

The sun is high in the sky; it must be late afternoon. I've been running for hours. My feet are cut and bleeding, and every step hurts so much it makes me wince. My stomach aches from hunger, but I can't stop. The adrenaline is fading, and I'm getting tired fast. Why is it so foggy here?

My feet slow when a river stretches in front of me. I drop to my knees and scoop up water with my hands, drinking as fast as I can. Then I flop back onto the wet grass, staring at the rushing water. I don't think I can go on without a break. I hiss as I put my feet in the freezing water.

"Hey, you there! Are you okay?"

I jerk my head. A brown horse is barely ten feet away. How did it get that close without me hearing it? On its back sits a young woman. Her pink hair bounces a little as she rocks the saddle. Her cheeks are red from the cold, and her blue eyes are sharp. She's... pretty.

"Yeah, I'm fine. I just got a little lost."

I force my voice to sound calm, even though my whole body wants to run.

"Are you sure?" She jumps off the horse and steps closer. "Those clothes aren't really made for this weather."

I glance down at my tank top and silky shorts and shiver. "My boyfriend and I fought, and I left... on impulse."

She smirks. "Impulsive, huh? I know a thing or two about that."

I force a small smile. "I ran too far, now I'm lost."

"You can come with me. I'll get you some proper clothes and food, and then we can look for your boyfriend."

I nod, trying not to let relief show. My feet hurt too much to argue.

"Seriously, you could've at least put some shoes on," she says, shaking her head. "Ever ridden before?"

"Nope," I say, moving toward the horse. It shifts and neighs when I reach for the reins. I ignore it and focus on steadying myself.

"Don't take it personally," she says, laughing as she jumps back onto the saddle. "He doesn't trust strangers. I'm Lyra, by the way."

I nod, keeping my voice calm. My heart is racing, my mind is thinking about escape, but I force myself to stay collected. Just breathe. Don't show her how close you are to falling apart.

"Shit, I was about to jump on your horse, and I didn't even know your name. It's nice to meet you, I'm Amara. How does this work?" I round the horse, standing next to Lyra's leg. My legs ache from running barefoot, but I try not to think about it.

"Here, put your foot in the stirrups, grab my hand, and I will pull you up, swing your leg around to straddle the horse."

"Got it." I nod, placing my foot in the stirrup and reaching up, grabbing her hand. I jump, and she pulls me up, and then I am straddling the back of the horse. Every muscle in my arms and legs shakes a little. "Oh God, we're up higher than I thought."

She laughs, "Stormy boy is tall."

"Stormy, I like it." I grip the reins tighter, trying to calm the tremble in my hands. For the first time in weeks, I feel... almost free. I fucking did it! But a small knot of worry curls in my stomach. Freedom feels good, but danger is never far behind.

"Hold on!" She takes off, making me yelp as I grab her waist. My heart races—not just from the speed, but from the thought of what could go wrong if I fall.

A few miles later, we enter a small town that looks like an old western town. On either side of the dirt road are two-to three-story wooden buildings. I stare at a bar as we pass. The guys standing in front whistle as we ride by. My muscles ache, but I force myself to stay alert.

A mile more and we stop in front of a two-story cabin with a big wrap-around porch. Completely different from the realm I saw through the portal.

"Welcome to my home. I'm warning you, my brother is a complete asshole to strangers." I swing my leg around and jump down, careful to land lightly.

"Not a big deal. Surrounded by assholes has kinda become normal for me." I force a smile, keeping my guard up.

"That sums it up. You were pretty close to the realm's capital. It's buzzing with stuck-up rich assholes there."

We go inside and immediately head upstairs. I notice the family pictures along the way, my eyes flicking to doors and windows, as I quietly note exits. She opens the first door on the right, and we enter a cozy room. A queen-size bed is pushed against the far wall, and next to the door is a wooden desk full of papers. Clothes are scattered across the floor.

"Sorry about the mess. I wasn't expecting anyone." She blushes as she looks around.

"It's not bad. My sister's room looks way worse." I nod, trying not to show how tense I still feel from the ride and running.

"The bathroom is through there." She gestures at a door further down the hall. "You can shower while I get some clothes and food."

I'm dressed in black trousers and a leather shirt that shows way too much cleavage since the top buttons refused to cooperate. We're sitting at a small wooden table in the kitchen. I'm eating soup, trying to ignore how awkward this feels while Lyra's brother, Kai, glares at me from across the table. He clearly finds it strange that I was running barefoot through the woods. Honestly, I don't blame him.

I've been here since lunch, and now it's nearly six. It's getting late. I need to move. Staying too long never ends well for me.

I clear my throat and straighten my spine. "Do either of you know how to get to the human realm?"

They both freeze. Lyra's eyes widen, her mouth opening like she's about to say something—but a loud bang cuts her off.

Everything explodes into chaos.

Guards rush into the kitchen, weapons drawn. Kai moves instantly, grabbing Lyra and pushing her behind him, demanding to know what the hell is going on. That's when I see him.

Xavior steps into the room.

There's something wild in his grey eyes, something feral and unrestrained. He looks furious and dangerous, like he tracked me here on instinct alone.

My heart slams into my ribs. I jump to my feet and bolt for the back door.

I feel sick for bringing this mess into their home, but how did he find me? I wrench the door open, and then his shadows wrap around me.

The door slams shut.

I spin around, lifting my chin even as fear claws its way up my throat. I won't let him see it. I won't give him that.

"Where do you think you're going, Amara?" Xavior growls. His anger fills the room, heavy and suffocating.

"Away from you," I snap. "You got what you wanted. Leave me the fuck alone."

"Your ex is the fucking prince?" Lyra shouts, peeking around Kai, staring at me as if I've completely lost my mind.

Xavior's mouth twitches. His gaze drags over me—slow, deliberate—lingering on my shirt, on the way it barely covers me. His expression hardens.

"Ex?" he says quietly. "I am far from an ex."

"You are," I snap. "I want nothing to do with you."

"Enough." The word lands heavily with its finality.

"You're coming home."

"No," I laugh, sharp and brittle. "You tried to kill me."

He tilts his head, studying me like I'm a problem already solved. "You're not dead," he says flatly.

I laugh again, the sound verging on hysterical. "You kidnapped me. You locked me up. You held me down and drained me until I blacked out."

His jaw tightens, irritation flashing across his face.

"And yet," he says coolly, "you're alive and healthy. Exactly where you're meant to be." His eyes meet mine, unblinking. "I had a plan. It worked."

I scoff. I cannot believe we are having this conversation. "I don't care if you had a plan. It changes nothing. We are over."

He growls and steps closer to me. His voice is low, but sinister, leaving no room for argument. "We are not over. You are mine." He grips my jaw, forcing my gaze up to his. "I did what needed to be done. Stop being so fucking stubborn." He turns to look at Lyra and Kai. "Thank you for keeping her safe." Then he bends and throws me over his shoulder.

"Kai, do something!" Lyra shouts, sounding desperate.

"What do you want me to do?" He hisses lowly, "he is a prince, with the royal guards. It would be suicide!"

Chapter Twenty-eight

Xavior sits me on top of an overly large black horse. In one smooth, practiced move, he settles behind me. I try to scoot forward, but he growls low in his throat and wraps an arm around my waist, dragging me back against him.

"I'm surprised you left without Ana."

I tense instantly. He chuckles like he feels it.

"Ah. You thought I took her home." His lips brush close to my ear. "No. She's still there. Don't worry, she's unharmed. And she'll stay that way as long as you're a good girl for me."

I grind my teeth together. I refuse to answer or give him the reaction he wants. I hate him.

"I'll let you keep those pretty lips shut for now," he murmurs, "but don't mistake my patience for permission. You won't ignore me much longer."

His arms close around me, his hands reaching forward to grip the reins between my thighs.

It's such an innocent thing. It shouldn't mean anything. But the way his large, veiny hands curl around the leather pulls memories to the surface—of the way those same hands once brought me to a pleasure so intense it made my vision blur, before everything shattered.

His warm breath grazes the side of my neck. I swear I can feel the steady beat of his heart against my back.

The way my body moves with the horse... how I bounce slightly against the inside of his strong thighs, makes my thoughts spiral somewhere dark. Somewhere I don't want to go.

I hate this man. I hate him with everything in me.

And yet, part of me wishes we were alone. Naked. Our bodies moving together the way I know they can be perfect, consuming, devastating.

I don't understand why my body betrays me like this, why it reacts so strongly to the weight of him pressed against me.

He releases one rein and places a broad hand against my lower stomach, fingers spreading slowly. I feel his chest rise, the shaky breath he lets out as he pulls me impossibly closer.

His hand trembles just slightly as he slips a single finger beneath my shirt, touching bare skin.

I know I should push him away.

But I don't.

Because how do you stop something when it feels this good?

I lick my lower lip, forcing my breathing to stay steady as I try to shove my filthy thoughts aside and focus on the only sound around us—the heavy pounding of hooves, dozens of them moving in sync, striking the earth like a relentless drum. Each step carries me farther from safety, closer to him.

Then his hand slides fully beneath my shirt, bold and unhesitating, his thumb brushing the underside of my left breast. His chest vibrates when a low groan escapes him, like he's been holding it back for too long. My body betrays me instantly. Without thinking, I arch my back, silently begging for more.

The moment stretches. I hope—stupidly—that he doesn't notice.

Of course, he does.

"Gods," he murmurs against my ear, his voice rough and ruined, "I've missed feeling your body pressed against mine. I've dreamed about it.

About *you*." His breath stutters. "Jerking off to the memories of us every fucking chance I get."

A shiver rips through me. Heat coils low in my stomach, my pussy spasms, sharp and demanding, my body reacting before my mind can catch up. I hate how easily he still does this to me. His hand moves higher, cups my breast, pinches my nipple just enough to make my vision blur. A moan tears from my lips—too loud, too honest.

The nearest guard glances back.

"Eyes forward," Xavior snaps. Every guard stiffens instantly, attention locked ahead. His tone softens only for me, dark and intimate. "Shh, my little vixen. Those sounds you make belong to me."

"Please..." The word slips out before I can stop it, thin and desperate. A small part of me screams to shut up, to pull away, to remember everything he's done, but I drown it out. The press of his body against mine is overwhelming. I feel weak for wanting this. I hate myself for it.

"What is it you need?" His hand lowers, teasing the waistband of my trousers, slow and deliberate. I moan again, tilting my head back against his shoulder, arching without shame now. When I don't answer, his voice cracks just slightly, his need bleeding through control. "Tell me. Please. Don't torture me like this."

"Touch me, Xavior."

That's all it takes.

His hand slides beneath my trousers, shoving my panties aside in a rush that feels almost frantic. I feel the faint tremble in his fingers, the loss of control he refuses to admit. We both hiss when his touch slips between my pussy lips, the world narrowing down to that single, dangerous point of contact.

"So, fucking wet..." he groans. The sound sends a sharp wave of heat through me. I spread my legs wider, needing more, giving him better access. He takes it immediately, pushing two fingers inside me and slowly pumping them in and out while his thumb works my clit, controlled and deliberate. "Just for me, right, baby?"

"Please," I beg, my voice low and breaking as I turn my head and bury my face into his neck. My breath comes uneven, my body trembling with want. I try to move my hips, but it's nearly impossible on top of the horse, the rhythm frustrating and desperate.

He kisses the top of my head, his mouth brushing my hair as he mutters filthy words meant only for me. "Such a naughty girl. Begging me to finger-fuck you on a horse, surrounded by my soldiers." I can hear the smirk in his voice, feel the arrogance of his control—but he still gives me what I want. His fingers move faster, deeper, and his thumb presses harder against my clit, sending sparks of pleasure shooting through me.

I start to cry out, the sound slipping free before I can stop it—but he slams his mouth over mine, swallowing the noise, claiming it. My body shakes against his, my senses narrowing down to his touch, his heat, the dangerous closeness of it all.

Then, out of nowhere, a harsh squawk cuts through the air.

The sound of a crow slices through the moment like a blade.

Xavior's fingers stop instantly.

The shift is immediate. His body goes rigid behind me, every muscle locking. I whimper when his hand slips from my trousers, the sudden loss almost painful. He yanks the reins hard, bringing the horse to a sharp halt. The soldiers react at once, stopping as well, dismounting without question.

Something about the sound has changed him.

Without a word, Xavior swings down from the horse. I watch, chest heaving, as his attention fixes on the large black crow nearby. The tension rolling off him is unmistakable, alert, dangerous, controlled. An audible gasp leaves me when he lifts his right hand—the same one that was inside me moments ago—and slowly licks his fingers clean.

The act is crude. Possessive. Deliberate.

He turns his head just enough to look back at me over his shoulder as he does it, grey eyes dark and knowing, like the interruption means something only he understands.

The horses finally slow and stop in front of a massive stone mansion. We rode straight past the towering gates of the Shadow Realm, where the king's castle looms over everything like a threat. Xavior's home sits on the outskirts—far enough to be quiet, close enough that he can reach the castle within minutes if needed.

That doesn't surprise me.

Xavior has always preferred silence, control, and distance.

The mansion itself is breathtaking. Gothic-arched windows stretch up the four stories, framed by dark wooden trim and antique brown stone that looks like it's been standing for centuries. A rounded turret rises from each corner, making the place feel more like a fortress than a home. It's intimidating, cold, and somehow beautiful.

I swallow hard, my throat tight. Anger floods me, sharp and relentless, but it's aimed inward at myself. I can't believe I let him touch me. How am I this weak? This man betrayed me. He kidnapped me. He drained me of my blood until I blacked out.

And my body responded.

Shame curls in my stomach as I replay it, the way my skin burned for him, the way I melted against his touch. I clench my hands into fists. I can't let myself be alone with him again, not close. Not pressed against him like that. I'm too weak. I know it now.

I hate that I know it.

Because the truth is, I love his touch. It's addictive, dangerous, like a drug I can't quit. I crave it. I need it. And that terrifies me more than anything else.

Xavior swings off the horse and turns to help me down, reaching for me like he owns the right. I don't let him. I throw my leg the other way and jump down on my own.

I wholeheartedly misjudge the landing.

I stumble straight into a solid chest. My hands instinctively grab fabric, and my eyes lift, taking in a stranger's face. He's tall, lean, strong, but soft in a way Xavior never is. Too soft to belong here. Pretty blue eyes widen as they meet mine, warm and curious instead of cold and sharp.

His curly, dirty-blond hair falls into his face, loose curls brushing his forehead. Full lips, his lower lip fuller than the top, high cheekbones. Strong arms that tighten around me, steadying me before I can fall.

For just a second, I feel... safe.

"Take your hands off her." The voice behind me is pure violence.

It's low and thunderous, a sound that seems to shake the earth beneath our feet. The stranger stiffens instantly. The interest in his eyes vanishes, replaced by fear. He drops me like I've burned him.

Another pair of arms replaces his, strong, familiar, suffocating.

Xavior pulls me back against his chest, possessively. I react without thinking, elbowing him hard in the ribs. He grunts, the sound more annoyed than hurt, and his grip loosens just enough for me to twist free.

I step away from him, heart pounding.

Behind us, somewhere in the distance, a crow cries out again, harsh and cutting.

Xavior stills.

Just for a fraction of a second, his body goes tight, his attention snapping somewhere beyond me, beyond the mansion. I don't understand it, don't know why the sound makes the air feel heavier, but whatever it means, he knows.

And that unsettles me more than anything else.

I storm off, but the raw power in his voice stops me. "Stop acting like a little brat, you won't like the punishment."

"I fucking hate you!" I shout, spinning around to meet his sharp gaze.

His smirk holds so much arrogance. "Keep telling yourself that while I still have that sweet smell of your pussy on my fingers."

My face turns hot, probably ten shades of red. I cannot believe he just said that in front of all these men.

And yet... my mind flickers back to the crow. Why did it stop him? The sound cut through everything, and suddenly, he went tense, like it meant something only he understood.

I force the question out before I can overthink it. "Xavior... what does the crow mean?"

His grey eyes narrow. He tilts his head, his voice drops low, clipped, and dangerous. "It's a message from the king."

The words hit me like ice. I don't understand the full meaning, but I know it's serious.

I smirk anyway, letting the tension slip into provocation. Dripping my voice with pure seduction, saying, "Oh Xavior, how can I not be turned on by all of these sexy, muscular men?" My eyes flick to the pretty boy standing next to him. "I would've let any of them touch me."

I wink, spin around, and open the wooden door. The animalistic growl follows me into the house as I shut it behind me.

I don't know the layout of this mansion, but I will find Ana.

Chapter Twenty-nine

I don't end up finding Ana, but I'm not far into my search when I am manhandled by Xavior. He is seething by the time he finds me and forces me back into my prison. He sets me on my feet, then presses my back against the door, caging me in with his arms on either side of my head.

"Do you think your little stunt was funny?" he shouts, his hand slamming against the door. It rattles violently, and I jump, my heart pounding just as hard in my chest. "Making my men think they can have you, like some type of whore?" His eyes darken by the second, turning almost black.

The words hit me like a slap, and I flinch before I can stop myself.

He sees it. Of course he does. His eyes squeeze shut as he takes a slow, measured breath, like he's trying to rein himself in. "I'm not saying you're a whore," he says, voice lower now. "Just what you said implied it."

"I want to see Ana," I say, forcing my voice to stay steady. "And I want to go home."

"No." He steps back, jaw clenched so tight I can see the muscle jump. I move away from the door, retreating further into the room, desperate for space, for air.

"You can't keep me here, Xavior. And you can't keep me from my sister. You're not being rational. This is crazy." I cross my arms over my chest, staring at the wall behind him because looking at his face makes everything harder.

"You're right," he says quietly. "This is crazy. But you make me crazy." His gaze burns into me. "I lost my rational thoughts after that fucking kiss. I'll bring her in the morning so you can eat breakfast with her. It's been a long day. You need sleep." He turns to leave.

"I will never forgive you," I spit, venom coating every word.

His back stiffens. He turns and strides toward me, fast and deliberate. I don't step back. I refuse to. I meet his eyes head-on, my heart racing but my feet rooted in place. His hands move with the speed of a viper, cupping my face. The tenderness of the gesture hits harder than his anger ever could. His thumbs brush over my cheeks, soft and possessive, filled with something dangerously close to love.

"My sweet Amara," he murmurs. "I don't need your forgiveness. I just need you."

"You are crazy, Xavior," I snap, even as my chest tightens. "This is insane. You have completely lost your mind."

He chuckles softly and presses a kiss to the top of my head, gentle and unearned. "You call it crazy," he says quietly. "I call it love. Get some rest, baby." He turns and leaves without looking back.

He's a fucking psychopath.

But a part of me likes it... a dark, twisted part of me likes the obsessive, controlling side of him, likes knowing I do that to him—that it's me who makes him lose control, who turns him into something unhinged and dangerous. And it's a part of me I will absolutely ignore.

I know it's fucked up that I find it attractive.

I stare longingly at the gardens below as I watch the sunrise. I fell asleep pretty quickly last night, but woke up at four this morning. Ever since then, I have moved the chair Xavior usually sleeps in to the window and curled into it with the blanket, trying to feel some semblance of comfort in the quiet morning.

I am scared for my future. I don't know what I'm going to do. He won't let me go. My dad will come for us, right? It's difficult to travel to a different realm, but not impossible with the right reassurances. I am sure the council will help him, unless he doesn't know where we are. Witches can use locator spells, but if someone jumps to a different realm, they vanish from the search.

For the first time in years, I feel as if I am losing control of my inner demons, the ones I keep locked in a small cage. A cage that now has a little crack, letting the hateful words I've suppressed over the years sink in. It hurts when they circle my thoughts, relentless, taunting me with every beat of my heart.

Reminding me I am not enough. That my own mom hated me when I craved her love, and now, I will never get it. The tears flow down my cheeks like a never-ending waterfall, and my chest tightens painfully as the words replay themselves over and over...

You are not good enough...No one will ever love you...That pretty face will only get you so far in life...You worthless slut, sleeping around with that boy, letting your grades slip...

My grades were definitely slipping when I was with Jaxon. That's the night I lost my virginity. She wanted a slut, so I gave her one.

You are a stupid, stupid girl... You thought a boy like him would want you? You are only temporary for boys... You will never *be the one.*

That was right after Jaxon broke it off with me. I sobbed as I ran home, lungs burning, vision blurring, praying that for once she would hold me.

Everyone says scars heal, that they won't stain you forever... but what about emotional scars? Do they ever really go away? Do they fade, or do they just learn how to hide beneath the surface? Can I escape this? Will I ever feel cherished, truly cherished? *Loved*?

I thought I was finally healing. I thought I was *finally* feeling the love I craved so *fucking* desperately. But the gods were cruel, and I imagine them sitting on their thrones now, laughing at my pain, at my tears, at how foolish I was to believe I deserved more.

"Don't worry, Mom," I whisper, staring up at the sky, my chest aching. "I hate myself enough for the both of us..."

A door slamming open jerks me awake. I groan as I move, uncurling my legs, my neck stiff and aching. I must have fallen asleep in the chair.

"Amara?" a small voice whispers. My back straightens instantly, and I wipe the dried tears from my face before looking over my shoulder.

"Ana..." I cry out, rushing forward and colliding with her body. We cling to each other tightly, her shoulders shaking as she sobs loudly, holding onto me like I'm the only thing keeping her upright. "I will get you out of this," I swear, rubbing her back over and over, trying to pour all my strength into her.

When I finally pull away, I look her over, scanning every inch of her. She looks unharmed. Just... sad. So unbearably sad. "Did they hurt you?"

She shakes her head, her lower lip trembling. "No. But I've been so worried about you."

"I'm okay," I tell her softly, even though I'm not sure it's true. "Don't worry about me." I smooth her hair back, needing to reassure her. I've never admitted it out loud, but she is my strength. Her cheery spirit, her loud personality. It annoys some people, but it keeps my inner demons from dragging me under completely.

Finally, I look past her. I knew he would be there. I can feel him before I see him. Xavior's back is pressed against the wall beside the door, his face blank, unreadable, as his eyes stay locked on me.

Hate coils tight in my chest when I look at him. But there's something else tangled in with it... desire, love. Even after everything he's done to me, to my sister, I still fucking want him.

His eyes flick toward the small table in front of the sofas. I follow his gaze. There's food waiting there. He wants me to eat.

That's another thing I hate. I know he cares. I know he loves me, in his own twisted, dangerous way. He's always watching, always making sure I eat, that I sleep, that I have what I need. And I hate how it softens my anger, how it blurs the edges of my hatred until I don't know where it ends and something else begins.

You call it crazy. Insanity.

But I call it love.

"Come, let's eat." I grab Ana's hand and pull her toward the sofa, not wanting to anger Xavior and risk him forcing us apart once more. We sit side by side. She doesn't reach for her plate, so I grab it for her and set it gently on her lap before taking my own.

We eat the breakfast sandwiches in silence. There's so much I want to say to her, so much I want to ask, but I don't. Not with him watching us.

"Do you think Dad is close to finding us?" Ana finally asks, breaking the quiet.

"I don't know," I admit softly, "but I know he's trying. And I know he won't stop until he finds us."

She glances at Xavior from the corner of her eye, then leans into me, her voice dropping to a whisper. "I want to go outside. I haven't felt the sun on my skin since being here."

I nod immediately. I want that too. I want fresh air, space, something that doesn't feel so heavy. I know she wants me to ask, and even though the thought makes my stomach twist, I'll do it for her. I lick my lips and turn my attention to him.

"Can we go outside?" My tone is sharp, full of attitude.

He raises a brow. I inhale deeply, grinding my teeth together, already knowing what he wants. So, I give it to him, adding a sarcastic, "Please."

The corner of his mouth twitches before a smirk settles into place. "Of course," he says smoothly. "Since you asked so nicely."

The moment we step outside, I close my eyes and breathe in deeply. It's exactly what I need: the fresh air, the faint warmth of the sun against my skin. It's chilly and overcast, but it still feels good. I tug my sweater down over my hands, shielding my fingers from the cold.

"Gods, I've missed this," Ana says. When I open my eyes, she's spinning slowly in a small circle, her arms stretched wide, soaking it in.

"Come on," I say, looping my arm through hers. "Let's stretch our legs."

We head down the stone path together, walking in a peaceful silence. For a moment, I feel content, just me and her, like it used to be. I try to ignore the presence trailing behind us. He stays a good fifteen feet back, giving us a sliver of privacy.

I'm grateful for that.

And even though I hate admitting it... I also feel safe knowing he's there.

Chapter Thirty

Amara

We've been outside for hours, just walking. Eventually, I head toward the garden, and Ana and I sit on the cold concrete bench across from the large, four-tiered water fountain. Water trickles softly, the sound steady and calming, almost hypnotic. We sit in silence, lost in our own thoughts, breathing in the faint scent of flowers carried on the cool air beneath the gray sky. For a moment, it almost feels normal.

"It's time for lunch."

Xavior's voice startles me. I flinch slightly, my heart jumping into my throat. He hasn't spoken a single word the entire time we've been out here. He never complained. Never rushed us. He just stood there, watching—well, watching me.

Ana pouts, her bottom lip sticking out as she looks at me, silently begging for more time. I shake my head. If we behave, if we don't push, maybe he'll let us do this again tomorrow. I stand first, brushing off my palms, and turn toward my dark shadow.

I keep eye contact with Xavior as I walk toward him, my steps slow, measured. There was a time when being close to him felt safe. I would give anything to go back to before—before the lies, before the betrayal—lying in those strong arms, feeling protected... cherished... loved.

I walk right past him, my feet slowing when I notice someone standing near the entrance to the mansion.

Axel.

My breath catches painfully in my chest.

He's standing there, very much alive. Exactly like he did the last time I saw him. But the peaceful air that once surrounded him is gone, tainted with something dark... sinister. His round cheeks still give him a boyish look, making him appear softer than Xavior, but the illusion doesn't last. There's something lethal about him now, something that makes my instincts scream at me to turn and run far, far away.

His gray eyes, just a shade darker than Xavior's, are wild, unhinged, locked onto something with an intensity that makes my skin crawl.

At first, I think he's looking at his brother.

But then Xavior steps behind me, his body pressing close, one arm wrapping firmly around my waist. The contact is possessive and grounding, and suddenly I know—Axel isn't looking at Xavior. He's looking past us.

My stomach drops.

I turn slowly, dread coiling tight in my chest, and horror crashes through me when I realize it's Ana who has his unwavering attention. She stands a few steps behind me, frozen in place, wide-eyed and innocent, completely unaware of the danger standing in front of her.

"No," I whisper instinctively.

I try to move, stepping in front of her, blocking his line of sight with my body, but Xavior tightens his grip, pulling me back against him, locking me in place.

"Don't," he hisses in my ear. "Let them be."

Panic explodes inside me as he starts pushing me forward, away from her.

"No, what the fuck do you mean?" I struggle against him, my heart pounding violently in my chest.

"Give them a moment."

My eyes widen, terror flooding every inch of me. "No. I will not leave her out here alone, with *him*!" My voice cracks as I twist my head, watching helplessly as Axel begins to stalk toward Ana.

She doesn't move. Just stands there, staring at him with that same innocent expression, like she doesn't understand why the air suddenly feels so heavy.

Axel stops in front of her.

Then he says one word,

"*Mate...*" The sound of it booms around us, unnatural, powerful, sending a violent shiver straight through my bones.

"No." I shake my head, the word barely a whisper, thick with dread. "No... no..."

Xavior suddenly lifts me off the ground, my back slamming against his chest, my feet dangling uselessly in the air as he turns toward the door.

"No! Gods, please, no!" I scream, clawing at his arms. "That monster cannot be her mate. Xavior, stop! Please, Xavior!"

My voice echoes even after the door slams shut behind us.

"I am sorry," he says quietly as he carries me down the hall. "But it is fate. We cannot intervene. That is between the two of them."

He sets me down once we're back inside my prison.

And just like that, Ana is gone.

I spin around, shoving him out of my way, but the door doesn't budge, it's locked. Panic crashes into me all at once. I grow hysterical, my hands shaking as I grab the handle, rattling it violently, twisting and yanking like I can force it to obey me if I try hard enough.

"Xavior, please, open the door. *Please*!" My voice breaks, desperation clawing its way out of my chest.

"Baby..." His voice comes from behind me, low and strained. "I am sorry, but I can't allow you to intervene. He won't hurt her. I swear."

He gently presses my back against the wall, trapping me there, his hands warm as they cup my face. His touch is careful, reverent, like he's afraid I'll shatter beneath his fingers. There's regret in his voice—real regret—and it hits me harder than I expect. It's the first real glimpse of him I've seen since waking up after practically dying of the man I fell in love with.

"I can't leave her out there alone with that monster!" I choke out, my chest burning.

"He is no monster," he says quietly, his tone firm but pleading. "I promise you."

He presses his forehead against mine, breath warm against my lips. "We'll check on her soon. Just... give them some time alone."

I let out a broken laugh, disbelief, and fury tangling together. "You're joking, right? How can I trust anything you say?"

He pulls back just enough to look at me. "You don't have any other choice than to trust me."

The words land like a slap. He shrugs like it's nothing, grips my upper arm, and starts dragging me toward the sofa. Rage surges through me, sharp and wild.

"You're wrong," I snap, ripping my arm free and stumbling back. "I do have a choice. I will fight you every step of the way."

The softness vanishes from his face in an instant. That crazed look—the one that terrifies me—returns to his eyes. He reaches out again, gripping my arm once more, his hold tight but not crushing.

"Do you think I wanted this?" he snaps, his voice cracking with something raw. "I didn't mean to fall for you. That wasn't supposed to happen." He exhales sharply, frustration bleeding through. "I never lied about who I am. It is still me. My feelings are real."

His grip loosens, but his words don't.

"I know what I did was unforgivable," he continues, voice heavy. "But I had to help my brother. His life was hanging by a thread because of your mother. You were the only key." His jaw tightens. "And I am sorry for everything I did, for what I was forced to do to you. But it changes nothing."

His eyes burn into mine.

"I am never letting you go."

The words steal the air from my lungs.

"I will never be yours," I whisper fiercely. "Don't you see the hate? The longer you keep us here, the deeper my hate will grow."

His eyes flash, pain cutting through them so sharply it nearly knocks me off balance. The anguish rolling off him is suffocating, consuming the space between us.

He shoves his hands through his dark hair, fingers tangling in the strands as he yanks, teeth clenched tight, nostrils flaring as if he's barely holding himself together. When his gaze lifts back to mine, it's tortured—dark shadows rolling beneath his skin, begging to be released.

My breath stalls.

I want to go to him. Gods, I want to. Every instinct screams to close the distance, to touch him, to comfort him.

But the reminder of what he's done... what he took slams into me. And I stay exactly where I am.

"I want to see her." I try blinking back the tears, but it's pointless. They spill anyway, hot and relentless.

He watches me for a long moment, something twisting painfully across his face, sadness, regret, or maybe guilt. Then he nods. "If you hear me out," he says quietly, "and then eat, I will allow you to go check on her."

My body slumps into the sofa like the fight has drained out of me. I nod, lifting the plate onto my lap with shaking hands.

"When I first saw you..." He trails off, eyes dropping to the wooden floor like the words are too hard to say. He takes a few slow steps toward me and lowers himself, kneeling in front of me. He reaches out instinctively, but I slap his hands away before he can touch me.

He exhales sharply and lets himself fall back, landing on his ass. His arms rest loosely on his spread legs, his head bowed in defeat. One hand drags harshly down his face.

I never imagined that a man like him so powerful and so feared could ever look like this. Broken and defeated. It shatters something inside me to see it, knowing I'm the one causing it.

"When I saw you," he repeats, voice rough. "I felt a pull toward you. I didn't understand it, didn't know what it meant. I only knew that I wanted you." His jaw tightens. "I avoided that feeling, shoved it as far down as I could. But the more time I spent around you, the harder it became to ignore it. And then that damn kiss..."

A broken, humorless laugh slips out of him. "It changed everything. I kept telling myself I had to do it for my brother. That it was his life or yours... the woman I love." He shakes his head, anguish pouring out of him. "An impossible choice."

Suddenly, he punches the floor, once, twice—hard enough to crack it. Blood begins to bloom across his knuckles. I flinch as he drags his bloody hand through his hair, smearing red against dark strands.

"How did I not die?" The question slips out before I can stop it. I've been dying to know, literally.

"As soon as your heart stopped," he says, voice steady despite the devastation in his eyes, "I was hooked up to an IV. I gave you about eighty percent of my blood. It weakened me, but I would have given you more. I would have given you everything if I had to." His gaze locks onto mine. "I was never planning on you dying. I would have given you every last drop before letting anything happen to you."

My breath stutters.

"Zane was there to make sure your life was the priority," he continues. "Not mine. Because I cannot live without you. The healers handled the rest."

"You did that... for me?" My voice barely exists.

"Amara, I will do—"

My prison door slams open.

Xavior's growl reverberates through the room, dark and violent, crawling under my skin. My heart kicks into overdrive as his eyes blacken, teeth baring like something feral has taken over him.

Two guards stand frozen just inside the doorway, terror written all over their faces. One takes a shaky step forward.

"It'd better be important," Xavior snarls, "or your blood will be on my hands."

My mouth parts as I stare at him, stunned by the threat.

"Of course, my prince," one guard rushes out. "It *is* important."

"Give me a minute," Xavior says to me, his tone softening instantly, the shift jarring. He leans down and presses a kiss to my cheek before turning back to them.

The guards lean in, whispering urgently. I can't hear the words, but halfway through, Xavior's eyes flick toward me, sharp, furious, protective.

He dismisses them with a sharp gesture and stalks back toward me, his body coiled tight.

"What is it?" I ask, panic clawing up my throat. "Is Ana okay?"

"She's fine," he says quickly. "But something of importance needs my immediate attention. I will be back."

"When?" I ask before I can stop myself.

"I don't know," he admits. "But I will not let them succeed."

"I'm sorry, my prince," one of the guards says, poking his head back in. "It's getting out of control."

Xavior turns sharply and stalks away. Just before he leaves, he looks over his shoulder at me—something unreadable flickering across his face—then disappears down the corridor.

The guards rush after him, pulling the door shut behind them... but it doesn't close all the way.

I stay perfectly still, barely breathing, staring at the narrow gap in the door. Waiting for someone to notice. To come back. To seal it shut.

No one does.

I inch closer to the door, peering through the small gap between the wood and the frame. My heart pounds as I scan the hallway, but I don't see anyone, no guards, no movement, nothing. The silence feels wrong. I push the door open, not caring about the loud squeak as it drags across the stone floor. If anyone hears it, I don't care. The guards must be busy dealing with whatever is happening.

I want answers, but finding Ana is my top priority.

I rush down the stairs to where I last saw her, my pulse roaring in my ears. As soon as my feet hit the landing, raised voices echo through the halls, shouting with anger and authority. Fear curls tight in my chest as I follow the sound.

In the center of the large sitting room, at least a dozen people are gathered. My eyes immediately find Ana, and standing directly in front of her, like a wall she can hide behind, is my dad. He's shoulder to shoulder with the other council members, their bodies positioned protectively, faces hard and unyielding.

Across from them stand Xavior, Axel, and several guards, the air between them thick with barely contained violence.

My dad found us...

"Where is she?" my dad asks calmly, but his voice carries unquestionable authority, the kind that commands obedience without raising volume.

"You can't have her."

Xavior's voice cuts through the room. His back is to me, but I can see his hands trembling at his sides, fingers curling and uncurling as shadows writhe beneath his skin, desperate to be unleashed. Power rolls off him in waves.

If I step forward, my dad will take me. That's what I want... right?

My chest tightens. *What am I doing? Of course, I want to go home.*

I step into the room.

Xavior's shoulders tense instantly, like he feels me before he sees me.

I take another step, and my dad's attention snaps to me. Relief floods his features, his stern expression breaking as he exhales sharply. He holds out his hand to me. "Come here," he says gently. "We're going home."

Before I can move, Xavior steps between us.

"Go back upstairs, Amara." His voice is strained, rough around the edges. Then, quieter—barely audible—"Please..."

My breath catches as my eyes meet his. After being trapped here for so long, after everything he's done, everything I've felt, I am torn clean in two. I want to go home. I should go home.

And yet... a part of me aches to stay.

Xavior's father steps forward, placing a firm hand in the center of Xavior's chest, holding him back. It's the only thing stopping him from moving.

The moment breaks.

I rush forward, past them, straight into my dad's arms. The portal ignites behind him, energy crackling and swirling, wind whipping around us.

"Anastasia is mine," Axel growls, surging forward, breaking free from the grip of the other council members.

"Go!" my dad shouts, pushing Ana and me toward the portal.

I stumble through, the world warping around me, pressure crashing in all at once.

"Amara!"

Xavior's voice follows me through the portal... raw, broken, and full of pain.

My heart cracks straight down the middle as the sound of him is ripped away, swallowed by the closing magic.

Chapter Thirty-one

Amara

Ana and I are sitting outside at a picnic table. We're at a safe house. My dad didn't think it was the best idea to go home, knowing Xavior would follow me.

I agree, but a small part of me also wants him to find me. Crazy, right? What is wrong with me?

"What happened? With Axel, I mean?" I turn to look at her. We haven't had much alone time since we got here three days ago. My dad didn't want us out of his sight. Not that I blamed him. I missed him, so I didn't mind.

"He's my mate, Amara," she says so quietly I nearly miss it.

I nod, feeling a chill in my chest. I'd figured as much, but hearing her say it aloud makes my stomach twist. "How does that make you feel?"

"Horrible. I hate it. How can I be mated to a murderer? The freaking leader of the rebel group—the one that murdered hundreds of witches, our mom. He wants me to forgive him, but I told him that will never happen. He's crazy, Amara." A tear slides down her cheek. I wrap my arm around her and hug her tightly. I don't try to tell her it's okay. I don't even believe it myself.

"Yeah, I guess that runs in the family." I look away, watching a bluebird flit above the trees, its wings catching the dull sunlight. The small moment of beauty almost makes me forget everything else for a second.

"How does it make you feel?"

"How does what make me feel?" My brows furrow, lips pressing into a thin line.

"Xavior being your mate." She turns to face me, legs crossed on the bench, her eyes searching mine.

"What do you mean? He is not my mate." I laugh, but it's hollow, bitter. The thought of it is absurd, impossible.

"He is. He even said so himself. I heard Xavior and Axel talking when he woke up. Xavior was catching him up on recent events. I, obviously, eavesdropped."

"There is no way." I shake my head, pushing down the fluttering feeling in my chest. "He was talking about someone else." But even as I say it, my body tenses, my heart betraying me. The thought of him as my mate twists something inside me. I push it away, hard. It doesn't matter if it's true—I cannot forgive what he's done.

"We're both screwed. You know that, right? We both have psychopathic, unhinged, hot-as-fuck mates. *So* hot."

"Agreed. Totally screwed. Fuck, I need a drink. Some food too, is there anything left from last night?"

"Yeah, there's some. I put slices in the fridge." We stand, gripping each other's hands as we walk to the small cabin. It reminds me of Lyra's place, only smaller, cozier. I hope she didn't get in trouble for what I did.

I head straight to the kitchen and grab two slices, feeling the warmth of the cabin as I microwave them. I breathe in, catching the faint smell of woodsmoke lingering from the fireplace. It's comforting, grounding. A small moment of normalcy in the chaos of our lives.

Even with Xavior, Axel, and all the shadows of that other world hanging over us, this tiny bubble feels safe. The weight on my chest eases just slightly.

The wind whistles gently through the trees outside, ruffling the leaves. The bluebird lands on the fence, watching us with bright, curious eyes. Even here, life persists. A reminder that maybe, somehow, we'll be okay.

"Look at what I found!" Ana shouts, stepping into the kitchen, holding up two dusty bottles of wine like trophies. Who knows how long they've been buried in the pantry, but honestly... who fucking cares?

We end up sprawled on the floral couch, each of us holding a slice of pizza and a plastic cup filled with wine. It feels ridiculous and sad and comforting all at once.

There's no TV. No internet. Not that it would matter anyway, we don't even have phones. So, we eat in silence, staring blankly at the wooden walls, the quiet pressing in around us. It's the kind of silence that makes your thoughts louder.

"Amara..." Ana finally says, her voice breaking. "How am I supposed to mate him? He's a bad person. He's dangerous." She lets out a shaky breath, her face crumpling with despair. "He's the reason our mom is dead. This isn't what I thought it would be. I don't know what to do."

My chest tightens. I don't have an answer for her. I don't think there is one.

"Girls, I have to go into town."

We both turn at the sound of our dad's voice. He's standing just outside, talking quietly with Tyler, his posture stiff, shoulders tense.

"Can we come?" Ana asks immediately, already on her feet.

"No." He shakes his head once, sharp and final. The frown on his face makes my stomach drop.

"Why?" I ask, setting my cup down on the side table and leaning forward. "What is it?"

"Alexander," Tyler warns quietly, shaking his head.

"I won't keep this from my daughters," my dad says firmly. "They have the right to know."

He steps fully into the room and stops on the other side of the coffee table, his expression grave. "They're both in town. Demanding to see you. Don't worry—I already declined the request." His eyes lock onto mine. "But you can't go into town."

My breath stalls in my chest.

He's here.

Of course he is. Of course, he found me that fast.

Chapter Thirty-two

Exhaustion claws through me as I drive toward the Blackwood Coven headquarters. My brother and I just got into town, and the rage simmering beneath my skin refuses to settle.

Do they really think they can take her from me? Keep her away from me? And what—believe I would just stand by and do nothing?

I grind the back of my teeth together, shifting in my seat, my jaw aching from how hard I'm clenching it. The steering wheel creaks under my grip.

I am out for blood.

I will kill every single council member if I have to. I swear to the fucking Gods, I will tear this world apart for her. I will rain blood down on them until there is nothing left but ash and regret. I drag my tongue along my upper teeth, already tasting the violence waiting to be unleashed. The Grim Reaper will be very busy tonight if they don't hand her over.

Axel is quiet beside me, but I know he's fighting the same war inside his head. They're going to reject us—both of them. I knew she would hate me for what I did. I expected it. Prepared myself for it.

But when she actually said the words... when I saw it in her eyes...

It broke me.

My life is unrecognizable now, turned upside down by my own hands, and I hate myself for it. I barely eat. Sleep is a joke. I close my eyes only to toss and turn, trapped in the same hell over and over again.

Every time I do manage to drift off, I see her fear.

She's afraid of me.

I can still taste it—sharp and suffocating, like it's lodged in my throat, choking me from the inside out. I've been beaten, burned, stabbed, and broken in ways most men wouldn't survive. But none of it compares to the pain of her looking at me with that much hurt, that much terror.

My hand tightens on the steering wheel until my knuckles ache, while the other drags down my face, rough and restless. I always knew she was too good for me. I knew it from the start.

That knowledge never stopped me.

Now she wants nothing to do with me. And if I were a good man, I would listen. I would walk away. I would leave her untouched by my darkness.

But I am not that man.

"Man," Axel groans, breaking the silence. He exhales hard. "What are we going to do? Give me some advice, something, fucking anything. I don't know shit about girls, other than how to please them. I never dated. Never kissed. Just fucked."

I let out a bitter huff. "I can't even save my own mate bond. How the hell do you expect me to give you advice?" My jaw tightens. "I tried keeping her prisoner. Thought control would fix it." I shake my head once. "That shit failed."

"Come on," he says. "You know more about the opposite sex than I do."

"Not really," I snap. "I never dated either. I just fucked girls more than once, unlike you." I glance at him briefly before returning my eyes to the road. "If they get pissed, you buy them something. Flowers, chocolate, or diamonds. Then you fuck them good and done."

I scoff, the sound hollow. "The Wixx sisters?" I shake my head. "Nah. That shit won't work. They don't fall for a pretty face with money. You have to prove you're worth their time."

My grip tightens again. "You might have a chance with Ana. She's the easier one to please. You did all that shit before you met her." My voice drops, heavier, darker. "Not me. I did it right to Amara's face."

I swallow hard.

"I screwed up. Big time."

"Okay," Axel says, already spiraling, "diamonds, do you think she's more of a necklace girl or bracelets?" He pulls out his phone like he's genuinely about to place an order. "I'd rather have her forgive me," he adds, voice roughening, "but if she doesn't... we're in this shit together."

I glance at him briefly, then back to the road.

"I know a place we can take them," he continues. "I never told anyone this, but I bought a private island. Mansion, fully stocked, heavily warded. Even the council can't get there without an invite." His mouth twists into something feral. "There's no way off. No portals, no tracking spells. Just us. They'll have each other," Axel says, almost convincing himself. "They'll learn to be happy. They'll calm down eventually."

I don't answer right away.

"Because I'm not letting her go," he finishes, quieter now, but dead serious.

"Damn straight," I mutter. "I'm not letting my girl go either." The words scrape out of my chest. "She's insane if she thinks I'll let her walk away from me. Live some pretty little life without me. Find another man who doesn't deserve her."

My vision darkens at the thought. "Nah," I snarl. "Fuck that."

The image of her touching another man—smiling at him, trusting him—has rage detonating behind my eyes.

"I'll fight any man who tries to take her from me," Axel says flatly. Then, without hesitation, "And fuck her on his dead body."

A slow, approving breath leaves my lungs.

"You should install cameras in her room," I add casually, like talking about the weather. "I did that to make sure Amara was in her room every night. Alone."

"Good thinking," he nods. "I have a friend sending me a tracker. Small chip—goes under the skin. Tracks movement, vitals, and location. Don't worry. I got you one too."

I glance at him, equal parts impressed and irritated. "I feel stupid for not thinking of that sooner. Would've saved a lot of trouble."

My brother and I have always been... unbalanced, violent, and too obsessive. Too willing to cross lines.

But now? Now I understand. We aren't just similar, we're mirrors.

We pull up in front of the glass council building, its sterile shine mocking the chaos burning inside me.

"Ready, brother?" Axel asks, staring straight ahead.

I open the door, shadows stirring beneath my skin.

"Yeah," I say coldly. "Let's go get our mates."

We stride inside, power rolling off us in waves. Alexander stands there with the other council members, already tense, already afraid.

I bare my teeth at him. He's lucky I can't kill him, not yet. Not until every other option is gone.

"You cannot keep us from our mates," I say calmly, though my rage is clawing to break free. "You know that."

"That is correct," Alexander says. "Mates are sacred. The council cannot interfere."

"Good," I growl.

"But," Alexander meets my eyes, "I can interfere as their father."

My shadows surge.

"They do not wish to see either of you," he says firmly. "They will reject you both."

Something inside me snaps.

Axel moves faster. He grips Alexander's shirt and lifts him clean off the floor, shadows coiling around his legs like living chains. "Where are they?" Axel roars, fury cracking the air.

Council members recoil.

Dan steps forward, pale but steady. "I'm sorry, Alex," he says quietly. "They went to Nightshade."

The name lands like a death sentence.

My smile is slow, dangerous.

"Then," I murmur, shadows bleeding into the floor beneath my boots, "that's where we're going."

Chapter Thirty-three

Amara

Tyler, Ana, and I enter the club, and it catches me off guard that this was my dad's idea. Of all things, he said we needed a distraction, somewhere loud, somewhere alive. Somewhere that wasn't filled with memories of shadows, blood, and fate.

I just wanted to unwind. Drink and laugh with my sister. Forget… if only for a few hours.

But this… this is not what I expected.

The bass is heavy, vibrating through my chest, lights flashing in dizzying colors as bodies press together on the dance floor. Men keep coming up to us, too close, too bold. Hands grabbing at my waist, my arm, trying to pull me into dances I don't want.

And every single touch feels wrong.

Not exciting, it's all wrong. Disgusting, almost. My skin crawls where they touch me, my stomach twisting, my chest tightening like I can't get a full breath. I keep pulling away, forcing smiles that feel fake, hollow.

It's an eye-opener.

If I never forgive Xavior... will it always be like this? Will every other man's touch feel foreign, repulsive, like my body is rejecting something it doesn't want?

The thought unsettles me more than I'd like to admit.

I rush to the bathroom, squeezing between a group of girls crowded around the mirror. They're fixing lipstick, adjusting dresses, pushing their boobs up, laughing loudly like the world isn't fucked up.

I stare at my reflection.

The red dress hugs every curve, tight and unapologetic. I chose it for myself. I wanted to feel confident. To remind myself that I still owned my body, my choices.

But my traitorous mind drifts...

Would Xavior like this? The thought hits me like a slap.

Stop thinking about him.

I turn on the cold water and splash my neck, letting it drip down my collarbone. I breathe in slowly and deeply, grounding myself. I nod at my reflection, like I'm trying to convince the girl staring back that she's fine. That she's in control.

Then I walk back out. The music is loud as I step onto the dance floor. I raise my hands over my head and sway my hips, letting the rhythm take over... not thinking or feeling. Just moving.

Ana stumbles over, a wide grin on her face, eyes glassy, holding two shots. She looks carefree, too carefree. How much has she had to drink? I don't know, but I know she's trying to do the same thing I am.

Forget.

"Thanks," I wink, taking both glasses from her and downing them within seconds.

"Hey! One of those was for me!" she giggles.

I shrug and hand her the empty glasses. "Trust me, I needed it more," I slur. The alcohol hits fast, warmth spreading through my veins, but even drunk... even like this... he's still there. In my thoughts. In my body.

Someone grabs me from behind, pulling me flush against him.

"Hey there, sexy," he whispers against my ear.

My stomach turns. "Hi," I say, forcing politeness, peeling his hands off me. "I just want to dance alone, but thanks." I try to step away.

He grabs me again. "Just one dance," he insists. "If you're not feeling it, I'll leave you alone."

"No," I snap, the alcohol sharpening my tone. "You'll leave me alone now."

His face hardens. "Bitch."

The word hits, sharp and ugly, and for a split second, my chest aches, not from fear, but from the sudden, unwanted thought of how different this feels compared to him. How even his darkness never made me feel this small.

And I hate myself for thinking it.

"Yeah? Well, fuck you!" I scream at his back.

My chest heaves as the music crashes around me, but all I want to do is dance—just lose myself for a few minutes. Apparently, that's too much to ask. If I can't dance, then I want to go home. Coming here was a mistake... a stupid one.

It's not helping.

I stand in the middle of the dance floor, surrounded by people laughing, moving, living, and I feel... broken, like something vital has been ripped out of me, and I'm just pretending everything is fine.

I grab Ana's hand, yanking her away from her dance partner. She stumbles, then giggles, immediately falling into rhythm with me.

"I love you!" she shouts over the music.

"I love you too!" I shout back. We dance, but my heart isn't in it anymore. The weight in my chest won't lift. I don't want to ruin her night, though. "I have to pee again."

"Again?" She laughs. "I can go with you."

"No," I say quickly. "Stay and dance. I'll be back."

She grins and spins away, already lost to the music again. There's a lounge at the back of the club. I'll sit in a dark corner, catch my breath, and pray no one bothers me. An idea sparks, bright and reckless. We'll go to the liquor store later, dance under the moonlight like idiots.

A grin spreads across my face as I spin around to go find Ana.

I push through the crowd, but bodies slow me down, pressing in from all sides. I'm halfway there when the air changes.

It's instant... heavy and suffocating. My spine stiffens as his power crawls up my back, cold and electric, snapping me sober in a heartbeat.

I turn my head—

And there he is.

Xavior storms into the club with Axel at his side, shadows clinging to them like they belong there. The lights don't touch them the same way they touch everyone else. Conversations falter, and movements slow. People don't know why they're uneasy, only that something dangerous just walked in.

They look exactly like the murderous assholes they are. My throat tightens as I swallow hard. His gaze cuts through the room, sharp and furious, searching.

Leave before he sees you, stupid.

But I can't move.

I'm frozen, pinned in place by the weight of him. I can feel his anger from across the room, thick and violent, rolling off him in waves. Then his eyes land on me.

The world narrows.

My breath catches, and my pulse roars in my ears.

Run.

I don't think—I bolt.

I shove through bodies, ignoring shouts and curses, my heart slamming against my ribs. I burst through the back exit and turn just long enough to look over my shoulder.

His dark eyes are still locked on me.

He plows through the crowd without hesitation, shoving someone aside without even breaking stride. A girl stumbles and falls hard to the floor, her dress riding up, panties on full display.

He doesn't stop, doesn't look back. He certainly doesn't care.

Well... shit. That was hella mean.

I don't wait to see more. I run. Because I don't know what he'll do if he catches me, and the memory of the spanks he once gave me hits me out of nowhere, heat slamming straight between my thighs.

No... nope. Absolutely not.

Not right now.

Chapter Thirty-four

Amara

I run into a dark alleyway. There's a group of men leaning against the brick wall, smoking cigarettes, their laughter low and ugly. Okay, bad idea. I spin back toward the door, fingers fumbling for the handle, but it doesn't budge.

Locked.

Fuck.

I straighten my shoulders and lift my chin, forcing myself to walk forward like I'm completely unfazed by their presence. Like my heart isn't slamming against my ribs, and my palms aren't slick with sweat. They start catcalling me as I pass, their words slurred and disgusting.

It's going fine until they push off the wall and start walking beside me.

Oh, come on. Can't a girl catch a break?

Note to self: don't get so hammered that you lose the ability to think straight.

I'm going to end up on one of those crime shows I binge-watch.

The title: A Drunk Girl Dies in an Alleyway.

They circle me.

I spin around, searching for an escape, but there isn't one. They close in, shoulder to shoulder, blocking every path out. One step closer, then another, and I back up until my spine hits the cold brick wall.

The man in the middle presses his body into mine and palms my ass.

"Don't touch me!" I hiss, shoving him hard in the chest.

The other two grab my wrists instantly, wrenching my arms above my head, pinning me there. Panic blooms in my chest, sharp and fast.

"He'll kill you," I snarl, teeth bared. "And I'll laugh as he does."

I know Xavior will be out here any second. I *know* he's close. He was chasing me.

They just laugh.

Welp. I tried to warn them.

"Sure, sweetheart," the man in the center says, his breath hot and sour. "Shall we have some fun, boys?" He winks, then nods toward the man on my right. "Pull up her dress."

"No, please... stop!" I struggle, trying to twist out of their grip, but the alcohol makes everything sluggish. My head spins, my balance falters.

They don't listen. The man on my right yanks my dress up, exposing my black lace thong. Then he spins me around, slamming my upper body into the wall so they can all see me.

"Damn," one of them whistles. "That's a fucking nice ass."

The others murmur their agreement.

I feel sick.

I can't believe this is happening. I'm so stupid. I *know* better than this. My magic is useless when I'm drunk, and it's unreachable, locked behind fog and dizziness. That's why I never let myself get like this.

Tears burn my eyes, my vision blurring as fear finally sinks its claws into me. Then...

The back door to the club slams open.

I see him.

Xavior steps into the alley. Relief hits me like a tidal wave. My knees threaten to give out. I suck in a shaky breath, finally.

His eyes lock on me. They travel down my body. And then he growls. It's a low, feral sound that makes every hair on my body stand on end. It's violent, animalistic. And it's not fear that races through me.

He moves fast, too fast.

He grabs the man behind me—the one still palming my ass—and with a brutal twist of his hands, there's a sickening crack as he rips the man's head clean off.

The body collapses to the ground like a rag doll. He releases the head, and it rolls across the alley, blood spraying, coating Xavior from chest to face.

I can't look away. Horror mixes with awe. He didn't use his shadows. I've always known he was powerful magically, but I never realized he possessed this kind of raw, monstrous strength.

And God... I'm so turned on. My thighs squeeze together, trying to ease the ache between them. What is *wrong* with me?

Xavior's gaze locks on me, and my chest tightens when I see how dark, how *hungry* his eyes have become. Then his attention shifts to the men—the one holding up my dress, the other pinning my arms above my head. They freeze, wide-eyed with fear. And I? I'm paralyzed, utterly frozen in shock. How had I never realized he was *this* strong?

A low, feral growl rolls from his chest, and both men step forward, knives raised.

Are they insane? Did they not just see what I saw?

"Stay," Xavior commands, his voice deadly calm. I tug my dress back into place and nod. I'm not leaving his side, not with my magic useless and myself this vulnerable.

The men lunge, knives flashing, but Xavior is faster. He grips both of their wrists at once, twisting with a precision that makes my stomach lurch. Their screams pierce the night as their bones snap under his hands. They collapse to their knees.

And then his shadows surge, black swirls wrapping around their bodies, constricting, merciless. I flinch, squeezing my eyes shut and covering my ears as the cracks of breaking bones and their desperate screams fill my senses. He has no mercy, not an ounce. Three men... gone.

And then he's behind me, arms wrapping around my body, pulling me against his chest. My breath catches as I inhale his scent, intoxicating and dangerous. I open my eyes just in time to see his jaw set, his gaze fixed straight ahead, lethal and unyielding.

He begins moving, carrying me with a strength that feels both terrifying and thrilling. We round the corner of the building, heading to the front of the club, and my pulse races as he strides toward a blacked-out car. The engine idles, door wide open.

He slides me into the passenger seat, pausing just long enough to buckle me in.

"What about Ana?" I whisper, panic clawing at me.

Xavior glances over his shoulder. I follow his gaze, and my stomach drops. Axel is there, carrying Ana over his shoulder like some angry, muscular caveman. She's kicking, yelling, trying to wiggle free, but Axel's grip is iron.

"Hey, let her go!" I scream as I try to push Xavior away, but he doesn't flinch. He doesn't budge an inch.

Axel tosses Ana into the backseat, holding her down as she struggles. My heart races. Fuck... we're screwed.

It's... like watching a memory of him—the way he'd hold me before, unyielding, possessive, dangerous.

Xavior climbs into the driver's seat, revs the engine, and we surge forward. The crowd scatters before us, no one daring to cross his path.

"Wait! What about Tyler?" Ana shouts from the backseat.

"That fucker can find his own way," Xavior growls, pressing the gas pedal. My back slams against the seat, but I don't move.

I lean forward, unable to help myself, and ask softly, heatedly, "Why don't you like him?"

"He wants you," Xavior says quietly. "Talks about how much he wants you when your father isn't around."

My mouth falls open. "Oh…"

"What in the living hell, *Anastasia*?" Axel snarls from the backseat. "You were dancing with that man like a fucking whore. You're lucky I didn't kill him, bend you over in front of everyone, and spank the shit out of you."

Okay… maybe Axel is worse.

Xavior would absolutely do those things, but he wouldn't spank me in front of a crowd. At least… I think he wouldn't. I sneak a glance at him, trying to read his expression, but he looks completely indifferent, as if Axel's outburst doesn't even register.

"Hey!" I snap, yanking at my seatbelt. I twist around, climbing over the console, rage flaring hot in my chest. "Don't talk to her like that!"

I barely make it halfway before Xavior's arm wraps around my hips, dragging me back hard and settling me onto his lap. The car swerves, tires screeching as we nearly clip the vehicle beside us.

"We can fuck whoever we want," I shout, fighting his grip. "And dance with whoever we want! We're single!"

Xavior laughs, it's a harsh, dangerous sound that sends a shiver straight through me.

"The fuck you can," he growls in my ear. "You're mine, little vixen. Definitely not single. You're stuck with me." His grip tightens, possessively. "If you even *try* to fuck someone else, their blood is on your hands. No one touches you and lives."

I gasp, squirming, but it's useless. He only pulls me closer, iron-solid beneath me.

In the rearview mirror, I catch Axel leaning toward Ana, his voice dropping to something low and intimate. She refuses to look at him, pouting, but he cups her face gently and starts pressing kisses along her jaw, down her neck. Her lips part, a soft whimper slipping free before she can stop it.

I turn away, giving them privacy.

Xavior's hand slides over my bare thigh, his thumb moving in slow, lazy circles. Goosebumps ripple across my skin, heat pooling low in my stomach. God... it feels so good to have him touch me again. I hadn't realized how badly I'd missed it... how much my body still remembers him.

Exhaustion creeps in, heavy and sudden. I let my head fall against his chest, his heart pounding hard beneath my cheek. I shift slightly, trying to get comfortable.

He groans low, deep in his throat.

I ignore it.

After a while, the car slows and comes to a stop. I lift my head as he shifts the car into park. Outside, a massive two-story brick house looms before us, balconies stretching across the second floor, a wide U-shaped driveway, and a fountain bubbling softly at its center.

"Where are we?" I ask, confusion twisting in my chest.

"We rented it," he says calmly. "For a few weeks. Until we go home."

I shake my head immediately. "No. Take us back to the safe house."

"No." He steps out of the car without releasing me, lifting me easily into his arms.

"So, what now?" I ask softly. "You're going to keep me prisoner again?"

I don't even bother struggling. I already know I won't win.

"No." He sighs, the sound tired, almost weary, as he heads toward the front door. "You're free to go out—as long as you come back to me."

I glance behind him. Ana is leaning against the car, tears slipping silently down her cheeks, while Axel cups her face, murmuring something only she can hear. His expression is soft, reverent, full of something dangerously close to devotion. I say nothing. They need this moment. And despite everything, I know Axel won't hurt her.

Looks like they're not the only ones who need to talk.

I inhale deeply. I can't avoid Xavior forever, especially if he truly is my mate. But that doesn't mean forgiveness comes easy. It doesn't mean trust is automatic. If I ever trust him again, it will take time.

Inside, he carries me past the staircase and living room, down a quiet hallway. He opens a door and flicks on the light.

The bedroom takes my breath away.

Soft gray walls, a massive bed centered against the far wall. To the left, two plush chairs sit before a brick fireplace, bookcases framing it on either side. Directly across from the bed, tall French glass doors.

For such a large room, it feels... intimate, almost warm.

"Do you like it?" he asks, setting me gently on my feet.

I take a step forward, my eyes roaming the space. "It's nice, cozy. Nothing will ever live up to your mansion," I mumble.

Honestly, it was my prison, but that didn't make it any less beautiful.

"If you ever want to go back," he says softly, "all you have to do is say the word." He pats the edge of the bed. "Sit."

I obey, lowering myself onto the mattress. He drops to his knees in front of me, his hands warm as they wrap around my ankle. Slowly, carefully, he unwraps the thin strings wound around my calf, loosening my heel. His fingers skim my skin, and the contact sends a sharp wave of pleasure straight through me, my toes curling.

He repeats the action on my other leg, but this time, once the shoe slips free, he looks up at me. His gaze holds mine as he presses a featherlight kiss to the top of my foot.

My breath stutters.

I love the way he takes care of me, with such tenderness, such reverence. It makes staying angry nearly impossible. I feel like I'm grasping at straws, fighting against something my body and heart both want. I can't make this easy for him. If I do, he'll think I'm weak, easily swayed. And I'm not even sure I *want* to forgive him. How does someone move past something like that? How do you ever fully trust again?

"We need to talk, Amara."

His clothes and skin are still splattered with blood. I force myself not to look at it.

"No, we don't." I cross my arms tightly over my chest and turn my face away, stubborn and scared.

"Please," he says gently. "I'm begging you. I can't do this anymore. It's killing me." The rawness in his voice makes my chest ache.

"Were you ever going to tell me we're mates?" I ask, finally looking down at him.

He drags a hand over his face. The act is full of frustration.

"I don't know," he admits. "If I'm being completely honest... I don't know." He exhales slowly. "I was going to tell you before you ran. When I told you to pack, I planned to take you to the mansion and explain everything. I hoped you'd understand. I hoped you'd help me. Then I wanted to take you to dinner—something romantic—and tell you about the bond." His jaw tightens. "But everything went to hell. And after that, I was scared. Terrified you'd reject me."

He reaches for my arms, gently uncrossing them, as if afraid I'll pull away. He laces our fingers together, holding on like he might lose me if he doesn't. I let him, feeling too exhausted to fight anymore.

"I can reject the bond?" The words tumble out of me fast. If that's true... then I don't *have* to forgive him. I don't have to choose him.

He freezes. "I feel like I just shot myself in the foot." A strained laugh escapes him. "You didn't know? Is that why you haven't rejected me?" His eyes search my face. "Are you going to do it now?"

"I don't know anything about mate bonds," I whisper. "I completely dozed off in class." My gaze drops to our joined hands. His are rough and callused, so much larger than mine. Strong, familiar, and... safe. "I honestly don't know what to do. I don't know if I can ever trust you."

He squeezes my fingers gently. "I know." His voice breaks. "I don't expect you to forget what I did. Or forgive me right away. Take all the time you need." His eyes lift to mine, desperate and unguarded. "Just... don't reject me. Please. I can't live without you."

He raises our hands and presses slow kisses to my knuckles, one after another, like a vow.

"I know I'm crazy," he continues quietly. "Possessive and unhinged at times." A faint, bitter smile touches his lips. "But I swear I can give you what you need. I can love you the way you deserve. Give me a chance to prove it. Give *us* a chance." His grip tightens. "I'll make it up to you. I swear on the Gods. They paired us together for a reason. We belong together. We were made for each other." His voice lowers. "I'll do anything for you. I fucking need you."

My throat tightens. "We can take this slow," he adds quickly. "I won't force anything. I promise."

I press my lips together, my thoughts spiraling. Do I open myself back up to him? Give him another chance to hurt me? His words crack something open inside me, something fragile and dangerous.

"I never lied about how I felt about you," he says softly. "I told myself I was pretending—but I wasn't. Everything between us was real. It *is* real." His eyes shine. "I love you, Amara. So damn much. I can't sleep. I barely eat. I'm broken without you." His voice drops to a whisper. "Tell me what to do. I'll do anything. Literally anything."

He lifts one hand and cups my cheek.

I lean into his touch without thinking, my eyes sliding shut.

And that scares me more than anything. I hate this wedge between us. I want him to hold me, to tell me we'll be okay.

"Can I have a couple of days to think about it?" I finally ask, pulling away from his touch before I lose my resolve.

He exhales slowly. "Better than the no I was expecting." His voice is quiet, tired. "I'll sleep in the guest room. It's upstairs—first door on the right. If you need anything..."

He gives me a small smile, but it doesn't reach his eyes. It looks forced like it costs him something. He leans down and presses a gentle kiss to the top of my head, then turns away without looking back. The door closes softly behind him. As soon as it does, I fall back onto the mattress, staring up at the ceiling.

I don't know what to think. My mind won't slow down with my thoughts buzzing and colliding. Maybe sleep will help. Maybe if I shut everything off for a few hours, things will feel clearer when I wake up.

I should go check on Ana. I want to, but I don't. She needs to hear what Axel has to say. She needs space to process it without me hovering. She'll come find me when they're done. Unless... she forgives him. Unless she stays with him.

I hate this for her.

She always wanted the fairytale. Dreamed about it since she was little. The soft kind of love. The kind with safety and promises and happily-ever-afters. And this is what she got instead.

I was always the one drawn to bad boys. Ana craved the boy next door, her prince charming. I never thought someone like that could give her what she actually needed. She likes being dominated, being told what to do. She hates planning, hates being in charge. She wants someone else to make the hard decisions for her.

And she needs protection.

She's naïve. She believes in people too easily. She has panic attacks when things get ugly. She needs someone strong enough to protect not just her body, but her mind—someone who won't hesitate when things turn dangerous. If Axel is even half as strong as Xavior, then I know he can do that.

The boy next door won't push her when she needs it. Won't force her to face hard things. Won't kill for her if it comes down to it. She needs someone like my dad. A leader. Someone who knows when to be gentle and when to be ruthless.

Sweet boys are for normal girls. Not girls with parents like ours. We'll always have targets on our backs.

I push myself off the bed and walk toward the double doors across the room, opening the one on the right.

Bingo.

I step into the closet and move toward the rack of clothes. My fingers slide along the fabric of his shirts, and I inhale without thinking, his scent filling my lungs, grounding me. I missed it more than I realized. I pull one of his long-sleeve button-ups from the hanger and wrap it around myself, pressing it to my chest. I close my eyes, pretending it's his arms instead. Holding me and keeping me safe.

Eventually, I let the shirt fall away and strip out of my clothes, leaving only my panties. I slip the button-up over my shoulders and button it halfway, the fabric hanging loose, soft against my skin, showing just enough of my chest.

I rummage through the drawers of the cabinet, but there's nothing there. Not that I expected anything, he just moved in.

With a quiet sigh, I crawl back into bed and curl into the silk pillows, burying my face in them. I fall asleep wrapped in the scent of my mate.

My mate...Holy shit.

Chapter Thirty-five

Amara

My eyes spring open, and for a second, I don't know where I am. The room is still dark, quiet, wrapped in that deep, heavy silence. I blink a few times, my gaze drifting, and then I see him.

Xavior is asleep in the chair beside the bed.

A soft smile curves my lips before I can stop it. This is the second time. Does he wait until I fall asleep and then sneak in just to sit beside me? To keep watch? I should feel bad about it—and part of me does—but mostly it makes something warm bloom in my chest. It makes me feel safe, needed, and wanted.

I stare at him for a long moment, memorizing the way his head is tilted slightly to the side, his arms crossed tightly over his chest like he's holding himself together even in sleep. Right here, in this exact moment, I know something with terrifying clarity.

I'm not going to reject him.

I'm not ready to jump into a full mating bond. I'm not ready to forgive everything. But I want this. I want *him*. The way I feel around Xavior is overwhelming, mind-blowing. It's everything I've ever wanted, everything I've ever craved, and it scares me how deeply it reaches inside me.

I let my eyes close again, a small smile lingering on my lips as sleep pulls me under once more.

When I wake up the second time, sunlight is pouring through the French doors, warm and bright, spilling across the floor. The chair beside the bed is empty.

For just a second, my chest tightens.

I swing my legs over the side of the bed and glance at the chair again, as if he might reappear if I look hard enough. It's silly, but the room feels quieter without him. Still safe, just... emptier.

I head into his closet and pull on a pair of sweatpants from the drawer. They're way too big, hanging low on my hips, but I don't care. I look around for a brush or a comb, anything, but there's nothing, so I finger-comb my messy hair instead. I grab a ponytail holder from my clutch and twist my hair into a loose, messy bun on top of my head.

Walking out of the bedroom, I head toward the kitchen, but the view from the dining room stops me in my tracks.

I slide open the glass door and step onto the stone patio.

Two round metal tables sit on either side, umbrellas folded neatly above them. To my right is a large gazebo filled with cozy furniture, a fireplace, and a TV mounted above it. To my left, a wide fire pit is surrounded by six black Adirondack chairs. Beyond it all lies a large pond with a fountain bubbling softly at its center, and past that, woods stretch endlessly into the distance.

It's stunning.

A quiet happiness settles over me, surprising in its ease. Every place I've ever called home has had nature wrapped around it. I've always needed the outdoors, the trees, the stillness. And apparently... so does he.

"Holy moly! This is freaking nice!"

I turn to find Ana stepping out behind me, her eyes wide, her face bright. She looks... happy.

Genuinely happy.

And that catches me off guard more than anything else has.

"I started the coffee and already heated the stove to make breakfast!" she says, turning back inside. I follow her, sliding the door shut behind me, my eyes instinctively scanning the room for Xavior.

"So..." I lean against the island, watching her move around the kitchen. "Tell me, how'd your talk go? Are you okay?"

"It was okay, I guess." She shrugs, opening the fridge and pulling out eggs, bacon, onions, and tomatoes.

My brows lift when she grabs my favorite creamer and flashes me a small smile.

Of course, he made sure it was here.

I wait for her to continue. She finally sighs. "The guys left earlier. Said they needed to take care of a few important things for the council."

My jaw tightens. "Speaking of the council... do they know he was the leader of the rebels?"

She exhales slowly. "Yeah. They do. They made a deal. He helps them hunt down the remaining rebels, and he doesn't serve any time."

I snort, bitterness sharp on my tongue. "Seriously? He gets a slap on the fucking wrist?"

"I guess it kind of sucks that he got off so easily," she says after a moment, "but it benefits me too. I get time with him. Time to figure things out." She shrugs, fiddling with the carton of eggs. "Xavior actually played a big role in the slap on the wrist. Besides helping them track down the remaining rebels, Axel has to do odd jobs for the council. Whatever they need."

"We went off track," I say gently. "How do *you* feel about him after the talk you had?"

I push off the island and start rummaging through the cabinets for plates. When I find them, my breath catches. Shelves are stocked with my favorite snacks, things I didn't even realize I missed until now. Something warm swells in my chest. It's stupid how much that tiny detail affects me.

I pull out two plates and a bowl, then grab the eggs and crack them carefully into it. I can't cook, but I can help, chop, prep, and make myself useful.

"We talked a lot," Ana says softly. "And I still don't know what to do. I'm confused. My heart and my body want one thing, and my mind wants another." She hesitates, then adds, almost reluctantly, "Okay... maybe half the time my mind wants him too." She clears her throat. "After we talked last night... we had sex."

"Ana!" I whip around. "I thought you said you weren't sure what you wanted."

"I'm not!" she snaps, defensive. "Don't judge me. The pull is too strong to ignore, and I haven't had sex in months."

"I'm not judging," I say quickly, softer now. "Trust me, I get it. I'm in the same boat, remember?" I watch as she drops butter into the pan, the sizzle filling the room, then she helps me chop onions and tomatoes. I grab bread and slide a couple of slices into the toaster, finally finding a fork to mix the eggs. "But sex won't help you decide."

She sighs. "You're stronger than me." She glances at me. "What about you? Have you decided?"

"Yes." I inhale deeply as I whisk the eggs. Before I can stop myself, I glance over my shoulder, checking the doorway, even though I know he isn't here. I always feel him when he enters a room. Always.

I'm not ready to tell him yet.

It's not because I want him to suffer. It's because I want to know him again—*really* know him—without the weight of this decision hovering between us. I need to be sure the man standing in front of me now is the same one I fell for.

"And...?" she presses, impatience creeping into her tone as she dumps the chopped vegetables into the pan and plants a hand on her hip, watching me.

I look away and hand her the bowl of eggs. "I decided to give him a chance."

Her expression softens.

"I don't trust him yet," I continue, my voice steady but quiet. "But I want to try. I want to give *us* a shot. He's my mate. It won't be easy, and I'm not pretending everything is okay, but I don't want to give up on us." I swallow. "Not when I see how desperate he is. The agony in his eyes. How deeply he regrets everything." I finally meet her gaze. "And that... that means a lot to me."

"That actually helps me a lot," she says, relief softening her voice. "I didn't even think about taking baby steps. I thought it was all or nothing." She exhales slowly. "I'm willing to give him a chance, test the waters before diving in. If he's okay with taking it slow, then I'll let him prove himself to me. Show me he's not just the bad man everyone says he is."

She grins, but it doesn't quite hide the seriousness beneath it. "Because I see it too, how much he regrets everything. He told me he never planned on attacking Mom. She showed up unexpectedly, and then all hell broke loose."

"Self-defense," I say immediately. "Anyone would've protected themselves in that situation." I pause, considering it. "He could still be a bad person, but as you said, give him the chance to prove that he isn't. A mate is once in a lifetime." I tilt my head. "Why did he start attacking covens in the first place?"

"His mom was murdered by witches," she explains plainly. "So, he wanted to rid the world of the evil ones. But the group he was part of... they grew too bloodthirsty. Things spiraled. They started attacking innocents." She shakes her head. "He never touched an innocent witch, though. He only killed those with black auras. And if he ever saw someone kill an innocent, he either kicked them out or killed them himself."

"That's... actually a good thing," I admit. "I get wanting to rid the world of evil." My chest tightens. "When did his mom die?"

"He was ten," she says. "They killed her right in front of him."

"Shit." The word leaves me on a breath. "That had to be horrific, watching your mom die like that, completely defenseless."

My thoughts drift to finding Mom's body hanging. That helplessness. The way it hollowed me out. I can't imagine the horror of actually *watching* it happen.

When the food is ready, we decide to eat outside in the gazebo. There's a large sectional with a couple of chairs positioned around the fireplace. We both rush for the corner seat, and I laugh when I beat her to it, sticking my tongue out in victory.

"I won't lie, Amara," she says, dropping dramatically into her spot. "The feeling I got last night at the nightclub—when I saw Axel shoving his way through the crowd, not caring who he hurt, just to get to me?" She fans herself, rolling her eyes back. "That killer look in his eyes?"

She groans. "I didn't even run. I *wanted* him to catch me. I stood there waiting. And then he punched the guy I was dancing with, knocked him straight out. I have never been so turned on in my life."

I burst out laughing. "I get it. Completely. I ran, but only because I wanted him to chase me."

The anger. The murderous rage. It's intoxicating. Knowing they'd do *anything* for you, even kill creates a high like no other. I loved the thrill of him hunting me down. He's my predator, and I'm his prey.

"I love his possessiveness," Ana admits softly. "I never thought I'd like someone controlling, but I do. I love that he's a complete asshole to everyone else, but with me? He's gentle and sweet."

"Yeah," I murmur. "It's because it's *him*." I think of Jaxon. "Jaxon tried to control me, overly possessive, jealous, and I hated it. Xavior does it, and I push his buttons just to see how far he'll go." My voice drops. "I love him. I hate this wedge between us. I pray it works, because it feels like I'm drowning without his touch."

"And the sex," she adds lightly. "If he's even half as good as Axel—"

"Mind-blowing," I finish for her.

"Yeah."

Our laughter fades as footsteps approach. Both of the men we were just talking about are stepping into the gazebo.

My heart slams violently against my ribs the second my eyes meet gray ones.

"What are you lovely ladies laughing about?" Axel asks, his gaze never leaving Ana.

I take the opportunity to really look him over. He's undeniably Xavior's brother, built bigger, broader, packed with more muscle, but a little shorter. His lips are slightly thinner, his cheeks rounder, and his blue eyes contrast sharply with his chestnut, shoulder-length hair.

The way he looks at Ana mirrors Xavior's intensity almost exactly.

My attention drifts back to my mate. His eyes are roaming over me slowly, deliberately, like he's committing every inch of me to memory. He steps closer, then kneels in front of me, his gaze locking with mine as he reaches out.

And then—he starts buttoning up my shirt.

I suck in a quiet breath.

"Oh, nothing," Ana says casually. "We were just talking about last night. You know, all the fun we were having before you brutes walked in and dragged us out like a bunch of cavemen."

She lifts her feet slowly, deliberately, placing them on the cushion beside her, showing off her long legs like she knows exactly what she's doing.

"Don't lie, my sweet," Axel murmurs. "You know you liked it."

He lifts her legs and drops onto the couch beside her, placing her feet in his lap as he leans back, completely at ease, like that's exactly where they belong.

Xavior finishes buttoning my shirt all the way up. I roll my eyes, biting my lower lip to keep my smile from giving me away. He rises and sits beside me, slipping an arm around my shoulders and pulling me into his side.

I let him because I need to be close to him.

I nestle into his chest, and he releases a soft sound—low, content—that sends a spark through my body. Something settles inside me. I feel full and whole. Like I've finally found my way back home.

I missed this. *I missed him.*

"Do you like it here?" he asks hesitantly. "I rented this place because when I saw the view, I thought of you."

"Yes," I whisper. "I love it. It's beautiful."

My eyes flutter shut when his thumb starts tracing slow, absent circles on my upper arm. "What did the council need?"

"They want the information Axel has," he says evenly. "To capture the rebels."

I open my eyes to glance at Ana, and she's gone. Both of them are.

I blink, scanning the gazebo. When did they leave?

I lean back, tilting my head to look up at Xavior. "I woke up last night."

He clears his throat and finally meets my gaze, a faint, but unmistakable flush creeping up his cheeks. "Did you?"

"Mhm. You were there," I say softly. "Sleeping in a chair beside the bed."

"Are you mad?" His voice is careful, like he's bracing for impact.

"No," I admit. "But I do want to know how many times you've snuck into my room."

His eyes slide away, jaw tightening just slightly, enough that I notice.

"I don't want to lie," he says tentatively. "But I feel like you'll be mad."

My brows knit together. "Why?"

He looks back at me then, really looks at me, his eyes dark and serious. "Don't get mad," he says, already knowing that won't help. "After I left you in the medical ward, I went into your room and installed cameras. I wanted to keep an eye on you." He swallows. "And at your parents' house... There were cameras there, too. I watched you sleep every night. For about an hour."

The words hit me like cold water.

"You—" I turn away instinctively, my body pulling back, but his grip tightens around me, anchoring me in place. "You installed cameras?" My voice wobbles despite my effort to steady it. "Did you watch me undress?"

"This sounds bad," he says immediately. "I know it does. I don't have an excuse." He exhales. "Yes, I watched you undress, but I looked away before you were completely bare. I only saw you in your underwear."

My chest feels tight. "Why?" I whisper. "Why would you do that?"

I don't even know what I'm feeling—anger, disbelief, something dangerously close to understanding. I'm glad he's not lying, not hiding it... but my privacy. It feels violated in a way I don't know how to untangle.

"I wanted to know you were okay," he says earnestly. "After you got hurt, I couldn't stop worrying about you. And I wanted to know you... how you lived, what made you smile, what made you sad." His voice roughens. "I followed you. Watched you."

"You mean you stalked me," I say, sharp now. "Invaded my privacy like some kind of psychopath."

"If that makes me a stalker, a psychopath, then fine." His voice is raw, unapologetic. "I needed to be near you. To keep you safe. But it was more than that." He leans closer. "Being away from you hurt. It drove me fucking insane. There was this invisible pull inside me, dragging me toward you. When you were out of sight, it just kept pulling and pulling until it ached." His hand lifts, cupping my jaw. "It only eased when you were close."

My breath stutters as my anger slips through my fingers like sand. I hate that my body betrays me, that I melt into his touch so easily.

"Did you know about the bond," I ask quietly, "when we first met?"

"At first, no," he admits. "I felt something, strong, but I didn't know what it was. After you got hurt, I suspected it, but I pushed it aside." His thumb brushes my cheek. "It wasn't until our kiss that I couldn't deny it anymore. The bond became too strong to ignore."

I stare into his eyes, my heart pounding so hard I can feel it in my throat. Keeping him at arm's length hurts more than pulling him close.

I need him.

My hand presses against his chest, right over his heart, and he groans softly in response.

"I've made my decision."

I feel him tense beneath my hand instantly, like every muscle in his body locks at once. I pull my hand back and look away, my chest tightening. I chew on the inside of my cheek, stalling, searching for the right words.

He doesn't move. Not an inch. His face is carved with dread, like he's already bracing for the worst.

"Tell me…" he pleads softly. "Please." He straightens, his hands coming to rest on my waist, grounding and warm. "Shit." He shakes his head and drags a hand down his face. "May I—may I add something before you decide?"

"No." My voice is quiet but firm. "I've made my decision. Nothing you say is going to change my mind."

I drop my gaze, staring at my hand still pressed to his chest. God, I wish he were shirtless. The thought slips in uninvited, distracting, dangerous. What would he do if I asked him to take it off?

"Amara, please. Just hear me out."

"I don't trust you completely," I say, the words heavy but honest. "And it hurts, Xavior. It really does." My hand slides up his chest, fingers curling at his neck as I cup his jaw, my thumb tracing along its sharp edge. "But do you know what hurts more?"

His breath stutters beneath my touch. "What, baby?"

"Not being in your arms," I whisper. "Not kissing you. It's killing me."

His eyes drop to my lips, pupils darkening, desire and relief warring in his expression. I can feel his restraint fraying.

"I want to give you another chance," I continue, my voice steady even though my heart is racing. "I want you to prove yourself. But if you hurt me again," I swallow. "I'm done."

He just stares at me for a beat, like his brain needs time to catch up. Then it happens, his eyes light up, raw joy breaking through, so intense it almost hurts to look at.

I'm not safe with him… but I don't want safe…

"Kiss me, Xavior."

He doesn't hesitate. He leans in and presses his lips to mine, slow and reverent, like he's afraid I might disappear if he moves too fast. He tastes me, teases me, his hands coming up to cradle my face, thumbs brushing my cheeks.

He pulls back just enough to breathe. "Fuck," he murmurs. "I'm the luckiest man on this fucked-up planet."

Then he kisses me again, harder, urgent, desperate, like he'll die if he doesn't.

"Xavior," I moan, my hands sliding into his hair, fingers tangling and pulling him closer. My tongue brushes against his, and the sound he makes, deep and wrecked, comes from somewhere primal inside his chest. Whatever restraint he was clinging to snaps.

In one swift motion, he flips me onto my back, pushing me into the cushion beneath me. He pulls away just long enough to grab my shirt and rip it open, buttons flying in every direction.

Chapter Thirty-six

Amara

Shadows swirl around us, tossing our hair with the wind they create. "We can't have anyone looking at what belongs to me," he mumbles, his gaze roaming my body. The way he looks at me makes my heart skip a beat. He makes me feel desired, wanted, and cherished all at once.

"Xavior." My voice is breathless, my body aching for his rough hands to trace my skin. "Touch me." He groans and lowers his head, pressing soft, searing kisses just below my ear.

"I want you to know that you're my everything, Amara. I know I don't deserve you. You're too sweet, too angelic, compared to my devilish ways. I never thought I'd have something so perfect, made just for me. A good man would let you go, but I won't. I can't live without you. You're my heaven, my angel, and I'm your hell, your demon—but I'll treasure and protect you with every fiber of my dark soul. I'm completely yours. I'll do anything for you; all you have to do is ask. I love you, with all of my black, sinful soul."

"I love you, Xavior. If you're my hell, then burn me. I'd choose you over heaven."

I moan through his words as his hands trail over me, calloused fingers mapping every inch of my skin. He leans closer, lips brushing my collarbone, tracing down my arms.

"Again, baby, please." His hair is tousled, his lips slightly swollen from us kissing, eyes soft with desire.

"I love you. I'm all yours, Xavior."

He closes his eyes, savoring my words. Then, without warning, he lifts me and gently tosses me onto something soft. The shadows vanish, and I realize we're in our room. He grabs his shirt and rips it off, muscles taut and gleaming in the dim light.

Kneeling before me, he slowly slides my sweatpants down. I lean on my elbows, watching him, my breath coming in ragged gasps. His grey eyes are locked on my bare pussy, nostrils flaring, pupils dilating, devouring me.

"So... goddamn beautiful." He exhales, pressing a kiss to the side of my right knee, moving deliberately upward, tracing a slow, hot path.

My body trembles, arousal flaring through me. I can't take this slow torture any longer. "Xavior, please," I gasp, desperate.

And then he gives me exactly what I need—his mouth sets me ablaze, tongue dragging across my achy clit. My body arches, white-hot sparks shooting through me, lighting me on fire. I cry out, eyes rolling into the back of my head.

"This is all I dreamt about, your sweet pussy on my mouth, you beneath me at my mercy, screaming my name as I devour you." His groan vibrates against my sensitive skin, swirling his tongue around my clit, sucking it into his mouth, scraping his teeth, ripping a loud whimper from my throat.

Every vibration of his voice shakes me to my core. He slips two fingers inside, curling them perfectly against my most sensitive spot, moving in and out with precise, maddening rhythm. "That—and the way you bounced on my cock..."

"Don't stop, please!" I whimper, needy and trembling. I open my legs wider, hips bucking, grinding against his fingers. I glance down, his eyes are fixed on me, watching my breasts bounce with every roll of my hips, drinking me in.

He moves faster, plunging his fingers deeper, tongue flicking and lapping at my clit with increasing urgency. Every stroke, every curl, every flick pulls me higher, closer to the edge, and I can't hold back, moaning his name.

"Oh, Gods... I'm..." My voice shatters as I throw my head back. Heat explodes through my body, flames licking my core as my orgasm slams into me, shuddering violently with every pulse.

He doesn't wait for it to fade. In a swift motion, he lifts me, spins me around, and places my legs on either side of his hips. I glance behind me. He's sitting up against the headboard, and I'm straddling him backward. Without warning, he thrusts hard into me. I scream, stretching impossibly around him, feeling full, overwhelmed... too big.

"I need to watch this ass bounce on my cock," he growls, eyes dark and locked on where our bodies connect. He spanks me, grips my hips, lifts and slams me back down, demanding every inch. Showing me exactly what he needs.

I plant my hands on his thighs to brace myself. I take control, lifting myself, and slamming down, over and over, leaning forward, pushing deeper, faster, harder. Every bounce, every roll, every squeeze of his hands pulls me closer.

"Shit, you should see yourself taking me. Ass jiggling with every bounce... so fucking sexy," he growls, primal, uncontrollable.

"You like that? Does my pussy feel good?" I tease, breathless, daring him.

"Fuck yesss... so fucking tight, so wet," he growls, and I shiver at the weight of his words, the ownership in his voice.

He pulls out of me, and I whimper at the sudden emptiness, my body aching for him. I was so close. He doesn't give me a second to protest before flipping me onto my back and rolling over me, thrusting back inside in one brutal, possessive motion. I cry out as his hands slam into the headboard above my head and he starts fucking me hard, and deep, like he's claiming me all over again.

I clench around his cock, and he hisses sharply. "Fuck. Come for me," he growls, voice dark and commanding. "I can feel how bad you want it. The way your tight pussy is clenching the fuck out of me." His thrusts grow heavier, meaner. "Look at me. Now, Amara."

My eyes flutter open, locking onto his burning gaze. The headboard slams against the wall with every thrust. He slows just enough to make it torture.

"That's it," he murmurs, rough and low. "Good girl. Watch me fuck my pussy. Take it, you're mine."

"Oh my God!" I cry out, fingers clawing into his shoulders as pleasure detonates through me. My body spasms violently, white-hot pleasure ripping through me like a hurricane, stealing my breath as another orgasm slams into me. It's overwhelming, bone-deep, soul-shaking. Stars explode behind my eyes as I scream his name.

"Yes," he growls, voice thick with satisfaction. "That's my good girl. That's it. Let go. Come all over my cock."

I shudder uncontrollably, my limbs going limp as he keeps thrusting through my orgasm, dragging it out, milking every broken gasp from my mouth. I'm completely undone. I'm addicted to this feeling, to him.

His shadows wrap around us again, but this time they're controlled, restrained, like they're obeying him the same way my body is. He thrusts once more, deep and unforgiving, and his cock pulses hard as he comes inside me, spilling into me fast and hot. His body shudders violently as he buries his face into my neck, breathing me in like he needs me to survive.

"Fuck," he pants, pulling back just enough to look at me. "I've never lost control like that before you. Never exploded like that." A dark, satisfied smirk curves his lips. "You do that to me."

I'm still trembling when he adds quietly, almost reverently, "Mine."

I laugh weakly, shaking my head as I melt into the afterglow, completely spent, still pulsing around him, knowing I'd give him that control again without hesitation.

I sit up, breathing raggedly, my wild eyes searching the dark room. Another nightmare, calm down. I press a hand to my chest, a low sob slipping free. *Mom.*

My nightmares are always the same—four unknown figures wearing large hooded cloaks, their faces hidden in shadow. I watch in frozen horror as they wrap the rope around her neck while she struggles. She turns to me, her eyes cold, and tells me how disappointed she is in me—how useless I am. Then, in the next second, she's hanging limp, swaying back and forth.

I look toward the man sleeping peacefully beside me, our legs tangled together. I had been resting on his arm when I woke. I know I won't be able to fall back asleep, and I don't want to wake him. He looks exhausted, worn down from too many sleepless nights. Slowly, carefully, I untangle our limbs and slip off the bed. Thankfully, he doesn't stir.

I make my way into the kitchen. *Jesus,* I'd kill for some chocolate chip cookies.

I remember when Ana and I were little—when one of us had a nightmare or got scared, Dad would make cookies and pour us warm glasses of milk. We'd sit at the counter, watching him mix the dough, sneaking bites while the rest baked in the oven.

I hate how distant he's become. He barely answers calls or texts anymore. I know he lost his wife, and I understand that kind of pain... but we lost our mom. We still need him. I miss him—*the old him*—more than I can put into words.

I open the fridge and smile when I see the cookie dough. I can't bake it, I'd probably burn the house down, but I can eat the dough and drink a glass of milk.

Arms full, I head outside and settle into one of the Adirondack chairs. I pull my knees to my chest, lean my head back, and stare up at the stars.

I wouldn't have survived the emotional guilt eating me alive without Xavior. I'm so tired. Emotionally drained. Everything hurts, and the only thing that eases the ache is him.

"I miss you, Mom," I whisper to the night sky. "So much. I know we never had a good relationship. I never understood why you treated Ana and me so differently... but I forgive you."

Ten minutes later, I'm nearly finished with the cookie dough when the air suddenly thickens, pressing uncomfortably against my skin. A sharp shout of my name cuts through the quiet from inside the house. The panic in Xavior's voice has me sitting upright.

The sliding door flies open, and Xavior storms outside, his gaze wild, nostrils flaring as he scans the yard like he's hunting for a threat.

"Xavior, what's wrong?"

His eyes lock onto me, and the tension drains from his body almost instantly. He stalks toward me, jaw tight.

"I thought you left." His gaze sharpens. "Why are you crying?"

I lift my fingers to my cheeks, surprised when they come back wet. I hadn't even realized. A small, humorless laugh slips out.

"I've been having dreams... more like nightmares about my mom. It's stupid, I know." I release a long breath. "I wanted cookies and some fresh air to clear my head, but then I remembered I can't bake without burning the house down. So... cookie dough and air."

He drops to his knees in front of me, cupping my face and gently wiping away my tears with his thumbs. "You should've woken me," he murmurs. "Come here."

His arm wraps around my waist, and before I can protest, he lifts me easily, turning us as he sits back down in the chair with me curled in his lap. I sink into him instinctively, fitting against his chest like I belong there.

"Tell me about your life," I ask softly. "Your family. I hardly know anything about you."

He shrugs. "There's not much to tell. My dad raised me. I always knew I had a secret older brother. My father would let us see each other when no one was around." He looks away. "My mom left in the middle of the night. She was never heard from again."

His arms tighten slightly. "My dad grew harder after that. I wasn't allowed to be around Axel anymore. My teens were nothing but training. I became exactly what he wanted—a machine that kills." His voice dips. "He wasn't happy when I told him I found you. My mate. He believes emotions make you weak. He wanted me empty."

"Does it upset you," I sigh, "that he doesn't approve of me?"

"No." His answer is instant, rough. "I don't give a fuck." He growls the words. "You're mine. My mate. No one gets a say in that."

I feel it too—that same fierce certainty. I know my dad doesn't approve. It doesn't matter.

"I'm sorry your mom left," I murmur, my face buried in his neck. I press a few soft kisses beneath his ear. His body shudders, and he exhales slowly, holding me tighter.

"Don't be," he says, voice low. "My father drove her away. Flaunting his whores, never caring if she saw. I always knew why she left." A pause. "I just hate that she left me, too."

I laugh as I dart out of the room. This time, I actually make it out. The first time, Xavior's shadows wrapped around me, dragging me right back into bed with him. He has zero interest in leaving our bed—which I normally wouldn't mind—but my stomach is screaming for food, and my head is already pounding from the lack of caffeine. I cannot do round three this morning without breakfast.

I sneak away while he's in the bathroom.

The door slams open behind me.

Xavior growls as he comes after me, and the kitchen and living room come into view just as shadows coil around my body, stopping me mid-step.

"I wasn't done with you, mate," Xavior murmurs huskily in my ear when he catches up to me.

"About time!" Ana calls over her shoulder. "Breakfast is almost done. I made biscuits and gravy this morning, Axel's favorite. Come help me get plates."

"Motherfucker," Xavior groans under his breath, making me laugh again.

I glance up and spot Axel leaning against the kitchen cabinet beside the stove, watching us with open amusement. He knows *exactly* why Xavior didn't want to leave his room.

I turn my head toward Xavior, our lips brushing as I whisper, "Behave. I'm starving."

"Fine," he huffs, sounding like a sulky little boy who just had his favorite toy taken away.

We step into the kitchen, and Axel pats Xavior on the back. "Stop pouting, bro. You'll be fine. Your dick won't fall off."

"That's the opposite of what you told me less than an hour ago," Ana says sweetly. "I believe you said, *'My balls will shrivel up and fall off if I don't come at least one more time.'*" She deepens her voice, trying—and failing—to sound manly.

Xavior and I burst out laughing.

Axel clicks his tongue. "That was a private conversation, my sweet. You'll ruin my reputation if you keep telling people how needy I am."

I turn my back on them to grab plates. *Is this how it'll be now?* Because I won't lie, I love it. We're relaxed and laughing, comfortable with our mates. We feel like a family again, something we haven't had in a long time. Dad's barely home anymore, and Mom... well. She's Mom.

"Oh, shut up," Ana mutters, rolling her eyes.

"Roll your eyes again," Axel warns, "and I'll spank that attitude right out of you."

Ana shoots me a mischievous look, and I wiggle my brows back at her. When I glance over, my gaze meets Xavior's, and my chest warms at how happy he looks, especially the laughter dancing in his grey eyes. He loves this too.

"You love my attitude," Ana teases Axel, hands pressing against his chest. "But if you want to spank me, I'll bend over for you."

She looks tiny next to him, her head barely reaches his chest, his shoulders are broad, and his arms nearly as wide as her legs. Xavior towers over me too, yet his lean frame is just as intimidating.

Suddenly, hands grab mine and tug me forward. I hadn't even noticed Xavior filling our plates while I was distracted by my sister and her mate.

He sets them on one of the round patio tables outside and pulls out a chair for me. I kiss his jaw before sitting down, warmth blooming in my chest.

"Tell me about him." I jerk my chin toward the house. I need to know Ana will be safe. With the way he looks at her, I highly doubt he'd ever hurt her—but I need to hear it.

"It's not my story to tell," he says evenly. "But I can assure you, she's in good hands. He loves almost as fiercely as I do, and he's unwaveringly loyal. He and I are a lot alike, even though we weren't raised together. A hard life does that to you." His arm tightens around me. "We don't trust easily, but when we do, our trust and love are fierce. So fierce you'll get sick of us. We'll die for you. Kill for you."

His voice drops, dark and unyielding. "The only thing I'll never grant you is freedom from me. I'll never let you go. Not even if you hate me for it."

"I'll never hate you," I say softly. "And I won't grow tired of you either. I'm yours. I'll never leave. Sometimes, when I'm angry, I'll need space, but I'll always come back."

"Good," he murmurs. His gaze drags over me, slow and heated. "Now hurry and eat—because the only thing I want to eat is you."

Fuck.

My nipples harden instantly, heat pooling low in my belly.

I nod and pick up my fork.

He groans. "Good girl."

Chapter Thirty-seven

Amara

I sink deeper into the hot, bubbly bathtub, muscles aching in the most delicious way. I'm so sore. He ate me until my head spun, until I couldn't take it anymore, until I begged. *Twice*. And then he finally fucked me so good I nearly forgot my own name.

The way he worships my body still blows my mind.

I hear the bedroom door open and then close again.

"Xavior?" I call out. He was supposed to get in the bath with me, but his phone rang earlier—his father. He's been gone longer than I expected.

"I'm sorry about that." Xavior steps into the bathroom, his expression tight, eyes hard. I don't need him to say it... the conversation clearly didn't go well.

"Is everything okay?" I sit up straighter.

He kneels beside the tub and presses a soft kiss to my lips. "Nothing for you to worry about, love. He's just pissed I'm not there working."

"If you need to deal with something important, I'll still be here when you get back."

"No." His voice is firm. "I want to spend time with you. At least one full day." His thumb drags slowly along my lower lip. "Is there anything you want to do?"

"Hmmm." A smile spreads across my face. There *is* something—something I've missed. Something Ana and I used to do every week before everything went to hell. "There is."

"What is it?" he asks.

"Bowling."

His brows knit together in confusion, and I burst out laughing. "You don't know what bowling is?"

"I can't say I do."

I reach up and smooth the crease between his brows. "Will you try it for me? We'll invite Ana and Axel. She loves it too."

"Of course." His expression softens. "Anything for you. Axel isn't the type to go out, but he owes me—he'll go."

"Oh, I'm not worried," I grin. "Once Ana hears about it, she'll drag him along—or leave without him. Fair warning, though: she and I are *extremely* competitive."

"So are we." His eyes light with interest as he stands and grabs a towel. "Come on. Get out. Whatever bowling is, you and I will crush it."

I rise from the tub, water sliding down my skin. "Bowling looks easy," I tease, "but I promise—it's not."

His gaze darkens as it drags slowly over my wet body. Desire flashes hot and unmistakable.

"One more round," he murmurs, licking his bottom lip. "I swear I'll be gentle."

"No." I snatch the towel from his hands, wrapping it around myself. "You are *cut off* for the rest of the day. My body needs time to recover; you barely let me leave the bed."

He groans low, and I roll my eyes, stepping past him. I don't know if I'll ever be able to keep up with his stamina.

But Gods help me—I love it.

I laugh as I watch Ana jump up and down after I ask if she wants to go bowling with us. Axel arches a brow in confusion and looks over at Xavior. We're sitting in the living room, facing them on the couch—well, *I'm* sitting on Xavior's lap.

"Yes, we are definitely going, aren't we, Axel?" Ana plops back down, leaning comfortably against his massive body.

"If you wish to go, then yes, we'll go," he murmurs against the top of her head before placing a gentle kiss there.

"Xavior and I are going to kick both of your asses," I say confidently, glancing over my shoulder at him. He smiles at me first, then his expression turns serious as he looks at our competition.

"We sure are."

"Whatever," Ana scoffs. "Axel and I will. Tell them, babe." She smacks his chest playfully.

Axel folds his arms across his chest and lifts his chin. "Damn straight."

"What do we get when we win?" Ana asks, eyes sparkling.

Of course she does. I just want to play for fun, but Ana never plays without placing bets.

"I don't know." I shrug.

"Losers have to strip down to their underwear in the middle of the bowling alley." Ana wiggles her brows.

"Definitely not happening." Xavior's arm tightens around me, his upper lip curling into a low snarl.

I bite my lower lip to hide my smile—relieved he spoke up before I had to—because that is absolutely not happening.

I clap my hands, a grin stretching wide as I lean forward, narrowing my eyes at Ana. "Losers have to eat an entire jar of peanut butter without a drink. Within an hour."

"That's cruel!" Ana gasps, then immediately points at me. "No, losers have to shove ice down their pants!"

I laugh. "Hard pass. Oh, wait. I've got one." I jump up and step closer, and she pops to her feet too, getting right in my face. "Losers have to ride the mechanical bull at that bar across town."

Axel and Xavior exchange a *'these women are insane'* look.

"That's insane," Ana says, staring at me like I've lost my mind—then her mouth curves into a wicked grin. "I love it. Deal. What are we waiting for? Let's get ready!"

"Seriously?" Axel mumbles as we enter the bowling alley.

I grin and glance at Ana. We share a look before taking off, rushing straight for the concession stand. You can't bowl before snacks—that's just common sense.

"Jarod!" I shout when my eyes land on a mass of wildly curly blond hair.

He jumps over the counter with a huge grin and scoops me up, spinning me around. He and his dad own this place. He used to date Brandon, and they'd gotten serious—*really* serious. Jarod and I grew close back then. He's the one who got me into bowling, taught me everything I know. We haven't talked much since their breakup. Brandon panicked when Jarod brought up moving in together and ended things.

"I missed your crazy ass!" Jarod laughs as he sets me down.

A hand clamps around my upper arm and yanks me back.

Before I can react, Xavior grips Jarod's collar and snarls inches from his face.

"Xavior, stop!" I grab his arm, trying to pull him back. "He's a friend."

"He shouldn't be touching you," Xavior growls, not releasing him.

"Please, stop. Jarod, meet Xavior—"

"Her mate," Xavior cuts in. I roll my eyes. He finally shoves Jarod away and pulls me into his chest, possessive and unyielding.

Jarod doesn't look scared. If anything, he looks amused. "Nice to meet you," he says easily. "No need to get possessive. She's really not my type." His gaze flicks over Xavior slowly. "You, on the other hand, are right up my alley." He winks.

"Jarod." I narrow my eyes, heat of jealousy flaring unexpectedly in my chest.

Xavior's voice drops, lethal and flat. "I don't care which way you swing. Don't touch her."

"Yes, sir." Jarod lifts his hands in surrender, then turns toward Ana, his grin widening.

He takes one step toward her. Axel steps in front of Ana without a word.

Unlike Xavior, he doesn't grab or snarl. He just *stands there*—solid, unmovable, his stare cold and dangerous.

Jarod chuckles. "Let me guess," he says lightly. "Her mate too... and no hugs?"

"That's right, boy," Axel says coolly. "I won't be as nice as Xavior. He didn't rip out your throat because of her. Me? I'll do it regardless."

"Got it." Jarod doesn't look fazed at all. He grew up around werewolves; he understands the jealousy and possessiveness that come with being mated to an alpha male.

I wish I were used to it too. This is hard. Will I really never be able to hug my male friends? That sucks, especially since most of my friends are male. At least he didn't get offended—neither did Brandon. His reaction matters the most to me.

Jarod clears his throat, his face reddening as he looks past my shoulder. "Is Brandon coming?"

"No... I'm sorry. I didn't invite him." Guilt twists in my chest. "God, I should've. We haven't spent any time together lately."

I don't add that it's Xavior's fault. I told him yesterday I wanted to invite Brandon over. He didn't like that one bit.

"Is he doing okay?" Jarod asks quietly. "Dating anyone new?"

I look away, unsure how to answer.

"Yeah," Xavior cuts in impatiently. "He's fucking some dude. Now, can we order food or what?"

"Xavior!" I smack his chest, forgetting for a moment how big of an asshole he can be. I shoot Jarod an apologetic look. "Why don't you go get our lanes?"

"No."

I close my eyes and groan. Maybe we shouldn't have come here.

Ana and I order snacks, and once that's done, I shrug Xavior's arm off my shoulders and stomp away. He keeps pace with me easily.

"Hey," he says. "Are you mad?"

"Yes," I hiss. "I honestly just want to leave. How could you be so rude? Are you always going to act like this around my friends? You kept me away from them, and now you won't even let me talk to them."

"I'm rude to everyone, Amara," he says bluntly. "I don't care if they're your friends or not—that won't change. But..." His voice softens just slightly. "I am sorry I cut into your conversation and kept you from them. I'll try to work on that."

He steps into my space, cups my face, and just like that, my anger melts away. I know he doesn't apologize often. The fact that he's willing to try means everything.

"Does that mean you'll let Brandon come over?" I ask quietly. "I miss him, Xavior. I know you don't like him, but he and I are close."

"No," he says immediately. Then sighs. "I mean—I'm not a fan of any male around you. But you can invite him over. I won't promise to be nice, but if he keeps his hands to himself, I won't be a complete ass. I don't want to control you. I want you to be happy."

He leans closer. "This possessiveness I have over you is hard to control, and I won't apologize for it."

"As long as you try," I say softly. "I wouldn't ask you to deal with another man around me if there were anything going on. He's just a friend. There's no reason for you to be jealous. I would never let another man touch me. Your touch is all I want."

"I know," he murmurs. "I trust you. It's them I don't trust."

Then his mouth curves into a dangerous grin. "Now show me how to bowl so we can crush them."

He jerks his chin toward Ana and Axel, who are already tying their bowling shoes.

Forty minutes later

My hand smacks my face as I groan. This is horrible.

Xavior throws another gutter ball, and Axel isn't doing much better. They *did* try to cheat, using their shadows to aim the bowling balls, but we shut that down fast.

"This is an awful game," Axel grumbles, glancing between Ana and me. "Why in the seven hells do you enjoy this?"

"Because it's fun," Ana laughs. "You just suck."

Xavior slumps into the chair beside me, arms crossed, jaw tight. I nudge him with my elbow. "What's wrong?"

He exhales slowly, rubbing a hand down his face. "I feel like I'm failing you."

I blink and turn toward him. "You're not. I'm having fun."

"You're the one getting all the points," he mutters. "You're the only reason we're winning."

"So?" I shrug. "It doesn't matter, as long as we win." I lean closer, lowering my voice. "Besides, imagine that big dude riding the mechanical bull."

I can't help smiling as a smirk tugs at his mouth, the tension easing from his shoulders. His eyes darken with amusement, pride slipping back into place. He opens his mouth to say something, but then his phone rings.

Chapter Thirty-eight

Amara

I frown when I check the time. It's nearly eleven. Xavior and Axel had to leave the bowling alley suddenly. Something important must've come up, and it's been hours. Too long. He hasn't answered a single text. A knot tightens in my chest.

I refuse to sleep until I hear from him.

The loud ring shatters the silence, making me jump. My heart slams against my ribs as I answer without checking the caller ID.

"Xavior, is everything okay?"

"Sorry to disappoint," a familiar voice says smoothly. "It's Jaxon."

My frown deepens instantly. I should've looked at the caller ID. "What do you want?" I ask, my tone sharp.

"Look," he says, sounding strained, almost desperate. "I know you found your mate, but I really need to talk to you. My mom is worse. The doctors don't think she's going to make it, and I—" his voice cracks just enough to sound real, "—I could really use someone to talk to."

Guilt flickers, I swallow. "We can talk tomorrow," I say carefully. "You can come over. I'll tell Xavior what's going on and—"

He cuts me off with a low, dark chuckle.

"You really think Xavior would allow you anywhere near me?" he asks. "He knows I have feelings for you. That'll never happen. Just meet me now. Please. I'm already outside, by the pond."

My blood turns cold. "Are you insane?" I hiss. "Coming here this late? What if Xavior were home? You know he meant what he said. He'd kill you without hesitation."

"I knew he wouldn't be home."

The words hit like a slap. My back straightens as a cold shiver crawls up my spine, sinking deep into my bones.

"You need to leave," I say, forcing steel into my voice. "Don't ever think I'll go behind Xavior's back to meet you. I feel horrible about your mom, I really do, but we can talk during the day, when he's home."

The line goes dead.

I pull the phone away from my ear, staring at the dark screen. My pulse pounds violently in my throat. A bad feeling settles in my gut. No... worse than bad. Wrong.

I hesitate only a second before calling Xavior. It goes straight to voice-mail.

"Hey, baby," I whisper, trying and failing to keep the fear out of my voice. "When will you be home? I don't want to worry you, but Jaxon just called. He's here, outside. I'm nervous. Please call me back."

My hands shake as I lower the phone. I leave our room and head toward the front door, checking the lock twice. My gaze drifts up the stairs. Should I wake Ana?

Don't be ridiculous, I tell myself. It's just Jaxon. He won't hurt me.

A soft sound breaks the quiet.

An unmistakable creak of a door opening.

Then slow footsteps.

My breath catches as I see a shadow move along the hallway wall—moving with purpose, heading toward my room on the first floor.

Fear crawls up my throat, choking me. I can't leave— I'm standing by the front door, but Ana isn't. I spin and bolt up the stairs, no longer caring about noise. He already knows I'm here.

I shake Ana awake. "Get up."

She blinks, startled. "What's wrong?"

"Someone's here," I whisper urgently. "Hide. Call Axel."

Her eyes widen. "What about you?"

"Don't worry about me," I say quickly, even though fear coils tight in my chest. "I'm pretty sure it's Jaxon. He called me earlier. I can deal with him, but just in case, I need you to hide."

She nods, scrambling to her feet.

I leave her room and close the door softly behind me. My pulse roars in my ears as I call to my magic, feeling it stir beneath my skin. Please don't let it come to that.

I move quietly down the stairs, pausing halfway to listen.

Nothing. No footsteps. No movement.

Maybe I'm overreacting.

Jaxon's always been headstrong, impulsive, acting before thinking. With his mom's condition worsening, he's probably spiraling.

I'm halfway down when he steps into view.

Jaxon leans against the wall casually, arms crossed, eyes dark and gleaming. His lips curve into a slow, wicked smirk when they land on me.

"God," he murmurs. "You look delicious, baby."

My stomach twists.

"What are you doing?" I demand, forcing my voice to stay steady. "You're not thinking straight. You need to leave. Axel and Xavior will be home any minute."

I descend one step at a time slowly and deliberately—like approaching a cornered animal.

"We'll be out of here before they show," Jaxon says lightly. "Although it's sweet that you're worried about me."

The front door bursts open with a deafening bang. My eyes widen as three men step inside. I don't recognize any of them, but the way they fan out makes my stomach drop.

"These are friends of mine from the city," Jaxon says casually. "I called them to assist me."

"Assist you with what?" My voice trembles despite my effort to keep it steady. "What is it you want from me, Jaxon?"

He tilts his head, his gaze dragging slowly down my body. "You're mine. You always have been. I only broke up with you to have some fun before asking for your hand in marriage. I had someone keeping an eye on you." His lips curl. "I was proud that you never moved on, but when I heard you were seeing him..."

His calm snaps, his face twisting into a snarl. "I came back thinking this would be easy, that you'd choose me. After everything we've been through." His expression softens unnervingly. "Don't worry, baby. I'm not mad at you. I know the mate bond makes it hard."

"Jaxon, don't," I whisper, shaking my head as I step back. "Please."

He clicks his tongue. "The mate bond is all in your head. You don't really want him. Remember what you used to say about what a prick he was?" His eyes flick to the men behind him. "Alright, boys. We're running out of time. Grab her."

I turn and run.

Ana is at the top of the stairs, her back pressed against the wall, knees pulled to her chest as she rocks, tears flowing down her face.

Warm fingers curl around my ankle and yank.

I go down hard—my face slamming into the edge of the step. Pain explodes behind my eye, my vision blurring as blood floods my mouth. I groan, clenching at the stairs as the world tilts.

I twist, kicking blindly. My heel connects with a man's face. He stumbles back, crashing into the other two and taking them down with him.

"Fuck," Jaxon snarls. "Do I have to do everything?"

I scramble, trying to crawl upward, but my body slams into the wall. Stars burst behind my eyes.

"Amara!" Ana screams.

I hit the stairs again, tumbling down them.

"Why are you making this so fucking hard?" Jaxon yanks my hair, forcing my head back. "Get up."

Pain rips through my scalp as he drags me to my feet.

"Please," I choke. "You're hurting me."

"I don't want to hurt you," he murmurs, smoothing my hair before pressing a kiss to it. "If you listen, I won't have to. I love you—but we need to leave." His grip tightens. "Now walk."

He shoves me toward the door.

I spin, swinging my right arm as I scream, "Lactus!"

Four bodies fly backward.

"Ana, now!" I shout. "Congelo!"

I repeat the word over and over, palms out, forcing my magic to pin them to the wall. Ana bolts down the stairs, but I can feel myself weakening—I can't hold all of them.

Jaxon starts to move. One of the others follows.

"We can't let her go," the man snarls. "The boss will be pissed."

"Not just him," Jaxon growls through clenched teeth, fighting against my magic. "You'll answer to both of us."

His cold eyes lock onto mine, and he smirks.

My throat tightens. I don't think I'll get away, but I have to get Ana out.

She grabs my hand and drags me toward the door. I stumble after her, my magic straining as the other two begin to shift. The further I get, the weaker my hold on them gets.

"Congelo!" I scream again, forcing it—forcing *everything*.

I cry out in relief when they freeze, but barely.

Ana jumps into the driver's seat and turns the key. The engine roars to life.

I'm almost there, but then a body slams into me.

I blink up into a familiar face.

No. No, *no*... he wouldn't...

"Brandon?" I whisper.

His eyes fill with regret.

Then his fist crashes into my face, and everything goes dark.

I blink a few times with a groan. Every inch of my body aches, like I've been hit by a train—especially the side of my face. I lift a hand to my left cheek and moan when sharp pain flares beneath my fingers.

What in the world...?

I force myself upright, blinking against the dizziness. Where am I?

The answer hits me as my nose wrinkles. A dirty basement. A musty, damp smell hangs heavy in the air. Somewhere in the corner, water drips steadily, each sound echoing and making the pounding in my head worse.

Drip.

Drip.

Drip.

I realize I'm lying on a clean mattress, a soft blanket tangled around my legs. The contrast feels wrong—too deliberate.

My breath catches as everything comes rushing back.

Jaxon is breaking into the house. The men. The stairs.

Oh, God... Ana.

I sit up fully, panic clawing at my chest as I scan the room. She's not here. Relief crashes through me so hard it nearly knocks me over. If she were here, I'd hear her. I'd feel it.

Brandon...

The thought burns. How could he? Was he the one watching me for Jaxon all this time?

I push myself to my feet and stumble away from the mattress. The room spins violently. I pause, clutching my head like it might keep the world from tilting apart.

The concrete floor is coated in a thin layer of mud, damp beneath my bare feet. This place looks abandoned—forgotten. The walls are cracked and stained, the small windows busted with bars on the outside. Thick cobwebs cling to the corners. One of them holds a spider far too large for comfort.

I shiver. I hate spiders—but they're the least of my problems.

My gaze drifts to the stairs. I'm not sure how they're still standing. Several of the wooden steps are partially broken, some missing chunks entirely. They lead up to a dirty white door.

I place my foot on the first step. It creaks loudly but holds.

I test the next—

The door slams open.

I jump back, curling my arms around my midsection. I won't lie—I'm terrified. Will I ever see Xavior again? Will he find me before it's too late? Will he be okay without me? Will he move on?

What is Jaxon planning?

Why is he doing this?

Tears flood my eyes when they meet Brandon's. I was praying it wasn't really him, but it is. He's here. I stumble backward, and a sob breaks free from my chest.

"You're awake." He steps down onto the first step, closing the door behind him. "How are you feeling? I brought you some food. I know it's not much."

He lifts his hands, and I see a bottle of water and a sandwich sealed inside a Ziploc bag.

"I know you probably have a ton of questions, but—" He stops short when he notices that every step he takes toward me, I mirror, retreating farther away. His brows knit together. "I…" He licks his lips. "I won't hurt you. Please. I'm sorry, but I owe him. He saved my life. I never thought it would come to this." His voice softens. "He loves you."

"No, he doesn't." My voice cracks. "Please, Brandon. If you ever cared about me. Let me go."

"I can't." His jaw tightens. "I do care about you. That's why I'm doing this. Xavior is a monster." He shakes his head like he's convincing himself. "It was only supposed to be fun. He's hot—I get it—and if I'd known it would turn into this, I never would've encouraged you to flirt with him. I just wanted you to have a little fun before you were tied down."

My stomach twists.

"But you belong to Jaxon," he continues quickly. "He'll take care of you. He'll love you." His voice drops. "I'm sorry I hit you. I was in the truck, waiting. I wasn't allowed to go inside. But when I saw you had the upper hand, I had to help him." His eyes flick away. "He doesn't trust me anymore—not after I encouraged your relationship—so I had to prove myself."

I shake my head slowly. "Our entire friendship was a lie. I'll never trust you. Leave me alone."

"No." His voice is firm now. "It was never a lie. I watched you for him, yes, but I could've done that from a distance. I wanted to be your friend." He steps closer again. "Did I tell Jaxon everything? No. Only what was necessary. The only time I truly betrayed you was when I realized your feelings for Xavior were growing. That's when I called him. That's when I told him to come back."

"I have a mate," I shout. "I don't want Jaxon. Why can't you understand that?"

"I do understand!" His voice rises, frustration bleeding through. "But you're not safe with him. He's dangerous. He's a monster." His eyes search mine desperately. "You can't tell me you truly care for him."

"I can," I snap, tears spilling over. "Because I do. He'll come for me, and when he does, you're all dead." My chest heaves. "He may be dangerous. He may be a monster. But he's *my* monster."

Chapter Thirty-nine

Xavior

"**S**hit, that was fun," I chuckle, sinking into the passenger seat.

"Hell yeah, it was, but I'm ready to go home and be with my mate," Axel says as he starts the car.

I grin, Amara's face flashing through my mind. She's probably fallen asleep waiting for me. The thought twists something warm and sharp in my chest.

"For the first time, I agree with you." I lean my head back against the seat. "Let's go home, brother."

"We're lucky sons-of-a-guns," Axel adds. "Our mates are gorgeous—and they forgave us even though we're crazy fuckers."

"Damn straight."

"Shit." Axel's gaze drops to his phone, his expression shifting. "Ana called a shit ton. I gotta call her back."

"Put it on speaker."

The moment the call connects, Ana's voice breaks through, frantic and panicked.

"Axel—Axel—" she sobs.

"Babe, slow down," he says quickly. "I can't understand you."

"Someone came into the house..." Her breathing stutters. "Amara—she's—" Her voice cracks, and she trails off.

My heart slams violently against my ribs.

"Where is she?" I demand, dread flooding my chest like ice water.

"I—I don't know!" Ana cries. "They took her. She fought them, she really did, and I just—I hid. I panicked. I couldn't move. I didn't even help her—I'm sorry!"

Each word hits me like a fist, slow and brutal. Took her. Hid. Didn't help. My chest tightens until it hurts to breathe. Shadows creep at the edges of my vision, crawling under my skin, thrumming with a hunger I can't contain. I can hear Axel talking, trying to calm her, but his voice sounds distant, muffled, like I'm underwater.

My hands shake as I grab my phone, seeing the missed calls. From Amara. One voicemail blinks at me. I play it, and her fear-filled voice rips into my ears. She needed me. She called for me. And I wasn't there.

We pull into the driveway hard and fast. Ana is leaning against my car, crying hysterically. I don't look at her. I can't.

My gaze locks on the front door, which is splintered and broken. And the blood on the ground beside the car burns my vision.

Something savage unfurls inside me. "Tell me everything," I snarl, my voice rough, my shadows writhing beneath my skin, hungry for blood.

We want blood.

I will do whatever it takes to get her back. There will be no mercy. No restraint. If I have to burn this entire town to the ground—every single soul—I will.

They will all turn to ash.

I throw my head back, arms spreading wide, and my shadows erupt in a violent surge, tearing free of me. The air shudders, the night itself trembling, as I release a roar that splits the world.

They took my mate. And the world will bleed for it.

Hours later...

Zane, Axel, and I cut through the woods in silence. They keep their distance. They have to.

My shadows lash around me in a wild ten-foot barrier, snapping and curling with a mind of their own. Snow melts beneath my boots, grass blackens and dies, and everything living in our path withers as we pass. I don't rein them in. I can't.

Axel steals glances at me when he thinks I won't notice, then quickly drops his gaze to the ground. He's worried. He should be.

"What's the plan to get your girl back?" Zane asks, breaking the heavy silence.

I don't slow. "No plan," I answer coldly. "I kill anyone who stands in the way."

Axel lets out a short chuckle. "Now that, I can do." Then his humor fades. "What about the boy—Brian?"

"Brandon," I growl, my teeth grinding together as my shadows spike violently.

"Right. Brandon," Axel says carefully. "Ana saw him take her. He'll be there. He's her best friend. What do we do with him?"

"I want to kill him," I admit without hesitation. "But Amara should decide."

Zane nods. "I agree. He betrayed her, but she cared about him. Killing him might hurt her more than help."

"If he becomes a problem," I say, voice lethal, "kill him. I'll ask for forgiveness later." I inhale sharply. "How much longer?"

"Her scent's getting stronger," Zane says. "We're close."

We stop abruptly. Something lies ahead in the snow.

Red stains bloom violently against the white. My heart slams as I recognize the fabric. I drop to one knee and grab the shirt, my hands shaking as rage floods my veins. I rip it in half with a roar that splits the forest.

A distraction.

Someone planted this.

Where is she?

Zane doesn't hesitate. He strips out of his clothes and shifts mid-motion, bones cracking as his wolf explodes free. I press my face into the torn fabric, breathing her in—her fear, her scent, *her*.

"I'm coming for you, baby," I vow.

Zane growls once before tearing off through the trees.

"I'm guessing that means he found something?" Axel mutters.

I don't answer. I launch forward, shadows screaming as I follow.

Chapter Forty

Amara

The sun disappears, my eyes are heavy, but I refuse to close them. I hate that I didn't ease my worry and asking Brandon if they have Ana. It's been a full day, and Xavior hasn't come for me. I know he's looking for me. I just hope he's okay.

The door slowly creaks open, and I roll to my side. Closing my eyes, pretending to be asleep, hoping it'll give me an advantage—or that whoever it is will leave.

The stairs creak under the weight of someone walking down. My hands squeeze the blanket, holding it closer to my chest. The closer they get, the more fear grows. My heart pounds violently, my hands shake, and a cold sweat covers me. Someone leans onto the mattress so close I can feel their body heat. Please, God, send whoever it is away.

"Oh, sweet, sweet, Amara. I know you're awake. You're shaking like a leaf in the wind. I truly forgot how beautiful you were while I was away." Jaxon's lips graze my neck.

I scream and start pulling away, but he flips me on my back and shoves something into my mouth, then forces my head up, tying it around my head.

"Fuck, you look so sexy with that gag. It's for my protection, so you can't use your magic on me. Your brain hasn't caught up to what your body wants," he sneers, his eyes dark and predatory.

I twist, trying to get him off me. My hands grab his face, and I dig my nails into his flesh.

He screams, "Bitch!" and punches me across the face, again and again.

I lose count. I cry, begging him to stop. The pain is unbearable. My eyes slowly close, breathing ragged, my chest heaving.

The darkness starts swelling when he grabs my jaw and shakes me. "Uh-uh, no sleeping for you. Why did you make me hurt you?" He brushes my hair out of my face and kisses the bruised area. The pain from his lips makes me whimper.

"Shh, I'm sorry, don't cry. I love you. I'll make you feel good, I promise. Remind you how perfect we are," he mutters, almost tenderly.

He pulls back and grabs my wrists, tying them together with ropes. Then he starts taking off his belt.

I shake my head, trying to use my legs to push away, but they're pinned beneath his.

"Don't act like you don't want me," he hisses. "You want a monster? I can be a monster." He punches my ribs. The pain steals the air from my lungs. It's unbearable. "You like that?" I shake my head; a small whimper slips out. "No? The more you fight, the more I hit you."

"How do you want it, babe? Fast and hard or soft and slow? I bet that monster is always rough with you. I'll be gentle, I promise." He slides his pants down.

He leans over me, hand gripping my throat, taking my air away. My lungs burn, and my eyes water. He smirks. "God, look at you, so pretty when you cry."

Then, suddenly, the door bursts open. "Get off her, Jaxon!" I hear Brandon's voice, distant but furious. I can't see anything. It's too dark... no, my eyes are closed. "Jaxon! What did you do?"

"No, get the fuck out, Brandon," Jaxon snaps.

"You think I'll let you force yourself on her? You said you'd take it slow! I would never have helped you if I knew this was what you were planning. God, is she dead?"

"No, she still has a pulse. We were just having fun with some breath play. Now get out."

The weight lifts from my body. I hear grunts, growls, and the sound of fighting. I want to open my eyes, but they're too heavy, pain fading slowly. Maybe I should sleep. I'm exhausted, trembling, and cold.

Someone grabs my arms, shaking me. "Please, Amara. I'm so sorry. This wasn't supposed to happen. Wake up! I'm calling him now."

There's a pause. "Ana? Oh, God. Ana, I messed up. Is he there?" Another pause. "Xavior, there's no time for threats. She's hurt. Oh, God. I don't know what to do, she's not opening her eyes! I'm sorry, I'm so sorry."

"Yes, there's a pulse, but it's weak," he whispers.

Finally, everything goes quiet. I feel like I'm floating. Peace. Yes, this is what I need, some peace.

Chapter Forty-one

Xavior

I tilt my head to the side, staring at the three men bound on the floor in front of me. They don't matter enough for me to remember their names. Zane, Axel, and I made quick work of them, too quick. Pathetic, really. None of them fought like men who believed they'd live through the night.

My gaze drifts to the basement door.

She's down there.

I hate that I haven't gone yet. Hate that every second I've spent up here has felt like my chest is being crushed from the inside. But I couldn't give them the chance to run. Couldn't risk one of them escaping while she needs me. I won't hurt them now—not yet. She needs me whole and focused.

She needs me.

Ana's sobs echo faintly from below, slicing through me.

"You shouldn't go down there," Zane says firmly, stepping in front of the basement door. His eyes flick toward me, cautious and afraid. "It's not a good idea."

"Don't make me hurt you," I growl.

I don't raise my voice. I don't need to. The promise is there—heavy, absolute. I will hurt anyone who stands between me and her.

Axel grabs Zane by the elbow and yanks him aside. "Move."

I don't hesitate. I take the stairs two at a time. The smell hits me first.

Blood. Fear. Her.

My shadows stir beneath my skin, agitated, furious, clawing for release. My eyes lock onto Jaxon's unconscious body slumped against the wall, and a snarl tears from my throat. Not now, later. He'll wake up just long enough to understand what he's done.

Brandon is kneeling on the floor, crying like the coward he is, rocking beside a thin mattress in the center of the basement. Ana's back is to me. She's hunched over something—someone—and my heart lurches violently in my chest.

Amara.

She's so still.

The healers warned us not to move her. Alexander is already on his way with more, but fuck... he's taking too long.

I force myself to move slowly, afraid that if I rush, I'll break something that can't be fixed.

My eyes take her in piece by piece.

Bare feet, bruised thighs. My vision blurs red when I see her underwear exposed, the hem of my shirt shoved up her body. I close my eyes hard, dragging in a breath I don't feel. I don't want to see this. I don't want to know what he did to her. Not yet. I feel tears burning in the back of my eyes.

When I open them again, my gaze moves further up. Bruises bloom across her ribs, angry and dark. My breath leaves me in a sharp, broken sound.

Then I see her face.

I cry out.

Her face is swollen, split. Almost unrecognizable. The woman who owns my soul reduced to this—broken because I wasn't there.

Ana turns at the sound of me. Her eyes are red, face streaked with tears. "Xavior," she whispers. "Come. She'll want you here with her."

I cross the room in three steps and drop to my knees beside her. As gently as I can, I lift Amara's head and rest it on my lap. She's so light it terrifies me, like she's already halfway gone.

"I'm so sorry. I didn't think he would do this. He said he loves her," Brandon declares. I ignore him. I don't care what he has to say, or about anything else.

I grip her closer and don't try to stop the tears.

I've never cried. Not when my mother left. Not when my father's fists taught me what pain was. Not when I buried the pieces of myself that I couldn't afford to feel.

But this?

This breaks me.

"I'm sorry," I whisper, my voice cracking. "I'm so sorry I wasn't there when you needed me."

I listen to her breathing—counting, tracking every shallow rise and fall of her chest. My fingers find her wrist, pressing gently until I feel it. A pulse, weak. Still there.

My shadows surge free.

They spill across the floor like living snakes, climbing the walls, curling inward around us. Thick, alive, and protective. They seal us off from the world, pressing close until no light seeps through.

No one can see in our little cocoon.

It's just her and me.

"I'll make them pay," I murmur against her hair. "I'll burn this world down if I have to. Do anything you want. Just don't leave me. Please... I can't live without you."

I feel them hovering at the edge of my barrier. Axel's presence prickles at my senses.

"Xavior," he says carefully. "The healers are here. You need to drop your shadows so they can help her."

He's too close.

I push the cocoon wider, forcing him back. He hisses in pain. "Fuck... that hurt."

Good.

"Xavior, please," one of the healers says, her voice strained. "She's not doing well. I can hear her pulse; it's weak. Let us help her." I growl at her. "I'll make you a deal: you can hold her while we work."

"Please, son." Alexander's voice cuts through, steady but heavy. "Your mate is dying."

The word hits like a blade. I look down at Amara. Her pulse is growing weaker, and her breathing turns shallow.

"I promise," he says softly, "no one will hurt her."

Slowly, and reluctantly. I draw my shadows back.

The healers rush in, murmuring urgently as magic fills the room. I don't hear their words. I don't care. My world has narrowed to the woman in my arms.

"She's bleeding internally," one says. "We need more power. We'll keep working while you carry her out. We have to move, now."

"Yeah," I nod, already rising with her held tight against my chest.

Zane steps closer. "We'll stay here. What do you want us to do?"

I don't look at him. "Kill them. Make it painful. I won't leave her side for them."

I pace the room, back and forth, back and forth, the motion the only thing keeping me from tearing the walls apart. I need her to wake up. I need to see those beautiful green eyes, that smile that lights something inside me I didn't know existed until her. It's been a full day, too long, and I can't take the waiting anymore.

Why isn't she waking up?

They healed her, but the damage was extensive. Even the healers didn't know if she would make it. A broken rib punctured her lung. Swelling in her brain. They worked on her for hours, switching out when their magic drained, forcing their power into her body until the wounds finally closed.

And still... she doesn't wake.

Thankfully, he didn't get far in his assault.

If Brandon hadn't stopped him, it would've been worse. That truth turns my stomach, rage and sickness twisting together until I have to clench my fists just to breathe through it.

I've refused to let anyone enter this room except the healers. No one else touches her. No one else breathes the same air unless I allow it. Ana and Alexander are furious about it, but I don't care. Their anger means nothing compared to the terror of losing her.

"Xavior." Axel's voice booms from the other side of the door.

"What?" I snap, dragging my hands through my hair for what feels like the hundredth time today.

"It's important, brother. This can't wait. Put your possessiveness aside. I'm coming in." The door opens before I can stop him.

Ana steps inside cautiously, her face streaked with tears. The moment she sees Amara, she breaks, a sob ripping from her chest. "I won't let you hurt my mate any longer," Axel says firmly, nudging her forward. "I gave you enough time. Go ahead, sweetness."

"This is what was so important?" I spit, fury flaring hot and sharp in my chest.

Ana reaches for Amara's hand.

"Don't touch her," I growl.

"I won't hurt her," Ana whispers, her voice small and trembling. "Please… just let me hold her hand. I won't touch anywhere else. I swear."

I stare at her for a long moment, weighing the risk, the instinct to bare my teeth and shove her away, battling with the truth staring back at me. My gaze drops to where her fingers are already intertwined with Amara's.

This is what she would want.

I give a short nod.

Ana exhales shakily, like she's been holding her breath the entire time, her shoulders sagging in relief as she gently tightens her grip on Amara's hand.

"No," Axel says quietly, breaking the moment. "This isn't the important thing. Although… we should talk. In private."

"I'm not leaving her," I say flatly, sinking back into the small chair I slept in, my eyes never leaving Amara's face.

"Alright," he relents. "Then listen. We finally got information out of Jaxon."

My head snaps up. "Information? What do you mean? I told you to kill him."

"You did," Axel says, smirking as he drops into the empty chair across from me. "We just didn't listen."

"Obviously," I grumble.

"Something didn't add up," he continues, growing serious. "How did Jaxon manage to get that much manpower? His background is clean. No criminal ties, no underworld connections. So why would three high-class criminals—men who had never worked together—suddenly help him?"

He pauses, watching my face carefully. "When Brandon said he'd never met or even heard of those men before, we started digging. Old records. Old favors."

I lean forward, elbows braced on my knees. "Go on."

Axel exhales. "This isn't going to be easy to hear, so don't go full killer on me."

My jaw tightens.

"Those men were paid by our father."

The words hit like a blade to the gut.

"Father found out Jaxon was stalking Amara," Axel continues. "Learned about his obsession. And instead of stopping it, he used it. They came up with a plan to get Amara away from you. He hired those men and created a distraction to pull you out of the house."

"But why?" I snarl. "Why would he do that? It doesn't make sense. Why does he care who I'm with?"

"We asked the same thing." Axel hesitates, then says quietly, "Jaxon told us Father said he was getting pissed that Amara was taking you away from work. That he needed your head back in the game."

My vision darkens.

"His words," Axel adds grimly. "'Get rid of the distraction.'"

The distraction...Amara.

A growl rips from my chest, low and feral. I always knew my father was cruel, controlling, and obsessed with power. But this? Using my mate as leverage? Trying to rip her from me like she's expendable? Does power really matter that much to him?

I rise abruptly.

"Ana," I say, my voice deadly calm as I turn back to her. "Do not leave her side. Not for a second. Call me the moment she wakes."

She nods immediately, tears shining in her eyes. "I won't. I swear."

I lean down and press a gentle kiss to Amara's cheek, my voice breaking despite myself. "I'll be back, my love."

Axel follows me into the hall. "What's the plan? You can't just kill him. The council will get involved. He's under too much protection."

I don't slow my stride.

"Accidents happen all the time."

The lights flicker on in my father's office as he steps into the room. His brows come together, and he frowns as he stares at me.

"Son, what are you doing here? Alone in the dark? Has something happened?"

He fakes concern. He doesn't know we killed his goons; he sent a few messages not long ago asking if the mission was completed.

"Yes, my mate, she left."

"See? I'm sorry to tell you I was right, but you should have known not to trust a woman. After all, your own mother left. I am dearly sorry either way. I tried saving you from this heartbreak; it's the same I had to deal with."

"It's not the same. Mother was not your mate."

At last, he moves away from me and goes to sit behind his large wooden desk. He lifts his hand with one small wave, dismissing me.

"Heartbreak is all the same, mate or not."

"I'm sure you're happy. You'll have me once more underneath your thumb. Doing whatever you ask of me."

He chuckles darkly. "I won't lie, I am quite happy about it."

"I wonder, father."

I pause, stand up, place my hands flat on the desk, and lean forward.

"How will you call me without a voice?"

"What do you mean? I—"

He is cut off when my brother lifts his shadows, the ones hiding him and Alexander in the dark corner behind the desk.

"Axel? Alexander? What is—"

"Hello, dear old friend," Alexander says. "You shouldn't have come after my daughter."

My father stands, releasing his shadows, understanding he's in danger.

My shadows clash with his, stopping them before they hurt Alexander, who begins to mumble a spell far too fast for me to understand. The spell throws my father back into his chair, keeping him locked in place.

I round the corner, never looking away from my father's horrified eyes—eyes that look so much like mine.

"How dare you hurt my mate. You thought I wouldn't find out? You thought I'd go back to answering every demand you sent my way? No. I would've been too busy searching the ends of the earth for her. You love my power so much, why don't I show you how it feels to be on the receiving end of it?"

"No, son! Don't—please! I'm sorry!"

"You're sorry?" I scream. "Sorry, sorry! Of course, you're sorry!"

I laugh, the sound dark and cruel.

"Where was this 'sorry' when you hit me? Beat me into submission? Or when you used to beat Mother in front of me? Or how about abandoning your own flesh and blood because his mother was too weak?"

I am seething, my body shaking. My shadows grow stronger, surrounding me. Papers on the desk fly, photos on the walls fall, lamps crash to the ground.

"Axel, now," I growl.

He steps forward, grips my father's jaw in one hand, grabs his hair with the other, and yanks until his head is tilted back.

Axel smirks down at him.

"Do you regret ever mistaking me for weak? I have more power than you ever had. I am extremely happy I can be a part of your falling."

Axel looks at me and nods.

I allow my shadows to enter my father's body. The task?

To make him weak—no voice, no control of his body. He'll be paralyzed, never being able to speak another demand. He won't even be able to chew his food. He'll be a vegetable.

I'll only leave him like this for a little while before coming back and finishing the job. Maybe even find my mother so she can come and give him a piece of her mind, since she'll stop hiding, no longer having to fear him.

A cruel grin lights my face as I watch his body begin to spasm.

We write symbols on the office wall, making it look like Axel's witch-hunting group was responsible for this.

We leave my father sitting in his chair. No one will find him until someone comes looking for him. He can no longer use his power to control anyone or hurt another innocent person.

I hate that I did his dirty work, but I was always afraid he would push me aside like he did Axel. I always craved being accepted and loved by someone. I never knew it until I met Amara.

I call Ana to make sure she hasn't left. I know she would never hurt her, but damn, I hate not being there—having someone else touching her, comforting my mate. That's my job, no one else's.

I enter the room with a cruel smirk still on my face. Jaxon's gag muffles his screams. His body thrusts, trying to break free of his restraints. The fear bleeding into his eyes makes my smile widen.

"Don't be so scared, Jax." I pause. "I can call you Jax, right? Anywho, don't be so scared. I'm not going to kill you. Yet."

I step closer. "I need to relieve some tension." I stop in front of him, removing his gag. "You don't mind being my punching bag, right?"

"You're fucking crazy!" He spits on my shoes. "You don't deserve her. She'll realize she's too good for you, and she'll leave. She already thinks you're a monster. But don't worry—when she leaves you, it'll drive you mad like it did to me."

He laughs, unhinged.

"I understand your obsession with her. When I realized how much I craved her touch, it was too late. That's what she does best... makes you drown in madness until you're a crazy psychopath needing another hit like a drug addict."

His eyes gleam.

"Instead of drugs, it's for her soft touch, those amazing tits, full lips, and fuck that ass, mmm—and best of all, that sweet, sweet, tight pussy."

"Don't talk about her," I growl.

I unleash my fury, using my hands instead of my shadows. Would it be easier to use them? Yes. But my fists can cause just as much pain and damage, and I get to relieve this pent-up tension.

She already thinks that you're a monster.

The words repeat over and over again. Is that true? I know a lot of people do, but I never cared what they thought.

I had to bring in a healer three times, pulling him back from the reaper's front door.

Chapter Forty-two

Amara

My eyes flutter open, and fear slams into me. Is he waiting for me? Is he going to hit me again? Did—God—did he touch me?

Bile rises at the thought, burning my throat. I start coughing, my eyes watering as I roll onto my side and throw up.

"Amara…" a throaty voice says behind me.

I squeeze my eyes shut. My mind is playing tricks on me again. He's not really here. Tears blur my vision as I cry out, clutching my chest. I'd give anything to see those gray eyes again, to see that rare smile, to kiss those full lips.

"Tonya!" the voice shouts.

A door opens a second later. "She's awake, but she's throwing up, shaking, and crying. What's wrong with her?"

"She could be in shock. She's been through a lot of trauma." A woman in a white dress steps into my line of sight, though she's blurry through my tears. "Amara, sweetie. I'm Tonya, one of the healers who's been keeping an eye on you."

"Heal—" I clear my throat. It feels raw. Why would Jaxon call a healer when he wanted me in pain?

"Yes, your healer," she says gently. "Here, drink some water. You've been in a coma for four days, so your throat is raw from not having any liquids."

I blink a few times before grabbing the glass and drinking all of it.

"I'll be right back," she says softly. "Let me grab a few things."

Panic explodes in my chest. If she leaves me—

"No, please!" I cry out. "He'll hurt me again. Don't leave me."

My body starts trembling uncontrollably. Strong arms grab me, and I thrash against their hold, screaming for help. "Please! Help me! Don't touch me!"

The arms twist my body, hands gripping my face. I gasp when I finally see who's holding me.

"Xavior?"

"I'm here, baby. I'm here." His voice breaks. "He won't ever touch you again. I swear on my life. You're safe."

His gray eyes are filled with tears. I lift my hands, cupping his cheeks, and I feel the sparks of our bond come alive.

"Xavior," I sob. "He took me, he—"

I lean closer, needing him, and he pulls me against his chest, wrapping me tightly in his arms.

"I know, baby. I know."

He rocks us together, his grip almost too tight, like he's afraid I'll disappear—but I don't mind. I need it just as much.

"Xavior?" I whisper once the sobs finally ease.

"Yes, my love?" He pulls back to look at me, and my heart throbs when I see the tears running down his cheeks.

"Take me home."

His eyes soften, and he nods. "I will, I promise. I own a secluded cabin. I think it'll be nice for you and me to get away for a little while. How does that sound?"

"A peaceful cabin... just you and me?" I manage a small smile. "That sounds amazing."

A few hours later, I'm finally released. Ana and Xavior are making a fuss. They won't even let me pee alone, even though my legs work perfectly fine. They walk me into my childhood home since I can't bear to go back to that house.

We haven't told anyone that we're leaving. It's only a few hours' drive to the cabin, but I know they'll be upset. I am too. I'll miss them, but we need this. I also learned that Zane's wolf pack lives on the property beside the cabin, so we'll be seeing a lot of each other.

"Sit. I'm going to make you food." Xavior guides me to the couch before disappearing into the kitchen.

I turn around and place my chin on the back cushion so I can watch him. He keeps glancing over like he thinks I'll flee. My heart swells seeing this side of him. I love how caring and sweet he's being. I also hate it—no, maybe hate is too strong of a word.

Physically, I'm not hurting. The healers did a great job. They told me to relax and be careful, but they also said I could return to normal, non-strenuous activities.

Mentally, though, I'm struggling.

I won't lie—if Xavior were to leave my sight for more than a few minutes, I might panic. He's keeping the demons at bay. They slowly creep in whenever he leaves me. I'm never alone, at least not without either Ana or Zane nearby, but it doesn't matter. As soon as Xavior leaves my line of sight, anxiety grips me, like the boogeyman is waiting to jump out at any moment.

He left to take a shower, and after fifteen minutes, I started having a panic attack. Thank God no one noticed, because he came back before it turned into a full-blown one. I didn't tell him. I didn't know how. I didn't want him to feel forced to stay beside me at all times, because I knew if I told him, he wouldn't leave.

I take a deep breath and stand, walking toward the kitchen just as he turns to place whatever he made into the oven. I keep my eyes on him, watching his reaction when he glances toward the couch.

His brows pinch together.

He spins around.

Guilt washes over me when panic flashes in his eyes as they land on me.

"What are you doing?" he asks, his eyes hardening as he stares at me, clearly angry that I moved without help.

I chew on my lower lip. "I want to go outside. I need some fresh air."

"Go back to the couch. I'll open the window."

"Xavior, please." I bat my lashes at him. "I won't step off the deck, and I'll leave the door open."

His expression softens. "How about this? Sit on the couch, and when the food is done—in about fifteen minutes—we'll sit outside and eat."

"Okay." I smile.

We haven't kissed since I woke up, and I'm in dire need of one. "What about a kiss?"

He grins, those dimples I love so much making an appearance. He walks over, cups my face in both hands, tilts my head, and kisses me—sweet and slow, like he's savoring it. He guides me back to the couch without breaking the kiss, and we fall into it together.

A groan slips from me, but he immediately pulls back.

"Shit, did I hurt you?" He leans away, scanning my body like he's searching for damage.

"No." I grab the collar of his shirt and tug him back down, pressing my lips to his again, but he pulls away before I can argue. The look in his eyes stops me cold.

"Do you see me as a monster?"

His jaw clenches. His body goes rigid as he looks away, like he's bracing himself for the answer he already thinks he knows.

I reach up, grab his face, and force him to look at me. "No, I don't. But even if you were a monster, I wouldn't care. Because you're mine—my monster, my knight, my mate, my everything. I'll never stop loving you."

A low growl rumbles out of him, thick with pleasure, and he crashes his lips to mine. I grab the hem of his shirt and start pulling it up.

He jumps back like I've burned him.

I frown, pushing myself up on my elbows. "What was that?" I can't keep the hurt out of my voice.

"I can't. We can't." He turns abruptly and marches toward the kitchen just as the alarm goes off, signaling the food is done.

"What do you mean, we can't?" I follow him and watch as he opens the oven. He made us a homemade pizza. He doesn't look at me.

That pisses me off.

I grab his arm and force him to turn around.

"I don't feel comfortable doing that after everything you've been through!" he shouts. "Can you not make it so damn hard on me?"

I flinch.

He turns away and starts cutting the pizza like nothing had happened.

I take a step back and nod. "Okay." My chest caves in.

I try to remind myself that he's been through hell too—that it wasn't just me who was affected—but fuck, it hurts. I understand why he doesn't want to. I really do. That doesn't make him snapping at me hurt any less. And it doesn't make me feel wanted.

I blink back the tears threatening to fall. "I'm actually not feeling so good. I'm going to lie down."

I see the pizza cutter slip from his hand. His shoulders sag as his head hangs low.

I leave the kitchen and am almost at the stairs when he finally calls out, "Amara, I'm sorry. I didn't mean to snap."

I don't respond. He follows me anyway.

I stop before shutting my bedroom door and don't bother turning to face him. "I want to be alone. Sorry for making this so hard on you."

"That's not what I—"

I slam the door in his face.

Chapter Forty-three

Amara

It's been an hour, and I've been sitting on the window seat with the window open the entire time. I'm starving, but I refuse to go downstairs. It feels just like before we got into a relationship—me hiding in my room, avoiding the dark prince I find extremely attractive.

My door slams open.

I jump, nearly off the seat, the walls practically vibrating from the impact. Xavior stands in the doorway; his grey eyes already locked on me. "I think it's time we stop this temper tantrum."

"You could've knocked, you know. I could've been changing or something." I cross my arms over my chest and turn back toward the window.

"Yeah, because it matters if I see you change." His voice is dry. "I've seen all of you, and it's all very much mine. And I *did* knock. A few times, actually."

"Oh, now I'm yours," I snap, "but downstairs you refused to touch me. You didn't want me."

His expression shifts instantly. He crosses the room in two strides and cups my face, forcing me to look at him.

"Is that what you think? That I don't want you?" His voice drops. "Jesus, Amara. I always want you. Fuck—my dick is constantly hard for you. I'm so used to it already."

Heat floods my face.

"I don't want to hurt you," he continues, his tone turning raw. "I read that women who go through an assault, like you did, sometimes have flashbacks. The healers told me to give you time before we did anything. I'm sorry for snapping. I was tiptoeing on a very thin line—trying not to lose control and take you anyway, regardless of what the internet and the healers said. That's not an excuse, and I'm sorry. I never want you to feel unwanted, because fuck... it's the exact opposite."

"You searched the internet?" I ask softly.

"Yes." His thumb brushes my cheek. "I didn't want to do or say anything wrong that would cause you distress. It's all I've read for days. Don't you understand by now that you're my entire world?"

Guilt crashes into me.

God, I feel stupid. Childish.

I lean forward, resting my head against his chest, smiling faintly as his heartbeat thunders beneath my ear. It's my favorite sound. He walks us backward until the backs of his knees hit the bed, then sits. I crawl into his lap without hesitation.

He places a small black velvety box in my hands.

My brows knit together as I lean back, confused. I watch him swallow, his eyes flicking between my face and the box.

"I'm not good at things like this," he says tentatively, "but I'm hoping you'll want to fully seal our bond—and be completely mine."

His fingers tremble slightly as he opens the box.

I gasp.

The ring is stunning. A large diamond sits at the center, shadows moving inside it like they're alive. The band is encrusted with smaller diamonds, dark and brilliant all at once.

"Is that—?"

"Yes." His voice softens. "Your father helped me. We sealed a small portion of my shadows inside it. You'll always have a piece of me with you."

"Oh, Xavior... it's beautiful. I love it." My voice breaks. "Yes, I'd love nothing more than to complete our bond and be completely yours." I sniff, and the first tear slips free.

His expression instantly shifts, shock, then fear. "Why are you crying? I was terrible, wasn't I?"

I laugh softly through the tears. "No. You were perfect. These are happy tears."

Relief floods his face. "Thank you." He takes the ring from the box and slides it onto my left hand with reverence. "For being patient with me. For forgiving me—even though I've done so many unforgivable things."

I scowl at him. "Not like you were letting me go. I know for a fact you would've done something stupid. Probably kidnapped me again."

A corner of his mouth lifts. "Yeah, I would've. But that's beside the point." His voice turns serious, raw. "You could've hated me, made this hard. But you didn't. You saw past the darkness and brought light into my heart and soul. You showed me what it feels like to be loved—not for my power or my wealth, but for me."

His thumb brushes over my knuckles, right above the ring.

"You brought happiness into my world," he continues honestly, "and I don't know how I'll ever repay that. But I'll spend the rest of my life trying. I'll make sure you're happy, never in need of anything, and I'll prove my love for you every minute of every day."

He kisses me.

My body ignites instantly, heat flooding my veins. I twist in his lap, straddling him without hesitation.

"I know what the internet and the healers said," I whisper against his mouth, "but you never asked me what *I* needed. Or wanted." My voice trembles, but I don't stop. "Make love to me. Make me forget. Please."

His breathing turns uneven.

"I can still feel him," I admit, the words spilling out. "His lips. His hands. His fist." My chest tightens. "Erase him from my memory—my body—with your hands and lips."

A low, dangerous growl rips from his chest. His face twists with fury, possessive and feral, but he doesn't hesitate. He grips me, lifts me, and presses my back into the mattress.

"You can still feel him?" His voice is rough, shaking with restraint. "Touching what's mine?"

He steps back, and I watch him strip with a heated gaze, every movement deliberate, controlled, lethal.

"Tell me where he touched you," Xavior says darkly. "Every place." His eyes burn into mine. "I'll replace every inch—with my hands, my lips, my tongue. Whatever you need."

"Let me see!" Ana runs into the kitchen, where I'm watching Xavior make pasta. We're all having dinner tonight, and I'm excited. I hardly see my dad anymore. I laugh and hold out my left hand.

"That is so pretty! Damn, Xavi, didn't think you had it in you to design such a pretty ring!" Ana pushes him with both hands. He narrows his eyes at her, and his shoulders go rigid like he's bracing.

"Ana." Axel pulls her away from Xavior.

"Oh, stop!" She wiggles out of Axel's grip and wraps her arms around Xavior, who gives me a 'help me' look. "He's my future bro-in-law; he loves me and would never hurt me. Tell me I'm lying, you big grump."

"No, I'll never hurt you, but please do refrain from pushing me." He deadpans; I can tell he's restraining himself. He hates being touched.

"See, I told you! He has so much love for me."

"Alright, Ana. Stop touching him before he makes you. Come on, let's sit on the patio." I grab her hand, leading her outside, and we sit on the patio steps instead of the table. She leans her head on my shoulder.

"So, how do you feel about being a princess?"

"Princess?" I blink slowly, trying to understand.

"You truly are something sometimes. Xavior is the prince, and you are his mate, so..."

"Oh, God. I can't be a princess! I'm not made for the royal life. I can't make big decisions. I'm a horrible influence on young girls." My chest tightens, and I clutch my hands together. Did it suddenly get hot? Why does it feel like an elephant is sitting on my chest? And why didn't Xavior say something? Maybe he thought I was smart enough to figure it out.

"Calm down! Xavior doesn't really do anything royal; it's all his dad. You don't have anything to worry about unless something happens to him. You have plenty of time to learn how to be royal."

I nod, taking a few deep breaths to calm myself. The heat in my chest slowly eases. "Yeah, I mean, his dad is in perfect health. He's not going anywhere anytime soon. God, I think I was close to a heart attack." I laugh, shaking my head. I grab my sister's hand, remembering I needed to talk to her before Dad arrives.

"I want to talk to you about something. We're telling Dad during dinner, but I want to tell you before that."

She jumps up and claps. "Oh God, are you pregnant? I'll be the coolest auntie; we'll get matching outfits and..."

"No, God no." I cut her off. "I'm not ready for that. I'm on birth control, so... Anyways, Xavior and I are leaving. He has a cabin. I don't know for how long, but we need some alone time."

She blinks slowly, opening her mouth a couple of times, but no words come out.

The back door opens, and Xavior steps out, looking grim.

"What's wrong?" I frown. He knew I was breaking the news to her and wouldn't have interrupted me if it wasn't urgent.

"There's an emergency meeting with the council."

"Oh." Disappointment seizes my chest. This is probably the last time I can have dinner with my family before we leave in a couple of days.

"I would like you to come with me."

"Why? I'm fine. Don't worry about me. Ana and I will still be here, I promise."

"I know you're okay. Come for me? I'm not ready to leave your side, just yet. I already packed your pasta in a to-go container so you can eat on the way."

"Okay." I squeeze my sister's hands. She gives me a sad smile, and it pierces my chest. "We'll talk when we get back, okay?"

I follow Xavior out, my heart heavy. The sadness in Ana's eyes clings to me, and I hate leaving her behind, even for a little while.

"I'm guessing that didn't go well?"

"She didn't take the news very well, though I shouldn't be shocked." I stare down at my hands, twisting my fingers together. "It's been just us most of our lives, with Dad and Mom always traveling." My chest tightens. I hate that I left her like that. I know being at the cabin is what I want—what I *need*—but leaving her behind is hitting harder than I expected.

"I hate seeing you heartbroken." He keeps his eyes on the road but reaches over, threading his fingers through mine. The simple touch steadies me. "What if she comes with us? There's more than enough room for all four of us. I bought the cabin for Axel and me for when we needed an escape. He's always loved it there."

"Really?" I turn toward him, hope blooming in my chest. "Are you serious? I know that's not what you wanted."

"It may not be what I wanted," he admits quietly, "but I'll do anything to make sure you're happy. And you being happy makes me happy."

"You are truly amazing." I smile and lean across the console, pressing a kiss to his cheek.

He exhales softly. "More selfish than anything. I do it for myself." His lips curve faintly. "I want to see that smile—the one that lights up my dark world."

Chapter Forty-four

My heart races as we drive past Brandon's apartment. He's still alive, but only because he called Ana for help and told them where I was. He's tried calling me, but Xavior refuses every time. I don't want to talk to him anyway. There's nothing he could say that would make me forgive him. All those years of friendship were a lie.

But truly... was I that gullible? Did I really crave acceptance so badly that I'd see past the lies the entire time?

I mean, come on.

Now that I think about it, how could I have been so stupid? He and I were never really friends, and out of nowhere, he wanted to hang out after Jaxon graduated...

Xavior squeezes my hand, and I know he sees me looking longingly at Brandon's apartment.

"Am I stupid for believing so many lies?" I lean back against the headrest and glance at him.

"No," he says gently. "You were lonely, and you needed something more. I know how it feels. I used to fall for lies, too. People I thought were friends... they were just using me for what I could give them. That's why I don't trust easily. But we have each other now. If you need a friend, I'm here. I can even dress up and pretend I'm a girl." He laughs. "We'll get our nails done and everything."

I laugh so hard I snort, imagining him in frilly clothes, and tears roll down my face.

"There she is." He winks and presses gentle kisses to the tops of my hands.

We step into Coven's Hall, and all eyes turn to us. My legs freeze. It isn't just the council members—the king of every being is here, the one who controls all the kings. The sheer power nearly chokes me, and the room suddenly feels too small.

"Hey, it's okay," Xavior says, moving in front of me. He blocks my view, shielding me. "I'm here, and they're not here to hurt anyone."

"No, we are not. Please, come. Let us start the meeting." A deep, impatient voice growls. I glance at Xavior, and my eyes fall on the Lycan King. Shit. Will he shift and tear me apart if I turn and run?

Xavior grabs my hand and guides me forward. We take a seat opposite the King's, though I notice one seat is empty.

"As you are aware, your father is... no longer fit to rule," the Lycan King says. My head snaps toward Xavior. What? "You are next in line to rule."

"And we will not honor our contract to continue. That agreement was with your father, out of respect for him, when your mother vanished," the Fae King adds.

I finally snap out of my haze. "What's going on? What contract?" All eyes lock on me, and I pray the ground will swallow me whole.

"Do not interrupt me." The Fae King snarls, his fist slamming against the table.

My eyes widen in fear, and I open my mouth to apologize.

"Do not disrespect her." Xavior growls as he stands, shadows crawling beneath his skin, restless and lethal.

The Fae King rises as well, eyes glowing as his hard gaze locks on Xavior's. Neither of them backs down.

I swallow hard. Are they going to fight?

"May I ask why your daughter is here?" the Vampire King asks, turning calmly toward my father, who doesn't seem the least bit concerned about the dominance battle unfolding in front of him.

"She is my mate," Xavior answers without breaking his stare from the Fae King.

All eyes turn to me once again.

"My apologies," the Fae King says, lowering his chin in respect. "I was not aware."

Xavior finally relaxes and sits.

"Good," the Fae King continues. "Then we do not need to concern ourselves with the contract, since you have found your mate."

"She doesn't know what's going on," Xavior says sharply, "and she hasn't agreed to anything."

"Tell me what *is* going on, Xavior."

My nervousness evaporates, replaced with irritation. He's hiding something—something big.

"Later," he says dismissively. "What if I do not fulfill the contract?"

No. I will not sit here in the dark.

"I will not be dismissed," I snap. "You will tell me what is going on, Xavior."

A low chuckle leaves the Vampire King. "Oh, I like her."

"If you refuse," the Warlock King says calmly, turning to me, "then I will explain. The contract—"

"Enough," Xavior growls.

He finally looks up. "They want me to take a queen. This contract was signed with my father when he refused to take one after my mother vanished. It will not be transferred to me." He doesn't even look at me.

His eyes are on the paperwork in front of him. His gaze sweeps the table. "I will not be taking a queen."

Something sharp twists low in my chest, like the bond itself recoiling, tightening until it hurts to breathe.

My chest caves in.

After everything...

All eyes turn to me. I refuse to let them see what that did to me. I straighten my shoulders, lift my chin, and stare straight ahead as my teeth grind together. Somewhere behind me, my father is shouting in outrage.

The sound fades.

My ears ring. I can't hear anything anymore. My heart pounds, my palms sweat, and I feel my control slipping through my fingers. The edges of the room blur, like my mind is already trying to escape before I do.

I stand.

Every gaze locks onto me again.

I bow in respect and turn to leave. I won't beg. I won't break. And I won't stay where I'm only a complication.

A hand grabs my arm. I ignore him—just as he ignored me.

"Where are you going?" Xavior hisses in my ear, his anger crackles, sharp and restrained.

"Let go of me."

"King Xavior," one of them says, "we must finish the meeting."

King Xavior.

"Sit down," he murmurs, low enough for only me to hear, "or I'll make you."

"I will take her," my father says firmly, stepping forward. "So, you may finish your meeting."

Relief floods me so fast my eyes burn.

I feel Xavior's fury, his stare drilling into the side of my face, begging me to look at him. His grip loosens as he turns back to the council. I thought I was standing beside him. I didn't realize I was standing beneath him.

I don't hesitate.

I rip my arm free and storm out of the room.

I remove my shoes and slip my feet into the water. I need to be alone.

My gaze drops to the ring on my finger, the diamond catching faint moonlight. I don't know what to think anymore. Did he change his mind? Or did he decide I'm not enough?

Maybe he doesn't think I'd be a good queen.

Whatever the reason, he should have talked to me first—should've warned me—instead of making me look clueless and stupid in front of everyone.

I know I should let him explain it. I know that. But even if he has a good reason for keeping me in the dark, it doesn't change the fact that he blindsided me. He *knew* what that meeting was about. He knew, and he still said nothing.

I sit there for hours. By the time I glance at the sky again, it's nearly midnight. He has no way to track me. I covered my scent, and I left my phone in his car.

I know I can't avoid him forever—but I can't bring myself to get up and go home yet.

The snap of a branch makes me whip around, my heart jumping into my throat.

"It's just me."

Brandon steps out from behind a tree, his hands tucked into the pockets of his jeans. "I heard you were missing and figured you'd be here. It's our spot, after all."

"What do you want?" I ask warily. "And how did you know I was missing?"

"I wanted to make sure you were okay." He shrugs. "Ana called and asked if I knew where you might go. Don't worry—I didn't tell them. I know how much you like your space."

I turn back toward the water. "Having a mate can be so... suffocating sometimes."

I hesitate. I know I shouldn't trust him. I know that. But right now, I don't want judgment. I want quiet.

"He keeps secrets," I continue softly. "I don't think he's trying to hurt me. But he completely blindsided me."

"What happened?" Brandon asks as he sits beside me, leaving a careful distance between us.

I tell him everything. When I finish, he lets out a low whistle.

"Yeah," he says slowly. "That would've crushed me, too. I can't even imagine how that felt." He glances at me. "I do believe he loves you. You should talk to him."

"I know," I admit. "But I'm tired of the secrets. And I'm not ready to hear the truth yet." I swallow. "What if he thinks I'd make a horrible queen? Is that why he doesn't want one? Or... what if he changed his mind about us?"

"I don't think it's either," Brandon says immediately. "And if it is, he's a damn fool. You'd be an amazing queen."

I snort. "Yeah, right. The entire realm would fall apart if I were queen."

"No, it wouldn't."

He wraps an arm around me, and I stiffen for half a second before I let myself relax and lean into him. I tell myself it's just comfort—nothing more.

"I'm so sorry, Amara," he murmurs.

A humorless laugh escapes me. "See? I'd be a horrible queen, because I forgive too easily—even when I know better. What if a murderer comes in crying for forgiveness? I'd cave immediately." I shake my head. "I forgave Xavior. And now my stupid ass is probably going to forgive you too."

"It's a good thing Xavior is such a savage," Brandon says dryly. "Extremely murderous."

Despite myself, I laugh.

For a moment, the night feels lighter.

And I hate how much I needed that.

Chapter Forty-five

Amara

Brandon pulls into the driveway. I already know Xavior isn't home. Ana told me he's out looking for me. Apparently, he thinks I left town.

"I swear to God, Amara, if you disappear again, at least *tell me*," Ana snaps as she yanks open the passenger-side door. "I get that everything's been insane and you needed space, but you could've texted me that you were safe or something."

"I didn't have my phone," I say quietly as I climb out. "Did you call him?"

"Not him," she replies. "I called Axel—so yeah, I'm guessing he knows now."

Her gaze slides past me to Brandon as he gets out of the car. Her eyes narrow, hands landing on her hips. "You told me you didn't know where she'd be."

"Yeah," Brandon says evenly. "And I knew that if she left without saying anything, it was because everything was closing in on her and she needed time alone, which she deserves. After everything she's been through, it was the least I could do."

Before Ana can respond, tires squeal sharply behind us.

I don't need to turn around.

"Here it goes," I mutter under my breath.

"Where the fuck did you go?"

Xavior storms toward us, fast and furious, fury rolling off him in waves. If I didn't know him, I'd probably be shaking right now.

Actually—judging by the look in his eyes—I still might.

I lift my chin anyway. "I needed time alone. Is that a crime, *King Xavior*?"

"You think this is funny?" he snaps. "I've spent the last few hours looking for you, thinking you ran off or that you were hurt."

"Whatever." I wave him off. "I'm not in the mood for your shit. I'm going to bed."

"The fuck you are," he growls, stepping into my space.

"What do you want from me?" I throw my hands up. "You told me no more lies. No more secrets. And then you turn around and keep me completely in the dark—*again*. You made me look absolutely stupid in a room full of the most powerful people in the realm."

He exhales slowly through his nose, dragging a hand through his hair like he's barely holding himself together. "I didn't know how to tell you."

"It doesn't matter now, does it?" My voice cracks despite my best effort. "You don't want me as your queen. So, what are we even doing?"

My chest tightens as the words spill out.

"I can't be with you if you don't think I'm good enough."

He flinches.

"That's not it," he says quickly. "I do think you're good enough. I just knew it wasn't what you wanted."

My breath catches as he continues.

"I overheard you freaking out about being a princess when you were talking to Ana. I didn't want you to feel forced into anything." He steps closer, his voice lowering. "You would be the perfect queen. You're smart, strong, brave—too forgiving sometimes—but that's exactly what my people... *our* people need."

His jaw tightens. "I should've told you. I was going to, on the way there, but you were already upset and I..." He exhales. "I chickened out. The way you found out wasn't fair. I'm sorry."

"I did freak out," I admit, staring at my feet. I can see now why he hesitated. "But I want to be there for you. I want to be everything you need me to be."

He chuckles softly. "Baby, you already are. You don't need a crown to be there for me." His thumb brushes my knuckles. "You're already my queen. You always have been."

"But it feels like they're forcing your hand," I say, looking away. The truth sits heavy in my chest. "I can't make you fight because I'm scared of failing."

"They're trying," he admits. "But this isn't about what they want. It's about what *you* want." He cups my face, grounding me. "I will always fight for that."

I lean into his touch despite myself—still hurt, still angry about the secret, but understanding now.

"Tell me what happened to your dad."

"They think the rebel group attacked him."

They think? My brows knit together.

"It's what we wanted them to think," he adds quietly.

"Xavior... you're confusing me."

"Your father didn't want you to know," he says carefully, "but I won't lie to you. You can't tell anyone."

My stomach drops as he continues.

"I found out he helped Jaxon take you. He was angry with me—I wasn't doing everything he demanded, and he wanted to remove the distraction."

"The distraction," I echo hollowly. I shake my head. "Me."

"Yes." His voice hardens. "So, your father, Axel, and I dealt with him for hurting you."

"You killed him?" I gasp.

"Not yet," he says calmly. "I paralyzed him." His thumb brushes my jaw. "Don't act surprised, my love. Anyone who tries to take you from me—anyone who hurts you—will face my wrath."

He presses a gentle kiss to my lips, as if to remind me that violence and devotion live side by side in him.

"What about the cabin?" I ask. "It's your home."

"We'll live in the castle, inside the shadow realm. It's not possible to live in the mansion, but we can visit. Take vacations." His gaze softens. "It *was* my home. Now, my home is wherever you are."

"Xavior?"

He hums against my lips, and I pull back just enough to meet his eyes.

"I want to be your queen. I might fail. I might mess things up. But I want to do this—with you."

His grin is immediate, bright, and entirely unguarded. His eyes sparkle.

"Okay," he says softly. "Whatever my queen wants."

He intertwines our fingers and kisses my knuckles. "And just so you know—we're both going to mess things up. We'll both fail at times."

His thumb squeezes my hand. "But we'll do it together. And we'll learn together."

My chest swells, nodding. "Together."

Chapter Forty-six

Amara

"**R**eady?" Xavior asks, looking at me, but I know he's asking all of us. I take a slow breath, nerves fluttering in my chest, and glance at Ana and Axel.

Ana squeezes Axel's hand. They look at each other and nod at the same time.

I turn back to Xavior and nod.

He lifts his hand and moves it in one smooth arc. The shadows twist and fold until they form a black circle in front of us. I step back, staring in awe as the shadow realm comes into view.

It's not the first time I've seen it, but it still takes my breath away. This time is different, though. I'm not being dragged through it. I'm not a prisoner. I'm actually excited to explore.

Still, it's dark and gloomy, gothic and beautiful in a way that feels almost unreal. I'll miss the bright colors of the human realm.

Xavior steps closer, and I pull my eyes from the portal to look at him. The doubt in his stormy gaze is impossible to miss.

"I know it's... different," he says quietly. "But I can make you happy there."

"I'm ready," I say, smiling.

This new chapter of my life is scary, and I know he's afraid I'll hate it—especially now that he's king and can't leave whenever he wants.

Ana and Axel step through the portal hand in hand.

I move closer to Xavior, catching the hesitation still on his face. "I'm okay," I say softly. "I haven't changed my mind."

He takes my hand, and together we step into the portal.

Just like the first time, everything blurs as we travel between realms. It feels like riding a roller coaster, only worse since we're not strapped in. The wind whips my hair violently, and I tighten my grip on Xavior's hand, needing the comfort.

We hit the ground hard enough that my knees buckle, but Xavior's arm wraps around my waist before I can fall.

That was definitely better than the first time.

We're standing in front of the gates leading into the shadow realm. Guards bow immediately when they see their new king.

Trumpets blare overhead, and I look up to see men in black uniforms sounding them from the towers above the gates.

"Your Majesty," the guard on the right says, stepping forward. "Would you like the royal carriage?"

Xavior looks at me, waiting.

I shake my head. I want to walk. I'd love to see everything up close.

"No carriage," he says. "My mate would like to walk."

"Very well."

The guard on the left waves his hand, and the massive gates slowly creak open.

I swallow as townspeople rush forward to see their new king. Whispers follow us as we walk.

Their clothes are nothing like ours. Women wear dresses with full skirts. Men wear dark pants and buttoned shirts, everything very formal. I suddenly feel out of place. I wish I'd known... I would've dressed differently.

We don't look like we belong, but they still bow as we pass, splitting apart to make room.

Xavior stares straight ahead, completely unfazed, his hand resting on the small of my back. A few people try to get his attention. He dips his chin in acknowledgment but keeps moving.

I realize he's used to this. He's always been their prince.

A group of kids suddenly runs up and stops right in front of us. Xavior tries to walk past them without reacting.

I squeeze his hand, stopping him.

He looks down at me, brow lifting slightly.

I nod toward the kids, and understanding crosses his face.

"Hello," he says, his voice coming out deep and intimidating.

I bite back a smile. Does he not know how to talk to children?

He glances at me, almost unsure, and I nearly laugh at the lost look in his eyes.

One of the little girls with blonde pigtails stares at our joined hands, and she steps closer to me, curiosity shining in her gaze.

"Are you the king's girlfriend?" she whispers, big blue eyes staring up at me.

"I'm the king's mate," I say with a smile. Her eyes somehow grow even bigger, her mouth forming a perfect O.

"She is my mate and your future queen," Xavior says. His voice booms, deep and deliberate, echoing through the street. He wants everyone to hear.

Gasps ripple through the crowd, whispers following as Xavior pulls me gently forward. I turn to wave goodbye to the kids, but they disappear from view as Ana and Axel close in behind us.

My gaze lifts to the castle looming ahead. It's massive and intimidating. The towering stones are overwhelming. My chest tightens. How am I supposed to find my way through something like that?

Two guards open the enormous double doors.

"Welcome home." An older woman stands just inside, smiling warmly at Xavior.

The inside of the castle reminds me of his mansion—the one where he kept me prisoner—but bigger. Dark stone walls. Dark wooden floors. Red and cream rugs stretching down endless halls.

"Moira," Xavior says, his smile turning soft as he steps forward and hugs her.

I blink. That alone surprises me.

"Moira?" Axel questions in surprise as he steps closer.

Her eyes widen as they trail over him. "Axel? Is that you?"

She rushes past me and wraps her arms around his waist. "You grew into such a handsome young man."

"Moira pretty much raised Axel and me whenever we were here," Xavior explains quietly to me. It makes sense now—the tears in her eyes, the way she clings to them.

"Moira," Xavior continues, "this is my mate. Amara."

She shoves Axel away—somehow, despite being shorter than me—and spins around so fast it startles me.

"Did you say *mate*?"

Her eyes rake over me slowly. My stomach twists. What if she doesn't like me? What if I'm not what she expected? I know Xavior wouldn't care, but I do.

"Oh wow," she breathes, then laughs softly as her eyes fill with tears. "Xavior... she's beautiful."

My shoulders relax.

"I'm sorry," she says, turning fully to me. "I'm talking like you're not standing here. You really are beautiful, Amara."

"She is," Xavior agrees, tightening his arm around my waist.

Axel clears his throat and pulls Ana closer. "I have someone I want you to meet, too. This is Anastasia—my mate. And Amara's sister."

"Oh goddess," Moira squeals. "Another mate!"

She spins toward them, completely abandoning us, and Xavior immediately takes advantage, pulling me toward the stairs without a word.

"That was rude," I mutter once we're out of earshot.

"They'll survive," he says calmly. "I want you to myself. Now hush—so I can take advantage of you."

I yelp as he suddenly scoops me up and throws me over his shoulder, carrying me the rest of the way up the stairs.

Chapter Forty-seven

Amara

I walk down the corridor, my steps echoing through the quiet space. It's nearly empty; I've only passed a few maids rushing around with their heads down. It's early morning, the sun barely rising, and I woke up alone, with the space next to me cold.

Now I'm wandering the castle, looking for Xavior, with no real idea where I'm going. He promised me a tour after Moira offered, but he declined it, saying he'd show me himself. That never happened. We've been here for two days, and he wanted me all to himself. Not that I'm complaining, but now I remember why I wanted that tour in the first place.

Everything looks the same.

I am so lost. Dark stone walls. Long stretches of corridor. No personal touches, no warmth. I'm pretty sure I've already walked past the same fake armored guard at least twice. Maybe three times.

I chose a green silk dress this morning—mostly because women here wear dresses instead of pants, and I'm still trying to blend in. The slit runs high up my thigh, the neckline dipping low enough to make me feel bold and slightly exposed. My hair hangs loose down my back, a golden leaf hairpiece wrapping around my head like a tiara. A matching cuff circles my upper left arm, right above my elbow. I look like I belong here... even if I don't feel like it yet.

After climbing down four flights of stairs, I finally reach what I think is the main floor. I turn right, deciding to explore while I search for Xavior. My steps slow when I notice the large portraits lining the wall. Each one is framed in gold and of men staring out with hard eyes, some younger, some older. All-powerful and very intimidating.

I don't stop long enough to study them. Something about their gazes makes my skin prickle, like I'm being judged.

Across the hall, I spot a coffee bar.

Relief floods me instantly. Coffee is exactly what I needed.

It's nearly empty this early, except for one man sitting with his back to me. His posture looks stiff, almost uncomfortable in the metal chair. I step into the room, my attention immediately snagging on the high-tech espresso machines: sleek, black, and covered in more buttons than I know what to do with.

I shake my head and move to the one that looks less intimidating. It has a touchscreen, complete with pictures of different coffees and lattes. Thank God.

I select my favorite, caramel macchiato, grab a to-go cup, place it where it needs to go, and hit start.

As the machine hums to life, I lean back against the counter and glance toward the man again. He hasn't moved. His shoulders are tense, like he doesn't quite belong in the space either.

Funny how that makes me feel a little less alone.

"Do they not make bigger chairs around here?" I blurt out awkwardly. I'm terrible at talking to people—especially strangers. I gesture vaguely toward him. "It looks like you're about to break it."

Oh my god. My face heats instantly. Why would I say that?

After a moment of painful silence, I panic and keep going. "I'm not calling you fat or anything. You're just... very big. You know. In the muscular way."

Please stop talking.

He growls, the sound low and irritated, and stands so abruptly the chair screeches across the floor. He spins around; face twisted like he's about to tear into me—but then he pauses. His eyes drag slowly over my body, lingering in a way that makes my stomach dip.

I do the same, unable to help myself.

He's gorgeous in a rugged, dangerous way. Raven-black hair, slightly wavy, just long enough to tuck behind his ears. Dark eyes that miss nothing. Full lips. A scar cuts down his forehead, just above his left eyebrow. Suddenly, the room feels much larger—and I feel very small inside it.

"I'm sorry," I rush out, needing to break whatever this is. "I really didn't mean to offend you."

"Who are you?" he asks. His tone is sharp, but curious. "I've never seen you around."

"Oh?" I arch a brow. "And you know everyone who resides in this realm?"

"I do." His gaze sweeps over me again. "And trust me, I'd remember you."

"My name is Amara. And you are?" The machine beeps behind me, signaling my macchiato is finished, but I ignore it.

"Commander Tyson."

We stare at each other. There's interest in his eyes, but nothing inappropriate, nothing I can call out. We're just talking. I don't need to announce I have a mate. That would be weird.

I turn away, grateful for the excuse, and grab my drink, needing space from the intensity.

"So," I say casually, turning back to him, "do I have to call you Commander Tyson, or will Tyson do?"

He's closer now, a lot closer. For someone so big, he moves silently.

"Tyson is fine." He reaches past me, placing his cup under the machine and selecting an option. His body crowds mine, his scent hitting me, woodsy, clean, with a hint of mint.

"Amara," he says slowly, "as in King Xavior's mate?"

I smile and nod. "Yes. Do you know him? Being a commander and all?"

"You could say that." He leans in, one hand braced on the counter. "He's one lucky bastard."

His eyes dip again, blatant this time.

A throat clears. And the air shifts, it's sharp and electric.

Xavior.

I feel him before I see him. His heat presses into my back as he steps close, wrapping a possessive arm around my waist and pulling me firmly against him.

"That's right," he growls near my ear. "I am one lucky bastard. And this," he tightens his hold, "is all mine."

My feet nearly leave the floor as he lifts me slightly. "I've been looking for you."

"I was looking for you too," I say, breathless. "But I found this place and met Tyson."

"It's *Commander* Tyson to you, Amara," Xavior murmurs, lips brushing my ear.

"For fuck's sake, Xavior," Tyson says with a low chuckle. "Stop being so possessive."

"Shut the fuck up," Xavior snaps easily. "Do you blame me? I mean—look at her."

He sets me back down, and I silently thank every goddess that my macchiato survives.

"Can we not talk about me like I'm not standing here?" I say, stepping out of Xavior's grasp and dropping into a chair. I cross my leg, the slit revealing my thigh.

When I look up, Xavior is staring, absolutely devouring me, and my naked thigh, nearly drooling.

That's not what steals my attention.

A black crown rests on his head, gothic and sharp, shadowy designs etched into the metal. The pointed edges look like they could cut skin if touched.

It makes him look lethal, powerful. And Gods... unfairly attractive, dangerously so.

Heat coils low in my belly as I rub my thighs together, and his eyes snap up to mine. His nostrils flare, gaze darkening instantly, and he fucking smirks.

"No, I can't." Tyson lets out a low laugh, shaking his head. "Fuck, Xavior. You were right... she's stunning. If she were mine, I wouldn't allow her alone in a room with another man."

"She isn't allowed," Xavior snaps. "She snuck off on me."

I roll my eyes. "You snuck off long before I woke up. And don't tell me I'm *not allowed.* This castle is full of men. It'd be impossible not to be alone with one at some point."

"You should've waited for me," he says, jaw tight. "I figured you'd still be asleep when I got back."

"What were you doing?" I take a sip of my drink and—shit. It's the best macchiato I've ever had.

I lean back in the chair, arching slightly, and drag the tip of my middle finger from my knee up my thigh in a slow, deliberate line. I don't look away from him. I watch his reaction instead.

His eyes track the movement instantly, and his breathing shifts. He licks his lower lip, exactly the reaction I wanted.

"I had paperwork to take care of," he says tightly. Then, sharper, "Excuse us, Tyson."

Xavior holds out his hand. I take it without hesitation.

"It was nice meeting you, Tyson," I say, lifting my cup in a small wave as we head out.

"*Commander* Tyson," Xavior scoffs.

Tyson's chuckle follows us. "Pleasure was all mine."

The moment we're out of sight, Xavior shoves me into a dark corner, his body slamming into mine. The wall is cold against my back, the contrast making me gasp as his mouth crashes into mine.

"Mine," he growls against my lips.

"Such a jealous, possessive man," I whisper, smiling into the kiss.

"I can't help it, baby." His hands grip my hips, lifting me effortlessly. My legs wrap around his waist, my dress riding up, the slit opening enough for cold air to brush my ass cheek. "Fuck—I need you."

He starts undoing his belt.

"Xavior, no." I glance past his shoulder, heart pounding. People pass in the corridor beyond us. All it would take is one turn of the head and they'll see us. "Not here."

This... *this* is where I draw the line.

He drops his forehead to my shoulder, inhaling deeply before griping, "Fine. Hurry, let's go."

He doesn't release me.

Instead, he fists the fabric of my dress, tugging the slit closed with a possessive swipe, and carries me out of the hidden corner and down the corridor, his stride fast and determined. Maids and guards scatter out of our way, casting knowing looks at one another as we pass.

Chapter Forty-eight

Amara

"What's the hurry?" I tease, wrapping an arm around his neck. I don't care what they think, or about the rumors that will be spreading like wildfire by the end of the day. Somewhere along the way, I stopped caring.

"I need you, my little vixen," he murmurs into my ear, voice rough and unrestrained.

His hand slides into my hair, gripping hard enough to tilt my head aside. His tongue drags slowly along the length of my throat, and a groan vibrates through his chest. "So, fucking sweet," he breathes. "My little ruin."

"Xavior..." I moan, my legs tightening around his waist as I arch into him.

The sound of doors opening then slamming shut grabs my attention.

I blink, lifting my head. We're inside a massive room now, the walls a dark, stormy gray. At the far end sits a towering throne on a raised dais. Its jagged, shadowed designs are the same as the crown on Xavior's head.

"Is this the king's—your—throne room?" I whisper.

"Yes," he says without hesitation. "*Our* throne room."

He carries me to the edge of the dais and sets me down, my ass barely resting on the sharp stone corner. It's at least two feet off the ground. He steps back just long enough to look at me—really look—before gripping my knees and spreading them apart in one fast motion.

He hisses, jaw tightening, dark eyes snapping up to mine. "No panties?"

Heat floods my face. "The slit wouldn't allow them."

"This dress," he mutters darkly, more to himself. "Will be burned." I nearly missed the words. He reaches up, grabbing the crown to take it off.

"No." The word leaves me breathless and urgent. "Fuck me wearing your crown, *my king*."

He freezes. Then he growls, low, dangerous, and unrestrained. Nostrils flaring as he draws in a slow, steady breath.

"Again," he orders, voice thick with promise. "Call me *your* king again."

"My king... fuck me, please." I plant my feet flat against the cold floor and widen my legs for him.

He keeps the crown on his head and fumbles with the strings of his black trousers, fingers trembling as he drags them down and steps free before leaning over me.

I tsk softly, shaking my head. "Shirt off, my king."

A dark smile curves his mouth. "Is my mate feeling bossy today?" He straightens, arms stretching behind him as he pulls his shirt over his head. My gaze drops instantly, drinking in every dip and line of his bare body, every hard-earned muscle, every shadow. My God... It's glorious.

"Do you like what you see?" His voice is rough with need as his hand trails up my thigh.

"Yes," I whimper, lifting my hips off the floor, desperate to get his fingers to their destination faster.

"Feeling impatient?"

"Mhm... please."

"Is this what you need?"

I jolt as his fingers slide between my thighs, dipping into my pussy, circling my clit in slow, torturous motions. I rock my hips, chasing the friction. "Naughty girl." He grips my hip, halting my movement with his free hand.

"Xavior," I growl, frustration thick in my voice, my lower lip pushing into a pout. "I need you. Please, my king."

He groans and shifts over me, bracing himself on one elbow beside my head as his fingers lower, pressing into my entrance. He thrusts them in and out with deliberate precision, his thumb circling my clit in a delirious rhythm. His gaze never leaves mine, dark and hungry. It makes my toes curl.

"So, godsdamn beautiful," he murmurs. "I love you. You are my entire world, Amara. I will bow to you, my queen. So will the world, if that is what you want... or they will burn at your feet."

"And I love you." My back arches as the pressure builds, spiraling fast. I'm right there. I whimper when his fingers suddenly slip free. My head falls back, the faint sting against the stone barely registering as I squeeze my eyes shut.

"Not yet," he growls. "You will come undone on my cock."

I scream as he thrusts into me, *hard*.

"Fuck," he snarls, head tipping back, eyes threatening to roll back as he fills me completely.

Watching a man this powerful unravel for me—because of me—is indescribable. I would do anything to burn this image into my memory forever. Every brutal thrust steals my breath, driving my pleasure higher and higher until my body can barely keep up.

"Tell me who you belong to." He drops his head, lips hovering just above mine, his movements turning wild, fierce, unrestrained.

"You!" I scream. "I belong to you!"

"Fucking right you do."

He crashes his mouth to mine, then suddenly pulls back, gripping my left ankle and lifting my leg over his shoulder. The new angle drives him deeper, each thrust demanding, punishing. I shiver as shockwaves of pleasure slam into my body with the force of a hurricane.

"Xavior," I cry, lips parted, mind unraveling. "I'm so close. I can't—" I can't think straight; I am at a complete loss from the delicious sensation.

"Come for me," he commands. "For your king."

And I do, my pussy walls spasm around him as the orgasm crashes into me with a demanding force.

"Fucking hell!" he roars, his cock swelling inside me before one final, brutal thrust sends him over the edge. He throws his head back, shouting my name as he comes.

He releases my leg and collapses against me, forehead resting against mine as we struggle to breathe, sweat covering our bodies.

My hand lifts, tracing the dark metal of his crown, following the engraved patterns up to one sharp point. I yelp as it slices the tip of my finger.

Xavior's eyes snap open. He catches my wrist instantly, pulling my hand away before drawing my finger into his mouth, tongue warm as he licks the blood clean.

"Be careful, my vixen." His voice drops low. "My crown is poisonous to those who are not meant to hold it. You'll be fine, the magic will sense who you are to me, but it's best to be safe."

He pulls his softening cock free but stays above me, his weight still anchoring me to the cold stone. I lift my hand and brush the damp strands from his gray eyes, but it's pointless since they immediately fall back into place.

"Why did you run off this morning?" I ask quietly. "And don't give me the paperwork excuse."

He smiles, bright white teeth flashing. "I was here, designing your throne. And I had guards giving me an update. They're still searching for my mother."

"My…" I clear my throat. "My throne? Your mother?" I'm not sure why the throne shocks me—I agreed to this, didn't I? Still, the words feel heavy. And everyone says his mother died long ago.

"Yes, my mother." His voice softens. "She ran away when I was ten. And your throne will sit beside mine, exactly where you belong."

He sits back on his knees between my legs, his gaze slowly tracing my body. "I will never get used to how perfect you are." A pause. "I have something to show you."

"Wait." I stop him before he can stand. "They say she died. I don't understand."

"It's a long story," he says quietly. "She didn't die. That's just what my father told everyone. My mother was... unhappy, and depressed. But when I was with her, something would light up in her dull eyes. She used to sing to me every night."

"Then why did she leave?"

His jaw tightens. "Their marriage was an arrangement. She fell in love with him. He never loved her back. He cheated, and worse, he took his anger out on her." His voice hardens. "He'll hit her. Every time I saw her, she was wearing a new bruise.

My chest tightens.

"She never let me see how much it hurt. She always wore a smile for me. I didn't understand until it was too late." His gaze drops. "After she left, he turned that anger on me. Now that he's gone, I want to find her. I want to know she's safe, and if she's taken care of."

"That's horrible," I whisper. "I'm so sorry." I reach for him. "You'll find her. I believe that."

He looks away, pain flickering briefly across his face before he stands, shutting that part of himself back behind stone walls. I don't take it personally. He's done talking, for now. He'll tell me when he's ready.

I bite my lower lip as I watch him pull his trousers up, muscles shifting beneath sweat-slicked skin as he crosses the room. Gods, he's unfairly beautiful. I force myself to look away before I beg him to take me again. Later...

I stand fixing my dress as I look around. The floors are dark gray marble, nearly black. Towering arched windows stretch at least twenty feet high, and between each one stands a gothic metal torch etched with the same shadowed designs as Xavior's crown. Two massive floor torches flank the throne, unlit for now. The room is intimidating, powerful, and stunning.

"Amara," Xavior calls.

I spin around.

I am caught off guard when I find him kneeling in front of me, one knee to the floor, the other bent, his posture stiff. In his hands rests a red velvet pillow. On it sits a crown.

It's breathtaking... similar to his, but larger, and more detailed. Beneath each sharp point glimmers a smoky black diamond.

"This belonged to the previous queen," he says softly. "My mother. As my mate, it now belongs to you." His eyes lock onto mine. "If you accept me, it... we will be fully mated. You will be my queen."

Tears blur my vision as I nod, smiling through them. "Yes. I accept. I will be your mate and your queen, Xavior."

"Good," he says, already rising. "Because I wasn't taking no for an answer."

And in two long strides, he's in front of me, lifting the crown and placing it onto my head.

I gasp.

Magic starts swirling around me instantly, teasing and alive beneath my skin. My blood heats, my pulse racing as power hums through me.

"Xavior," I breathe. "What's happening?"

"The crown is accepting you," he says, awe threading his voice. "And so is our bond. You can wield my shadows now. We are one."

"Wait, what?" I shriek, lifting my hands as something stirs beneath my skin. "Oh my God—"

My eyes widen as shadows slither up my arms like living snakes, curling and coiling. It doesn't hurt, but the sensation is strange, tingly, electric.

It's unlike anything I've felt before, it's *power*. Completely different than my magic I wield as a witch, *darker*. This is deeper and stronger.

And unmistakably his.

"Can you please stop doing things like this without at least a warning?" I snap, still reeling. I don't understand why he didn't tell me before I accepted.

"I'm sorry." He rubs the back of his neck, almost sheepish, his gaze tracking the shadows as they creep past my elbows. "I knew you'd freak out. I didn't want you to decline."

"Am I turning into a shadow wielder like you?" My eyes follow the dark trails as they climb higher, nearly brushing my shoulder.

"Yes. You'll be part shadow wielder, part witch." When I look back at him, his own shadows are stirring now, responding to mine. "It's complete. Being my mate, my queen, suits you. You look absolutely stunning."

I look down at my arms. The shadows stop at my left elbow, but my right arm is almost fully claimed, the darkness reaching up toward my shoulder, just shy of my neck. I trail my fingers over them. Like Xavior's, they move beneath my skin, alive, restless.

"It'll take some time to get used to them," he says softly. "Both the way they swirl and how to use them, but let's try. My shadows are itching to meet yours."

"How?" I ask, lifting my gaze. He's smiling, wide, and unguarded. I've never seen him look this happy.

"Hold out your hand," he says. "Either one."

He lifts his, and I mirror him with my arm extended, palm up. "Imagine them moving out, just like when you use your magic."

"Okay." I nod, picturing them spilling free the way I've seen his do.

Nothing happens.

I stare harder, but nothing is happening. My brows pinch together as I grind my teeth.

Xavior chuckles. "You're trying too hard. Close your eyes, breathe."

I do, inhaling and exhaling. I feel him move closer, his chest pressing lightly against my back.

"Good girl," he mumbles near my ear. "Now breathe slowly and ask them to come out and play."

I exhale slowly, imagining them moving out of my hand, but nothing seems to happen. *Come out, it's okay...* A faint tingling sparks at my fingertips.

Yes, come play...

"Open your eyes, baby." I do, my breath catching in my throat as I stare.

"Xavior... wow."

Our shadows are swirling together.

I can tell which are mine. His shadows are a deep gray, nearly black, where as mine are lighter, threaded with tiny silvery flecks, like distant stars scattered through smoke. Not star-shaped, just glimmers.

They circle us slowly, then faster, rising and curling around our bodies like a living storm.

"They're beautiful," I breathe, glancing over my shoulder at him.

He leans in and kisses me gently, like this—like *us*—is sacred.

Chapter Forty-nine

I groan; the banging echoing around the room wakes me.

"This better be fucking important." Xavior growls.

He gets up and marches to the door, swinging it open, wearing only a pair of black boxers.

"I apologize, my king," the guard says, bowing before straightening. His gaze drifts past Xavior and lands on me.

I clutch the blanket tighter to my chest, suddenly very aware that I'm completely bare beneath it.

Xavior glances over his shoulder, his expression flashing with fury when he realizes how little I'm covered.

"Do not look at her," he snarls, stepping sideways to block me from view. "I am running out of patience. What is it you want?"

"There is a woman at the front gate," the guard says carefully. "She is demanding to be let in. She claims to be your mother. Normally, we wouldn't disturb you, but we know you've been searching for her."

Xavior goes still. "Thank you," he says after a beat. "Put her in the throne room. I'll be down shortly."

He slams the door shut and immediately starts dressing. I throw the blanket aside and rush for the closet, grabbing the first thing I can find to wear.

"What are you doing?" he asks.

I turn to see him buttoning his shirt, watching me. "What does it look like?" I say, "I'm coming with you."

"You don't have to," he says gently. "It's early. Go back to sleep."

"Xavior, don't." I shake my head, already knowing he's about to argue. "I want to be there for you."

He stares at me for a moment. I meet his gaze, holding firm. He's always there for me. It's time for me to return the favor.

Finally, he nods sharply and steps closer, pressing a kiss to my forehead. "Fine. Please hurry."

I pull a simple green dress over my bare skin. "Ready," I say, moving toward the door. "I just need to brush my hair and put on sandals."

His hand wraps around my elbow, stopping me.

"You will not walk around this castle without panties again."

He drags me back into the closet, opens a drawer, and pulls out a lacy pair before dropping to his knees.

I lift my feet one at a time, letting him slide them on, biting my lip to hide my smile.

"You think this is funny?" he mutters. "I'll lose my mind knowing you're wandering these halls bare between those thick thighs. Or that a gust of wind might lift your dress and show everyone what belongs to me. Then I'd have to rip their eyes out."

"The slit on this dress isn't that high," I say reasonably. "I don't think that'll happen."

"And what if you fall?" he counters. "What if it slides up and shows what's mine?"

"Xavior," I sigh, smoothing the skirt down as he stands. "You're being dramatic."

"Dramatic or not," he says firmly, spinning me around and giving me a gentle push, "you're wearing panties. Now go brush your hair."

I stare at my reflection as I run the brush through my long hair.

The dress is a halter, leaving my back bare and putting my new markings on full display. The shadows along my arms look like living tattoos, one arm fully covered, the other only partially.

I look badass, sexy even, and I feel confident.

I've never once felt confident in my life. It feels good, empowering. I smile when Xavior steps behind me. His finger traces the shadows along my right arm.

"Do you like them?" he asks quietly.

"I do," I say softly. "I love them."

My chest swells with warmth. With him beside me, the confidence feels unshakable.

"We look like a perfect power couple."

A slow smile spreads across his face. "That," he says, "is something I completely agree with."

He takes my hand. "Now come on. Let's go."

"How will you know if she is really your mom?" I ask.

We're staring at the double doors that lead into the throne room. Xavior paused before opening them about five minutes ago. I think he needs a moment to just... breathe.

"This is how."

He releases my hand and reaches into his pocket, pulling out a folded piece of what looks like paper. He presses it into my palm, and I carefully unfold it.

It's not paper. It's a picture.

Of a little boy, maybe nine years old, and a woman. Gods, she's beautiful. She looks just like Xavior. There's no mistaking it. This has to be his mother, and the boy beside her must be him.

She's wearing a flowing white gown, dark raven hair half up and half down, a wide smile stretching across her face, wrinkling the corners of her eyes. They're dark, though I can't make out the color. The boy is dressed in brown pants and a white button-up, his dark hair a wavy mess.

"She's beautiful," I murmur, unable to tear my eyes away. The longer I stare, the more I notice it—the way her smile doesn't quite reach her eyes. They look dull, lifeless. Life has been cruel to her for far too long.

The boy, though, looks happy and full of life.

I silently pray the woman behind those doors is truly her. She deserves happiness. A real smile. A life with her son, no longer hiding from a dark, miserable past. They both deserve that reunion.

"Are you ready?" Xavior asks quietly. He wraps an arm around me, pulling me tight against his side.

"Whenever you are," I say softly. "Just remember. No matter what happens, I'm here. I won't leave you."

He nods, then unwraps his arm only to lace his fingers through mine. With his free hand, he waves through the air.

Shadows surge from him, slamming into the doors and forcing them open.

Guards stand in a loose circle around a woman in the center of the throne room, her back to us. She's wearing a black lace dress, with her hair twisted into a low bun. My pulse spikes, and my breathing turns shallow as she slowly turns around.

Xavior's grip tightens, almost painfully, like he needs an anchor to keep himself upright. We both release a breath at the same time.

It's really her. The woman from the picture. Only now her eyes aren't dull or broken. They're bright and alive. She looks healthy and happy. Her dress is clearly high-end, elegant.

"Xavior, my son, it's me," she says softly, her voice close to breaking. He stiffens but doesn't respond. After a heavy moment of silence, his mother's lips press into a frown as her gaze shifts to me. "And you must be his mate. Everyone speaks of how beautiful you are, but none of it does you justice. Amara, correct? I am Celeste, Xavior's mother. It's a pleasure to meet you."

I offer her a tight smile. "Let's skip the pleasantries and get to the point. I want to know why you haven't visited Xavior, especially when you seem to be doing so well for yourself. And knowing the kind of man his father was." I arch a brow, my gaze dropping briefly to her elegant dress. It may be rude, but I have no kindness left when it comes to my mate. He was broken, abandoned, and abused by his father, and she was living like this? Who leaves their child with a monster?

"I would also like to know," Xavior says, finally snapping out of his stunned silence. I step closer, as if I could protect him from whatever comes next.

Celeste's shoulders slump as she lets out a hollow laugh. "I don't even know where to begin..." She looks away, sighing. "I wanted to come back. Gods, Xavior, I truly did. Your father pushed me out. He told me that if I didn't leave, he would kill us both. He wanted the throne. I was weak, but my word still held weight. So, I left. He sent me money, ordered me never to return, and promised that if I did, he would kill you. I couldn't go back to my family. He wanted me erased. A divorce would have disgraced him, and he used my love for you as leverage. I watched you from afar, made sure you were safe. I wanted to reveal myself so many times, especially as you grew older, but I was terrified he'd hurt you. The moment I learned he was no longer a threat, I came here. I understand if you don't believe me, but I pray that one day you can forgive me. I would have endured every beating with a smile if it meant staying by your side."

By the time she finishes, tears run down her face. I believe her, but I still need answers. This woman was once powerful. "Why didn't you use your magic against him when he hurt you?" The question sounds harsher than I intend, but I need to know. I won't let anyone hurt Xavior again.

"I did the first time," she admits, her voice trembling. "After he secured our marriage, after Xavior was born, you were six months old then. I protected myself. When he recovered, he told me that if I ever used my magic again, he would punish Xavior instead. I couldn't risk it. So, I took every blow without fighting back." Her voice breaks on the last word.

My tears threaten to break free as my chest aches for her. I don't know what I would've done in her place, but I know if I had a son, I'd do anything to protect him. I glance up at Xavior. His jaw is clenched, muscles ticking beneath his skin. His anger is suffocating, barely contained.

Turning away from Celeste, I gently cup his jaw and whisper, "Xavior."

He exhales sharply, like he's been holding his breath for years, and looks down at me. The tension drains from him the moment our eyes meet.

"Are you okay?"

"As long as you're by my side." He pulls me closer, and I rest my head against his chest, wrapped in the warmth of feeling safe... and loved.

Epilogue

Six months later...

Amara

"**G**uess what?" I whisper huskily in Xavior's ear. He's sitting at a picnic table with Kai, Axel, and *Commander* Tyson. I was hanging out with Lyra, Ana, and Celeste, but I'm bored and want his attention.

A couple of months ago, I finally worked up the nerve to visit Lyra... the girl who helped me when I needed it most. We've been close ever since. Our little circle consists of Ana, Lyra, and now, Celeste. Somehow, I've also grown really close to Xavior's mom.

Ana and Axel are finally fully mated, and honestly, seeing them so happy makes me happy too. I feel good. Safe and loved. Xavior is everything I needed and so much more. He's amazing, so fucking amazing. He still stares at me every second of the day, still needs me close. I can't leave his side too long without him becoming anxious... or be alone in another male's company... he is still so possessive... and I still love it. Gods, he's obsessed with me no matter what... sex... cuddling... everything under the moon. I'm his everything, and he always makes sure I am aware of it.

Last week, we went home to visit Dad. He's still grieving Mom. I visited her grave alone. It wasn't easy, but I said what I needed to say.

She was wrong. I matter. I am enough.

I never got answers from her—why she hated me—but I don't need them anymore. I'm done carrying that.

Xavior tilts his head. "What?"

"I'm not wearing any panties."

His back straightens instantly, and his eyes drop to my thighs. I'm wearing a ridiculously short skirt and a tank top. I take a step back, grinning.

"Amara," he warns, voice low.

I turn and run.

I'm laughing as I take off down the hill, straight toward the forest... the same one I once ran into trying to escape him. This time, I want him to catch me.

"Amara, get your sweet ass back here," he growls. "Or I'll punish you. Don't make me chase you."

I glance over my shoulder. He's following, slow and confident, like he knows exactly how this ends.

Cocky bastard.

My back hits the rough bark of a tree as I stop to catch my breath. I'm seriously out of shape. I haven't kept up with my morning runs like I used to. I just need a second.

I push off the tree to keep running, but Xavior's massive body steps into view.

I spin and sprint in the opposite direction, barely making it a few feet before something slams into me. Strong arms wrap around me, and we twist as we hit the ground... he takes most of the impact.

I scramble to get up. I don't make it far before his hand clamps around my ankle and yanks me back. My skirt and shirt ride up as my bare stomach drags over branches and dirt, stinging as they scrape my skin.

It hurts, but my cheeks ache more from the grin I can't stop.

"You are a naughty, naughty girl," Xavior tsks. He hooks a finger into the string of my panties at my hips and snaps it against my skin. Leaning over me, he lowers his mouth to my ear. "Do you know what I do to naughty, lying girls? I spank them. You're going to count each one until we reach ten or we start over."

"Yes, daddy," I moan, my eyes widening at the word even as it leaves my mouth.

"Mmm, that's right," he groans lowly. "I'm your daddy." He pulls back, lifting my hips until my ass is in the air, his palm rubbing slowly over my cheek. "Let's start."

The first slap lands hard, sharp enough to make me gasp. "One…"

Another. "Two…"

"Three." My voice wavers as heat pools between my thighs.

"Four…" Gods, it hurts so good.

"Five…" My knees shake.

"Six, please, daddy—"

"Please what, baby?" His hand comes down again, making me whimper.

"Seven," I breathe. "I need you." I spread my knees wider, arching my back. "I'm so wet for you."

"Fuck," he growls. "Since you've been a good girl, and you asked so nicely."

My panties tear, and cool air brushes over my exposed clit. I hear his trousers next, the sound rushed and messy. I bite my lip, loving how desperate he is for me.

He shifts behind me, and a moan tears out of my chest when the head of his cock presses against my entrance.

"Is this what you need, baby?" He nudges into me just enough to tease.

"Gods, yes," I whimper, pushing back, trying to take more of him. I need him to fill me, to stretch me.

A deep, broken groan leaves him as he slams forward, burying himself inside me in one brutal thrust.

I scream, the sound echoing through the trees as birds scatter. The stretch burns, pleasure crashing into me so hard it makes my head drop forward. My forehead hits the ground as my eyes squeeze shut.

He pulls almost all the way out, then drives back in, rough and unforgiving. Every snap of his hips sends sharp pleasure ripping through me. I can't think, can't breathe, can only feel him pounding into me like he's claiming every inch.

"Come here," he growls.

His hand tangles in my hair and yanks me upright. I hiss at the sting as my back presses to his chest. His mouth finds my neck, teeth grazing, sucking hard. He loves leaving marks on me—and I love wearing them.

He grips my chin. "Look at me. I want to see those eyes."

I turn my head, meeting his grey eyes.

"*Fuck*," he mutters, crashing his mouth to mine. His hips move faster, harder. "Fuck... fuck... this pussy... squirting... it's too much." Each word sounds torn out of him. A desperate plea...

He growls and shoves me forward again, forcing my face back into the forest floor. His thrusts turn wild, powerful, desperate.

"Come for me, little vixen. *Now*."

The angle, the force of his vicious thrust, his voice, it's too much. His cock hits exactly where I need it. My mouth falls open as my body locks up, my pussy clenching around him.

"Xavior!" I scream as the orgasm rips through me, wave after wave crashing down.

I feel his grip tighten on my hips as his body shudders. He roars, spilling inside me, marking me.

My knees give out, but he catches me before I fall, flipping us so I'm on top. I collapse against his shoulder, both of us breathing hard, the forest quiet around us.

"Why do you call me vixen?" I murmur.

He exhales, fingers brushing my back. "That fire in you. That mouth. That body. It fit." A pause. "The first time I watched you kill those men with that fire whip—fuck, it was hot. I knew then that you were going to be the temptation that ruined me." He smirks against my hair. "And you did ruin me, little vixen, deliciously so."

The end...

About J.S. Rodriguez

J.S. Rodriguez lives in the beautiful countryside of Pennsylvania with her amazing husband and their four wonderful children. A lifelong romance enthusiast, she proudly calls herself a romance junkie who is fueled by strong coffee, good music, and the occasional spontaneous dance break.

Born in California, Rodriguez spent much of her childhood moving from place to place. Those early experiences sparked her deep love of reading and storytelling, eventually planting the dream of becoming an author. As she grew older, that dream only intensified, shaping her passion for writing heartfelt, imaginative romance.

Rodriguez now enjoys life in a spacious farmhouse, where the peaceful view of the creek from her front porch often inspires her stories. When she's not writing, she loves baking with her family, unwinding during cozy, lazy afternoons, and cherishing quality time with the people she loves most.

Also by J.S. Rodriguez

Throne of Sin and Desire

Dimitri

I am a demon, the bastard son of Lucifer. I take everything I want; I make sure no one goes unpunished for their crimes here in hell. I rule, I judge, I punish, and execute. Everyone here in hell is afraid of me and never gets too close. I love it. I have never liked people close to me until her. She makes me want to be better, but I am too damaged. She is too good for me. I do not deserve her, but I can't let her go. I crave her touch. Her scent is addicting, and she is the only one who can bring me to my knees. I'll burn the world down for her.

Rosa

I am broken.

My adoptive father hates me and blames me for the death of my adoptive mother. I am hurt and feel lonely. I have my best friend, Cassie, and she is the only one who keeps me sane. I can't wait to leave this town full of bad memories to get a fresh start. But then, I met him. Now, I crave his touch. He is everything I didn't even know I needed. I can finally breathe when I'm around him, but he keeps pushing me away. He doesn't believe he's good enough for me.

Wicked Little Witch

Azrael

Fuck... I need to do something I have never done before..., pray and pray that I will not give into in to her wicked spell. She is made straight from the devil himself, made to be a temptation you cannot fight, and she will cause you to sin for a simple little taste of her sweet nectar. She has me feeling things I have never felt before. I will not give in; I hate her and everything she is.

Bella

My mom is dead, and now my sister and I are on the run, hiding in the shadows so my own father doesn't find us. My life turns has been turned upside down when I met after having met AzraelXavior. He helped me, and now I'm in his debt, and he will not let me leave until I hold up my end of the bargain. God, I hate him... or at lease least that' is what I keep telling myself.